DATE DUE

Demco

BLOOD
DEFENSE

OTHER TITLES BY MARCIA CLARK

FICTION

The Rachel Knight Series

Guilt by Association

Guilt by Degrees

Killer Ambition

The Competition

NONFICTION

Without a Doubt
(with Teresa Carpenter)

BLOOD
DEFENSE

MARCIA CLARK

THOMAS & MERCER

Text copyright © 2016 Marcia Clark

Published by Thomas & Mercer, Seattle

www.apub.com

Amazon, the Amazon logo, and Thomas & Mercer are trademarks of Amazon.com, Inc., or its affiliates.

Hardcover ISBN-13: 9781503936195
             ISBN-10: 1503936198

Softcover   ISBN-13: 9781503954007
             ISBN-10: 1503954005

Cover design by Salamander Hill Design Inc.

Printed in the United States of America

PROLOGUE

LA NOW!.COM

BREAKING NEWS: Actress Chloe Monahan and Roommate Found Stabbed to Death

Actress Chloe Monahan, a regular in the hit drama series *Dark Corners*, and her roommate, Paige Avner, were found stabbed to death in their Laurel Canyon apartment. Officials say they have no suspects at this time. We'll post updates as more information is available.

THE BIZ.COM

Cops Say Comeback Kid Actress Chloe Monahan and Roommate Killed by Burglar

Reporters for *The Biz* have learned that Chloe Monahan's apartment was burglarized just two months before she and her roommate were murdered. Police Chief Wes Sanders says they are looking into the possibility that the burglar came back for another run and killed the girls when they unexpectedly came home. In the meantime, the outpouring of sorrow and rage from friends and fans has crashed

Monahan's Facebook page and her one-million-plus Twitter followers have flooded the social network with messages of grief and demands for justice.

GET THE ASSHOLE WHO DID THIS! #justiceforchloe

OMG I LOVED HER!! #tragedy

MY FAVORITE ON DARK CORNERS! NOOOOO! #chloeforever

ONE

I raced into the studio and hopped into the empty chair in front of Bonnie, the makeup wizard. I had just five minutes till airtime. She gave me an exasperated look as she whipped the red nylon cape around me.

The television in the makeup room—always tuned to the studio's news programs—showed a reporter standing in front of Chloe Monahan's apartment. I turned to look. Bonnie grabbed my chin and turned my head back. But I couldn't help myself. My head swiveled around again when the reporter snagged the lead detective for a sound bite. Bonnie gave an exasperated huff. I turned back to face the mirror again. "Sorry."

I kept thinking they'd come up with some new leads. Or actually, any leads—period. So far, there was nothing but speculation, and most of it centered on the burglar theory. The only other possible suspect I'd heard mentioned was a drug dealer. But no one was giving that idea much play—in large part because the source was Amanda Trace, the snarling muckraker who hosted *Justice on Fire!* Even Tony Banks, a frequent guest on her show and one of my fellow criminal defense attorneys, disagreed and pointed out that Chloe had been clean for nearly a year. Tony could kiss that guest spot good-bye. No one was allowed to argue with Queen Trace. Which was one of the many reasons I refused to do her show. Her producers started calling after my first appearance on Sheri's show, *Crime Time*, and though I've turned them down consistently, they still haven't given up. I don't know whether they're admirably tenacious or mush-brained robots who have me on speed dial.

I heard Chloe Monahan's voice on the television and the shock of it made me jerk my head toward the screen again—but it was just a clip from her interview on *Ellen*. Bonnie put her hands on her hips and fixed me with a death ray. "Once more, Brinkman, and I'll let you go out there looking like a raccoon in drag."

My sparring partner for the evening, lawyer Barry Stefanovich, sauntered in and flopped down into the seat next to mine. "Actually, that sounds kind of cute." Bonnie shot him a dagger. Barry blew her a kiss and turned his chair to face me. "Hey, Sam." I didn't think I could rock the "raccoon in drag" look, so I kept still and just wiggled my fingers at him. He nodded at the television. "When they get the guy, are you going to try for it? It's gonna be huge."

Which is always good for business. And as Michelle, childhood BFF, paralegal, and the lone "associate" in my firm, the Law Offices of Brinkman and Associates, would say: "Take the damn case; we need the money." Ordinarily, it would be a no-brainer. I've handled uglier cases that had no publicity benefits, but this was different. I'd been a fan of *Dark Corners*—and of Chloe in particular. I'd seen her on the late-night talk-show circuit. She was cool, very real, not actress-y. And she was funny. In that weird, sort of ridiculous way we have of bonding with people we see only on television, I felt like I knew her. So my human side said, *No frigging way.* But the lawyer in me said, *Isn't that why you got into this business to begin with? To stick up for the underdog?* I shook my head. "I don't know."

The production assistant ran in, her long single braid swinging behind her. "We've got to get you guys seated. Barry, you're in Studio B. Samantha, you're in Studio A."

Bonnie yanked off the cape and I vaulted out of the chair. Barry and I fell in behind the assistant as she led us down the hall. "Are we going to talk about Chloe Monahan?"

The assistant shook her head. "*We* are, but you guys aren't. There's no real news yet, so Sheri's just doing personal stuff with some of Chloe's friends."

I raised an eyebrow. Since when did they need real news to justify the slugfest? Barry gave me a knowing smile behind the assistant's back as he ducked into his studio.

I trotted into Studio A next door and sat down. Dane, the audio guy, was waiting for me. He clipped the mike to the lapel of my blazer, handed me my earpiece, and left. The door closed with a solid, air-compressing *thunk*. When you see me on television, it looks like I'm sitting in some cool twenty-sixth-floor office with a panoramic view of the Los Angeles skyline at sunset. Really, it's just a dark coffin-size room with a printed backdrop. Claustrophobics would bounce off the walls.

And thanks to the magicians in the makeup room and a shot that catches me from only the chest up, I look like I just stepped off the red carpet. You can't see the safety pin that's holding my skirt together, the scuffed pumps that've been resoled four times, or the old coffee stain on my blouse—which is still missing the last two buttons because I can't face up to the chore of searching through the overstuffed bag of spare buttons crammed under my bathroom sink.

I pulled out my cell phone to do one last Twitter blast.

I'm on LIVE with Sheri! Talking the Samron case: 14 Yr Old who shot her brother—tune in! #HLN

I've been doing the cable news circuit for about six months now. Contrary to popular opinion, it's not a paying gig, so only the young and desperate do it—or the already successful types who have the time to do it for fun because they're paying the young and hungry to do the real work. It's a real time suck, and if it'd been up to me, I'd have said *no gracias* when one of Sheri's producers first approached me. But Michelle elbowed her way in between us and said, "She'd love to!"

I'd been pissed. "I don't have time for that crap, Michy."

She'd hissed under her breath. "Are you nuts? This 'crap' is how you snag the kinds of cases that'll finally put us in the black. You can't afford *not* to."

So far it's netted me only a couple of DUI cases and a lot of requests to take on pro bono work. But it *is* kind of fun. A limo picks me up, hair-and-makeup wizards make me look fabulous, and I get to hammer other lawyers without having to worry about getting locked up by the judge. Where does any of that go wrong?

But since it still hasn't proven to be a cash cow, I limit myself to one or two shows a week. A lot of the lawyers who do this cable circuit are hoping to get their own show. I have to admit, I think about it, too, every now and then. It'd be nice not to have to worry about whether I've got enough money to feed Beulah, my ancient Mercedes, who—in addition to having a rear passenger window that no longer rolls all the way up and an ugly dent in the right rear fender (which, coincidentally, showed up the day a client got convicted of murder and his girlfriend threatened to kill me)—is a gas hog.

And it'd be a real personal coup if I could wind up living as well as my mother—*without* having to slide underneath a rich old guy every night. But I love what I do; I *believe* in what I do. Sticking up for the little guy is why I went to law school.

So I keep doing it, hoping to score my big break. A shrink who was on one of the shows with me a few months ago said the real reason I did the cable circuit was because I needed to prove that I was "somebody." Probably to my parents. I told the shrink I'd never met my father, and the only thing that would make my mother think I was "somebody" was if I married a rich "somebody." And then I told him I thought *he* did these shows because he was a self-important ass waffle who probably

got his degree from an online "university" in Belize. I hadn't meant to pop off like that—not that it didn't feel good to take down that self-important, patronizing jackass. But I figured that was the end of my brief stint as a talking head. Which just shows how green I was. The producers booked me for three more shows on the spot.

As I was finishing a tweet, Dane, the audio guy, spoke in my earpiece. "Could you give me a ten-count, Samantha?"

"Sure." I counted to ten while I scrolled through my Twitter feed.

Go get 'em, Samantha! #onetoughlawyer

Love you, Samantha! #onehotlawyer

Your a cunt. #SamanthaBrinkmansawhore

I retweeted the first two and answered the last:

You're a cunt. You are=you're.

Dane was back in my ear. "Okay, Samantha, coming to you in ten. Heads up."

The case we'd be banging around tonight was a simple one. Fourteen-year-old Linette Samron, who'd had enough of her bullying big brother, Ryan, "borrowed" her dad's 9mm and plugged him three times. If it'd been you or me, we'd be dead. Ryan, however, was in "stable condition" and resting comfortably.

It's the Law of Douche Bags. Douche bags walk away with enough holes in them to look like a colander, while good guys go down for the count with one random punch to the head.

Sheri—one of my favorite hosts; I love her tough, funny 'tude—came to me first. "Samantha Brinkman, you're our expert defense attorney. Linette's lawyers are claiming it was an accident. What do you think of their strategy?"

"I think Linette would be better off hiring Justin Bieber. Three shots? An accident? Look, she wins on popularity, not the law. She's the David to his Goliath. They've got a boatload of evidence that Ryan beat her up in the past. She needs to put it all out there and go for self-defense—"

Barry jumped in. "Come on, Samantha. They can't sell self-defense. She went and got the gun and then hunted him down—"

"So what? A jury who hears about those beatings is a jury who'll say screw the law and screw him. She walks. A jury who hears a lot of BS about trigger pulls and safety malfunctions says, 'Screw her.'"

Sheri leaned in. "Then, Samantha, you're banking on an emotional verdict, aren't you?"

"Sheri, since when *aren't* we?"

Sheri threw it to Barry. "You agree with that?"

Barry smiled. "There's no disagreeing with that. It's just a matter of how you go about it. But Samantha's right: the more the jury hears about those beatings, the better for her."

Which now, thanks to us, they just had.

When my last segment wrapped, I went to the makeup room to find Barry. We'd agreed to join the producers for drinks after the show. The television was playing clips from Chloe's most recent talk-show appearances. A voiceover was talking about the rough times Chloe had been through before she got the gig on *Dark Corners*.

She'd been a child star, but in the years after her show went off the air, she'd hit a downward spiral that ended at the tip of a needle. Before she scored the role in *Dark Corners*, the only time she appeared on television was when she landed in court for one drug bust or another. It made her murder an even bigger heartbreaker. I nodded at the screen. "She was really in the shits for a while, wasn't she?"

Barry nodded as he wiped off his makeup. "One of her lawyers is a poker buddy. Said she was heading down the OD track for sure when Paige took her in. He said Paige and that role saved her life." Barry

looked up at the television, his expression sad. "Kind of a tragic irony, isn't it?"

More than tragic, it was depressing. "Life is one unfair bitch."

Barry's cell rang. He frowned at the screen. "I've gotta take this. You go on ahead. Save me a seat, okay?"

"You got it." I headed out, thinking about the icy tequila with lime in my near future.

It was already dark by then, and the studio was on the east side of Hollywood. Not the best neighborhood for a nighttime stroll, but I'd found a shortcut after doing *A.M. Hot Spot* last Monday morning. But the minute I turned onto the smaller street just south of Sunset, I realized that what'd looked fine in daylight looked a lot different at night. I told myself to stop being such a wuss, but my stomach tightened with every step. I scanned the street as I moved, noticing for the first time the abandoned house with broken windows on the corner, the empty lot on the right where used condoms and discarded syringes glowed in the moonlight, and dark alleys on either side of me. I felt like the idiot in those scary movies who makes you want to yell at the screen when she gets into the car with a—*duh*—serial killer.

And then I hit a stretch of road that was totally pitch-black. That was it. I decided that I'd rather be an alive wuss than a dead tough guy. I'd just turned back to head for Sunset Boulevard when I heard the fast slap of running feet coming up behind me. At that same moment, two white men in red do-rags and baggy jeans—the kind that have loops sewn inside the legs to hold shotguns—stepped out of the alley to my left and came toward me with deadly eyes that said anything could happen in the next sixty seconds. A strangled little scream squeaked out of my mouth as I jumped back—and almost fell into the team behind me. I could feel their hot breath on my neck, and the smell of their sweat, oily and sour, wound its way over my shoulder like a snake. The bile rose in my throat.

A heavy-looking metal pipe slid down out of the sleeve of the taller of the two men in front of me. He slapped the pipe against his thigh, stepped close enough for me to smell the cigarettes on his breath, and said in a low, tight voice, "Shut the fuck up, bitch."

And in that second, a surge of anger burst through the fear. This cretin was telling *me* to shut the fuck up? I wanted to rip his stupid head off his neck. I was about to reach for my gun, but then I remembered I didn't have it. And I noticed we were standing at the mouth of a dark alley. It wouldn't take five seconds to pull me into it. Another five and I could easily be dead. I didn't see any lights on in the trashed-out houses nearby, but even if anyone was home, I seriously doubted they'd be in any shape to help me. Rage gave way to reason as I considered my options.

If I'd had a wad of money on me, I could've hoped that they'd just take my purse and be happy with the score. But as usual, my cash on hand would barely cover one drink. Still, it was all I had to bargain with. I started to take my purse off my shoulder. Seeing my move, the other man whipped a .44 out of the pocket of his hoodie and put it to my head. As the cold steel barrel pressed against my temple, I saw my face exploding in a red mist.

A voice behind me that sounded like gravel churning in a Cuisinart snarled, "You don't move, bitch."

I stood frozen, my hand still at my shoulder. There was something familiar about that voice. Could it be . . . ? If I was wrong, I'd be dead. But I had to take a chance.

TWO

I put as much attitude into my voice as I could muster and spoke over my shoulder. "Deshawn Johnson, what the *hell* do you think you're doing?"

Silence. Oh God, I was wrong. This was it. This was how I was going to die. I should do something, jump on someone's instep, make a fast turn and head-butt someone, but my brain was stuck on the barrel jammed against my head. The pounding of my heart was all I could hear.

Then, a figure stepped around from behind me and moved next to the guy holding the gun to my head. "Ms. Brinkman? Shit. What *you* doin' here?"

The man holding the gun—whose haircut reminded me of Vanilla Ice—looked from me to Deshawn. "You know dis bitch?"

"She's my lawyer." He waved a hand. "Y'all back off."

Vanilla Ice stepped back and slipped the gun into his pocket as the other one slid the pipe back up his sleeve.

My brain signaled for all systems to stand down, and the adrenaline ebbed—a little too fast. I had to swallow to keep from vomiting. I pulled my jacket around me and folded my arms around my waist.

After a few deep breaths, the throbbing in my head started to recede . . . and then I got mad again. Really mad. You know what I hate almost as much as getting jacked? Working my ass off on a case and seeing all that hard work get flushed down the toilet.

I'd spent a lot of nights putting together the motion I'd been working on for Deshawn. If I won, he'd be home free. But if the cops caught Deshawn out here jacking people, "home" would be Wasco State Prison for twenty-five to life. My motion would matter about as much as a squirt gun in a hurricane.

I stepped up close to him and tried to keep my voice low. "Are you kidding me with this shit? I busted my hump on that motion, your mom probably went into hock to pay my freight, and you're out here crime-ing." Deshawn looked down. I pulled my phone out of my purse. "Matter of fact, I'm gonna call her right now and let her know—"

"No!" He grabbed my hand. Mama Johnson was no one to mess with, and we both knew it. He looked around, remembered that his homies were watching, and whispered, "Come on, you don't gotta do that. Why you want to upset an old lady that way?"

I swear if we'd been alone, I'd have smacked him. "*Me?* Did *I* call you up and tell you to go out and jack people tonight?"

Deshawn sighed and threw a glance at Vanilla Ice. "It's just a favor for Lil' J. He's trying to buy a ring for his girl. That gun ain't even loaded."

"But you'd still get twenty-five to life." I nodded at the pocket of Vanilla's hoodie that sagged with the weight of the gun, and at the other guy's sleeve where the pipe was still peeking out at the cuff. "That's a gun, and that's a deadly weapon. You're a third-striker, Deshawn." I pointed to my temple—the same one that had hosted the barrel of a gun just minutes ago. "*Think*, man. You've got no slack here." Deshawn nodded, then looked down at the ground again. "You couldn't tell Lil' J to check out a layaway plan at Zales?"

Deshawn shrugged. "Lil' J's not much of a saver. We said we'd do one, maybe two hits—don't let no one get hurt—and he'd have to make do with whatever we got."

"That's good parenting, Deshawn. Way to set limits."

He started to smile. "Really?"

"No."

Deshawn stared over my shoulder, taking some time to try and save face. "Okay, okay. Tell you what, I'm goin' on home now. I promise. Just don't call my moms."

I took a few seconds to make it look like I was thinking about it. I wanted to make Deshawn sweat a little. I looked at his posse. They were watching us, a little bit wary, a lot curious. "I need you all to do Deshawn a favor and make sure he goes straight home. Now. No detours. Got it?"

They nodded. A pack of hyenas would be more reliable, but you've got to work with what you've got. I scanned the pockets of Deshawn's hoodie. "You strapped?"

He held up his hands. "No. I swear."

I gave him a skeptical look. "Let's see those pockets." If they got stopped on the way home and the cops found a gun on him, he'd be toast. Deshawn pulled out the pockets of his hoodie. They were empty. I pointed to his jeans. "Those, too."

He gave an exasperated huff. "Come on, man. I told you, I'm clean." He saw the expression on my face, sighed, and pulled out his jeans pockets.

As he did, a baggie full of white-ish powder fell out. I snatched it up, opened it, and sniffed. "Heroin? Seriously?" Deshawn had never been into junk. Coke, yes. Pot, yes. But heroin, never. I closed my fist around it, just in case anyone was watching. "This is enough to bust you for intent to sell. What on earth are you dreaming?"

Deshawn shook his head. "It's not what you think. This is just business. That shit's pure, man. I step on it hard enough, I'll probably clear fifty, maybe even a hundred grand."

I stared at him, wondering how he'd managed to stay out of jail long enough to get busted again. "I don't even want to know how you scored this much pure shit. But your shop is now officially closed for business." I dropped the baggie into my purse.

Deshawn's eyes got big. "What? No! You can't! You know what that cost me?!"

"A lot less than it'll cost if you get caught with it."

He put out his hand. "Come on, man. Give it back. That's a lot of money."

"Just be glad I'm not calling your mother."

Deshawn's shoulders drooped and he gave me a glum look. He motioned to the others. "Come on. Let's go."

Lil' J leaned toward me. "Hey, uh, you got a card or something?" The others chimed in. "Yeah." "I'll take one." "Me, too."

I passed my cards around. "Cash retainers only, no checks, no credit cards." I doubted that they'd be able to swing my fee, but I didn't want to discourage what was probably the only responsible thing they'd manage to do that month—or that year.

They started to walk away, but Deshawn paused. He looked up and down the street, stepped back, and whispered, "Anybody else gives you trouble, you call me. Hear?"

THREE

The next day, I finished my morning round of court appearances early and got back to the office in time for lunch. Michelle had brought in my favorite: coffee.

I pulled up the old secretary's chair I'd liberated from the public defender's office when I quit to go into private practice and sat next to her desk. "Nice Scünci." This one was red and blue—color coordinated with her cobalt-blue sweater. She always wore her hair up in a ponytail, and I always gave her shit about it. Michelle has the kind of fresh-faced, cheerleader-y looks that still gets her carded at bars. And the tiny scar over her left eye—courtesy of the mugger who'd pistol-whipped her nine years ago—only heightened the effect.

Michelle shot me a look. "Shut up. Jury on Ringer still out?" I nodded. "They asking any questions?"

"Not a peep." Which was not a good sign. A quiet jury is a convicting jury.

The *whomp whomp* of a ghetto bird fired up. A daily—and nightly—occurrence in this 'hood. I picked this office because it was cheap and close to the Van Nuys courthouse. It seemed like a win-win, until I found out the building was smack-dab in the heart of Barrios Van Nuys turf, one of the biggest gangs in the county.

Michelle was saying something, but I couldn't hear her over the din of the helicopters. I shook my head and pointed to the ceiling.

Michelle shouted. "How'd he do on the stand?"

"Not bad." For a rapist-bully-asshole. His eighteen-year-old victim, Aidan Mandy, a homeless kid Ringer had found hanging around a fast-food joint looking for a handout—money, food, or drugs—had a prior bust for solicitation. So Ringer's claim that it'd been a consensual business deal might've been a winning gambit. Except Aidan wound up in the emergency room with injuries so bad it'd take years before he fully recovered—if he ever did.

Ringer claimed he hadn't hurt him, that Aidan must've tricked with someone else after Ringer, but I didn't believe it, and I didn't think the jury would, either. I kept my defense short and tight, put on a couple of "Ringer's so nice" character witnesses from the insurance company where he used to work, and rested. I expected the jury to convict any minute now.

The helicopters began to move away. Michelle waited for the noise to die down. "Well, I hope he gets nailed. He's a disgusting douche."

No argument there. "But I did give a pretty good closing if I do say so myself. Want to hear it?"

Michelle hit a key on her computer and started typing. "Depends. You care about having phone service? If not, I'm all ears. Otherwise, I've got to get your claim in to the court this second because we're about a month overdue on the bill. And you need to pay your car registration."

"Fine, never mind." I glanced at Alex's office—AKA, the storage room where we kept our ancient, incredibly slow copying machine. We'd probably be better off using carbon paper. I noticed the door was closed. That meant he was out. The room was so small you had to leave the door open or you'd wind up breathing carbon dioxide in about ten seconds. "Where's our intrepid investigator?"

I just hired Alex Medrano, a former client, to be my investigator. He's got no training or experience, but he's smart and has mad hacking skills. And I figure he can't be any worse than the useless slugs I hired in the past.

"Working from home. He's trying to get those records you asked for on Deshawn's case."

"Oh yeah." I would've tried to track them down myself, but it required serious cyberpunk chops—and a decent computer. I had neither. I started to head for my office, but Michelle held up a hand.

"Are you sure about hiring that guy? I mean, he's a thief and a hacker."

I looked around at our Office Cheapo furnishings and smacked my forehead. "Damn, you're so right. How could I so endanger our financial empire?"

Michelle glared at me. "I'm not saying he'll rip us off, smartass. I'm saying what if he gets caught? It might look like we're in on it and—"

I shook my head. "Never gonna happen. Trust me." Alex had hacked into the company computer to "liberate" two 750Li's from the BMW dealership where he was a salesman. But he hadn't done it for himself. It was a story straight out of *Les Misérables*. Alex's father had died of a sudden heart attack, then his mother had a stroke and needed full-time nursing care, which they couldn't afford, so his brother, Carlos, had to quit work to take care of her. And his little sister, Leticia, was about to graduate high school. She'd been offered a scholarship at Penn State, but it wouldn't cover her dorm fees. If Alex sold those cars, it would take care of all of them for at least a few years. So he did steal, but he wasn't really a thief in my book. I told Michelle his story.

She had a skeptical look. "That's a pretty sad tale of woe. You check it out?"

"No. Why would he lie?" I shot her a dagger. "Of course I checked it out."

Michelle paused for a moment, then nodded and turned back to her computer. "Okay, back to work. Get me your time sheets on Ringer. One way or another, he'll be done soon."

I saluted and headed into my office. My office decor is best described as early "I don't give a damn," because I don't. Plus, there's no one to impress. My clients are almost always in custody. Most of my cases are court appointments—basically public defender cases that the public defender can't take for one reason or another. So I have the minimum: a big desk and lawyer's chair (I scored them on the cheap at a storage locker sale) and a couple of unmatched chairs in front of my desk that sit lower than mine (so I can look imposing). The only thing on my desk other than my computer is a bottle of tequila shaped like a skull—a present from a former boyfriend—and a little jade "money tree" with tiny gold-colored bells hanging from the branches. Michelle gave it to me for inspiration. It hasn't done much for us so far.

I spent the rest of the afternoon pulling together the paperwork for Michelle and working up the cases that I probably wouldn't be able to plead out. Alex showed up at six o'clock. He looks nothing like any real-life investigator I've ever seen. But Hollywood would cast him in a hot second: thick black hair swept to the side, olive skin, and eyes like black diamonds. It'd broken Michelle's heart when I told her he was gay. But she knew better than to argue; my gay-dar almost never fails me—and it hadn't this time, either.

I walked out to the anteroom. "You don't look joyous. No luck on those records?"

He shook his head.

"Look, don't sweat it. If you can't, you can't. We'll just have to—"

"Oh, I can." His tone was calm, utterly self-assured. "It'll just take a little more time. When's Deshawn's hearing?"

I liked his confidence. And I knew it was justified. It was only a fluke that he'd been caught stealing those BMWs. He was that good. Which was why I'd been able to make him a sweetheart deal for no time and straight probation: he'd agreed to show the cops how he'd done it. "His hearing's set for next week."

Alex made a *poof* sound. "I'll have it for you in two days." He gestured to the monitor of Michelle's desktop, which was splashed with the latest headline on the double murder in Laurel Canyon. "They've been thumping Chloe's and Paige's murders nonstop."

I nodded. So nonstop it filled the airwaves, the Ethernet, and every tabloid rag in the supermarket. You couldn't get away from the case if you tried. "But it's all background stories on Chloe. They still don't have anyone."

Michelle, always on the hunt, looked at me with fire in her eyes. "Oh, they will. Trust me. And when they do, you've gotta go for it." I didn't answer. "Sam, I'm not kidding."

"I know."

Michelle looked at me with frustration. "I don't get it. You took Ringer for no publicity."

I was about to say that Ringer hadn't killed his victim. But that wasn't the issue. The issue was Chloe. And Paige. Something about them hit too close to home.

FOUR

But I couldn't stop following the coverage of the "Canyon Killer" case, as the press had dubbed it. So far, the only new announcement was that the girls had been stabbed to death with the same weapon—a carving knife that was missing from the butcher block on the kitchen counter. The police media liaison said it was too soon to speculate about who'd done it or why. But the usual pundits disagreed. They immediately pronounced that the use of the carving knife showed the murders weren't premeditated, that the girls had probably walked in on a burglar. When their apartment was burglarized two months before, the perp had gotten in through an open sliding glass door. That same door was found open after the police discovered the bodies.

Predictably, most of the coverage was devoted to Chloe Monahan. The tabloids in particular were feeding nonstop off the tragedy of a young actress who'd managed to pull herself out of a drug-infused abyss and climb her way back to the brink of superstardom only to have her life brutally cut short.

To top it off, they'd dug up a whole new, heart-grabbing wrinkle. Though no one knew it at the time, when she was a child star, Chloe had been the sole support for her family, which included a younger sister, an absentee father, and an abusive mother. The makeup artists, who now felt the truth must be told (but only to a tabloid that was notorious for checkbook journalism), said they'd kept special concealer on hand to cover the bruises. Those stories probably explained why Chloe's mother hadn't surfaced to suck up some of the limelight.

But her roommate, Paige Avner, got almost no ink. Pretty but not glamorous, Paige had been a part-time print-ad model and waitress. Nothing to be ashamed of, but not the stuff of fairy tales, either. Her story was largely eclipsed by the searing drama of Chloe's life. What little press she did get was centered on the fact that she and Chloe had met when they were kids on the set of *All of Us*, where Paige's mother had been the on-set tutor. Apparently, they'd remained friends ever since. Paige's mother, Nina, gave a brief, heartrending statement about the loss of her only child—all that was left of their little family. Paige's father had died of cancer years ago.

So the victims were about as blameless as it gets, their only crime being that they were unlucky enough to be home when some asshole decided to rip them off.

There was no suspect in custody, so the sharks hadn't started to circle yet. But they would—the moment there was an arrest. It had all the makings of a media circus, and the bigger the circus, the better it is for business.

But big enough to be worth sitting next to the animal who'd done it? I wasn't sure. I had friends in the public defender's office who were true believers, who didn't care how many victims their clients had disemboweled, who thought they were all just poor, misunderstood unfortunates. And some are, though more often they're just schlemiels who don't think past the next five minutes—which is largely why they get caught. But there's a small percentage who are nothing but born predators. And for them, no amount of good parenting, quality schooling, or therapy sessions will ever make a bit of difference. That doesn't mean I don't fight for them just as hard. I fight like hell. It just means I never forget who they are. Or that justice really should prevail, though too often, it doesn't.

I didn't mind the fact that the Canyon Killer would be the most hated guy in the country. I knew going into this business that I wasn't going to score a lot of Valentine's cards. Being troll-bait for haters is part of the gig.

And I don't have to love the client. I don't even have to *like* the client. Sometimes, I really *hate* the client. Doesn't matter. I'm there to take care of society's refuse, the ones nobody wants—or ever wanted. And if I have to slash and burn to do it, so be it. When I walk into court, I'm not concerned about justice, the rule of law, or making sure it's a fair fight. Fuck fair. I'm there to protect my client. That's where my duty begins and ends.

But Chloe—and by association, her best friend, Paige—felt too real, too close to me. And whoever murdered them was likely a real monster. The idea of sitting next to the douche bag who'd done it made me sick. So I didn't ask Michelle to monitor the case, I didn't ask the courthouse reporters for the inside skinny, and I didn't call my producer buddies for media scoop.

* * * *

It'd been a grind of a week, and by Friday afternoon I was dragging like a dog on its way to the groomer. My last appearance of the day was a misdemeanor vandalism case. My client, Naille Tarickman, an eighteen-year-old "street artist," had been busted for "enhancing" the side of a liquor store. I wouldn't ordinarily have taken a case that picayune, but his mother, Harriet (we call her Hank), was one of the few—okay, the *only*—cop I actually liked, and she'd asked me to step in. She'd insisted on paying my retainer, but I planned to tear up the check when I finished the case.

I'd managed to get declarations from the store owner and a couple of neighbors saying they'd pay Naille to paint the whole 'hood if they could—and they'd be glad to come in and testify. When I showed them to the prosecutor, he folded like a cheap card table and dismissed the case.

Naille took off to celebrate with his friends, and Hank and I talked in the hallway for a few minutes. I asked her if they were zeroing in on the burglar who killed Chloe and Paige yet.

Hank looked around, then leaned in. "Don't say anything, okay?" I nodded. "It wasn't the burglar."

"Then who?"

"A cop. A detective in the Hollywood Division."

I've got to admit, I did not see that coming.

I wasn't necessarily any more interested in taking the case, but the sheer oddity of a detective being the bad guy got my attention. All day Saturday I kept an ear tuned to the news while I ran the million errands and chores that'd piled up all week.

Michelle had called in the morning and left me a message saying, "Call me back, we have to talk," but I didn't have time until almost eight o'clock that night. Doing laundry at the local Fluff 'n' Fold takes forever on a Saturday. Between that, grocery shopping, the dry cleaners, and giving Beulah a bath, my whole day had been shot. And now I was starving. I hoped Michy might be, too. "Hey, sorry I didn't get back to you earlier. I've been running my ass off all—"

"We've got to talk."

"But first we've got to eat."

I told her to meet me at Barney's Beanery, kind of a roadhouse diner. It's close, cheap, and funky. And I love the history. It's where famous rockers like Janis Joplin and Jim Morrison used to go. It also used to be a redneck haven. Less so now that it's situated in the heart of Boys' Town, AKA West Hollywood.

When I got there, I found Michy already seated near the window, with a basket of fries and chicken fingers on the table in front of her.

I barely had a chance to sit down before she leaned in and spoke, her voice low but intense. "You heard about the Canyon Killer being that cop, Dale Pearson, right?" I nodded. "You ever run into him in court?"

"Nope. Pretty weird that it's a cop."

"They're saying he was well respected."

I rolled my eyes. "They always say that when a cop gets busted."

Michelle snorted. "No, they don't."

"Yes, they do. Anyway, he was supposedly dating Chloe—"

Michelle nodded. "I heard they met when he showed up to handle her burglary."

I finished off a chicken finger and wiped my mouth. "Kind of creepy, him dating a crime victim, don't you think?"

Michelle stared at me. "I'd think that would happen all the time. Cops, firemen, they come in and save you and—"

"It doesn't happen all the time."

"Whatever. And, so what? It's not like he was married. Where else is he supposed to meet women?"

I reached for another chicken finger. "At a bar. Where he can get drunk and use bad judgment like the rest of us."

Michy deadpanned me and moved on. "They're saying he stabbed Chloe in the chest, and Paige in the back. Some neighbors heard him fighting with Chloe that night, so the police figure he stabbed Chloe in the heat of the argument, then had to get rid of Paige."

"You wouldn't think a cop would be that sloppy—"

"It was a fight, not a planned hit."

I shrugged. "I guess. Their building have a surveillance camera?"

Michelle popped a fry in her mouth. "I doubt it. From what I saw on the news, it's just a dumpy little place. Exterior hallways, an open carport."

In short, a lot like mine.

Michelle glanced around the restaurant, then leaned forward, both hands on the table in front of her. "You've got to go for it. This is the case we've been waiting for, Sam. It'll get us a ton of publicity, put us in the big leagues. And it'll bring in some decent money—"

"Cops don't have money, and his buddies on the force aren't going to take up a collection for a guy who murdered his girlfriend."

"I bet he'll have enough money to hire *you*. And when he taps out, the court's gonna have to appoint you. Come on, Sam. It's a no-brainer. Win-win."

I'd thought of all that. But there was just one fly in the ointment. "No way he'd hire me. Everyone knows how much I hate cops—"

"That's exactly why he *should* want you. Gives him more credibility."

I wasn't so sure he'd see it that way, and to be honest, I still wasn't sure I wanted the case. I shook my head. "He'll never go for it—"

"He might. You've got a solid rep around the courthouse. He's bound to have heard of you."

"Exactly my point. Why pick a cop hater—"

Michelle grabbed my forearm. "Sam, you haven't paid me in two months, they're about to turn off the electricity, and we're behind on the rent."

I sighed. She was right. I picked up the last of the fries as I nodded, very reluctantly. "I'll give it a try. But don't go paying any unnecessary bills. This is a long shot at best."

"Good." Michelle sat back. "Besides, it's possible he's not guilty."

I laughed so hard I had to put down my fries.

I went to bed that night still conflicted about whether I wanted to try and get Pearson's case. If it'd gone down the way the news reports said, the jury was going to shred this guy so hard there wouldn't be enough left of him to bury.

And even if I did go for the case, how would I pitch myself to Dale Pearson? As I drove to work Monday morning, I tried to come up with an intro. But all the lines sounded like bad come-ons for a hookup: "I know I've got a rep for hating cops, but it's different with you . . ." Or like phony ass-kissing: "You've probably heard I'm not a big cop lover, but I'm actually a big fan; you're one of the good guys . . ." And I'd know that . . . how? I was still trying to come up with a line I could deliver without laughing—or gagging—when I got to the office.

But the minute I walked in the door, Michelle waved me over to her computer. "Never mind about Pearson. He's hitched." She pointed to the news clip.

I read over her shoulder. "Dale Pearson, 51, a veteran LAPD detective who has been declared a 'person of interest' in the double homicide of Chloe Monahan and Paige Avner, has reportedly met with attorney and former police officer Errol Messinger. Messinger has made the representation of police officers a specialty since leaving the force in 2002. Stuart Holmes, a Los Angeles attorney who has worked with Messinger in the past, said, 'This case is Errol's bread and butter. He's the perfect lawyer for Dale Pearson.' District Attorney Skip Whitmer has said his office is reviewing the evidence and that a decision as to what charges will be filed will be made by the end of this week."

Messinger. It figured. He was the go-to guy for naughty cops. And of course, Stuart Holmes, his bun boy, was there to cheer him on—in the hopes of getting on the case as his second chair. "How did Holmes manage to get Messinger's dick out of his mouth long enough to give that statement?"

Michelle gave a short laugh. "According to certain 'celebutantes,' it just takes a little practice." She sighed. "So much for our shot at the bigs."

I shrugged. "Probably for the best."

FIVE

Other than finding out that someone else had snagged the Canyon Killer case, it was a day like any other. But for some reason, by the time I got home, I was so tired I barely had the energy to heat up a can of chicken noodle soup before falling into bed. So I thought I had a shot at making it through the night without having the damn nightmare again. No such luck.

In my dream, I'm plunging the carving knife into his chest again and again and again, grunting with each blow until my clothes, my face, and my arms are covered in blood. I stand back to let him fall, the handle of the knife slick and wet in my hand. But he doesn't fall. He smiles. That sick leer of a smile that always made my insides freeze. I'm paralyzed for a moment, but then the hot rage surges through me again, and I lunge forward to slash his throat with a swift backhand motion. Blood gushes from his neck. But he's still smiling. Frustrated, furious, I sob as I bury the knife in his stomach. Once, twice, three times, heaving with the effort of each thrust. Finally, I yank out the knife and stand back. Still he doesn't fall. Exhausted, gulping for air, I raise the knife again, but suddenly, I can't reach him. He's a giant. I stare up at him, terrified. Then, in one swift motion, he grabs my arms, lifts me up, and pins me against the wall. His hands feel like steel clamps. I fight to break free, my heels kicking against the wall. As I twist my head back and forth, I feel a blast of hot, fetid air. His mouth opens wide—a huge, cavernous black hole—and I feel the darkness begin to engulf me. Trapped, terrified, I scream and scream, but all that comes out is a pathetic little whisper.

I woke up to the choked gurgle of my own voice, my heart pounding, my throat raw. I rolled over on my back still gasping for air. I used to believe the dreams would go away over time, once the memory of the living nightmare faded. But it's been years now, and the dreams still come almost every night. The only thing that ever changes is the weapon. I've used a gun, a piano wire, a machete—even an ax. Doesn't matter. It always ends the same way, with his hands clamped around my arms, and me, paralyzed, terrified . . . doomed.

Now, I curled up and shivered under the covers. My favorite sleeping T-shirt, the one with a smiling Janis Joplin, was soaked with sweat. I looked at the soft glow of sunlight that peeked through the gap in the curtains of my bedroom window—a reassuring slice of reality that reminded me that the monster was out of my life. I might not be able to get to him, but he couldn't—wouldn't dare—try to get to me. Except in my dreams.

I stumbled out of bed the next morning, tired and groggy. I had a headache that felt like someone had pounded a spike through my forehead. It took three cups of coffee to get my brain clear. By the time I left for the office, it was nine thirty. I hate being late.

I ran downstairs, jumped into my car, and jammed the key into the ignition. Beulah slowly groaned to life. Dealing with her on days like this made me want to scream. I needed to fly—or at least make it from zero to sixty in less than five minutes. But that just wasn't Beulah's way. I was turning onto Beverly Glen Boulevard to head over the canyon when Michelle called. "You almost here?"

"Almost," I lied.

"Just left home, huh?" Michelle knows me way too well. "Good. Because you need to get downtown. Your jury came back."

It'd been three days since the jury had gone out on Harold Ringer's case. It wasn't the longest I'd ever had a jury stay out, but it was close. "Sure took their time."

"Yeah. And I hope they hammered your guy. That scum-sucking pig. No offense."

"None taken. My guess is you'll get your wish."

It'd taken hours of coaching to make Ringer come off halfway decent on the witness stand. "Okay, I'm heading to court."

Happy at the prospect of not having to see him again after today, I dialed up a Steely Dan album on my phone and sang along to "Don't Take Me Alive." When I got to court, I saw that the victim, Aidan Mandy, was sitting in the audience with a victim-witness counselor from the DA's office. He looked frail, vulnerable, his skinny frame hunched over with his hands clasped in his lap. It hurt to look at him. I signaled to Jimmy, the bailiff, to let me into the holding tank.

Ringer was pacing in his cell. His square face, normally ruddy, was pale, and I noticed a film of sweat on his forehead. As I approached the cell, I saw that his hands were shaking and he was swallowing hard, his breath coming in shallow gulps. Prison was going to be a rough ride for him, and he knew it. He moved up and gripped the bars. "What do you think?"

Now that I was closer, his body odor, sharp and rancid, made me turn my head. I shrugged. "You never know with a jury. But we did all we could—"

The bailiff poked his head in. "Wrap it up. Judge says we're ready to roll."

Five minutes later, Ringer was seated next to me at counsel table as the judge called for the jury. I watched their faces as they came out. The foreman glanced at me, then hurriedly looked away. A bad sign. I studied the judge's expression as he checked the verdict forms, but he was stone-faced. He handed the folder to the clerk and said, "Will the defendant please rise?"

I stood and helped Ringer up. He was shaking so badly now, I could hear the chains on his ankles rattling.

The clerk read the verdict in a quavering voice. "We, the jury in the above-entitled cause, find the defendant, Harold Ringer . . . not guilty."

The courtroom went dead silent. I blinked for a moment, then stared at the clerk. I couldn't have heard that right. But then a cry came from the audience. "No! You can't! You're wrong!"

I turned to see Aidan standing, red-faced, as he clutched the back of the bench seat in front of him. Tears began to roll down his face as he stared at the jury in disbelief. A stab of pain shot through my heart. The judge called for order, and the victim advocate put an arm around Aidan's shoulders. He sank back onto the bench and put his face in his hands. I turned away and glanced at the jury. Some of the jurors looked shame-faced; others looked sad. The judge thanked the jury without much enthusiasm and told them they were discharged. A few minutes later, the show over, the courtroom emptied out.

Ringer had been subdued, but now he snapped back to his old obnoxious self like a rubber band. He fist-pumped the air. "I *knew* it! I knew they'd never believe that little faggot!"

I glared at him. "You didn't know it ten minutes ago."

"I was just nervous. But I *killed* up on that stand. I was a fucking rock star!"

Disgusted, I started to pack up my briefcase.

Jimmy, the bailiff, gave me a look of sympathy as he came over to escort Ringer back into lockup. "I've got his court clothes. They his? Or yours?"

I sometimes had to provide a decent-looking shirt and pants for clients so the jury wouldn't see them in their orange jumpsuits. But Ringer had brought his own. He wasn't wearing them now because once the jury has a verdict, there's no point in bothering. "They're his. You got them in lockup?" Jimmy nodded. I thought for a moment. "Give 'em to me. I'll take them over to Twin Towers, put them with the rest of his stuff. Is he going to process out today?"

"Yeah. Should be out by five o'clock or so."

Jimmy took Ringer by the arm. I picked up my briefcase and nodded to my client. "I'm taking off. Good luck." Ordinarily, I'd make arrangements to get him a ride home, but as far as I was concerned, this jerk could walk.

Ringer gave me his old, snotty smile. "Yeah, thanks."

A few minutes later, Jimmy emerged from lockup with a dress shirt and a pair of slacks on a hanger. I took them and headed out to the Twin Towers jail.

When I got down to the property room, I handed the clothes to the custodian. She took them and sighed. "I need to check these?"

"Nope. Bailiff cleared everything. They're good to go." She turned to get a plastic bag to store them in. I held up a hand. "Don't bother. He'll be down here any minute. He's going home."

She raised an eyebrow. "Congratulations. I guess."

"Yeah. I guess."

SIX

I told Michelle and Alex about Ringer when I got back to the office.

Alex looked stunned. "Seriously? Why?"

Michelle's mouth fell open. "No way. How could they walk that filthy worm?"

I shook my head. "I'd like to think I'm just that good—"

"Actually, you are. But still." Michelle gave a sharp sigh. Her e-mail pinged. She went to her computer and held up a hand. "Listen to this. 'Errol Messinger has given a statement saying that due to previous commitments, he will not be able to take Dale Pearson's case.'" Michelle looked up. "You'd think Messinger would've known that before he met with Dale."

I smiled. "Oh, he knew. He's just saving face. Pearson turned him down."

It might've been the thrill of the hunt. That same animal instinct that makes you grab for the last blouse on the bargain table even though it's a hideous shade of puce, is missing a button, and you know deep down that you'll never wear it.

Or maybe it was because I was feeling invincible after the win on Ringer's case. I wasn't sure. I just knew in that moment that I was going to go for it. "Do you guys have a number for Pearson?"

They cracked wide grins. Alex pumped a fist in the air. "All right!"

But when I went into my office and picked up the phone, I hesitated. I told myself to just do it. Just make the call. But I was still standing at my window, staring at the sliver of sky that peeked between the buildings when Michelle buzzed. Her voice was low. "This is so bizarre. Guess who just called? Dale Pearson. Line one."

"I . . . uh . . ."

"Take the damn call, Samantha."

I clicked over. Dale Pearson introduced himself and asked me if I knew about his case. I told him of course I did. He got right down to business.

"I'd like to discuss the possibility of you representing me."

His voice was deep and smooth, like old single-malt scotch. And it had the authoritative timbre of someone who was used to giving orders. But it stopped just short of the macho, condescending tone some cops have. Then again, I reminded myself, he was on his best behavior.

"I'm not sure I can, Dale. I've got a pretty heavy caseload." It was a strategic move, a way to keep the upper hand. If I did take his case, I wanted him to know he was lucky to get me.

"I kind of figured you would. But I thought I'd give it a try before I moved on to the others who've lined up, because you came highly recommended by someone I trust."

Someone recommended me to a *cop*? Couldn't be anyone who really knew me. "Who?"

"Rick Saunders."

Now I got it. I'd had a case with Saunders before. He was an honest cop. If Saunders really was a buddy, Pearson might not be all bad. It'd be easy enough to verify. I checked my calendar. "Why don't you come by the day after tomorrow?"

"I might already be in custody by then. Can you spare any time today? I can come in as late as you want."

We agreed on five o'clock. I walked out to tell Alex and Michelle. "He's coming by at five o'clock. You guys don't have to wait. I'm sure he won't feed my body to the shredder."

Alex *tsk*ed. "Your shredder's way too small."

Michelle shook her head. "And you're high if you think we're going to miss this."

I figured. "Give me everything you've got on Pearson. And Alex, see if you can find out whether he's tight with this LAPD detective Rick Saunders."

Michelle tapped a few keys on her computer. "There. Go read."

It wasn't much. Dale Pearson, fifty-one years old, had been married and divorced twice. Nothing unusual for a cop. Or a trial lawyer. We're notoriously bad marriage material. One daughter from the first marriage, Lisa Milstrom, who was seventeen now. He'd graduated cum laude with a BA in political science from UCLA. So he hadn't always wanted to be a cop. Whatever he'd been planning to do, it took him just one year to figure out it wasn't happening and sign up with the LAPD.

And he'd done well. He'd made detective within five years, which was pretty fast. He'd done stints in West LA, Rampart, and South Central before winding up in the Hollywood Division.

And then he'd killed two women.

The day moved as slowly as all days do when you're waiting for them to end. I read up on the latest state and Supreme Court decisions, answered some letters and e-mails, and prayed my mother wouldn't call.

At ten after five, the buzzer sounded. Michelle spoke into the intercom, our only form of security. Dale Pearson announced himself and Michelle buzzed him in. I'd left the door to my office open so I could listen in while he met Michelle and Alex. It's always telling how someone treats "the help." If he was a jackass with Michelle and Alex, he'd be toast.

responded to the call. What was a homicide detective doing on a burglary call?"

"I was doing a favor for Chuck Demeter; he's on the burglary desk." He shook his head. "Talk about no good deed."

"That's when you met Chloe." He nodded. "Do you always date your crime victims?" Dale's face darkened. This wasn't good. "Look, you might have to take the stand. If you can't even handle *my* asking you questions like that, you'll get shredded when the DA gets in your face. So let's try that again. If you've dated other victims, some of them might come out and say you used your position to push them into it."

He exhaled, but his expression was pained. "No, I've never dated a crime victim before."

"But since you've been working in Homicide for the past ten years, I'd guess victims are off the table. Hopefully. What about witnesses?"

He shook his head. "No. No one."

"Tell me about that burglary." From what I'd heard, the burglar had been Suspect Number One. Our first strategy would be to dig up evidence that showed the police should've stuck with that theory instead of zeroing in on Dale. "Was there forced entry?"

"No. The girls had a small balcony with a sliding glass door where they kept a few potted plants. They said they liked to leave it open to let in the air, and they forgot to lock it when they went out that night. When they got home, they found it pushed open wide."

I could relate. I left my windows open all the time. Even in my office. "What'd he take?"

"Just jewelry. But it looked like pretty nice stuff. Chloe had photos. A diamond necklace, two-carat diamond studs, a tennis bracelet. I can't remember exactly what she said it was worth. Something like ten grand, I think."

"Did you believe it was worth that much?"

Dale shrugged. "Seemed about right to me, but that's the insurance company's problem. I just take the report."

"Did they have anything else? Like a TV, a laptop, a stereo?"

"Yeah, but they weren't high-end, and it would've been tough to get anything big over that balcony. It didn't seem like a planned hit to me. The building's nothing special. Neither is the neighborhood. You wouldn't go there thinking you'd find anything worth stealing."

"So you think this guy happened to spot the open sliding glass door and decided to take a chance?"

"Yeah. That's why I had the place dusted from top to bottom. The job was strictly amateur hour, so I figured he had to have left prints."

"But he didn't."

"I think he probably did. The print guys just couldn't find any that were usable."

"Did that have to do with your print guys or the conditions in the apartment?"

Dale sighed. "Spangler isn't the best tech in the world. But the wood on the balcony was rough and splintered, and it'd been raining, so everything was damp." He shrugged. "I think the jerk just got lucky."

"How could Chloe afford that jewelry? From what I read, she was pretty close to homeless just a few months earlier. I would've thought she'd have pawned that stuff long ago."

"Me, too." Dale's expression was sad. "But they might've had sentimental value, gifts from friends back when she was still big-time—"

"Did she tell you who gave it to her?"

"She said a bunch of different people. Her manager, a boy-friend . . . she didn't give me any names. But she didn't flinch when I told her I'd have to run the photos to see if they turned up in any pawnshops."

So however she'd acquired that jewelry, it was legit. "What can you tell me about those neighbors who say they heard you and Chloe fighting that night?"

Dale stared down at his hands for a long moment. When he looked up, there was real pain in his eyes. "That they're telling the truth. We did have a fight. A big one. Chloe was high. She'd started using again in the past few weeks, and we'd gotten into it a few times. But that night it really got ugly. She slapped me, started scratching and clawing at me. I tried to hold her off, but she just kept coming. I—I hit her." He rubbed his face, and his hand covered his mouth briefly, as though he wanted to stop the next words from coming out. "Harder than I meant to—"

"Where? In the head? The stomach?"

"I think . . . the side of her head. It's all kind of a blur now. We'd both been drinking." Dale swallowed hard. "I started to leave, but she came at me again. She took a couple of swings. I think I shoved her, but I might've hit her again . . . I don't know. I just know she fell down."

"Did anyone take photos of you?"

Dale nodded. "When I got arrested. But it'd been more than a week by then. I don't know if the photos will show much." He looked at me, his eyes pleading. "You've got to believe me—when I left her apartment, she was alive. I know she was."

"Did she say anything?"

"Yeah, when I said I was sorry, she told me to go fuck myself."

"Where was she? On the floor? On the bed? What was she doing?" The more detail he could give about how she'd looked when he left her, the more credible he'd sound.

Dale paused and let his gaze drift over my shoulder. "She was on the floor. And she was starting to push herself up."

"Do you think she was high that night? And when you say she was using, I assume you mean something serious, like meth or heroin?"

"Heroin, yeah. I don't know for sure that she'd been using that night. But she seemed high. It should be in the tox report."

We wouldn't get the toxicology and autopsy reports for a while. It'd be good if the tox report backed up his story, but it wasn't of critical importance right now. There was no question about cause of death. Chloe hadn't overdosed; she'd been stabbed to death. "And where was Paige during all this?"

"Out. On a date with a guy they called Mr. Perfect. I saw her when I came to pick up Chloe that evening. Chloe said she probably wouldn't be back till morning."

"Who's Mr. Perfect?"

"I don't know. They never used his name. But I figured he was married because I remember hearing Chloe drop a comment about Paige not really needing to get all fixed up for their dates, since they never went out anywhere."

So he lived in LA. "When you and Chloe got back to the apartment, Paige was gone?" Dale nodded. "And you never saw Paige again." Dale shook his head. "So you're saying someone else must've come in after you left and stabbed them both?"

Dale's expression was bleak. "I know how it sounds, but that's what had to have happened."

He was right; it did sound impossible. But it was the only story that would get him off the hook. As much as it sucked, I knew I'd have to run with some version of it.

"Did Chloe ever mention anyone she was having problems with? Anyone who threatened her or—"

"No."

"What about her dealer? Maybe she owed him money or pissed him off because she wouldn't buy from him anymore . . . ?"

"It's possible. And I'd bet whoever she's been buying from lately is working on the show, because a couple of times when I picked her up at the studio, she seemed loaded."

I'd have to check that out. And I'd have to get every detail he could remember about Chloe and what she did every day, especially in the last week or so. The more I knew about her, the better my chances of finding someone else I could pin this on. "What about Paige? Did she have any enemies that you knew of?"

"No. But I do know she was no druggie."

"What about jealous boyfriends? Or Mr. Perfect's wife?"

"I wouldn't know about boyfriends. And Mr. Perfect never came to the apartment. Plus . . ." Dale trailed off.

"Plus, what? You'd have heard if the wife had found out?"

"No, I probably wouldn't. But if the wife knew about Paige, knew where she lived, why go to her apartment to get into it with her? Why not wait till Paige was in a place where she didn't have to worry about a roommate or neighbors?"

Good point. And that probably let out Mr. Perfect, too. But we'd try to find out who he was anyway. A married man could make a great decoy to throw at the jury. "Do you know of anyone else Paige might've confided in? Someone who'd know who Mr. Perfect was?"

Dale shook his head. "But I know what I'd do if I were running this case: I'd talk to the people she worked with, check her Facebook page for friends and hangouts, see what's on her phone or her computer. And, of course, any family you can find."

I knew this was coming. And I didn't mind. Matter of fact, I'd have been a little worried if he didn't try to give me some pointers. He was a detective; it's what he did. But I had to get him thinking from the other side of things now—he wasn't a cop anymore; he was a defendant.

"Here's the thing, Dale. We have to be careful who we talk to and what questions we ask. From what you're telling me, it's entirely possible the cops don't know about Mr. Perfect. So we can't tip our hand. Because if they find out about him, they'll do everything they can to prove he's not a possible suspect. They'll try to find an alibi for him, or witnesses who'll say his wife knew about Paige and didn't care or . . . whatever. We don't want that. The more straw men we can point to, the better. We're not looking for the truth or the real killer. We're looking for reasonable doubt. Got it?"

He stared at me for a moment, his expression stricken. It was a tough adjustment being on the other side of the lawsuit. But after a few seconds, he nodded with a look that was respectful . . . admiring, even. It caught me off guard.

"I just remembered something," Dale said. "Given what you told me, I don't know what you want to do with this, but Chloe was on the phone with her sister, Kaitlyn, when I came over. They were pretty close. You might want to check her out."

"We'll wait and see what the cops get out of her first. I don't want her telling them what we asked about. And we'll check out Paige's connects on the down low. Alex, the guy you saw when you came in, is a fabulous investigator."

"You just hire him? Because I didn't see him on your website."

"Yeah, he's new, but he's a real score." And when his guilty plea got into the system, he'd also be a real felon. But I saw no reason to overshare. "For now, just for the purpose of giving quotable quotes to the media, I'm going to say we're looking into the burglar theory." I didn't see how that could hurt anything. Since they didn't get any prints, they'd never catch the burglar.

Dale nodded. "You think the case is going to stay this big?"

I stared at him. *You killed a beloved actress and her best friend. Hell yeah, I do.* "I think it's likely, yes." I mentally reviewed the information he'd given me. We'd covered all but one area. The coroner wouldn't be able to narrow down the time of death to any less than two hours. But if the time of death was more than two hours after Dale left, we'd have a shot at selling his defense. "So you left immediately after the fight?" Dale nodded. "You know what time that was?"

He shook his head. "Late. After midnight."

"Where'd you go?"

"I went home." Dale sighed. "And yes, I live alone."

It figured. "An apartment or a house?"

"A house."

Getting worse. "Run into anyone on the way? See any neighbors when you got home?"

"No and no." He sighed. "I know. It's a shitty alibi."

"The kind innocent people usually have. At least that's what I tell my juries." I gave him a little smile. His smile was strained. "Have you heard about any of the evidence they found yet?"

"No." He raked his fingers through his hair. "It's crazy to be on this side of a case."

I didn't say, "You ain't seen nothing yet." He didn't need any more depressing news right now. "Let's take tonight to think about this. In the meantime, speak to no one. Not the press, not another cop, not your friends. For now, you have no friends. Not even Rick Saunders."

He looked upset. No, more than that. He looked wounded. "You're not going to take my case?"

I'd been more than ambivalent about it before. But in that moment, I knew what my answer had to be. "I will take your case. I just wanted to give you the chance to sleep on it."

A look of relief spread across his face. "I don't need to; I already know. You're the one I want."

I stood up and held out my hand. "Then I guess we're in business."

Dale got up and gave it a hearty shake. "Thank you. I can't tell you how much I appreciate this."

With the decision made, my wheels started turning. "You've got two exes and a daughter. Anyone lighting candles and chanting for your death?"

Dale gave a rueful smile. "Put it this way, they won't go out of their way to hurt me, but I wouldn't recommend you put them on the stand."

"What about your daughter, Lisa? Any child-support issues floating around?"

Dale looked insulted. "No. Never." He saw my expression. "Tracy never even had to ask. I paid in full and on time." His face immediately darkened. "But if you're thinking of putting her in front of a camera, the answer's no. I won't have Lisa dragged into this."

The sudden raw force in his voice made me lean back as though he'd shoved me. "If anyone 'drags' your daughter into this, it'll be the press, not me—"

As quickly as he'd heated up, he cooled down. The abrupt switchback was startling. His voice was calm, contrite. "Sorry. The thing is, I only just started getting to know her a couple of years ago. When Tracy and I broke up, she took the baby back east to be with her family. Lisa was just six months old. Between work and money issues, I never got the chance to see her. They moved back to LA two and a half years ago, and I've been trying to make up for lost time—"

"And they're okay with it?"

"Yeah, really cool, actually. Lisa is a great kid—no thanks to me." Dale rubbed his face, his expression miserable. "The minute I heard the cops were looking at me for this, I called to tell her and Tracy that I didn't do it. They said they knew, but . . ."

But they didn't. And now, at the very least, they'd start wondering. "I get it. And your other ex?" I knew his marriage to Tracy had barely made it past the honeymoon. But his second marriage had stuck for seven years.

"Bobbi'll be okay. No really bad blood or anything. But she won't be much help."

Damn. A loving ex would've been a nice touch in a case like this. But at least I didn't have to worry about any bad press. The exes went on the back burner for now.

"I'll need my retainer up front. It's fifty thousand. I'll probably run through that before we get to trial, so Michelle will work out the fee and payment schedule with you tomorrow."

I walked him out of my office and had him sign the retainer agreement Michelle had already prepared. He nodded to Michelle and Alex, then shook my hand again.

"Thank you, Ms.—"

"Samantha."

He looked at me and said in a soft voice, "Samantha." He turned to go, then stopped in the doorway. "I know you don't believe me right now, but I'm not like your other clients. I really didn't do it."

I nodded, but his lightning-fast mood shifts weren't reassuring. And I didn't think he'd want to hear the truth: that's exactly what my other clients say.

EIGHT

I convened the troops after he left. "What do you think, guys?"

Michelle leaned back and folded her arms. "The same thing I've been thinking."

I looked at Alex. He shrugged. "I'm not sure I should have a vote here, but I'd definitely take the case if I were you."

Michelle held out her hands, presenting Alex. "And there you have it."

"Then I guess it's unanimous."

Michelle finally smiled. "Hallelujah. And by the way, he's easy on the eyes. That'll help."

It really would. Being attractive matters everywhere—getting jobs, getting laid, and yes, getting acquitted by a jury of your peers. No one can resist a pretty face. As long as it's not *too* pretty.

Back in my first year of private practice, I had a bombshell of a client. Tall, blonde, built like a Victoria's Secret model. She was charged with grand theft. A teller for a very large chain of banks whose title ends with the name of a country, my client used her position to filch personal account information from almost a hundred customers and then gave it to her boyfriend. He pocketed more than sixty grand before they got caught.

The judge gave me every ruling, every jury instruction, and every lesser-included charge I asked for—and not because he was impressed by my legal genius. He practically stepped on his tongue every time he took the bench. But the jury hammered her. Hard. I talked to them afterward, and in stray comments here and there, I found out why. The women hated her, and the men saw her as the girl they could never get.

Dale Pearson looked good but not spectacular. So we were safe, at least in that regard.

I decided not to tell them about that flashpoint moment when I mentioned his daughter. It might mean something—but it might not. And there was something . . . satisfying about the way he was protective of Lisa, even if it was a little over the top.

I gave them a quick rundown of what Dale had said. Then I got into our immediate chores. "Alex, I'll need you to call the IO so we can arrange to surrender Dale when the DA files charges." I explained what an IO was—the lead detective, also known as the investigating officer—and how to find out who it was.

Michelle cut me off. "I'll get Alex up to speed on that stuff, Sam. You just do your thing." And thankfully, Michelle knew the ropes, because arranging for Dale's surrender was going to be serious business. The arrest of a veteran detective would have reporters swarming the skies in jet packs. I started to head back to my office, but Michelle held up a hand. "Don't forget you have Sheri again tonight. The car should be here any minute."

"Cancel it, Michy. I've got real work to do."

Michelle gave me her lightning-bolt glare. "I absolutely will not. You need her on your side now more than ever."

That was true. "I can't talk about the case."

"Hello? You think I didn't tell them that?"

Of course she had. Michelle wasn't just on top of things, she was always three steps ahead. "And they're cool with it?"

"Oh yeah. You're about to be kind of famous. They'll take you any way they can get you as long as that lasts."

As if on cue, the office phone rang. It was my limo. I wasn't in the mood for goofy TV talk, but the ride was a nice consolation prize.

Sheri was still obsessing over the Samron case. This time we chewed on parental responsibility—the girl's father had left a loaded gun in his nightstand.

It was only one segment, but Barry and I got into it, and the fur really flew, which made Sheri's producers happy. I guess if they're happy, I'm happy. But it'd been a long day, and I got into the limo looking forward to a drink. When my phone rang, I figured it was Michelle. She usually calls to give me a critique on how I did and to let me know if I'd generated any new business.

So I stupidly answered the call without looking at the screen. Not that it would've helped. My mother is onto my screening ways, so her number comes up BLOCKED.

Her voice, nasal and grating, was loud enough to scale even the heavy traffic on Sunset Boulevard. "Samantha? Your hair looked so flat. When was the last time you washed it?"

"Thirty years ago, Mom. When the beehive went out of style." Most conversations with her begin this way. She fires the first salvo, then I spend the rest of the time trying—and failing—to get off the defensive. Talking to my mother was about as much fun as chewing a ball of tinfoil with a mouthful of fillings.

"Don't be a smartass. *Someone's* got to tell you the truth. And must you always do the smoky eye?"

I pulled down the mirror and looked. "That's the way I like it."

"And I don't like that shade of lipstick on you. Didn't I tell you to ask for a neutral?"

I was sure she did. She always gave me a litany of To Dos. I gritted my teeth. "How about the *case*, Celeste? Did you hear what I was talking about?"

"I don't remember."

For the nine-billionth time, I wondered if she did it on purpose. It was all I could do to unclench my jaw long enough to tell her. "The girl's father left the loaded gun in his nightstand."

"Oh, enough already. Everyone's always blaming the parents for everything. I'm sick of it."

I bit my lip so hard I could feel my teeth making a divot. This from the woman who'd never taken the blame for anything. "Sometimes they *are* to blame. That gun should've been locked up."

"Oh, for Christ's sake. She's not a baby. She's fourteen years old. More than old enough to know better."

"She did know better. Better than to think her useless parents would ever protect her. They let that wolverine of a brother brutalize her for years."

"Parents are only human. They can't be everywhere and see everything."

Or in Celeste's case, much of anything. Of course, we weren't just talking about the show. But I wasn't in the mood to go for the real elephant in the room. And, as always, I'd been gritting my teeth so hard I'd given myself a headache. Time to get to the reason for her call. "What do you want, Celeste?" As if I didn't know.

My mother invites me whenever they have an empty seat at one of their dinner parties. My stepfather, Jack Maynard, is a huge commercial real estate mogul, and he does a fair amount of entertaining to keep the wheels of commerce greased. Because he's a decent, glass-half-full kind of guy, he insists these invitations are her way of reaching out to me. I know better. She just wants me because her buddies love to hear "insider" stories about the hot cases around town.

"I'm having some people over for dinner this Saturday. Nothing fancy, just a little get-together for some of Jack's upper-level managers."

First of all, in a mansion the size of two football fields, there's no such thing as "nothing fancy." You need to cater just to have someone move the food from the kitchen to the dining room. Second of all, if they were sacrificing a Saturday night, it would be at least a hundred of Jack's closest friends. So this dinner was neither simple nor small. "Sorry, I can't." I considered telling her I'd just picked up a big case and I was too busy for one of her soirees. But she wouldn't care. On a scale of one to ten—ten being most important to Celeste—my career rated a negative four. "I've got a date."

"With that singer?"

"He's a musician who also happens to sing."

"What's the difference? He's a zero."

Meaning: he's got zero money. "He's a good guy." I knew what was coming. I mouthed the words as she said them.

"A 'good guy' won't put you in a nice house. A 'good guy' won't buy you a nice car—"

"No. He won't. *I* will, Celeste." But self-reliance was not a concept she embraced. Her lifelong aspiration had been to become *de*pendently wealthy. The truth was, I'd already broken up with the musician. But I had no intention of telling her.

"You might not always want to work. You never know—"

I turned onto my street. "I do know. I've gotta go."

"You can show up late. Or just come for drinks."

"I really can't." The sad, inexplicable thing was, I knew I'd probably go anyway. And so did she.

NINE

When I got home, I changed into sweats and poured myself a double shot of Patrón Silver—a gift from a client who'd cleaned house when she went into rehab. The press was well on its way to making Dale's case a daily feast, and the jury pool was out there listening. I'd need to start using those reporters to talk to that pool right away—about burglars and drug dealers and maybe ex-boyfriends. Basically, anything that would point the finger at someone else.

I thought about where we should start digging, made some notes, and put myself to bed early. I wanted to hit the ground running.

The next morning, I was up by six thirty. I finished my first cup of coffee, then called Dale. He sounded wide awake and clear headed. I told him I was arranging to surrender him at the station so we could avoid a parade. "Has the press found your house or your phone number yet?"

"Not yet."

"They will. So try not to do a lot of running around. If anyone does call and you accidentally pick up, just refer him or her to me. You've got my number handy, right?"

"Yeah."

"Get your place in order. Have they searched it yet?"

"Yeah. First thing they did. Left it a friggin' mess."

"They seize anything I need to worry about?"

"Just my set of murder knives."

"That's a real knee-slapper, Dale. But watch out with the jokes. If the wrong person hears you, it won't play well. So I'll take that as a 'no'?"

"No. I mean, they did what I'd expect. They grabbed my comb and the clothes I wore that night. I'm sure they *will* find my hairs and clothing fibers at the scene. But, so what? It's no secret I was there that night. Hell, I was there a lot of nights."

True. But still, if they found his hairs or clothing fibers on her body, it wouldn't help. "They'll probably toss your place again when the DA files, which could be any minute. So stand by. I'll be back in touch."

I showered and dressed in camera-worthy slacks and a blouse. Alex called while I was eating breakfast. "I've got the IO. His name is Wayne Little."

I'd heard the name, but I'd never had a case with him. "Did he say when he thought the DA would get him the paperwork?"

"He thinks by this afternoon. And he said he'd call us as soon as he gets it and arrange a time for Dale to surrender. They're planning to book him at Twin Towers."

That figured. They'd need all the security they could get for a cop, and Twin Towers had maximum-security modules. "Got it." I looked at my watch. "Okay, I'll see you at the office."

I ended the call. I was about to go to my computer and start typing up my notes for the To Do list when I got a premonition. I headed for my car instead.

And that is why, when Detective Wayne Little showed up at Dale's house with an arrest warrant at eight thirty a.m., I was there waiting for him. I pointedly looked at my watch. "Guess the DA put a rush on that paperwork, after all. Thanks for the heads up."

Detective Little, his arms hanging loosely from a square, dumpy body, just shrugged and answered in a flatly unapologetic voice, "Sorry 'bout that. We kind of got busy."

Meanwhile, other detectives were cuffing Dale. I counted the blue-uniformed and sports-jacketed bodies. "*Eleven* men?" One of them started reading Dale his rights. I stepped over to him. "He's not waiving." I turned back to Little. "I assume you've got a search warrant as well?" He nodded. "I'll have one of my associates on hand, just to make sure nothing gets . . . lost or dented." Police can be careful or they can leave the place looking like it'd been through a hurricane. Judging by their last visit, the latter seemed more likely.

Starting now, I'd be making notes of every shitty thing they did. It'd all be part of my campaign to show the viewing public, AKA the jury pool, how Dale Pearson had been unjustly accused and mistreated—and by his own "family," no less. I called Alex and told him to come over and stand watch while they served the warrant. "Keep your eyes open for any unnecessary roughness, and take notes and pictures."

"Got it. I'm on my way."

The officers milled around trying to decide who'd take Dale, who'd ride in the follow-car, and who'd stay and help serve the warrant. In the meantime—*of course*—the press got wind of what was going down, and a crowd of reporters was starting to gather in the street. "I'd like to talk to my client for a moment."

Wayne Little looked like he wanted to argue. I hoped he did. It'd be another line on my List of Shitty Things They Did to Dale. I gave him a bland smile.

He finally seemed to realize this fight was a bad idea and waved to the officers holding Dale. "Let her."

The officers stepped back a few feet, and I whispered in Dale's ear. "The press is out there. I want you to walk out standing tall, no stooping, no hiding. Don't say anything, and for God's sake, whatever you do, don't smile. Got it?"

He took a tense breath and nodded. "What're they doing about security for me in the jail?"

"They have to put you in maximum. But I'll remind them how much it'll cost if you so much as stub your toe." I wanted to tell him not to worry, but that would be impossible—and insane. His life was going to be in constant jeopardy.

I went over to Little. "You've got special security arranged for him, I assume?"

Little scratched his round, balding head and spread his fingers along his chimney broom of a mustache. "Uh, yeah. I mean, we're putting him in max."

"That's the least you can do. And right now, when things are hot and fresh, I'd advise you to do the most." I drilled him with a look. "Because if anything happens to him . . ."

He gave me a heavily lidded glare. "I'll see what I can do." He walked away, trying to act like he was dusting me off, but I saw him pull out his cell phone.

By the time we left, the press had filled the entire street. The only free space was the area around the squad cars. And that was only because there were uniforms keeping them away. The cops marched Dale out as though he were Lee Harvey Oswald. All six of them. There was no way anyone within range could've gotten a shot at Dale without taking out an officer first. I appreciated the security, but I wasn't sure whether they really thought they needed that much manpower or they just wanted to be on camera.

Dale was pretty well hidden inside the phalanx of uniforms—which was fine by me—but the press screamed out questions anyway.

"Are you pleading not guilty?"

"Did she try to break up with you? Is that why you killed her?"

"What's your defense going to be?"

"Do you have an alibi?"

Then, one lone voice on the fringe called out, "How come they didn't let you surrender at the station?"

I'd been walking behind the group of officers holding Dale, but now I stopped and turned to see who'd asked a sane question for a change. It seemed to have come from a tallish, slender guy with curly brown hair that looked like it hadn't been combed since Kanye West dissed Taylor Swift at the Grammys. He was standing away from the crowd, off to my right. I fell back and waved him over. "Who are you?"

He jerked back as though I'd slapped him. "Who are *you*?"

Fair question. "I'm Dale Pearson's lawyer."

"You got a card?"

"Do you?"

He paused, then reached into his shirt pocket and handed me a business card that said his name was Trevor Skotler and he was a contributing reporter for Buzzworthy. I recognized the name. It was an online news mag that was starting to seriously encroach on Huffpo and the Daily Beast. This could be useful. I gave him my card. Then I told him how they'd done an end run so Dale wouldn't have a chance to surrender.

"No shit."

"No shit. And they'll be tossing Dale's place pretty soon. My associate is going to be here to make sure they don't play 'Thrash This Pad.' You going to hang around?"

"For a bit."

"I'll tell him to look out for you." And I'd tell Alex to point it out to Trevor if he saw the cops step out of line. With a little luck, my new buddy Trevor might help me fire the first salvo in the war for juror sympathy.

Off to my left, I saw one of the detectives put a hand on the back of Dale's head, preparing to duck him down into the squad car. "I've gotta go."

TEN

I followed the caravan that took Dale to the station to make sure there were no "accidents" during the booking process. Dale had buddies on the force, but this was sheriff's territory. Dale was LAPD. There was no love lost between the two cop shops, so Dale couldn't expect to get any sympathy here. And I'd be about as welcome as a parrot at a spelling bee.

I sat in the waiting room, scrolling through my e-mail to distract myself while cops walked by, shooting me daggers.

By the time Dale got through booking and into his orange jumpsuit, I'd read, dumped, or answered every e-mail, Twitter message, and Facebook note; watched all the latest bits on Funny or Die (using headphones); and checked out the clothes on the HauteLook, MyHabit, and Urban Outfitters websites.

I watched the guards lead Dale into the attorney room, one on each side. Orange isn't an easy color for anyone to work, but it was a real fashion "don't" for Dale, and the monster lighting didn't help. Neither did the shock of being on the wrong side of the handcuffs. The skin on his face looked like a deflated basketball, and his chest had the caved-in look of someone who was collapsing from inside. But he didn't seem to have been knocked around. Not yet, anyway.

The deputies walked him in, and he sat down heavily. He stared, slack-jawed, as they chained him to the floor and the table. "How'd the booking go? Any unnecessary roughness?"

Dale was staring around the airless little room as though he'd landed on Mars. It took him a few seconds to focus. "Uh, no . . . no."

I leaned down to catch his eye and waited for him to look at me. "Listen to me. I want you to get this. If you've got any ideas about being some kind of martyr who covers for his buddies in the Thin Blue Line, send them to Warner Brothers. That crap only works in Hollywood. If anyone gives you a hard time—and I mean *any* kind of hard time, including not giving you enough bread to go with your gravy—you tell me about it. Got it?" He didn't answer, didn't even move. "Blink once for yes, twice for no." Finally, he blinked. Once. "Good. Now let's try this again. How did the booking go? Any damage I can't see?"

He shook his head. "What about bail?"

Now I knew just how shaken up he was. He knew the answer as well as I did. "It's a double. It's a capital case. There is no bail."

Dale sighed and shook his head. "Of course."

"Now I'm going to remind you: no matter who it is, no matter what anyone says, no one here is your friend. No one. If you need to talk or even just vent, call me. If I can't come, I'll send Alex or Michelle. And if anyone wants to come visit, you send them to me first. I'll vet them." Dale looked confused. "Your case is going to be on every news channel, all day, every day. Your grandmother's second cousin's adopted nephew is going to be looking to cash in on you. Every ex-girlfriend, ex-boyfriend, ex–best friend—"

"Okay, okay. I get the picture. I won't talk."

Probably by tomorrow he'd have his feet under him a little better, but right now, he was reeling. I wrapped it up by telling him we'd be working night and day on his case.

"Thanks, Samantha." He gave me a wan smile.

I signaled the deputies that we were done, and they came to get him. As they led him out, he looked back at me. Most clients—even some of my gangbanger clients—get scared the first time they're led away. Dale looked like a child lost in a department store. I gave him the most reassuring smile I could muster and called out, "I'll see you tomorrow."

I headed for the door, planning what I'd say to the press. It was time to start winning the hearts and minds of our jury pool. I'd planned to walk slowly when I got through the door so the reporters could catch up, but I didn't have to worry. I couldn't have missed them if I'd cut out of there at a dead run. A whole contingent was waiting by the exit, and they jumped me the moment I stepped out the door.

"Ms. Brinkman, what's your defense going to be?"

"Are you going to try and get him a deal?"

I recognized a few of the reporters from other court cases, and my new buddy Trevor from Buzzworthy.

This was it. I planted myself in front of the microphones and put on my serious-but-not-scary face—a steady gaze with just a hint of upturned lips. "I have no plans to make any sort of deal in this case. Dale Pearson is innocent of these charges, and we look forward to the opportunity to prove that in a court of law."

One of the female reporters I'd seen around the courthouse called out, "Edie Anderson here for Channel Four News. Are you taking this to trial by yourself? Or will you be adding other lawyers to the team?"

"I don't plan to add any other lawyers to the team, Edie. You know what they say about too many cooks." And Dale wasn't a millionaire, so the only lawyers willing to jump in would just be publicity whores. They wouldn't do any real work or give a damn about the case.

I gave her a smile, and she grinned back at me. "Thanks, Samantha."

"My pleasure." I stepped around the throng and headed for my car. A small group trailed behind me still shouting questions, but I just kept walking. No nods, no headshakes. I'd said what I wanted them to air. I didn't want to give them any other choices.

It'd already been a long day, and it wasn't even half over. I had just fifteen minutes to get to Department 130, where I had a pretrial conference on a drive-by shooting. My client, Ricardo Orozco, a Grape Street Boy gang member, had opened fire on a house that was supposedly the home of the shot caller for the Southside Creepers, their archenemy.

Except it wasn't, and Orozco wound up killing a three-month-old baby and maiming a seven-year-old girl. I inherited the case from another lawyer who'd told the court he and Orozco had had an "irreconcilable breakdown in their relationship." Translation: the lawyer hated him, and no amount of money was worth the grief. Or maybe Orozco had threatened him. But by that time the case had been lingering on the docket for almost a year, and Judge Mayer was desperate to get it off his desk. He begged me to take it. The unspoken quid pro quo was that he'd approve all my billings and throw some good cases my way. As Michelle put it, I couldn't afford to say no.

But it had taken just five minutes with Orozco for me to know it was a mistake. This shooting was so bad, even his fellow Grape Street bangers were ashamed. One was even quoted as saying it was "disgraceful." But Orozco? At our first meeting, he'd looked at me with flat, dead eyes and said, "I didn't do it. But I ain't sorry it happened. That baby'd just grow up to be another Southside Creepers piece of shit. Oughta hang a medal on the dude who did it." At our second meeting, he'd laughed about the little girl he maimed. "Man, you should see the way she stumble around. Little *puta* look like one of them damn zombies from *The Walking Dead*. Ain't nobody ever gonna fuck her gimp ass."

Just breathing the same air as him turned my stomach. I'd tried to make a deal, but the DA told me not to waste my breath. He was going for life without parole. And now I had to give Orozco the bad news that there was no deal. Even worse news for me, because it meant I'd have to sit through a trial with this foul piece of swamp sludge. I told the jail deputy to stay close as I knocked on the door of the holding tank and braced myself for the face-off.

Orozco, his thick hair slicked back, dark and shiny with grease, was sitting on the bench in his cell. He leaned against the wall, his tatted arms folded across his chest, legs stretched out in front of him. His mouth twisted in a lazy sneer of a smile when he saw me. I motioned for him to come to the bars. Moving as though he had all the time in the world, he shuffled up and gave me a head bob. "S'up?"

The sickly sweet smell of his hair goo made me breathe through my mouth. "The DA won't deal. We're going to trial."

Orozco tilted his head back and looked down his nose at me. "I don't think so. When you last talk to him?"

"Yesterday."

He gave a mirthless chuckle. "Go back and talk to him now. Tell him I'll plead to ex-con with a gun, low term."

I stared at him, read the superior look on his face, the confidence in his voice, and put it together. "I'm assuming Castaneda had an accident." Castaneda was the sole eyewitness. So much for witness protection. "That won't help you. They'll just read in his testimony from the preliminary hearing."

Orozco gave a derisive snort. "Castaneda ain't got killed. He jus' finally got his mind right." He flicked his fingers at me, shooing me away. "Go on. Talk to your DA buddy." Orozco turned and walked back to the bench.

ELEVEN

Orozco was right. Jerry Ratner, the DA on the case, was furious. "Problem is, Castaneda didn't just say he wasn't sure anymore. He fingered someone else who looks a lot like Orozco—and the guy doesn't have an alibi." Jerry threw the file on his desk. "Castaneda was practically the whole ball game." Jerry peered at me. "I don't suppose you'd know how Castaneda happened to have this epiphany?"

"I don't know any more than you do, but I can make the same guesses." The only question was, how did those gangbangers find such a good fall guy for him to point to? But I didn't think Jerry was in the mood to ponder it right now. "Look, it's not my place to tell you how to do your job, but if you take this dog to trial, you'll probably lose. Don't you think it'd be better to let it get dismissed and refile when you get more evidence?"

I was doing my job, taking care of my client, but I was also talking sense, and Jerry knew it. He looked miserable, but he nodded. "We've got him on the gun possession, though."

"He'll plead for a county lid."

Jerry got red in the face. "One year? Fuck that." But after a moment, he sighed. "Get him to take low term. He at least has to get state prison out of this. I'd rather dismiss than let him fart around in county jail for a year."

"I'll do what I can."

As it turned out, it was an easy sell. Orozco preferred state prison to county jail. A lot of defendants did. Living conditions were better, and bangers like Orozco always had lots of *familia* there.

When I walked into the courtroom, I saw that Randy was the bailiff on duty. I went over and handed him my cell phone. "You may as well take it now." Somehow, my phone always seemed to ring when he was on duty. He took it away from me so often, I told him he should share the bill.

Randy took my cell and dropped it on his desk. "Gee, Sam. If only there was a way you could stop that from happening."

"I know, right?" I shrugged. "At least this way we know I'll be safe this time."

Randy pulled the lockup keys out of his desk. "Glad you're taking a plea on Orozco. Can't get that piece of garbage out of here fast enough."

As Randy headed to the holding tank, I glanced at his desk and noticed the custody assignment sheets. I quickly flipped through the pages. Then my phone lit up with a call. I didn't recognize the number. Probably the press.

Randy came out of the holding tank with Orozco and saw me at his desk. "What are you doing?"

"Someone called; I was just trying to see the number." I moved to counsel table and Orozco walked over, a shit-eating grin on his face. I turned away and opened my file so I wouldn't have to talk to him. It'd be good to say *adios* to Mr. Orozco.

Judge Mayer came out, and Jerry took the plea and waivers through gritted teeth. The judge gave Orozco an icy glare as he accepted them. With the exception of Orozco, there was no joy in Mudville. The judge pronounced the sentence of two years in state prison.

"Your Honor," I said. "My client would like a 'forthwith.'"

The judge nodded. "My pleasure. The sheriff's department is to have Mr. Orozco transported to state prison forthwith."

When I got back to the office, Michelle was at her computer and Alex was reading over her shoulder. She looked up. "How's Dale doing? And what happened with Orozco?"

I told her about Orozco and that Dale was shell-shocked. "It's going to be rough on him in there. Did you happen to catch my news hits?"

Michelle smiled. "Yep. You did great. Nice sound bites."

"*Gracias*. Has the DA sent over any discovery yet?"

"No," Michelle said. "But they sent over an e-mail confirming that the arraignment's tomorrow at eight thirty. Want me to call?"

"Don't bother. They'll give it to me in court." I sat down on the edge of Michelle's desk. "Alex, you check the girls' Facebook pages, Twitter feeds, every site you can think of that'll give us information on them, their friends, their family—you get the drift. Michelle, get us the contact information on where they worked: Paige's restaurant, her modeling agency, and her agent, if she has one. And get Chloe's studio people, her agents, managers—everyone who had contact with her."

I brought them up to speed on what Dale had told me about the girls. "So we're looking for possible enemies, rivals, jealous exes. We want fall guys. Someone else we can point the finger at. I'm not sure we really want to find Mr. Perfect—"

"Unless we can show he has no alibi," Alex said.

I pointed to him. "Exactly. We just need to find out who he is so we can check that out—"

Alex had been taking notes on his iPad. "And I could start sniffing around Chloe's studio to check into who her dealer might've been—"

"Hold off on that for now. We don't want to make any moves until we see some discovery and find out what we're dealing with." I headed for my office.

"I hate to go all Fashion Police on you," Michelle said. "But the press is definitely going to be in that courtroom tomorrow, right?" I nodded. "Do you know what you're going to wear?"

It sounds like a silly question. It's not. The image is the message. I have to look successful, even a little flashy. Because if I look good, my client looks good—good as in "not like a murderer." Also, I needed to steal focus from Dale. He'd be in his orange jumpsuit for this appearance. The less anyone saw of him looking like an inmate, the better. Especially since the victim's side of the courtroom was going to be dazzling. Lots of celebrity supporters—some legitimate friends of Chloe's, some just looking for free camera face time. I had to give our side as much shine as I could to balance things out.

"I figured I'd wear my usual: the black pencil skirt and the silk pinstriped blouse." Skirt by Tahari, blouse by Calvin Klein. They were the only designer-ish clothes I had.

Michelle nodded. "Good enough."

"Alex, did you get Dale's suits and shirts?" Part of the reason I'd asked him to stay behind while the cops searched his house was to collect all the clothes we'd need to dress Dale up for his future court appearances. Alex nodded. "What do you think? Will they work?" After today, Dale had to look like a million bucks every single time the camera found him.

"Not bad. He did pretty well for someone on a cop's salary. I can work with it."

I wasn't surprised. Dale had style.

Of course, that didn't mean he wasn't a killer.

TWELVE

By the time I left the office at eight o'clock, I was bone tired. So it figured that the very last thing I needed was the first thing that happened. Beulah died on me. The yellow engine light went on three blocks from home, and she just stopped. There was a station a few blocks from my apartment where I could get her towed, but there was no way she'd be roadworthy by tomorrow morning. I called AAA to come get her. Luckily, the driver took pity on me and dropped me at my apartment.

I slogged up the stairs to my tiny one-bedroom apartment. My building is small, just fourteen units on a hillside street above the Sunset Strip, but I scored a unit on the second floor that actually has a partial view of the city. There's no elevator, no security, the carport is wide open to the street, and the washer and dryer are under the building in a dark little room where I just know I'm going to find a dead body someday. And someone's always using the machines anyway, so I usually wind up at the local Laundromat. But for all that, it's home. My little slice of heaven.

I dropped my purse on the kitchen table and went to the refrigerator. It was slim pickin's. Some dicey-looking cottage cheese, an apple, and half of the roast beef sandwich I'd bought at the courthouse snack bar. I took out the sandwich and ate standing up at the sink as I tried to figure out how I'd get to court tomorrow. I couldn't ask Michelle to take me; she had to man the office. But maybe Alex? I didn't know whether the Jetta he was driving now belonged to him, but it was worth a try.

Alex had an even better idea. "I've got a connect to A-1 Limos. If I tell him who you are and where you're going, I bet he'll do it for free. It's good publicity for him."

"That would be awesome. Call me back when you know."

An hour later my phone rang. It was Alex.

"You're all set. He'll pick you up at seven thirty. And I told him to wait and bring you back to the office. You've got to look good in both directions."

"Kind of a maxim for life."

I heard Alex laugh for the first time. "Sure is. Good luck tomorrow."

"See you at the office."

I was going to court in style. Yeah, baby.

I turned on the television, kicked off my shoes, and sat down on the couch. The news came on. I muted it while I sorted through the mail. I hate television news. It's just a disaster report. And it's the crassest form of ratings grabs out there.

My cell phone buzzed on the kitchen table. I went over and looked at the screen. It was Michelle. "Hey, Michy. What's up? You okay?"

"I'm better than okay. The cops left a message with the answering service. Our buddy Harold Ringer OD'd last night."

"Wow. On what?"

"Heroin. Sounds like a hot shot. Can you believe it? First night of freedom. I hate to sound callous, but it couldn't have happened to a nicer guy."

I chuckled. "No argument." We talked for a little while longer, and I promised to try and get more details on Ringer in the morning. When we ended the call, I poured myself a double shot of Patrón Silver, on the rocks with a twist of lime, then found a rerun of *Breaking Bad*. I put up my feet and took a long, deep sip.

* * * *

Going to court in a limo was even better than taking one to the studio. It made me feel like a rock star, and I drank it up all the way to the courthouse. I stared out the window at the palm trees and passing cars, reveling in the fact that I didn't have to navigate the rush-hour traffic. I could sure get used to this. Too bad I wouldn't get the chance.

As we pulled up to the curb, I saw that the press and gawkers were crowded around the front doors. I was a little worried about the gawkers. You never know when a nutbag might decide the world would be better off with one less lawyer. "I'll be about an hour."

"That'll work." He handed me his card. "Here's my number in case you're out sooner. You really that cop's lawyer?"

"Yeah."

He shook his head. "Sounds like they got that guy three ways from Sunday."

"Not when I get done they won't." I gave him my card. "Just in case."

He looked at it. "Hey, you mind signing it?" He pulled out a pen and clicked it. My first autograph. I felt like a doofus signing my own card. He tucked the card into his jacket. "Thanks. And, uh . . . good luck."

His tone didn't just make it clear that he thought I'd need it—it said he thought luck was the last thing he wished for me. Not exactly the send-off I needed right now. I got out and had to push my way through the crowd. None of the reporters recognized me till I got to the door and pulled it open. A squirrelly-looking little guy with a microphone jumped in front of me. "Hey, you're the lawyer, right? Love that skirt. Are you going commando?"

I knew I should ignore him. Don't lose it, don't lose it, don't lose it . . . I lost it. "Tell me, Smurf, you ever ask the guys that question?"

"Heck yeah!"

I glared at him. "Liar." I stepped inside and let go of the door, hoping it'd hit him in the head. The lobby was packed with people waiting for the elevator, so I decided to take the stairs. The arraignment court was only five floors up. But—my bad—I belatedly realized that when you're in four-inch heels and a tight skirt, there's no such thing as "only" five floors. By the time I came out of the stairway, I was sweating. I ducked into the ladies' restroom for some damage control.

But as I searched through my purse, I realized I'd forgotten my compact, my concealer, and . . . everything else. All I could hope to do was hide the sweat, so I grabbed a paper towel and dabbed my face. Two of the women reporters I'd seen at the jail yesterday came in. The one with the blonde bob stretched out her hand. "Samantha? You probably don't remember me. I'm Brittany Marston. With Channel Seven."

"I do remember you. You covered that McDonald's shooting last year, didn't you?"

"Yeah. Great memory. You know Edie? Not that I should introduce my rival."

Edie laughed. "Too late, she already knows me." She looked at the paper towel in my hand. "You are not rubbing that thing on your face."

I gave her a weak smile. "I forgot my makeup."

She dug a compact out of a huge, black fake-alligator purse. "Here, let me do that for you." She patted her purse. "I have everything in this suitcase, so from now on, you let me know if you have a cosmetic emergency."

She made a few expert swipes, and I went from sweaty to smooth in mere seconds. I laughed. "Cosmetic emergency. If ever there was an oxymoron—"

They made huge mock gasps. Brittany's eyes were wide. "There is no greater emergency!"

Edie rolled her eyes. "Unfortunately, in our business it's kind of true."

I sighed. "Bet the men in your biz don't have to worry about that."

Brittany snorted. "Wrong-o, baby. They pack almost as much as we do. If you're ever in a pinch again and we're not around, believe me, you can ask them for help. I promise they'll hook you up."

I laughed. "Thanks. Guess I'll see you out there."

But as I headed across the hallway, I noticed there were large, wet rings under my arms. The biggest arraignment of my career and I come in sweating like a linebacker. Perfect.

The master calendar arraignment court seats three hundred. It's the biggest courtroom in the building because it's the first stop for all the cases set downtown. And instead of two counsel tables that face the bench, it has a big U-shaped table that stretches from one side of the courtroom to the other. The right side is for the defense; the left is for the prosecution. Against the wall on the right side is a glass-enclosed section with a bench. That's where the custodies sit. And that's where Dale would be when he got arraigned.

A bunch of deputy DAs were milling around, but I didn't see anyone I recognized. Big as it is, this courtroom is always packed to the gills in the morning. But today was even worse than usual. It was standing room only, and a camera crew was set up in the well between the table and the judge's bench.

Greta, one of my friends from the public defender's office, was running the calendar for the office cases today. I headed over to her. "Hey, Greta! How come you're on calendar?"

Greta, being Japanese, had that great hair, which she totally took for granted and threw up in a bun most of the time. "Larry's in trial. But I know why *you're* here." She leaned in with a conspiratorial smile. "So what's it like handling a cop?"

Cops almost never have public defenders. They retain their own lawyers—who are almost always former cops. "It's kind of Bizarro

World. I feel like I'm hanging out behind enemy lines." I looked at the lawyers crowded into the space behind us. "Do you think I can get priority?"

"I think you'll get priority whether you want it or not. I heard the judge is dying to get the press out of here." Greta laughed, a gentle tinkling sound.

My laugh can most accurately be classified as a guffaw. I don't even know how to make a little bell sound like Greta's.

I noticed that the sheriff's deputy was bringing out the custodies. "Excuse me. Gotta go see my guy."

I moved close to the dirty glass. Dale's face looked like it had weights attached at the jaw, and with the dark circles under his eyes, he looked like a basset hound. I hoped the smudged glass would hide some of that from the camera. His eyes roved around the courtroom before coming back to settle on me. I smiled at him and he struggled to smile back. Before I could say anything, Judge Magnuson came out, his robe still unbuttoned and flying behind him. The bailiff called everyone to order.

After a single, irritated glance at the camera crew, the judge quickly pulled a file off the top of a depressingly big stack. "Case of *People v. Pearson*. Counsel, state your appearances for the record."

Greta was right. He really did want us out of there. "Samantha Brinkman for the defendant."

I searched the opposite side of the courtroom to see who'd be my worthy adversary.

There was a gaggle of prosecutors huddled behind counsel table with their backs turned. Now, one of them stepped out. "Zack Chastain for the prosecution."

I couldn't believe it. I stared, hoping that somehow it'd turn out to be someone else. But no such luck. It was Zack. Dark, lean but wiry, full lips, and longish black hair that fell charmingly over one eye, you could practically see the DANGER sign flashing above his head. Not that it mattered. I didn't know a single woman who'd ever heeded it.

He walked toward me. "Let the record reflect I'm now handing the first batch of discovery to defense counsel. Pages numbered one through one hundred fifty."

He approached my side of counsel table and held out the sheaf of pages, just a hint of his trademark wolfish smile twitching on his lips.

I took the pages from him and faced the bench. "I can't say whether I've received one hundred and fifty pages, Your Honor, but I have received a stack of paper."

The judge waved me off. "That'll do for now. Your client is charged with two counts of murder and the special circumstance of multiple murder and murdering a witness. Waive further reading of the complaint and statement of rights, counsel?"

"So waived. My client will enter his plea at this time." I nodded to Dale, who was now standing.

He straightened up, looked straight at the camera, and spoke in a voice as loud and strong as a trombone. "I plead not guilty, Your Honor. To all charges."

I'd say I couldn't have scripted it better except that I *had* scripted it. And I'd made him rehearse it. But I had to hand it to him—he really delivered. I backed up to the glass enclosure and whispered to him. "Nice job. I'll see you back in lockup."

Judge Magnuson assigned us to a trial court, gave us a date for our next hearing, and looked down at the camera crew. "Show's over." He called the next case.

Greta caught my eye as I pulled out my cell phone. "Oh, girl, you done stepped in it now. Zack Chastain? You better not let any women on your jury."

"Now I know for sure God's a woman. And she obviously hates me."

A younger, but already tired-looking deputy public defender came up to Greta, and I headed back to the lockup to give Dale a little TLC. I had only a few minutes. I needed to get downstairs and give the press a sound bite to counteract whatever Zack was saying—because there was no doubt he'd be saying something.

Dale was handcuffed to a chair next to the sheriff deputy's desk. I was glad to see he wasn't in the cage with the rest of the prisoners. If he were, he'd probably be bleeding out on the floor by now. "Hey, you did great out there."

He looked tired. His knee was bouncing a mile a minute, and his eyes were scanning the room in a continual arc, back and forth. "Thanks."

"What time did they get you up this morning?"

"Four. And I couldn't sleep. They never turn out the lights."

"Yeah, it sucks. The only thing I can say is that you'll get used to it." Dale nodded, but his expression said that didn't even qualify as cold comfort. "Sorry. Hey, I meant to ask you, did you ever meet Chloe's folks? I heard her mom's a psycho, but what about her dad? I know he left when she was two, but he must've come back at some point."

"Her dad's dead. Got killed in a drunk-driving accident about three years ago."

"Only three years ago? Then how come he wasn't around when—"

"She was the star on *All of Us*?" I nodded. His eyes had been darting around the room, but now he looked directly at me. "Maybe because he was a fuckup, but he wasn't a big enough jerk to think he could just waltz back into her life when she got famous."

He looked into my eyes for a long beat. I was about to ask him if there was more to it than that when the deputy came over to us. "Time to roll it up. Next batch is coming in."

I patted Dale's arm. "I'll come by tomorrow, after I've checked out the discovery. Be safe."

He gave me a serious look. "You, too."

He really meant it. That was a first, a prisoner worrying about me.

THIRTEEN

I hurried out to catch the press. Trevor's head stuck up above the crowd. I'd give him a quote, but right now I needed cameras. I spotted Brittany and Edie near the front steps. They were doing stand-ups and had their backs to me. I slowly headed their way. Brittany's cameraman pulled his head up from the lens and said something to her. She turned around and hurried toward me. Edie and a few others noticed and followed.

Brittany got to me first. "The DA gave you a pretty good chunk of discovery. Can you tell us what you know so far?"

I spoke straight into the camera. "I haven't had the chance to get into it yet. But I can promise you, we will be working day and night to bring out the truth: that Dale Pearson is innocent."

Trevor was right behind her. "Do you have any other suspects in mind?"

"We're certainly looking into that burglar." I didn't want to get into any specifics until I saw what Zack had given me.

Edie jumped in. "But the police are saying they don't believe it was a burglar."

"It wouldn't be the first time the police have made a mistake. They didn't spend five minutes looking into the possibility that the burglar was the killer. In fact, they never even tried to find him. As usual, they jumped on the easiest target—the boyfriend—and ignored all the evidence that pointed to someone else. So since the police won't do their job, we'll have to do it for them." I looked around at the crowd that'd gathered. "That's all for now, folks."

I let the cameras follow me as I got into the limo. It was a much classier exit than trudging up the hill to the cheapest parking lot. I hoped it sent the right message: successful lawyer = innocent client.

This time I had a different driver, an older, balding man with a round face and a Brooklyn accent. He pulled away right on cue, as I was rolling up my tinted window. "Hey, I saw you on TV. Actually, on this thing." He held up his cell phone.

I looked at the image on his screen. "That was yesterday. At the Twin Towers jail."

"So you'll be coming to court a lot, then?"

I could practically hear the wheels turning in his head. "Yeah. And I love this, but I can't afford it."

"I think the boss might be able to work something out for you."

I had a feeling the boss was very nearby. "Like?"

"Like how about we give you fifty percent off and you plug us on your website?"

"That's a good deal, but I still can't afford it, and my website's only for legal services. But thanks, I appreciate it."

He concentrated on navigating through the crowded streets until he got to the freeway. "Tell you what, you pass out my cards, I'll drive you for free."

"Seriously? For how long?" I could spare Beulah, save on gas . . . it was too good to be true.

"For the next month. But just for court. What do you say? Deal?"

"Deal." He pulled a stack of cards out of the glove compartment and held them over his shoulder. I took them and smiled at him in the rearview mirror. "Your boss really knows how to work it."

He chuckled. "Yeah, he's a pretty sharp guy. Besides, any friend of Alex's is a friend of mine. He's good people."

"He sure is." I looked at his cards. "Nice to meet you, Xander."

"You too, Ms. Brinkman."

"Samantha."

"Samantha. You got it."

The morning had given me only a glimpse of the shit storm that was heading my way. Freebies like this were the lonely pockets of sunshine. I took a few minutes to lean back and enjoy the scenery, then took out the discovery Zack had given me.

It was time to find out exactly what I'd gotten myself into.

When I walked into the office, Michelle was on the phone. She rolled her eyes as she spoke into her headset. "All I can do is give her the message; I can't promise when she'll get back to you." As she ended the call, the phone rang again. "Brinkman and Associates." The other line rang. Michelle put the first one on hold, answered the second one, then put it on hold, too. She blew her bangs off her forehead and looked up at me. "It's been like this all morning. Ever since they saw you in court."

"They who?"

"The press. And hopefully a few paying clients. Fingers crossed."

I handed Michelle the discovery for scanning. "Study time. I'm changing into my sweats." We had to get on top of the reports immediately, because we were about to get buried in them. The phone lines kept ringing as I headed into my office. Day one and it was already crazy. I changed into my sweats, then opened the door. The phone was still ringing nonstop. "Michelle? Let the service pick up, and get Alex."

They plopped down in the chairs in front of my desk. Alex opened his iPad.

Michelle flipped to a clean page on her legal pad. "From the look on your face, I'm guessing it's worse than we thought."

I sighed. "According to the reports, the neighbors said Dale and Chloe fought a lot in the past few weeks. And a couple of witnesses in the building next door thought he was stalking her."

Alex looked up and frowned. "Dale warned us about that, didn't he?"

"Not the stalking part. But that's not our biggest problem. They did a video of the crime scene—for our viewing pleasure." Or rather, for the jury's. It was a painfully effective tool, and from what I'd read in the crime-scene reports, this one in particular was going to be graphic. I popped the DVD into my computer and turned the monitor so we could all watch. "And I took a look at the autopsy report. I'll tell you about it when we get to that part."

I hit play.

It was a small apartment. The kitchen and dining areas were on the right, and the living room, which led to a tiny balcony, was straight ahead. A short hallway between the living room and kitchen led to a bathroom on the right and two bedrooms on the left.

The video zeroed in on a set of knives in a butcher block on the kitchen counter. One slot that looked about the size of a carving knife was empty. I pointed to it. "They think that's where the killer got the murder weapon. The coroner says the perp used the same knife for both victims. The cops never found it."

The living room was neat. No drawers pulled out, no couch cushions thrown around. The camera moved down the hall and into the first bedroom on the left. Chloe lay on the floor, faceup, eyes half-open, her body twisted to the right, knees bent and turned to the left. I paused the disc and studied the scene. She was dressed in jeans and a white long-sleeve T-shirt—which was now soaked in blood. One hand was stretched out to the side, and the other lay just below her stomach, as though it had been clutched at her chest and then fallen. She looked so small and crumpled—like a marionette whose strings had been cut mid-dance.

"Jeez," Alex said. "That's a lot of blood. How many times did he stab her?"

"Coroner counted four stab wounds. Two nonfatal, two very fatal strikes that went straight to the aorta."

I hit play, and the camera pulled back to scan the room. All of the dresser drawers were open, and it looked like someone had gone through them in a hurry. Two pairs of jeans and a few camisoles were on the floor. The lamp on the dresser had fallen on its side, and three small silver-framed pictures lay on the floor next to a broken flower vase. The camera zoomed in on a hoop earring that'd come off Chloe's ear and landed on the floor next to her head. "Looks like she fell against the dresser when she and Dale were fighting."

"But why the ransacking? What was he looking for?" Michelle asked.

"I'll be saying that's a sign the burglar did this and he was looking for more jewelry."

Michelle gave me a skeptical look. "And they'll be saying Dale was trying to make it look that way. Awfully violent for a burglar."

Alex pointed to the blood that'd run down Chloe's arm. "And it looks like he stabbed her while she was on the floor."

I countered. "So the burglar panicked. He's high on . . . whatever. The girls come in, surprise him, he freaks out . . ." I looked from Alex to Michelle.

She shrugged. "I guess. But I don't love it."

Alex raised his eyebrows. He didn't say anything, but his expression said he agreed with her.

I hit play again. The camera moved out of Chloe's room, down the hall, and into Paige's bedroom. The eerie quiet made it feel as though we were following in the murderer's footsteps.

There was similar ransacking here. All the dresser drawers had been pulled out; a brassiere spilled over the edge of one drawer, and some T-shirts had been thrown to the floor. The drawer in Paige's dressing table had been yanked out and lay upside down on the floor, and the closet door stood wide open. We didn't see a body until the camera moved to the far side of the bed. Paige lay on the floor, facedown. She was in a white robe, and a towel partially covered her head. She'd probably had it wound around her hair, turban style, before the attack. According to the crime-scene and autopsy reports, she'd been freshly showered. Blood had seeped through the back of her robe, and there was a huge pool of blood under her head. A cell phone lay a few feet away.

Michelle blew out a breath. "Stabbed in the back? And what's with all the blood under her head?"

"He cut her throat. Twice."

Bad as it'd sounded in the reports, seeing it was a hundred times worse. The attack was gruesome—and the girls looked painfully young and defenseless.

Alex pointed to the cell phone. "Think she was trying to call the cops?"

I nodded. "Seems so." I studied the rest of Paige's room. "The only good news is that there's a fair amount of ransacking here, too, so that might give our burglary theory more traction."

"Anything missing?" Alex asked.

"According to the reports, no. But how would the cops know? It's not like there was an empty TV stand. If the burglar took cash or some other small stuff like jewelry, the only way they'd know something was missing is if someone close to the girls told them. And from what I've seen so far, no one did."

I hit play again. The camera zoomed in on blood impressions near the foot of Paige's bed. It slowly followed a short, faint blood trail to her body. I paused the DVD. "According to the autopsy report, she fell near the foot of the bed first, then dragged herself to the side of the bed."

It was a hideous mental image, the victim bleeding out and desperately trying to crawl away from her killer. The image of Dale's face came back to me, his eyes warm and smiling. If he'd done this, he was one hell of a sociopath. In which case there might be—no, probably were—other victims. Jeezus. It was a whole new reason to get this case to court as fast as possible. Before any more bodies turned up.

"Where was Paige when the killer cut her throat?" Michelle asked.

"The coroner says she got cut once where she fell, but it was a superficial wound. Just enough to bleed out a little. The final, fatal cut to the throat was done at the side of the bed."

Michelle shook her head. "Sorry, this feels a lot more personal than a freaked-out burglar."

I sighed. It really did.

The next frame clicked over, and we were back in Chloe's room. The camera zoomed in on a crime-scene tech who was holding a print brush and pointing to two black spots on her dresser. I hit pause. "Dale's prints. Just the pinkie and ring fingers on the left hand. But since they'd been dating for two months, those prints don't worry me."

I clicked through the frames until the camera moved back into Paige's room. "These prints do." The camera focused on the same crime-scene tech, who was now pointing to black spots on top of Paige's nightstand, which was just a foot away from her body. I let the disc play as the camera followed the crime-scene tech to the drawer of the dressing table that'd been thrown to the floor. He was pointing to three more black spots. "And especially these."

I paused the disc again. "I know Dale might've gone through their apartment with the crime-scene tech back when he took the burglary call. But prints on that drawer and the nightstand probably mean he was in that room recently, because those areas get a fair amount of use."

Michelle sighed. "And I'd think Paige would've cleaned that nightstand fairly regularly."

Alex shrugged. "Even if she didn't, that burglary happened two months ago. If Dale left his prints there when he was investigating the burglary, wouldn't you think they'd have rubbed off by now? A nightstand, a dressing table—they get a lot of use."

I nodded. "Though prints can hang around for a long time if the conditions are right."

"Did they get any of his prints on that butcher block in the kitchen?" Michelle asked.

"No. But he wouldn't have to touch it to pull out a knife. And a cop would know better."

Alex frowned. "So wouldn't a cop know better than to leave those prints in the bedroom? How come there's no evidence the place was wiped down?"

I pointed to him. "Exactly. And that's one of the points we'll make. But keep an eye out for follow-ups from the crime-scene tech saying he went back for a second look and found wipe marks."

Michelle scanned her notes. "What about DNA?"

"They've got Dale's skin under Chloe's nails, his sweat on her arm, and a trace of his blood on her right index finger. That all fits with them having a fight."

"Any on Paige?"

"No. Which I'd call good news, except she got stabbed from behind. There was no sign of a struggle, no bruising or scratching on her body. The coroner's theory is that she was stabbed in the back first, then stabbed in the throat after she fell. So there wasn't much contact. And Dale's hair is short. He wouldn't shed much."

Michelle nodded. "Makes sense. Paige was just a witness who had to be killed. Wrong place, wrong time. Not a girlfriend who'd been driving him crazy. He'd have known to be careful."

Alex rubbed his neck. "So we can use the ransacking to say the burglar did it, and if there's no evidence anyone tried to wipe the place down, we can use that to say the killer couldn't be a cop. Any other good news?"

"We have the usual stuff that doesn't fit." Every crime scene has it. The cops pick up everything in sight, so there are always pieces of evidence that don't match up to anything—or anyone. "They got some stray hairs on Paige's robe that don't look like hers or Dale's. But there were no roots, so there's no DNA. Can't even tell what gender the hairs are. And it's a terry-cloth robe, so hairs would stick to it for some time. They could belong to anyone—the cleaning lady, a friend who borrowed the robe, someone who used the dryer in the apartment building before she did."

"What about Chloe? Any stray hairs on her?" Michelle asked.

"Not on her body. A couple on the floor. But that's just as bad. Could've been left there anytime, by anyone. Even if they match the ones on Paige, it probably won't take me very far."

"What about prints?" Michelle asked.

"They found two that don't match anyone on the door of Paige's closet—"

Michelle looked up from her legal pad. "That's something. The video shows the door was left open."

"Yeah. But again, we can't say when those prints got there. And there were some stray prints on Chloe's dresser—but same thing. They could've been there for days, weeks, even months."

Alex frowned. "So what're you going to do?"

"Oh, I'll still argue that stuff proves someone else was there. The question is, will anyone buy it? Would you?"

He looked down at his iPad. "Not so far."

"Anyway, the tox report might be our only bit of really good news." I pulled it out of the stack of discovery Zack had given me. "Paige had a low level of cocaine and a .06 blood alcohol level. I don't know what we can do with that yet. And they found semen in Paige's body that indicated recent sexual activity."

Alex looked up. "Mr. Perfect?"

"Maybe. Chloe had a low level of heroin in her blood. So Dale was right. She was kind of loaded. That might help us with the homicidal drug-dealer theory. So how about this? Chloe owed him money, and he went to the apartment looking for it. Or for the drugs he'd sold her."

Michelle frowned. "Maybe."

But no matter whom I tried to lay it off on—a burglar or a drug dealer—I'd have to concede that Dale and Chloe had a fight, and that he'd knocked her around. Juries don't like guys who punch their girlfriends—especially if that guy is a cop.

It wouldn't be enough to slam the shoddy investigation, pound the table about lazy cops, or point to some vague, possible straw man.

I needed a real suspect.

FOURTEEN

I gave Alex a copy of the discovery so he could get up to speed on the witnesses, because I'd be taking him with me to do the interviews. I never talk to witnesses alone. If they decide to "forget" something on the witness stand, I need someone who can testify to what they told me—and that can't be me.

Michelle went back to man the phones, which had slowed down some. Alex went to his office, and I went back to work. An hour later, I heard Michelle tell someone in the anteroom to take a seat. A few seconds later, there was a sharp rap on my door, and Michy stepped in. "You've got a visitor—"

"No press. I don't have time right—"

"It's Dale's daughter. Lisa Milstrom."

I glanced at the paperwork on my desk to make sure there were no grisly crime-scene photos. "Send her in." I hadn't intended to talk to her until we got closer to trial, but since she was here, I might as well see if there was a chance she might be a good character witness—or maybe good camera fodder on the cable news circuit. Dale wouldn't like it, but I couldn't afford to worry about that. He needed all the help he could get.

Michelle waved her over, and a slender girl in a blue-and-black maxi dress and boots walked in. I introduced myself and reached out to shake her hand, expecting to wind up holding the dead fish I usually got from kids. But Lisa's shake was surprisingly firm. A little cold and clammy, but firm. I studied her face as she settled into one of the chairs in front of my desk. Her long, light-brown hair and delicate features showed she took after her mother. But I saw a little of Dale in her high cheekbones and slightly bent nose.

I sat down and folded my hands on the desk. "Nice to meet you, Lisa. What brings you here?"

Her tongue darted over her lips as she glanced around the office. When her eyes finally settled on me, she took a deep breath. "I—uh, I just wanted to tell you that my dad didn't . . . I don't think he did this." Lisa cleared her throat and sat up straighter. "I mean, I know he couldn't have done it."

She'd tried to deliver the message with solid conviction. But it was laced with fear and wobbly hope. I could tell she thought I knew the truth, but she was too scared to ask. It impressed me that she had the courage to come here on her own—and that she cared enough to do it for a dad she hadn't really known for most of her life.

There was no way I was going to tell her how bad it looked for him, but I didn't want to lie to her, either. "I promise you, we'll do all we can to prove he's innocent." I didn't want to let her start asking questions, so I steered the conversation away from the case. "Your dad told me you just moved here a couple of years ago. How do you like LA?"

Lisa shrugged. "It's okay, I guess. It was a drag at first, when I didn't know anyone."

"When was that?"

"Freshman year."

"That must've been rough." I felt for her. Being a freshman was bad enough. But being a new girl on top of that was a real bitch. A real lonely bitch. Still, she seemed pretty together. Nothing like the hot mess I'd been when I was in high school.

She dipped her head and sighed. "It totally sucked. But it's a lot better now. And Dad really helped. He took me out to dinner, took me to the station." Lisa spoke with a look of pride. "He even took me on a ride-along."

I smiled. "I did a couple when I first joined the public defender's office. Kind of crazy, isn't it?"

She returned my smile, and her face finally relaxed. "Yeah. I really loved it." She tilted her head and gazed over my shoulder. "It kind of made me think . . . it might be kind of cool to be a detective."

"Absolutely." But I doubted she'd follow in Daddy's footsteps. She didn't seem the type—too soft, too nice. I guess that might've been my bias showing. In any case, it looked like Dale had been a positive force in her life. But in the next moment, the memory of those gruesome crime-scene photos flashed through my mind. It was hard to reconcile them with the man who'd shown up for Lisa. Hard—but not impossible. It's a truth you learn early when you're on the defense side of things: very few people are all bad. I once defended a serial killer who cared for a whole family of rescue dogs. "Sounds like it's been good getting to know him."

Lisa nodded. "It has—not that I don't like my stepdad."

"When did your mom remarry?"

"Three years ago. That's why we moved back here. Lonnie's a sound editor. He works at Paramount." She paused and dropped her eyes, a guilty look on her face. "He's a nice guy, but . . ."

"He's a stepdad."

She looked at me with relief. "Exactly."

I could relate. I hadn't met my stepdad, Jack, until I was a junior in high school. He was a great guy, but I'd had a hard time warming up to him—even without the competition of a real father coming into the mix.

We chatted for a little while longer about school and her plans for college. I let her do most of the talking so I could get a bead on her, see how she'd play in court or on camera. But there was one question I'd had on my mind since Lisa had walked into my office. I held off until she was about to leave. "What does your mom think about all this?"

Lisa pressed her lips tightly for a second. "She doesn't believe he did it, either. But . . ." Lisa trailed off. "She said he did have a temper." She added quickly, "Not that he ever hurt her or anything. She just said she didn't want to believe it but that anything's possible." Lisa tilted her chin up, her expression defiant. "But I told her she's wrong. I know he didn't do it. Just because I haven't known Dale all my life, that doesn't mean I can't tell."

Her loyalty was as touching as it was painful. I did my best to give her an encouraging smile, and as I walked her to the door, I told her again that we'd be fighting for him. "It was great to meet you, Lisa."

She stepped back and gave me a swift hug. "I'm so glad he has you. I know you'll win." She headed out through the anteroom and stopped with one hand on the door. She looked from me to Michelle. "Thanks for—for everything."

I waved, and as the door closed behind her, Michelle said, "Nice kid."

"She really is."

Michelle and I exchanged a look: if we lost this case, it'd crush her.

FIFTEEN

I went back to work, feeling the weight of Lisa's faith in me. At four o'clock, Michelle came into my office. "We just got another batch of reports from the DA, and one of them is an interview with Chloe's sister, Kaitlyn. I think you should take a look at it." She stared at my open window and rubbed her arms. "It's like a refrigerator in here. Must you?"

"As always, yes. I must." I like to leave my window open. It keeps me awake. And Michelle complains about it every time.

Michelle folded her arms, her lips twisted with irritation. "And we just lost our Wi-Fi connection."

We needed to upgrade, but we couldn't afford it. "Again?"

"Again." Michelle sighed. "I'll have to go down to Apex and use their computer."

Our downstairs neighbor, Apex Printing, almost never had customers, but they had an industrial-strength connection, and they were pretty generous about letting us use it. But hanging around there wasn't a smart move. The few customers they did have showed up only after five o'clock—sporting tats, piercings, and bone-crushing rings on most fingers. Michy and I pegged it as a drug front the day we moved in. I expected the DEA to raid the place any minute. "Let me call the carrier and see if I can get us a deal on an upgrade."

"I tried, Sam. They won't do it."

"Can't hurt to try again." Michelle rolled her eyes and walked out.

I'd been down to Apex a few times in the past month, just being neighborly. And, of course, dropping off my business cards. Someone in that place—whether the employees or their customers—was bound to need my services sooner or later. The last time I was there, I'd asked an employee about their Wi-Fi carrier, saying I was shopping for a new one. He'd said theirs was the best and logged on to show me. Now, I remembered noticing the length of his password. These guys weren't exactly tech wizards. I had a hunch. I used my iPad to find their network provider and typed in *AP8182458989*. The business initials and their phone number. Stupid. Obvious. And right. I was in.

I went out and told Michelle. "Hey, good news! I got us the upgrade. Same provider as Apex." I handed her the Post-it sticker with the password.

"That's fantastic!" Michelle took the sticker and logged on. Two seconds later, she spun around and stared at me with narrowed eyes. "You stole their password."

I shrugged. "A little. But hey, we deserve it."

"If they catch us, Sam—"

I waved her off. "Please. Piggybacking on their Wi-Fi's the least of their concerns." Michelle shook her head. I put my hands on my hips. "What? Now you don't have to go hang with a bunch of cartel mules *and* you've got a great connection. You're welcome."

As I headed back to my office, I heard her say something under her breath about us "winding up in a block of cement."

I called out over my shoulder, "They're not that creative, Michy."

Michy called back, "Real comforting, Sam."

I sat back down at my computer and jumped on with the Apex Wi-Fi. It was the fastest I'd ever connected to the 'net. I should've done this months ago. I scrolled down, looking for the e-mail from Zack.

I'd been hoping we'd get Kaitlyn's statement soon. Dale had said Chloe was on the phone with her when he came by that night. I found the statement. "Damn it!"

Michelle came in. "What?"

"Chloe told her sister she was going to break up with Dale that night. Damn it!" Fighting over a drug habit is one thing. But fighting over a breakup is classic murder motive.

"I take it Dale never mentioned anything about a breakup?"

"No."

"Maybe they got stuck on the drug thing and she didn't get around to it."

Maybe. Hopefully. Because I didn't want to believe Dale was holding out on me so soon. "You know where to find Kaitlyn?"

"She works afternoons at a Starbucks near Santa Monica Community College. The four p.m. to nine p.m. shift."

"Thanks, Michy. I might hit her up tomorrow."

It was eight thirty when Michelle and I packed up to leave for the day. Alex was still in his office, hard at work. I stopped at the doorway. "Hey, don't kill yourself. You're not getting paid by the hour. And we need to get on the road early tomorrow."

Alex smiled. "I already finished the discovery. I'm reading up on PI techniques now. What time?"

I'd so lucked out with him. "Make it eight o'clock. You'll have to pick me up at my place. Beulah's still not running." I pulled out a ten-dollar bill. "And bring coffee."

He took the money and saluted, and Michelle and I left. She was giving me a lift home.

My cell phone rang just as Michelle pulled out of the parking lot. The caller ID said Blocked. I knew what that meant. I could've let it go to voice mail, but I decided I might as well bite the bullet now.

Michelle looked at me. I mouthed, "Mommy dearest." She shook her head. "Give her my love."

Celeste came at me like I'd told *People* magazine she wore knockoff Louboutins. "It's just a publicity stunt, right? You're not really going to do it!"

"Do what?" I knew what she was talking about, but I didn't want to make this any easier on her than I had to.

"Represent that awful murderer! I just saw you on the E! channel news. That man is dangerous. What if he comes after you?"

"He's in jail, Celeste. He can't come after anyone."

"But he might have people on the outside who can do it for him!"

"He's a cop. Not a Crip. Or John Gotti. And why would he come after me? I'm on his side."

"Because he's a *criminal*, Samantha. He doesn't need a reason. He's insane. Otherwise why would he kill that sweet actress and her roommate?"

"Whatever happened to presumed innocent? You know, it's possible he didn't do it." Not likely, but possible.

"Please, Samantha. They'd never charge a *detective* unless they knew for sure he'd done it—"

There was that. But I'd rather chew ground glass than agree with her. "They make mistakes just like everyone else." Her they're-all-guilty attitude was nothing new—and besides, I agreed. I moved on to what *was* new. "Since when do you care what I'm doing or who my clients are?"

Her voice grew sharp. "Don't take that tone with me. I care about everything you do."

The hell. "When it affects you."

There was a long beat of silence. "You always think the worst of me, Samantha."

"I think the reality of you, Celeste."

Her voice was rising. "Well, you're wrong! I'm telling you this for your own good. Don't take this case. Get away from that man—that cop! Do you hear me? Let it go!"

I was one block away from my building. "I'm about to pull into the garage; I'm going to lose the signal."

"Listen to me, Samantha! Have I ever said this to you before?"

She'd said plenty of other obnoxious and undermining things, but she was right. This was a new one. "I'll think about it. 'Bye."

I ended the call, and Michelle pulled up to the curb in front of my building.

"I take it your mother is less than thrilled with you taking the case."

"Your powers of deduction are, as always, astounding."

"Why don't you tell her you need the money?"

"Because she'd tell Jack to give it to me, and I'd rather cut off my right hand than take money from her."

Michelle sighed. "What time do you think you'll get back to the office tomorrow?"

"Can't tell. I'll call with updates."

When I got upstairs and changed into my sweats, I kept my promise to Celeste. I did think about it. Not about getting off the case. About why she wanted me to.

I'd had thirty-three years of up-close-and-personal experience with Celeste Brinkman (changed from the original "Charlene" because she thought Charlene was a "hillbilly" name). Enough to know that this had nothing to do with her concern for my safety. When she got this whipped up about something, it always had to do with her. Her image, her status, her convenience.

Conclusion? Someone at the country club or her Pilates class must've dropped a comment that made her believe my taking the case would make her look bad.

As earth-shattering as that event might be for her, I was willing to let her deal with it. Because that's the kind of evil, selfish bitch I am.

SIXTEEN

I had the friggin' nightmare again and woke myself up with the sound of my croaking scream. It took four cups of coffee to loosen the grip of the ugly images and stop the shakes, so I was running a little late. Of course, that meant Alex showed up fifteen minutes early. "Sorry, Sam. I just wanted to make sure I didn't keep you waiting."

"No problem." That's LA. You're either an hour early or two hours late. Two large coffees were in a cardboard tray on the passenger seat. I was probably pushing it with a fifth cup, but I'd rather have a caffeine buzz than a nightmare fog. "Plain, right?" I'm not a fan of all that latte, frappe business. Just give me the caffeine and no one gets hurt. Alex nodded. "Thanks."

Alex was wearing slacks and a blazer. He took in my outfit as I pulled on my seat belt. "Jeans and a black leather jacket? Don't you want them to believe you're a lawyer?"

"Sure, but I also want them to talk to me." I eyed his outfit. "A suit doesn't say, 'Relax and spill.'"

He looked skeptical but didn't argue. "First, Laurel Canyon, then Santa Monica to see Kaitlyn, right?"

I nodded. Laurel Canyon used to be one of the hippest places on the planet, creatively speaking. Joni Mitchell, Jim Morrison, Mama Cass, Glenn Frey—everybody lived there back in the day. The Canyon Country store on Laurel Canyon Boulevard still has a psychedelic sign. But now it's more of a mixed bag. The canyon has peaks and valleys. Literally and figuratively. The higher up you go, the better the view and the ritzier the properties—like multi-million-dollar-type properties. Steven Tyler lives in one of those. I heard Justin Timberlake does, too. So it still has cool people—albeit, bazillionaire-type cool people.

But the lower parts don't have a view, and they can be pretty raggedy. Some of the houses look like they're not much more than caves with plumbing. And I'm guessing about the plumbing.

Chloe and Paige lived all the way at the bottom of the canyon on the Hollywood side. The last stretch where Hollywood Boulevard dovetails into Laurel Canyon Boulevard. It had the hip-sounding address but none of the coolness factor. Their building was one of many two-story clapboard-style affairs that were thrown up back in the sixties without much attention to charm or detail—or, according to our police reports, soundproofing.

Alex turned left onto Laurel Canyon Boulevard. "Where do you want to start?"

"Let's hit the building next door." I read from the police report. "Nikki Ingalls in 1C claimed she saw Dale driving up and down the street almost every night—with a 'creepy look on his face.'"

"How'd she see the 'creepy look' if he was driving by at night?"

"Well, Supergirl has X-ray vision. But on the off chance she's not an immortal, that's what we'll have to find out."

High-profile cases attract and repel all types. Our Nikki might be a wannabe actress/model/game-show host looking for free face time, or just your ordinary loser horny for attention—or she might be a nutjob who thought most people looked "creepy." The possibility of an honest, sane witness was too statistically insignificant to even make the list.

Apartment 1C was on the ground floor of a faded, pink two-story building on Hollywood Boulevard that had a couple of sun-bleached plastic flamingos on the small stretch of lawn. All of the units had windows that faced the street. Nikki did have a decent-enough view. But I noticed that even though there were streetlights on both sides of the street, none of them were close to 1C. And they weren't all necessarily working. We walked up two concrete steps to a tiny front patio area and found a gray door that had a silver 1C hanging just above the peephole. I knocked and stood back to give Nikki a chance to check us out. Also to give her a chance to check out the gorgeousness of Alex. According to the police report, she was in her thirties and lived alone.

I heard footsteps thud on the wooden floor inside. There was a pause, and then the door opened. She was wearing tight navy-blue sweatpants and a sweatshirt that had the arms and most of the midriff cut off. She pushed back a hank of chin-length, overprocessed platinum hair and leaned against the door with a lazy smile. "What can I do for you?"

Her eyes were so occupied with Alex that she didn't even realize I was there. So I took a perverse pleasure in bursting her bubble by speaking up. "Just give us a few moments of your time."

The lazy smile went away. She gave me an irritated squint. "What for?"

"We're looking into the case involving Chloe and Paige, and we hoped you could answer a few questions." I try to hold off on saying that I'm working for the defendant for as long as possible. It's something you pick up after having fifty-seven doors slammed in your face.

Nikki's eyes strayed back to Alex. The lazy smile switched back on. She still had hope.

Knowing how to work witnesses is an important part of an investigation. I hung back to see how Alex would handle it. He played her like a clarinet. He started with a sincere, from-the-heart look. "Ms. Ingalls, I'd really appreciate it if you could spare us some time. I promise just five minutes and we'll get out of your hair."

She melted like a dropped ice-cream cone on a hot sidewalk. "Okay." She turned and gestured for us to follow her inside. "But we need to make this fast. I've got an audition in an hour, and I have to get ready."

Alex and I exchanged a look behind her back as we headed for the ratty, blue-chenille couch in the living room. Sometimes I wish people weren't such clichés. Other times, I'm glad they're so predictable. Nikki sat down on the ottoman chair across from us and ostentatiously crossed her legs—toes pageant-pointed and everything. I noticed her toenails were painted bubblegum pink and had sparkly designs on the big toes. I wondered if she'd ever get around to asking us who we were.

She oozed another smile at Alex. "I told the police I saw the suspect around here a lot."

Alex made a show of taking out his notepad, even though his pocket recorder was on. It was a trick I'd learned early in my career, and I'd taught it to Alex yesterday. Those recordings stay secret; I use them only to beef up the notes I take in front of the witness. Nothing that hurts my client gets written down, because if I wind up calling the witness, I have to turn over a report of what they said. And it looks better to the jury if they see that we take written statements just like the cops do. Well, sort of like the cops do.

Alex took out his pen. "Did you see Dale Pearson on the night of the murder?"

"No. I was at Hyde Lounge that night."

In her dreams. Just like the fantasy age she'd given the police. Nikki had left thirty-five behind at least ten hard years ago. And there was no way she was hanging out at a club as pricey as Hyde Lounge.

But Alex gave her a twinkle of a smile. "Hyde Lounge. Very cool. Do you remember when you first met Dale Pearson?"

She pouted and pulled on her lower lip. "About two months ago? I ran into him behind the building. The parking areas are next to each other."

"How did you know who he was?"

"Because he told me. I figured he'd just moved in, so I introduced myself. You know, being a good neighbor and all."

And probably hoping to be a really *great* neighbor.

Alex gave her an understanding smile. "Was he friendly?"

Nikki made a face. "No. He was kind of rude. Told me he was in a hurry and said to have a nice day."

"When was the next time you saw him?"

"Maybe a week? Two weeks later? I saw him drive past my place, heading east on Hollywood Boulevard, then he turned around and drove back toward Chloe's place."

"How did he look? Happy? Sad? Upset?"

"He looked . . . intense. Like he was searching for something. Or for *someone*." She gave Alex a meaningful look.

"Who do you think he was looking for?"

Nikki gave an elaborate shrug that hiked her sweatshirt up enough to show the bottom of her bra. It was an act that couldn't have found a less interested audience, which amused the hell out of me. And Alex—gotta hand it to him—played the part beautifully, giving her the eye bounce she'd aimed for. This boy was a natural.

Nikki gave a pouty frown. "I don't know. Another guy, maybe? It seemed kind of stalk-y to me."

Huh? So he was driving up and down the street to . . . what? Catch his rival? Wouldn't it be simpler to just park outside her building?

"When did you see him next?"

"I'm not sure. Maybe a week? Two weeks later? Same thing. It happened a couple more times. And he had this . . . look on his face. It was kind of scary."

My bullshit-o-meter was in the red zone. I had to jump in. "By scary, do you mean angry?"

Nikki glanced at me, then turned back to Alex. "Creepier than that." She gave a little shiver. "But it was angry, too. That's why I thought he was, like, suspicious of Chloe."

I could definitely see why the acting career hadn't taken off. "Do you know if anyone else in the building noticed Dale Pearson looking like that?"

She barely glanced at me as she answered. "I think Sheila did. Sheila Wagner. She's in 2C." Nikki jerked a thumb at the ceiling.

I didn't remember reading about any Sheila Wagners in the police reports. "What did she tell you about Dale?"

I'd asked one too many questions. Nikki frowned at me. "Hey, who are you guys?"

Alex stepped in with an extra dose of smooth. "I'm sorry, Nikki. I thought we told you already. We work for the defense." He pulled out a card. "Here you go."

She took the card. It was one of mine. I hadn't had time to make cards for Alex yet. Nikki looked at me, her eyes narrowed. "You guys are on *his* side?"

Busted at last. "I'm his lawyer. Alex is—"

"I'm an investigator." Alex stood up and we headed for the door. He paused at the entry and gave her a buttery smile. "If you think of anything else, please feel free to call. Anytime."

I watched the tug-of-war on her face. Distaste for the sleazy defense lawyer fought with desire for the gorgeous investigator. Gorgeous investigator won.

As we moved down the sidewalk, Nikki leaned against the door-jamb and gave Alex her best sex-kitten smile. "I'll definitely do that."

Alex waved to her. I kept walking until I heard the door close, then stopped. "Nice job, Alex. Good to know you're willing to slut it up for the team."

"You kidding? That was nothing. I sold high-end cars, remember?"

SEVENTEEN

We knocked on the door of apartment 2C, but Sheila Wagner didn't answer.

I was leaning in, trying to listen for signs of life, when the door to apartment 2D opened and a young guy, barefoot and naked to the waist in low-slung jeans, stepped out. A cigarette hung from the corner of his mouth, and his hazel eyes squinted at us above the smoke. He was hot in that dirty, up-against-the-wall kind of way. Back in my high school days, I would've gone for this guy in a fast second. His eyes flicked off Alex and landed on me. I was happy to take *my* turn to slut it up for the team.

I gave him a smile. "We're looking for Sheila Wagner."

"You probation officers?" I started to shake my head, but he laughed. "Joking. Sheila's, like, a nun."

In this neighborhood? "A nun?"

He gave a little chuckle. "No. She's a librarian. But same difference, right? She's probably just out walking her dog. Give it a few; she'll be back."

"Actually, we're here to talk to people about Dale Pearson."

"Dale." He took a long pull from his cigarette and blew it out through the corner of his mouth. "Am I supposed to know him?"

"He's the one they arrested for the murders." He still looked puzzled. "Of Chloe and Paige."

He nodded slowly. "You guys don't look like cops." I told him who we were. He nodded. "Nah, I never saw the dude. Saw Chloe, though. We had drinks a couple of times when I first moved in."

"And?"

He looked out at the street. "She was a nice girl but a mess. There was something, I don't know . . . broken about her." He took another drag of his cigarette. "Like she'd seen too much in too few years."

It was a much more nuanced insight than I'd have expected from this guy. And I got the reference. "The Stones. '19th Nervous Breakdown.' You a musician?"

He nodded appreciatively as he looked me up and down. "Trying to be."

I pushed down the electric surge from that look.

A female voice from inside his apartment called out. "Babe? What's going on?"

He gave me a slow smile. "Duty calls."

I held out my card. "Just in case you think of something."

He took the card and glanced at it. "Or in case I get in trouble?"

"Or that."

As he went back inside, I heard the skittering of dog toenails scratching up the walkway. A medium-size chocolate pit bull on a leash came into view. At the other end of the leash was a slender woman with long, almost waist-length brown hair. "Sheila?"

"Yes. Can I help you?" She looked flushed and a lot younger than I'd expected. Late twenties at most. The name *Sheila* seemed like it should belong to someone in her sixties at least.

I told her who we were. She gave a little frown. "Didn't the police put my statement in a report?"

So the cops *had* spoken to her. I noticed her dog was sniffing at my boots. I took a step back just in case he decided to get a little more intimate. "Not that I saw. I got your name from Nikki."

Sheila's frown got deeper. "Don't worry, Trixie doesn't bite."

"I wasn't worried about the biting so much."

Sheila nodded and gave the leash a little tug. Trixie backed up and lay down. "I didn't really have much to say. I was at my folks' house the night of the . . . the night they died."

"Did you know Chloe or Paige?" I was waiting for her to invite us in where we could sit down and talk in private, but she didn't seem inclined.

"Just to say 'Hi' to. But you might want to talk to C.J. I think he went out with Chloe."

"C.J.'s your next-door neighbor?" Sheila looked over my shoulder at his door and nodded. The way her eyes lingered, I got the feeling she looked at his door a lot. "What did you tell the police?"

"Just that I'd met Dale Pearson a couple of months ago. My car got a flat up in the canyon, and I was waiting for Triple A to come. I had Trixie and Dixie with me. That was before Dixie passed. We were on our way home after a hike in Runyon Canyon, and they were really thirsty. They're fifteen years old, so I was getting worried. Dale was the only one who stopped to see if he could help."

Finally some good news. "And did he? Help, I mean."

"Yes. He was super nice. Changed the tire, gave the girls some water—they loved him, and they don't usually like men all that much. When I told him where I lived—"

"He asked where you lived?"

"I volunteered." I guess my expression said more than I wanted it to because she nodded. "I know, dumb move. But he seemed so . . . safe. Anyway, I said I couldn't believe I got a flat less than a mile from home, and he asked me if I lived near Chloe's building. When I told him I lived next door, he asked whether I'd ever been burglarized or if I'd seen anyone suspicious hanging around the night of Chloe's burglary."

I liked what I was hearing more and more. And the fact that Sheila's statement hadn't shown up in any of the reports less and less. "What'd you tell him?"

Sheila smiled a little. "That the most suspicious people I've seen in this neighborhood are the ones who live here." Her eyes drifted back to C.J.'s apartment. "I've never been burglarized, but I have this little motion detector." Sheila looked down fondly at her motion detector, who seemed to have fallen asleep on Sheila's foot. "And back then I had her sister, Dixie, too. But I really don't see much. I work at the library all day, and when I come home, I shut the world out."

"So you don't know any of your other neighbors? Other than Nikki and C.J.?"

Sheila shook her head. "Really just C.J. I met Nikki only because I was coming home with Trixie when that police officer was leaving her place. She pointed me out to him."

"Did you ever see Dale after that day?"

"A couple of times, as he was coming or going. We just waved and said hi."

"Then you never saw him driving up and down the street at night, looking around?"

Sheila frowned. "No. Never. But like I said, I don't see much of anything at night. I come home, have dinner, go to bed."

"Did you tell the police officer that you'd met Dale?"

"Oh yeah. I did. But he didn't seem all that impressed. He seemed kind of impatient, like, 'Yeah, yeah, whatever.' You know?"

I sure did. And pretty soon, thanks to fifty-some-odd news channels, so would everyone else.

EIGHTEEN

We headed to Chloe's building, which was next door to Sheila's. I didn't need to know Chloe's address to figure out it was where she'd lived. The entire sidewalk and grass median in front of the building was filled with flowers, teddy bears, candles, and hand-painted signs that wept with love for Chloe, and anguish at having lost her. When we managed to weave our way through it all, I saw that the building was a little more worn than Sheila's, dingy white with peeling green trim, and it was positioned so that the side faced the street and the back faced the canyon.

I wanted to get an idea of the layout, so we walked down the open corridor that led past the first-floor apartments. There were six units on the first floor and six on the second floor. Chloe and Paige lived on the second floor in apartment 208.

There was only one witness I wanted to talk to here. Others had said they'd heard Dale and Chloe fighting, but the most detailed, and damaging, statement had come from Janet Rader. She was the prosecution's key eyewitness—or rather, ear-witness. I'd debated whether I should even bother talking to her. Even if she tried to hedge on the witness stand, the DA would get her to confirm what she'd said to the police—which was plenty. But I had to see if I could find any weak spots.

"I'll take this one, Alex. But feel free to step in if you think I'm missing something."

He nodded. I knocked on the door. There was no answer. I waited a few seconds and raised my hand to knock again, but the door unexpectedly opened, leaving my fist in midair. A slender young man stood in the doorway. I'd expected an older woman in her seventies. I told him we were here to speak to Janet Rader about Chloe Monahan and Paige Avner.

"Oh, you want my mother." He looked from me to Alex. "You don't look like cops. Who are you?"

"We represent Dale Pearson, and we're speaking to all the witnesses listed in the police reports." I always try to make it sound like everyone else has talked to me.

"I—I don't really think she's up to it. Maybe she could call you?"

Alex chimed in. "It'll take only a few minutes, really—"

A voice came from somewhere behind the young man. "Evan? Who is that?" He told her. "It's okay, let them in. I'll talk to them." A taller, stocky woman with short graying hair, wearing black rubber nurse's shoes and polyester slacks, came to the door and gestured for us to come in. "I don't want you saying in court that I refused to talk to you."

She'd obviously been a witness before. When witnesses refuse to talk to me, I always make them admit it to the jury. It shows they're biased against me. Sometimes that helps. More often, it doesn't.

Evan started to follow us into the tiny dining area off the kitchen, but Janet waved him off. "I can handle this myself. You go finish figuring out what's wrong with my computer."

"You sure?"

"I'm sure. Now go."

He went. Janet put on a pair of round wire-rimmed glasses that had been hanging from the neck of her T-shirt and gestured for us to sit down at the dining table. "I assume you want to hear about that night."

"I do." I took a notepad out of my purse. "How well did you know Chloe and Paige?"

"I didn't know them beyond saying hello when we passed on the walkway. But I saw their comings and goings quite a bit. I used to be a manager at Target, but I'm retired now, so I'm home a lot."

"Did they have a lot of visitors?"

"Not lately, no. When Chloe first moved in, she seemed to be pretty popular. A lot of young men came around."

"How do you know they were there to see Chloe? Why not Paige?"

"Because I'd see them leave with Chloe."

See them leave. There weren't any windows that offered a view of the walkway. "How did you see them leave?"

"Through the peephole in my door. And sometimes I'd see her coming or going with them when I was out doing chores or laundry."

Aha. Janet was the Gladys Kravitz of the building. Every apartment building has one. "Did you ever meet Dale Pearson?"

"Well, of course. He was here almost every day."

"Can you describe your first meeting?" I expected to get some vague I-don't-know type of answer. Wrong.

"He was knocking on their door, and when no one opened up, he kept on knocking and knocking. I thought he'd break the door down, so I went out and told him they weren't home. He got really angry, said Chloe knew he was coming."

"Was he yelling?"

"No. I could just tell he was . . . well, let's say very annoyed."

Okay, let's. "Did he leave after you told him they weren't there?"

"No. I told him to come back later, and he gave me a dirty look—"

"What did he say to you?"

"To me? Nothing. But then Chloe came home, and he really laid into her. Asked her where she'd been and why she didn't call to tell him she'd be late." Janet paused. "It doesn't sound like much now, but it was the way he said it. He wasn't yelling at the time, but there was . . .

heat in his voice. It felt as though if I hadn't been there, he would've really gone off on her. There was something kind of, I don't know, scary about him."

I wished I could say Janet seemed like the type to embellish, but she didn't. It made me wonder whether Nikki was a little more accurate than I'd given her credit for—and how many more witnesses the cops would dig up who'd paint a similar picture of Dale. "How long ago was that?"

"About a month ago."

"Did they get into a fight?"

"Not that time, no."

"But they fought at other times? Before that last night?"

"Several times. From what I could hear, it sounded like he was upset about her doing drugs." She shook her head. "Can't blame him for that."

"How did you manage to hear all that?"

"They left their sliding glass door open a lot. I do, too. These apartments aren't big, and they can get pretty stuffy. Anyway, the night she died, they had a terrible fight, worst one ever. I figured she'd break up with him sooner or later, and I was right."

"She broke up with him?" Janet nodded. "You heard her say that?" That hadn't been in Janet's statement.

"Loud and clear."

"Then why didn't you tell the police about it?"

"I thought I did." Janet frowned.

I didn't want to believe her. But it wasn't just the flat certainty in her voice. It was the fact that I knew Chloe's sister had said she intended to break up that night, too. This was bad. Worse than bad. A hair-trigger temper and a classic motive. The likelihood of being able to pin this on someone else was getting slimmer by the minute. I looked at her sliding glass door. The drapes were closed. "Were they yelling at the time?"

"Almost from the moment they walked in the door." Janet looked down at her hands, which were folded in her lap. "I knew I should've called the police. But they had so many fights. And he's a police officer. I never would've thought he'd . . ." Her voice trailed off.

I'd known she was going to be a tough witness for us. But now I knew Janet was going to cream us. I had to find out how much more damage she could do. "Did you happen to see Paige that night?"

"I might've heard her come home. But I can't be sure. I went to bed early that night. The fighting's what woke me up."

"Then you think Paige came home before Chloe?"

"Maybe. I'm really not sure about that."

"Do you know what time you woke up? I mean, because of the fighting?" Maybe she could help us fix a time that would show Dale was out of there too early to have killed them.

"I can get close. By the time I got up, they'd been fighting for a while. I decided to make myself some warm milk, and I remember looking at the clock on the oven. It said one thirty in the morning. It can be off by a minute or two, but not much more."

Shit. The coroner put the time of death between one a.m. and four a.m. "Did you go back to bed after that?"

"Not right away. I stayed in the kitchen and drank my milk. That's how come I heard their front door open and close. When I went to look, I saw him walking down the hallway toward the stairs."

"Did you notice anything unusual about him?"

She shook her head. "I couldn't see much. I was looking through the peephole, and his back was to me."

I needed to regroup and think for a minute. "Do you mind if I go out on your balcony?"

Janet pursed her lips and folded her arms. "Be my guest. You'll see. You can hear everything clear as a bell when the glass doors are opened."

"I'm not doubting you." I kind of was. Or maybe just hoping. "I just want to see what the balconies look like. I assume all the apartments have the same floor plan?"

"As far as I know."

Alex and I crossed the living room, and I pulled the drapes aside. It was a small but serviceable balcony with a wood railing. A rusting hibachi sat in the right corner. Chloe's apartment was on the left, and her balcony was within arm's reach. No doubt about it, if both of their sliding glass doors were open, Janet could easily have heard every word. I told Alex to get some pictures.

As I looked around, I noticed that the ground behind the building was higher and that all the units had identical balconies. I'd wondered how a burglar could've gotten to a second-floor apartment. But now I saw that it'd be easy. Anyone who was reasonably agile could stand on the railing of the balcony below and pull himself up to Chloe's balcony. And the area was pretty much sheltered from view. The carport was at the other end of the building, and the houses behind it didn't have windows facing this way.

I went back inside. "When did you go back to sleep?"

"I stayed up for another ten minutes or so after Dale left. So around two a.m., I guess."

"After Dale left, did you hear anyone else come to their apartment?"

"No."

Janet's son came back into the room. "You're all set, Mom." He shook his head at us. "You know, before that cop got arrested, I thought the killer would turn out to be that guy in 212."

"Who's that?"

Janet pursed her lips together. "A drug dealer. Everyone knows it, but they're all afraid to call the police."

"Did you ever call them?"

"No. I'm just an old woman living alone. Who knows what he'd do if he found out I'd reported him?"

The son spoke up. "I told her not to. There's no point in her taking a risk like that. The cops aren't going to bust him just because my mother thinks he's a drug dealer."

I wouldn't be so sure. But he was probably right that it was safer for Janet to stay out of it.

I moved toward the door, and Alex followed. "Thanks for your time."

Janet took a parting shot. "I never understood what a man that age was doing with a young girl like Chloe. I didn't expect him to kill her, but I knew right from the start nothing good could come of it."

I didn't bother to argue with her. Clearly nothing good had come of it. And right or wrong, I knew I'd wind up with a fair number of "Janets" on my jury.

NINETEEN

Alex looked down toward the end of the corridor. "Are we going to check out that dealer?"

"Heck yeah." I might be able to claim he was yet another suspect the cops failed to investigate. The more of those I could dangle in front of the jury, the merrier. I took in Alex's navy blazer and button-down shirt. "But I'll take the lead. No way he'll answer the door if he sees you."

"According to the book, business attire inspires more confidence and respect—"

"Wait. What book?"

"*The Comprehensive Guide for Private Investigators*. It says—"

I rolled my eyes. "I don't care what some out-of-work ex-cop says. *I* say you dress for your audience. Always go native."

Alex opened, then closed his mouth. "Got it."

We walked down to number 212. I motioned for him to stay out of range of the peephole and knocked on the door. I heard music playing inside. It sounded like jazz—Miles Davis.

A voice came through the door. "I gave at the office."

"I'm not asking for money. I want to talk to you about Chloe and Paige."

"You a cop?"

"No. I'm a lawyer." I pulled out my business card and held it up to the peephole.

I heard the deadbolt turn. The door opened a crack with the sliding chain lock still on. I poked my card through, and a white male hand reached out and took it. The voice—it sounded somewhere between old and young—said, "Never heard of lawyers going door to door. Seems kind of desperate."

I sighed. "I represent the defendant."

The chain came off and the door opened. A pot-filled cloud floated out. It was so heavy I thought I might get a contact high. "You represent that cop?" I nodded. "Tough case." He noticed Alex. "He with you?"

"Yeah. He's my investigator."

Alex put out his hand. "I'm Alex Medrano." They shook.

"Chas Gorman. Come on in."

Chas led us to a brown lumpy-looking couch, and he plopped down in a recliner. Our host was a beanpole, skinny and well over six feet tall. His dirty-blond shoulder-length hair was combed back off his face, which was almost handsome. High cheekbones, regular features, but his eyes were a little close together. Funny how just a millimeter can make all the difference. He was barefoot and dressed in jeans and a Thelonious Monk T-shirt.

The source of the pot cloud stood on the coffee table. It was an elaborately beautiful bong, painted in metallic blues and greens. The furniture looked like garage-sale rejects, the carpet had gaping holes, but the bong and the flat-screen were top of the line. He picked up the bong and took a lighter out of his pocket. "Want some?"

Alex nodded. "Sure, man."

What the . . . ? Damn. I'd told him to go native, and he'd taken it to heart. Chas fired it up, and they both took long pulls. I waited for them to exhale. "You talked to the police?"

"Hell, no. Under no circumstances." He set the bong on the coffee table and leaned back in his chair. "What do you want to know?"

"Did you know Chloe and Paige?"

"A little. Chloe came over for a hit a few times when she first moved in. But she hadn't come around for the past three or four months. I liked her; she was cool. Bummer what happened to her."

"That's one way of putting it. Did you see any of her friends? Or boyfriends?"

"Just that cop . . . I mean, your guy."

"You ever talk to him?"

"Nah. Just saw him around a few times."

"What about Paige?"

"I really dug her. She was sweet. I asked her out once, but . . ."

"It didn't happen?" Chas shook his head. "Did you ever see her with a guy?"

He frowned and reached for the bong. "I seem to remember a dude with a motorcycle helmet. I think he picked her up here a couple times."

"Recently?"

He fired up the bong again and took a long pull, then offered it to Alex—who took it. Shit. He was going to be useless. And hungry. Chas spoke while he held in the smoke. "A couple months ago?" He answered his own question. "Yeah."

"That was the last time you saw him?" Chas nodded. "You never got his name?" He shook his head and let out a stream of smoke.

"Can you describe him?"

"About my height, maybe a little shorter. Longish hair, brown . . . and that helmet. It had, like, red flames on the sides." He thought for a moment. "That's about it."

"You see his bike?"

Chas nodded. "Saw him riding it when he left."

"What'd it look like?"

"Beat up. And loud. Was it a Harley?" He thought for a moment, then answered his own question again. "Don't know."

"Were you home the night of the murders?" He nodded. "Did you hear anything unusual?"

Chas looked at me through slitted eyes. "I heard loud voices. But I couldn't make out words or anything."

"Did you see Chloe and Dale come home?"

"No." He yawned and patted his open mouth. "Can't even tell you if they were the ones fighting. I just know people in the building are saying it was them."

"Did you see Paige come home?"

He frowned. "No. But for some reason . . . I think she got home before Chloe." His words were coming out slower and slower.

"Why is that?"

Chas worked his dry mouth. "Good question. Gotta get some water. You guys want some?"

I declined. Alex, of course, said, "Yeah, thanks."

Chas pushed himself off the recliner in slow motion and shuffled into the kitchen. He came back with two bottles of water, handed one to Alex, then flopped back into his recliner. He poured almost the entire bottle down his throat in one long gulp.

When he wiped his mouth on his sleeve, I took another run at him. "What makes you think Paige got home first?"

Chas stared at a spot on the wall just over my head, his mouth slightly open. "Uh, I'm not sure. But I think. Someone maybe knocked on their door."

"And that person who knocked, he got inside?"

He frowned. "Yeah, I think . . . because I heard the door close."

"Was that before you heard the people fighting? Or after?"

"Um . . . I think it was before."

Before? That wouldn't help. "Do you know if it was before or after midnight?"

Chas scratched his chin. "Somewhere around there. Midnight-ish." He chuckled to himself. "I was blazing with a buddy, so I wasn't, you know, looking at the clock."

I suppressed a sigh. The reliability of any of this was so dubious. "Are you sure it was Chloe and Paige's door? Could it have been the people next door to them, or two doors down?"

Chas tilted his head back and gave a soft chuckle. "Not the guy in 206. He's in his nineties. I'm not dissing the dude. We'd all be lucky to get there. But no one's coming to see him past, like, lunchtime." His eyes closed. I thought we'd lost him, but then he stretched, arched his back, and sighed. "The people in 207. It could've been their door, I guess."

"Who lives there?"

"A guy and his girlfriend. They're not home much. I think they must travel a lot. Mail piles up at their door all the time."

Alex grinned. "That was cool the way you put that together."

Chas grinned back. "Hey, man, maybe I could be an investigator." They shared a chuckle.

I shot a look at Alex. Just what I needed right now: Cheech and Chong. "Do you know if the couple in 207 was home that night?"

He yawned again and stretched his arms over his head. "No clue."

"The person who knocked, did you hear him say anything?"

"I don't think . . . wait, did I?" He looked up at the ceiling again. "Uh, no. Don't think so."

How much of this could I trust? The guy was a major-league stoner. *Maybe* someone had come to *an* apartment. And maybe it was Chloe's. But maybe not. *Maybe* it was around midnight. And he thought it was before Chloe got home. But maybe not. I looked at Alex. I'd been about to ask if he had questions, but he had a sloppy smile on his face. I bumped around a little longer to see if Chas remembered anything else, but he could barely get three words out between yawns that were so cavernous I thought he might pull something. Finally, after a string of questions that elicited "I don't know" and shrugs, I gave up. He was tapped out. The reliability of what little information I'd gotten out of him was up for grabs. But one thing I was sure of: Chas would never play as a possible suspect. He couldn't have stayed awake long enough to kill anyone.

I stood up and tilted my head at Alex. It took him a second to get the hint, but he eventually got up. I smiled at our host. "Chas, thanks. I really appreciate you talking to us."

He followed us to the door. "Anytime, man. Always happy to talk to a lovely lady." He patted Alex's back. "You too, dude."

Alex gave him a lopsided smile. "It was real, man."

When we got out to the corridor, I told Alex to head to the car. "You go sleep it off. I'm going to hit up number 207."

He drew back and looked at me like I'd grown a third arm. "Sleep what off? I'm not stoned. I didn't inhale. That would be totally unprofessional. But you said to go native."

I laughed. "Nice." We headed to 207. As we passed number 208, Chloe and Paige's apartment, I looked at the door. The crime-scene tape was gone, but I could still see black print powder around the doorknob. I had a feeling that apartment wouldn't be rented anytime soon.

A woman in her twenties answered the door at 207. She didn't know Chloe or Paige other than to say "Hey" when they passed in the corridor, and she and her boyfriend had been out of town at the time of the murders. No help there. And the old guy in 206 hadn't heard or seen anything that night. Not surprising, since he could barely hear us from two feet away.

We headed to Alex's car and I thought about what we'd learned from Chas. "Well, that motorcycle guy obviously wasn't trying to hide the fact that he was seeing Paige. And it doesn't sound like he has the money to buy her diamonds."

Alex nodded. "Besides, I'd have figured Mr. Perfect would be more . . . perfect."

"Yeah, the motorcycle guy isn't him."

Alex unlocked the car. "Janet's going to shred us. And Chas thinks someone was at their place *before* Chloe got home with Dale. That doesn't help."

"Janet will absolutely shred us. And timing is the least of our problems with Chas. If he were reliable at all, it'd be great to prove someone came knocking on the door that night—no matter what time he says it happened."

"Then you want me to serve him a subpoena?"

We got into the car. "Look at you, all knowing the legal lingo. No."

Alex looked at me, perplexed. "The book says we should always have subpoenas ready in case—"

This book business was going to drive me nuts very soon. "Yeah, Alex. But what do you think the jury's going to do with a witness like Chas? He's probably got a conviction or two, and even if he doesn't, he's a major stoner and he's not sure of a friggin' thing."

"Then we can't use him at all?"

"I'm not saying that. We might be able to use him for something. Just not for court." I already had an idea.

My phone rang. It was the mechanic. Beulah had made a full recovery. Well, as full a recovery as a car that has 157,000 miles can make.

Alex dropped me off at the station, and I sent him back to the office.

I'd have to get downtown to Twin Towers and talk to Dale about . . . everything. Not the least of which was why he hadn't bothered to tell me about his breakup with Chloe.

Or as the prosecution would put it: his motive.

TWENTY

I wanted to get to Twin Towers first thing in the morning, but Deshawn's hearing was at nine a.m., and there was no way Judge Raymond would let me put it over. A former marine and a slavishly devoted cop-lover, Judge Raymond was a prosecutor's dream come true. And my worst nightmare. He wasn't exactly a big fan of mine, either. Which is why I got to court a half hour early. I knew he'd jump at the chance to slap me with a fine.

Deshawn rolled in at five minutes to nine. That was early for him, and no doubt thanks only to his mother, Tamika Johnson, who was sitting in the audience, her eyes boring into Deshawn's back. Deshawn had spiffed up for the occasion in black loafers, dark slacks, and a white shirt and tie—thanks again, I was sure, only to Tamika. He turned to glance at her every few minutes, feeling the wrath of her glare. Deshawn feared no one the way he feared his mother.

Seconds later, Rita Stump, the prosecutor, wearing a dress from Forever 21 (no one told her it was just a name, not a promise) and an irritated expression, marched into the courtroom. The cop, Bruce Ambrose, rolled in behind her. He was one of those red-necked (it's not a pejorative in this case; his neck was actually red), fleshy cops who looked like a heart attack waiting to happen.

He'd busted Deshawn for a seat-belt violation, then claimed to have seen something "funny" about his glove compartment. The ensuing search turned up a handgun that Deshawn swore wasn't his.

Ambrose got on the stand, and Rita took him through the fairy tale he'd written in his police report. Then it was my turn.

I started by having him describe what was so "funny" about the glove compartment. He claimed it didn't seem to "line up right." I made him get specific about it—which edges didn't line up, how far off they were.

He stared at me with cold, hard eyes. "It looked to me like there was at least half an inch between the dash and the top of the glove box."

"And yet the glove compartment was fully closed, wasn't it?"

"It was closed."

"Amazing feat of engineering, wouldn't you say? That it could stay closed—"

"Objection!" Rita jumped to her feet. "Counsel's sarcasm is inappropriate."

I held up my hands. "I'm just asking for his opinion. I mean, he's clearly an expert in glove boxes—"

The judge gave me a menacing look. "Ms. Brinkman, you'll knock off the personal comments *and* the sarcasm or we'll stop this hearing and start contempt proceedings."

I turned back to my buddy Ambrose. "And of course, you took photos of that glove box so we could all see how 'funny' it looked—"

"No. I didn't."

I let that sink in for a moment, then moved on. "This wasn't the first time you met my client, was it? You've had a few run-ins in the past."

"I wouldn't call them run-ins. I had information that indicated to me he might've committed a crime on two previous occasions, and I detained him for further questioning."

But the descriptions of the suspects in those cases didn't even remotely fit Deshawn. The first suspect was five foot seven, 150. The second one was even more ridiculous: he was five foot six—and Hispanic. Deshawn was six foot three. I told Deshawn to stand up next to me. "Your Honor, for the record, I'm five foot six." I stared up at Deshawn. I glanced at the judge and saw that I'd made my point. Time to move in for the kill.

I picked up the gun Ambrose claimed to have found in Deshawn's glove box and took it to the witness stand. "Officer, would you read the serial number on that gun for us?"

He stared at me for a moment, then slowly read it.

"Thank you. Now I'm going to show you a police report that was prepared about a month before you arrested Deshawn."

"Objection! Irrelevant!" Rita bounced up again. "What does a police report on a different case have to do with—"

The judge cut her off. "I think we're about to find out. Overruled."

I put the report in front of Ambrose and pointed to the bottom of the page. "Please read those last two lines for us." I watched to see if his lips would move. They didn't. But when he finished, I saw him swallow hard. "That report was prepared one month ago by another LAPD officer, correct?"

"Yes."

"And it shows that another officer seized this very gun from a suspect named Julio Ortiz and booked it into evidence one month *before* you stopped Deshawn Johnson, doesn't it?"

Ambrose darted a look at Rita, then licked dry lips. "Yeah."

I pulled out the follow-up report on Julio Ortiz and showed it to Ambrose. "If this gun had been released back to Ortiz, it would say so in this report, wouldn't it?" Ambrose nodded. "But it doesn't say that, does it?"

Ambrose stared at the report for a long moment. "No."

"So can you explain to us how a gun that was booked into evidence a month *before* you stopped Deshawn Johnson wound up in his glove compartment?"

"I . . . someone must've taken it out of evidence."

"And that someone had to be a cop, didn't it? You guys don't let people like Deshawn or me go check stuff out of the locker, do you?"

"No."

"Any idea who that cop might be?"

Ambrose stared straight ahead. "No."

"But there's a video camera in the evidence locker, so we could find out, right?"

Ambrose turned a scary shade of red and gave me a death glare. "I guess so."

"Did you ever have the gun tested for prints or DNA?"

"No."

"But being a good police officer, you handled it carefully so as not to wipe off any prints or DNA that might be there, right?"

"I don't know. I wasn't really worried about that. It was in his glove box." Ambrose's face got so red I thought the top of his head would blow off.

The courtroom had gone dead silent.

I glanced at Rita, then turned to the judge. "I'd ask the court to order that the videotape of the evidence locker be produced and that this weapon be tested for prints and DNA. By a neutral agency, like the sheriff's office." I sat down. *Your move, Rita.*

The judge looked like he'd just taken a bite of rotten fish. He turned to the prosecutor. "People?"

This time, Rita didn't bounce. She didn't even stand. "I have no questions."

Judge Raymond didn't want to do it. I could see it was killing him. But he had no choice. "I'm going to issue those orders." He glared at Rita. "It's not my job to tell you how to do yours. But if I were you,

I'd give my superiors the heads up that the judge will be ordering an investigation. They might want to do one of their own." He glared at Ambrose. "And I'm ordering you to go back to the station forthwith and tell your captain what happened here." He banged his gavel. "We'll be in recess."

Rita stomped out with Ambrose trailing behind her. Neither of them looked at me. They knew as well as I did that the lab wouldn't find Deshawn's *anything* on that gun. This case was history.

Deshawn started whooping and fist-bumping the minute we got outside the courtroom, but I held up a hand and gave him the facts of life. "Deshawn, listen to me: Ambrose went to a lot of trouble to set you up. That's how bad they want you. You've had a target on your back for a long time, and it just got ten times bigger. You keep crime-ing, they'll get you for sure. And next time you won't have me."

"I hear you. I really do. Starting now, I'm out of the life for good."

I knew he meant it. Now. But I also knew that tomorrow, or the next day, Lil' J or Big Blue or whoever would show up and say, "I just need [fill in the blank] just this one time," and he'd go for it. As the saying goes, it was in Deshawn's nature.

TWENTY-ONE

It was four o'clock by the time I got in to see Dale. There are only seven attorney "rooms"—really just cubicles—in each module, and they were all full when I got there. I had to wait a half hour for one to open up. Dale looked better today. His face didn't sag as much, and there was more life in his eyes. He wasn't all the way back to the man I'd met in my office, and he probably wouldn't be as long as he was in here. But he was doing better. Which was a good thing, because I was going to have to get into it with him.

I picked up the phone. "Hey. They treating you okay so far?"

"Probably as okay as they can. They put me next to a juicehead who sleeps all day. And farts. But it could be a lot worse." He looked in my eyes. "How are you doing? I've been worrying about you. You must be getting some serious flack for representing the monster who killed America's sweetheart."

I'd never had a client in custody ask how I was doing. Especially one who was facing a sentence of life without parole. "I've gotten some . . . interesting comments on my website and on Twitter. But it goes with the territory. Don't worry about me; I can handle it."

I told him about our interviews.

He remembered Nikki—who hadn't been subtle about her irritation at not getting a rise out of him. "But what she told you was true. I was driving around the neighborhood. I thought the burglar was a local amateur who might decide to try it again."

"That'll work."

"It's the truth. I told you, I'm not like your other clients, Samantha. I'm not going to lie to you."

I gave him a long look. "Holding out on me is *exactly* what my other clients would do. How come you didn't tell me Chloe broke up with you that night?"

He blew out a breath. "Janet, right?"

I nodded. "And Chloe's sister confirms it. During their last phone call, Chloe said she was planning to break up."

He raked a hand through his hair. "I should've told you. I'm sorry. I guess I was worried that you'd make more of it than it really was. The truth is, we were *both* through with each other. She was getting back into the junk, and I couldn't just stand by and watch her throw her life away."

A jury would probably buy it, since the toxicology report backed him up. But it'd help if someone else could back up his claim that she was a regular user. "Did anyone else know she was using again?"

"I'd bet her sister knew. But I doubt she'll tell you. In my experience, next of kin tends to clam up when it comes to things like that." He gave me a searching look. "Speaking of family, how does yours feel about you taking this case?"

What a weird question. "Uh, my mom wasn't thrilled."

He flicked a piece of dust off the counter in front of him. "What about your dad?"

Even weirder. What was this about? "I think my stepdad's okay with it." Celeste would've made a point of telling me if he wasn't.

He looked up at me and cocked his head. "What about your biological father? Is he in the picture?"

This was getting stranger by the second. "No. Never met him. Look, about the drug dealer—"

"What if you could? Meet him, I mean. Would you want to?"

What the . . . ? "I don't know. When I was a kid, I wanted to." Actually, I'd dreamed of it day and night. Even now, the old feelings came rushing back. The pain of feeling alone, vulnerable, at everyone's mercy, of wishing I had someone in my corner. Someone strong and fierce, who'd protect me . . . who'd make them all pay. I pulled myself back with effort. "Why do you care?"

"I know him." He looked at me with soft eyes. "So do you."

I stared at him. "What the fuck . . . ?"

Dale took a deep breath. After a long moment, he said, "It's me." His eyes searched mine as he continued. "I'm your father."

I heard the words, but they made no sense. It was as though he was speaking backward. When my brain managed to unscramble the sounds, I was sure I'd heard wrong. "What? What the hell are you talking about?"

He spoke gently. "I'm sorry, I didn't mean to blindside you like this. But I couldn't seem to find the right time. I met you and then . . . everything happened so fast."

"Couldn't find the right time?" I felt a little dizzy, like the room had just tilted forty-five degrees. I shook my head slowly, thinking I must be dreaming. This couldn't be real. I looked down at the pen in my left hand, poised over a legal pad. I looked around at the cubicles, at the observation window where a guard was standing—and watching me. I was definitely not dreaming. The words echoed again in my brain: *I'm your father.* How could it be?

I'd forgotten to breathe. Light-headed, I gulped for air. Finally, I looked at him. I took in the strong chin; the widow's peak; the dark-brown, almost-black hair—all of it so like mine. And so unlike Celeste, with her blonde mane. Then I remembered seeing him sign the retainer agreement; he was left-handed—like I was. But I still couldn't wrap my brain around it. I stammered, "H-how do you know? What makes you think . . ." I couldn't manage all the questions that flooded through my mind.

Dale looked at me apologetically. "I know it's a lot to take in. Are you sure you're ready for this?"

I wasn't sure of anything right now. But I nodded slowly.

Dale searched my face for a moment. "Okay. I dated your mother when we were in college. We went out for a while, then she broke up with me. About a month later, she called to tell me she was pregnant and needed money for an abortion. I gave it to her, offered to take her to the doctor, help her out afterward, but she shut me down. Said it was her problem and she could handle it. I called her a week later to see if she was okay, but she didn't answer. And I never saw or heard from her again. I had no idea she'd had the baby."

I shook my head. "No, that's not right. Celeste got pregnant after a one-night stand. She went to a party, got drunk, slept with a guy whose name she never knew."

"*That's* what she told you?" Dale shook his head, then a little smile crossed his lips. "Celeste. She was Charlene when I knew her. But I'm not surprised she changed it. She hated the name, thought it sounded too hillbilly."

Hillbilly? He was definitely talking about Celeste. But it just wouldn't sink in. I had another dizzy spell. I'd stopped breathing again. I inhaled. Better. My brain started to work. "Why would she say she didn't know the father? Why tell me he was just a one-nighter?"

"I don't know for sure, but I have a good guess. Maybe because if you knew the truth, you might find me. And then I'd be coming around—which was the last thing she'd have wanted." Dale hesitated, his expression pained. "Look, Samantha, I don't want to speak ill of her—"

Most of my pistons were firing now. This had to be bullshit. I snapped at him. "Really? 'Cause I do. All the time. But why wouldn't she want to keep you around? We were broke. She needed the money.

And besides, she'd have been thrilled to have a free babysitter." Getting tied down with a kid was the last thing in the world she'd wanted.

He sighed. "I didn't have money—certainly not the kind she was aiming for—and she didn't want a low-rent loser in her life. It's one thing to be a single mom with a little girl. A lot of men wouldn't mind stepping into that picture. But it's another to be a single mom with a child and an ex-boyfriend who's always around. She was looking for a guy with big bucks, and she didn't want anything to get in the way of that."

That explanation made me slow down and reconsider. It was exactly how she'd think. Celeste was all about the money. I'd spent my childhood watching her pan for gold with one boyfriend after another. "Then why'd she go out with you to begin with?"

"I looked better off than I was. I went to UCLA, and she went to Cal State Northridge. I had a better car than I deserved—an Audi that I'd inherited from a cousin who had some money. And when I met her, I didn't have to work. But when my dad got laid off and I had to get a job, Char—I mean Celeste—saw that I was almost as broke as she was. It took her about five minutes to decide we weren't 'right' for each other." He shook his head. "And actually, she was right. We weren't. I don't know why it took me so long to admit it. I guess I was just deluding myself that she was someone else. Someone who'd wake up and realize love was more important."

Everything he was saying about her fit. That was her. That was Celeste. But I still couldn't believe it. This couldn't be true. It was some bizarre coincidence. It had to be. And there was an easy way to prove it. "Would you be willing to take a paternity test?"

"Absolutely. And I don't blame you for being skeptical. They can swab me in the infirmary and send it . . . wherever you want. If you get a private lab, you'll have the answer in a day or two."

Just the fact that he'd agreed to do it so readily was a jolt. He might be mistaken—I was sure he was—but he wasn't lying. "How . . . when did you . . . figure this out?"

"When I found out I might be charged with the murders, I put together a list of lawyers and checked out everyone on it—their whole life history." He saw my raised eyebrow and nodded. "I know. I'm a little OCD. It's how I cope, by trying to know everything. When I saw your birth date and that your mother was Charlene Brinkman, I couldn't believe it. But the timing was too perfect, and I knew she hadn't been seeing anyone else."

I gave him a skeptical look. "How can you be so sure?"

Dale shrugged. "We were together all the time until she broke up with me. And after that, I still saw her around, heard about her from mutual friends. She wasn't with anyone." He sighed. "Look, I know this is hard for you. It's a lot to take in. Tell you the truth, I didn't believe it myself at first." Dale paused and shook his head. "It was so crazy. To find out that not only did I have another daughter but . . ." His voice trailed off as his gaze took in my hair, my eyes, my face. "But when I met you in person, I knew it was true." Dale frowned. "Anyway, like I said, I'll be glad to take the test—"

I cut him off. "Is that why you hired me?"

Dale pulled back abruptly. "What? No! It's why I almost *didn't*. I met with five other lawyers, and I was still thinking about going with the last one before I met with you—"

"Messinger?"

"Right. But I wasn't that impressed with him. And this is my life we're talking about. I wanted the best." He looked at me with a mixture of pride and sadness. "You were it." He looked down and rubbed a spot on the counter in front of him. "I'm sorry about all of this. Especially having to meet this way." He looked up with a little smile. "But you just blow me away. I can't believe I have a grown-up daughter who's so brilliant, so beautiful." His eyes misted and he blinked fast, then cleared his throat. "Not that I take any credit for it."

In that moment, my mother's phone call, her strange fury at my taking the case, came back to me. It all made sense now. She knew that even if Dale didn't tell me, if the press dug hard enough, they could find the connection. Then everyone would know she'd dated—and had a child with—a murderer. In her mind, she'd never live it down.

Dale spoke again. "Samantha, if you want to get off the case, I'll understand. It was probably crazy to think this could be okay. I just felt like in the middle of this friggin' nightmare, it was the one ray of light." He shook his head. "I guess going from cop to murder suspect in the space of a week left me kind of . . . unhinged." He dropped his gaze down at the counter again. "I considered not telling you, but I couldn't risk you finding out on the four o'clock news." He looked up at me. "I can only hope that you'll forgive me."

I couldn't find any words. I had no coherent thoughts. My feelings were so tangled I couldn't even name them. When I spoke, my lips felt numb. "I—I need to think about this. I'm . . . not sure what I should do." Dale's case had to get to trial as soon as possible, and it wasn't just a trial strategy. Maximum security or not, his life was in danger here. "I'll figure this out. Tonight. I'll let you know tomorrow."

I hung up the phone and signaled for the guard to let me out.

TWENTY-TWO

I wound up in my car with no memory of having left the jail or walking through the parking lot. It probably wasn't safe for me to be on the road, but since traffic was bumper-to-bumper and moving about three miles an hour, I couldn't get into any serious trouble.

I barely noticed how I was inching along as my brain fumbled with the surreality of what I'd just heard. I remembered how I used to fantasize about who my father was when I was a kid. Especially during the dark time. I'd dream he was a martial-arts fighter or a Navy Seal or a Green Beret, who'd come to save me and never let anyone hurt me again. My knuckles turned white on the steering wheel. I made myself take a deep breath. In. Out. Let it go.

And then another realization hit me. It was one thing to be the lawyer for the man who'd killed two innocent young women. But it was a whole different world to be his daughter. The gruesome crime-scene pictures flashed through my mind. Then Janet's words came back to me—how she described his flashpoint temper, his fights with Chloe. I tried to square it with the man who'd looked at me with such pride and . . . tenderness. But he was charged with a brutal double homicide. And it looked like he'd done it.

I felt nauseous—like I'd just stepped off a Tilt-A-Whirl. My head swam with all the implications. It took me an hour and a half to get home, but I was so preoccupied, I didn't notice. It was after seven by the time I got back to my apartment, and only then did it dawn on me that I was supposed to check in with Michelle. She'd left a message saying that requests were coming in for interviews, and reporters were looking for background information on me.

The irony hit me almost as hard as the fresh wave of panic. Now I had a whole new vista of "background information" to worry about.

The press hadn't dug up the connection between Dale and me yet, but it'd been only two days. If they cared enough to keep digging, they'd figure it out eventually. I knew I should call Michelle, tell her what'd happened, and figure out what to do. But the thought of putting it all into words was more than I could handle.

I drew a hot bath, took a few sips of pinot noir, and curled up in the tub. I must've fallen asleep because when my phone rang, I couldn't remember where I was, and my right arm had fallen asleep. By the time I pulled myself out, the call had gone to voice mail. I dried off, threw on my sweats, and listened to the message. It was Michelle. I looked at the number. She'd called from the office, and it was after eighty thirty. It wasn't fair to go incommunicado this way. I had to call her back.

I took a deep breath and tried to make my voice sound normal. "Hey, sorry I didn't check in. It's been a bitch of a day and I was fried."

There was a beat of silence. "You sound funny. Did it go okay with Dale?"

I guess it was partly the wine. But mostly it was the right person with the right touch at the right time. I began to cry. "I—I don't know where to start."

"I'm coming over. Have you had dinner?"

I'd forgotten about that. "Uh-uh."

She hung up.

I wanted to make myself get some work done, but I couldn't focus. My mind kept toggling between Dale's apologetic expression and the crime-scene photos, between the man Janet described and the man I'd just seen. The killer—my father. I whispered the words. *My father.* I could barely choke them out.

I lay down on the couch, exhausted. I'd done all the coping I could stand for the moment. I turned on the TV and watched a rerun of *Friends.* Michelle showed up a half hour later. She pulled me into a hug and held on for a long time. I felt the spring in my chest start to uncoil and took a full breath for the first time since leaving the jail.

She stepped back and held me by the shoulders. "Ready to tell me?" I shook my head. "Okay, then try to eat something."

She'd brought us two thick roast beef sandwiches and coleslaw. It looked delicious, but I had no appetite. I picked at the coleslaw and listened while Michelle chatted about media calls and office business, but I barely heard her.

She finished half her sandwich, then poured us both a glass of wine. "Have some. Do it now." I took a long slug. "Can you tell me now?"

I sighed and rubbed my eyes. "God, Michy. It's so crazy." I told her the whole story. Just hearing myself say the words out loud made my head spin. "And now I don't know what to do. If it's true, I have to get off the case. I don't think I can handle this. I mean, shit. My *father.*" For the first time in my life, the word wasn't just an abstract concept. It belonged to a real person.

Michelle's eyes had gotten wider and wider, and by the time I finished, her mouth was hanging open. She was silent for a few moments, absorbing it all. Then she frowned. "*Can* you even represent him? I mean, isn't it a conflict or something?"

"No. If he wants to keep me, there's no legal reason why I can't stay on the case."

I heard my own words as if someone else was speaking. I still couldn't believe this was happening to me. It felt like a crazy dream, except I wasn't waking up. "But I just keep thinking that I finally met my father—and he's probably a psychopathic killer." I put my head in my hands. "Who knew that Celeste would turn out to be the good parent?"

Michelle sat stunned for a moment. Then she gave a little giggle. She clapped her hand over her mouth, but another one escaped—then another. And now the giggles swelled into a long, rolling belly laugh. Between gasps, she said, "Celeste . . . the good . . . parent."

Only then did it hit me what I'd just said. I started to laugh and didn't stop until tears streamed down my face and I couldn't breathe.

When we'd both recovered, Michelle stared down at her glass for a long moment. "Okay, let's talk about what to do now. If you heard anything I said when I first got here, the media is hot after your ass. Someone's going to find out about this no matter what you do. So if you're thinking you can keep it quiet by stepping away from the case, I'd let that fantasy go."

I knew she was right. "But if I jump out right now, the story will go away a lot faster."

"That's true. Drink your wine."

"I already had a little before you got here."

"Drink it anyway. You're way too sober." I smiled and took a sip. "If you get off the case, that's a story in itself. The press will want to find out why, and once they dig, they'll figure out who he is. How will that look?"

"Like his own daughter thinks he's guilty."

"Right. It'll screw him hard if you get off the case. And if he really isn't guilty and he gets convicted, will you ever forgive yourself?"

I thought about that. Probably not. Not even if he *was* guilty. "I guess I have to stay on, then." But if I thought the case had been a high-pressure situation before . . . just thinking about it made my stomach ache. I agonize over all my cases, but the pressure of defending my own father was a bone crusher. Every little detail I missed, every mistake—no matter how small—would keep me awake every night for the duration of the trial.

And if I lost, every night for the rest of my life.

TWENTY-THREE

When I woke up the next morning, I thought about the paternity test. Dale was more than willing to take it, but it would cost money, and there was a much cheaper, faster way to find out if it was true.

I called my mother. "Why didn't you tell me Dale was my father?"

There was a long pause. "So he told you."

That did it. I'd pretty much already accepted that it was true. But any lingering doubt was gone for good now. Dale really was my father. "Yeah, he told me. Why didn't *you?*"

"Because I hoped you'd get off the case. Or at least that he'd have the decency not to tell you."

"The decency? Why *wouldn't* he tell me? Some reporter was bound to figure it out eventually. Thank God he told me instead of letting me get blindsided by the press. But that never entered your mind, did it?"

Another long pause. "I just wanted to protect you."

"From what? The truth was going to come out regardless. You weren't protecting me. You were trying to protect yourself—and your image. As always."

"Well, now that you know, you're going to get off the case, aren't you?"

"No, I'm most certainly not—"

"He's a murderer!"

"You don't know that. And why did you lie to me about your relationship? Dale wasn't a one-night stand. You dated him for months."

"I did what was best for you!"

"You mean like you did when we moved in with Sebastian?"

Sebastian. One of her many boyfriends before she married Jack.

She sighed. "Oh God. Are we really going to get into all that *again*?"

"Sure. As soon as you stop pretending you ever did anything for my benefit! And by the way, why *didn't* you have the abortion?"

"Because I didn't want one. I just told him that so he'd leave me alone."

I knew I should let it go. I already knew the real answer, but for some reason, I needed to make her admit it. "You were too far along, weren't you?"

There was dead silence for several seconds. When she answered, her voice was weak. "No."

She was usually a better liar than this. I'd caught her off guard. Suddenly I was weary of this whole conversation. No. More than that. I was weary of all of it. Of constantly looking for someone who simply wasn't there and never would be. "I've got to go." I hung up.

The weird queasiness I'd felt when Dale told me he was my father washed over me again, and I bent forward, my forehead on my knees. When it passed, I sat up and looked at the clock on the oven. I needed to get to the office. But everything felt off somehow. I couldn't feel the floor under my feet, and as I glanced around the room, nothing looked the same—my hands, the kitchen table, the phone. What was happening to me?

I looked at the phone again. And then it came to me. Something had broken free inside me—an awareness of who and what my mother was. It'd always been there, but I'd kept it locked away, where I wouldn't have to admit the whole truth of it, what it meant. But now that I'd let it all in, I could never unknow it. My mother was a narcissist who'd never wanted me and didn't even particularly like, let alone love, me. And it didn't matter what I did, how many of her parties I went to, how many cases I won, how successful I might be. That would never change. As I let the reality of that settle in, a question slowly took shape: Then why keep showing up? Why keep taking her calls, listening to her criticize everything I did, wore, or said—deluding myself that a day would come when the loving mother would appear?

The answer was unavoidable: there was no point. Nothing good ever came from contact with Celeste. Even our phone calls were like crawling naked across a field of broken glass. Then why not stop? I barely breathed as the simplicity of that answer spread through me. I was an adult. I could choose to stop beating my head on the stone wall. I could fire my mother. As painful as it was to admit that my mother didn't care for me and never had, I'd known it for a long time. But the realization that I didn't have to keep trying to fix that, to keep showing up in the hope it would change, was liberating. I felt lighter. It was as though I'd cut the rope around my neck that'd been tied to a barge of misery. A barge I'd been dragging around my whole life.

I stood up and looked around the room—at the calendar of Mickey Mouse cartoons on the wall, the blue-and-red skull-head magnets on the refrigerator, the yellow oven mitts hanging above the kitchen counter . . . everything—the colors, the shapes—seemed more vivid, brighter. I knew it couldn't really be this easy, that I'd crash from this strange high soon enough. But for now, I let myself enjoy this unexpected silver lining.

It was time to get to the office, but I wasn't ready to see anyone. I needed to be with myself, make sure I knew how I felt. So I took drastic action: I put on my running shoes and went out for a short jog. I didn't do it often. For me, it was like medicine; I did it only when I had to. But it worked. After the run and a hot shower, I was ready to face the world. I headed to the office.

When I dropped the bomb on Alex, he was momentarily speechless. His eyes big, he finally said, "Your *father*? Are you kidding?" I told him I wasn't. "Are you okay?" I told him I was—sort of. "What are you going to do?"

"I'm staying on the case. But we need to handle this right. My guess is, with all the heat this case is getting, someone's going to find out sooner or later. So I think we should get out ahead of this and release the story ourselves."

"Probably so," Alex said. "How do you want to do it?"

I knew what I didn't want. "I don't want to make this a six-part piece in *Vanity Fair* about Samantha Brinkman and her fucked-up life—"

"As if you'd get *Vanity Fair*," Michelle said. "Probably more like the *PennySaver*—"

"Whatever." I shot her a look—though I agreed with her. "The point is, the shorter the better. So I'm thinking television news, where I can squeeze it down to a ten-second sound bite."

Michelle nodded. "And make a friend. Smart move. Which reporter do you like?"

"I'll give this one to Edie. Tell her to meet me in front of the courthouse at eleven thirty."

Michelle scrolled through the press contacts on her computer. "You heading downtown?"

I nodded. "I've got to tell Dale I'm keeping the case."

I started to head out, but Michelle held up a hand. "Don't you think you should call Lisa before this hits the airwaves?"

I paused, one hand on the doorknob. "Lisa? Why?" Then it hit me. Lisa Milstrom was my half sister. I actually had a sibling now. I'd so wished for a brother or sister when I was a kid. I remembered how jealous and lonely I used to feel when friends complained about being tortured by their younger this or older that. This wouldn't be the same; Lisa and I hadn't lived together and never would. But it was a connection, and I liked it. "Right. I'll call her from the car after I talk to Dale."

It felt strange, uncomfortable, to see Dale now. The problem was, I didn't have time for these feelings. I had to focus. I was his lawyer, and defending him was going to take all my energy. I hadn't told him that I'd met Lisa, and I decided that I wasn't going to do it now. One revelation at a time.

I got into Beulah and tuned in to a jazz station. Wayne Shorter's "Night Dreamer" came on, the perfect salve for my overworked psyche. And traffic wasn't bad. I made it downtown by ten o'clock. I'd resolved to keep this meeting short and to the point.

Still, I headed into Twin Towers feeling a little shakier than I wanted to. When they brought Dale out, he looked pale and drawn. We picked up the phones.

He studied my face. "Are you going to stay?"

"Yes." He closed his eyes and exhaled. I told him I was going to release the story myself. "I don't know what that'll mean for you in here, but brace yourself."

"Thank you, Samantha. You told your mother?" I nodded. He closed his eyes for a moment. "That had to be terrible. I'm sorry . . . about all of this. Well, not all." He gave me a warm look. "But I can't imagine how this has been for you."

"Funny, that's exactly what Celeste said."

"Really?"

"No. For her, the words *I'm* and *sorry* have never come up in the same sentence. So thank you. But now we've got to get down to work. Your preliminary hearing is next week. I'm going to go see the people on Chloe's show today. Do you have any names I should look for in particular?"

Dale had been watching me with concern. But when I shifted into work mode and asked for names, he went along with it. "If you mean the names of anyone she had problems with, I don't. But if you're thinking about looking for her dealer . . ." He shook his head. "I still don't. I'd just guess that it's someone on the crew. I wouldn't think any of the cast members would want to risk it."

"Or be bothered. They make enough money; they don't need to deal on the side. We might try to see Kaitlyn today, too. Any tips? Dos or don'ts?"

Dale sighed and shook his head. "I saw her only a few times, but she seemed very sweet. She's a much softer person than Chloe. But good luck getting her to talk to you."

"I know. We'll see about her."

I told him I'd be back tomorrow and headed for the courthouse. On the way, I called Lisa and told her she had a new sister. Hearing myself say the words felt almost otherworldly strange, and Lisa took a few beats to wrap her head around it. But she recovered and grooved into the idea pretty quickly. "Cool! Hey, maybe I can come watch you in court." I wasn't sure this case was the place to start, but for now, I just said that'd be great.

TWENTY-FOUR

When I got to the courthouse, Edie was already out front with her cameraman.

"Samantha, thank you so much for giving me the story. I'm dying of suspense. Michelle wouldn't say what it's about."

I smiled. "Ready?" She nodded. "Dale Pearson is my biological father."

Her jaw dropped. "Your what?" I nodded. Edie immediately turned to her cameraman. "Roll it. Let's go!" She let me make the announcement, then asked, "So you knew when you took the case, right? I assume your mother must have told you."

That was exactly what I figured people would think: that I took the case because I felt sorry for my guilty, estranged father. Or that Dale had hired me because he knew I was his daughter. So I had my story ready. "Actually, no. My mother doesn't follow this kind of news much, and she never suspected that Dale might be the fling she had in college. And Dale and I didn't figure it out until after he hired me and I started reviewing his background." Edie asked about my mother and Dale, how they'd met and how long they were together. "Didn't Dale know he had a daughter somewhere?"

The question played right into my hands. I needed to make it clear that Dale never knew about me so people wouldn't think he was a deadbeat asshole who'd abandoned a pregnant girlfriend and her baby. "Dale never knew about me. By the time my mother found out she was pregnant, they'd broken up." I had to push down the gag reflex to add, "She didn't think it'd be right to obligate him to take care of a baby they'd never planned to have."

It was total bullshit, but I had to make Celeste sound noble so she'd go along with my story. When we finished, Edie thanked me with shining eyes. "Thank you, Samantha. I really owe you one. This is going to be huge. So just for your sake, a word of warning: if you don't want to spend the next week giving interviews, you'd better lay low."

"That's the plan." And we both knew that piece of advice wasn't just for my sake. By telling Edie I didn't intend to talk to anyone else, I'd just given her an exclusive. Now everyone would have to credit her and piggyback on her footage. "I have news about the case, too."

She turned to the cameraman. "Are you still rolling?" He said he was. She turned back to me and raised her microphone again. "Do you have some new development on the case?"

Time to make use of Chas. "I have evidence that someone else came to Chloe and Paige's apartment late that night."

Edie's eyes widened. "Can you tell us who that person is?"

"Not yet. But we will soon."

"I assume your witness must be someone in the building. Who is it?"

"I'm sorry, I can't give out that information just yet. But again, I will. Very soon."

"Thank you!" She turned to the camera. "For those who just tuned in, that was Samantha Brinkman, the attorney who's representing accused murderer Dale Pearson, with some incredible news."

Edie took another few seconds to wrap up, then grabbed my hand. "Thank you for this. And congratulations on finding your father. That's fantastic!"

"Thanks." I turned to go.

"Just tell me off the record, who's the new witness? I promise not to tell."

"I'm sorry, but I can't. Not yet."

"Okay, just promise you'll let me be the first to know when you go public with it."

I didn't want to commit, so I just smiled and trotted away. I had only a limited number of party favors to pass around, and I needed more than one reporter in my corner. Plus, I didn't want anyone finding out that my new, secret star witness was a loadie who'd probably dreamed the whole thing.

I headed out to meet Alex at the Warner Bros. studio lot in Burbank. The plan was to see if someone on Chloe's show could give us a lead on who'd been her dealer. But no such luck. I couldn't tell whether they really didn't know or just weren't inclined to tell me. Either way, that line of inquiry was a bust.

The one thing everyone did seem to know was that Dale was my father. Edie's piece had already aired as "Breaking News!" and apparently, it'd gone viral. Every single person I talked to stared at me like I was a circus freak and "just had to ask" what it was like to have a murder suspect for a father, and did I "think he did it?" It didn't take long for me to get sick and tired of it, and by the third interview, I snapped and said, "Yeah, he did it. And I hear it runs in the family." The witness's eyes got big and round. I sighed. "*No*, I don't think he did it." Alex suggested that from now on, I stick with a simple "No comment" and let Michy handle the press calls for a while.

But I did find out that Chloe might've been seeing one of the young writers, Geoffrey Brocklin. No one knew how serious it'd been, but they'd spent a fair amount of time together on the lot. He might've had an idea who was selling to Chloe, but he wasn't around. He was off writing a script. We'd have to track him down when he came back.

And I showed everyone photographs of the jewelry that'd been stolen in the burglary. No one had ever seen Chloe wearing anything that pricey. Alex and Michelle had checked out every photo they could find of Chloe—at press parties, A-list parties, and wrap parties. She wasn't wearing the jewelry in any of them.

Alex shook his head. "I don't get it. Why have jewelry like that if you're not going to wear it?"

I'd been thinking about that for a while. "I have a hunch that jewelry didn't belong to Chloe."

"Then why'd she report it as hers?"

"To cover for someone else. Like her roomie, Paige. And Paige didn't want to report it because it was a secret gift."

We got to Alex's car. He stopped and looked at me over the hood. "From Mr. Perfect?"

I nodded. "That's my theory. And if I'm right, it's just more proof that he's got to be married." And a married lover opens up a rich vein for all kinds of possible fall guys I can toss into the mix: the man himself, his wife, maybe even adult children. Any one of them could lose it with the "home wrecker." I told him, "Let's move on Paige. I want to try and figure out who Mr. Perfect is."

Alex headed out of the lot. "Don't you want to see Chloe's sister? She could probably tell us if Chloe was using on a regular basis."

"But she won't. Families aren't exactly delighted to see us, Alex. Especially when we're looking for information that makes the victim look bad."

"Even if the cops might have the wrong guy?"

"They never think that. They'll think we're just trying to get our client off. Which we are." And that's why I almost never talk to the family of the victim. There's no point. "Besides, we don't have time to waste on long shots. The preliminary hearing is next week, and I have to find a zinger that'll get people to start doubting the prosecution's case."

"So where am I going?"

"Beverly Hills." Alex had plumbed Paige's social media, but she hadn't been a big "sharer." All he found for the past year were a few photos from a trip she took to Napa Valley with Chloe and her sister, Kaitlyn; a group photo with other waitresses at Majesty; and a couple of photos with fellow models. No personal postings about her life or anyone in it. Paige was smart to play it close to the vest. As many have learned the hard way, there are too many jerks out there who'll abuse the access to all that information.

But it left us with relatively few threads to pull: her modeling buddies, the other waiters at Majesty, and her mother. I didn't think the latter could help us even if she'd wanted to. I doubted Paige would confide in her mother about a relationship with a married man. That basically left us with her coworkers.

I called Michelle and asked her to get us permission to talk to the waitstaff at Majesty. She called back ten minutes later. "The manager's a real piece of work. But I got him to give you a few minutes to—and I quote—'see if anyone is willing to talk to you.' And the story about you and Dale went nuclear. Listen to this." The sound of phones ringing nonstop came through. "It's been like that all day. By the way, did you really tell someone all your relatives are murder suspects?"

"Shit. Yeah. I kind of lost it. Tell 'em that was a joke." I got the address of the restaurant and the manager's name and told Michelle I'd check in after we got kicked to the curb.

TWENTY-FIVE

Majesty was one of those high-end restaurants that did the minimalist swank thing. Very subdued décor—original abstract art and clever hanging lights that were virtually sculptures. I noticed the chef and sous chefs were already working in the kitchen, and delicious smells were floating through the air.

The manager, Bernard Shore, reminded me of the English butler character in one of those old movies. Slicked-back steel-gray hair, a pinched nose, and permanently pursed lips. He even gave a prissy sniff when he saw us at the door. Bernard made us come in through the back door and pointed to the closest table to the bathroom. "You can sit there."

I looked at all the empty tables. Message received. "Why don't we start with you?"

Bernard's expression showed he'd like to tell us why not. But he said, "Fine," in a bored voice.

We were all still standing. Bernard didn't wait for a question. "Paige was a beautiful girl and a hard worker. She never gave me any trouble. That's all I know."

I pulled out my notepad. "So you hired her without knowing anything about who she was? Where she worked before? Whether she had a rap sheet?"

Three twentysomething guys and a woman about the same age came in through the back door carrying aprons. The waitstaff was starting to show up.

Bernard gave me a hard look, then deliberately turned his gaze over my shoulder. "I know she got her BA at Cal State Northridge. And she used to work at Ciao on Sunset." Bernard's sour expression told us what he thought of that restaurant.

"Did you know who she was friendly with? Who she might've been dating?"

"I had no idea and no wish to know."

Alex looked at Bernard and leaned in, trying to force the man to make eye contact. It didn't work. Another two young guys and two women with aprons came tumbling in, laughing.

I tried again. "Then she wasn't particularly friendly with any of the staff here?"

Bernard gave an irritable sigh that blew the smell of industrial-strength mouthwash into my face. "I didn't take any notice of that. I'm not a den mother; I'm the manager of a high-end restaurant. What my employees do on their own time is their business. As long as it doesn't affect their job performance, they can socialize with pelicans for all I care."

I stared at Bernard. His eyes remained fixed over my left shoulder. I turned to see what was back there. Just the door. I'd noticed some of the waitstaff throwing us glances while we talked to Bernard.

Alex spoke up. "Did Chloe ever come in here?"

"No." Bernard glanced at his watch. "I have to get to work. You've got ten minutes to talk to the staff—if they want to—and then you'll have to leave."

I smiled at the manager and held out my hand. "It's been lovely chatting with you."

He ignored my hand and headed for the kitchen.

The waiters and waitresses had gathered at a large round table near the front of the restaurant. Alex was scoping them out. "I think one of the guys is on the team."

I gave him an apologetic look. "I hate to play the gay card, but . . ."

"I don't."

We walked over to the table. I followed a few paces behind to let Alex storm the beachhead. When he introduced us, their expressions ranged from wary to downright hostile. More fun was on its way. The guy Alex had clocked sized Alex up, then turned his head. So much for the gay card.

I stepped up and talked fast. "Look, we're not here to dig up dirt on Paige. A lot of questions are coming up about the case against Dale Pearson. It's not as slam-dunk as the press makes it seem. And if Dale Pearson didn't do this, then the person who did is still out there. You want to make sure you do everything you can to get that guy, don't you?"

A couple of them nodded. A couple of them shrugged. But the rest weren't buying it. One of those, a woman whose hair was pulled into a tight bun on top of her head, and who looked like the oldest of the bunch, stood up. "I know he's your father and all, but as far as I'm concerned, you're defending a murderer. I get that you're just doing your job. But I don't have to help you do it."

She walked off. Alex's "teammate" gave him a cold look and left with her. A couple of others seemed inclined to do the same but stayed seated—probably out of curiosity. One of the younger-looking waiters, who had a tattoo of an iron cross on his neck and wore black-framed glasses, watched them leave, then turned back and studied Alex and me for a moment. "I'll talk to you, but I doubt I'll be of much use."

We took the two now-empty chairs. I asked whether anyone knew whom Paige was dating. The tattoo guy in the glasses, who said his name was Greg, spoke first. "I think she had a friends-with-benefits thing going with a guy." He looked around the table. "Remember that dude on the motorcycle?" There were nods and *Oh yeah*s. "I think he was an actor or something. But she never really talked about him."

The waitress with freckles and a ponytail added, "I thought I remembered her saying he was a stuntman, but he might've been an actor."

But no one knew his name. "Did you ever hear about her dating someone who was famous? Possibly married? Someone she called Mr. Perfect?" The ponytailed waitress gave me a dirty look. I shook my head. "I'm not looking to slam her for it. I have information that she was seeing someone like that and he might have a reason . . ."

Greg nodded. "We get a lot of famous people coming in here. But I never knew about her dating anyone famous. Or married."

The others agreed. A young girl, tall and thin, with long dark hair and exotic features, came in through the back door. The ponytailed waitress pointed her out. "That's Tonya. I think she and Paige used to hang out."

Bernard had emerged from the kitchen and was shooting us daggers. I gave him a friendly wave. He tapped his watch, then turned and went back into the kitchen.

I got up and started to pass out my cards, but the ponytailed waitress held up a hand. "Wait, um . . . I hope you don't mind my asking, but what's it like? You know, him being your father. Is it totally weird?"

I was no stranger to the power of the media, but the speed with which this story had spread was breathtaking. It felt like I'd been asked that question a million times during the past few hours, but I still had no better answer than the simple truth. "Yeah, it really is." I told them to give me a call if they thought of anything else, then we headed over to Tonya.

Now that I got a better look, I realized I'd noticed her in the group photo on Paige's Facebook page. She'd been in the background, but there'd been something about the way she stood, like a deer poised to bolt at the slightest sound, that made me take a second look. Otherwise, I probably would've skipped right past her, because her face was closed off in a way that said, *Don't notice me.*

Tonya looked a lot younger in person than she did in the photo. Alex and I introduced ourselves. She glanced from me to him without expression, but I could feel the tension in her body, and I knew she was about to tell us to buzz off.

I talked fast. "I know we're probably the last people you want to see, but we only want to figure out who did this." I gave her my spiel about the possibility that Dale was innocent and wrapped up with a line I use with reluctant witnesses. "And I promise we'll keep whatever you say confidential."

That was a big fat lie. Well, sort of a big fat lie. If she didn't have anything helpful, I really would keep it confidential. And if it hurt us, I'd take it to the grave. But if she said anything I could use, I'd haul her into court and pry her statement out of her with Crisco and a crowbar.

Tonya tucked a strand of hair behind her ear. "D-do you really think someone else did it?"

"I think it's very possible. But I need to get more information." I gave her a gently pleading look.

"I don't really know anything. I didn't see her the night of the . . ." Her lip began to tremble. She bit down on it.

They'd obviously been close. This was exactly the person I was hoping to find. Someone who might know Mr. Perfect. I had to go easy on her, though, or she'd shut us down. "How long had you known her?"

"About six months. She was really nice to me."

"Did you guys ever hang out after work?"

Tonya nodded. "A little. We'd go out for drinks, stuff like that."

She'd tried to make it sound occasional, no biggie, but she was a lousy liar. It'd been more than "a little" and more than just drinks. "Did you know who she was dating?"

Tonya's eyes slipped over to Alex, then came back to me. "No."

Yes. But she clearly didn't want to talk in front of Alex. I looked at my watch. "You probably have to get back to work. Why don't we meet up after? Drinks are on me. But it'll just be you and me. Alex won't be able to make it. Are you okay with that?"

She nodded. I suggested we meet at the Tower Bar on Sunset. It had private corners and it'd probably be quiet on a weeknight by the time she got off. I took her contact information. She said she could get there by ten thirty.

Maybe, finally, I'd found someone who could give me an inside line on Paige's life.

And especially on Mr. Perfect.

TWENTY-SIX

Alex dropped me off at the Tower Bar at ten o'clock, and I got a table by the window. It was a cool, clear night, and the view of the city was downright transporting. I stared out at the sparkling lights and thought about all the ugliness that lay under the cover of darkness.

After the waiter took my order for club soda and lime, I thought about Tonya—the way she'd looked in the group photo and the depth of her grief when she'd spoken about Paige. I had a feeling I knew what her story was.

Fifteen minutes later, Tonya showed up, in jeans and a black sweater, her long, dark hair now down around her shoulders. She ordered a glass of chardonnay. I offered to buy her dinner, but she shook her head. "I ate at the restaurant. I'm good."

We chatted about Majesty—what the tips were like (really good), what Bernard was like (really douchey)—and then I got down to business. "So I get that you and Paige were pretty close."

"Um . . . kind of, yeah."

It was a quiet night, just four or five occupied tables. The waiter was back with her wine in less than a minute. Tonya took a sip.

"You met her on the job?"

Tonya nodded. "She helped me get hired."

I was going to wait for her to get a little more lubricated before I played out my hunch. But if she was the type who had a hollow leg, I could be waiting all night. I decided to go for it.

"And you needed her help because you're underage, aren't you?" Her eyes widened. She said nothing. "It's okay. I'm not the cops. You can tell me. How'd you get the fake ID?"

"Paige. She was there when the manager interviewed me. I told him my purse got stolen and I'd lost my ID. He said he couldn't hire me until I replaced it. I would've given up. But Paige caught me on the way out the door and told me she could help."

When that hunch played out, I knew I was right about the rest of it. "So you're what, seventeen?"

"I'll be eighteen in June." She gave me a rebellious smile as she took another sip of wine.

"Where'd you run from, Tonya?"

She froze. "I d-didn't. Why are you saying that?"

"Was it your stepdad? Your uncle? Your dad?"

Tonya stared at me for a long moment. Her eyes, wide and frightened, darted around the room. When they came full circle, she looked down at the table and whispered, "I don't know what you're talking about."

"Yes, you do. And it's okay. You're safe." I waited for her to make eye contact. When she finally did, I continued. "I get what you've been through. Don't worry, this stays between us." Tonya slowly nodded. "So who was it?"

"My stepbrother."

I had to fight down the burning flash of anger. I wanted to kill that son of a bitch with my bare hands. Tonya looked down at her wineglass. After a few seconds, she glanced up at me. "So how did you know? Were you—"

"Sorry. Just a sec." The waiter had arrived. I'd waved him down thinking Tonya had better start drinking some water before she got back in her car. Now I decided I could use a drink myself. I had to calm myself down and refocus. No one realizes how common this shit is. Or how serious the damage. I ordered a glass of pinot noir and a glass of water for Tonya. When he left, I asked, "Did Paige know?"

"Not at first. I never meant to tell her, but one night after we'd been partying, I got pretty wasted and . . . messed up. It just came out."

"Were you at Paige's place?"

"We were that night, but we didn't hang there much."

"Did you ever see Dale there?"

"That's the . . . cop?" I nodded. "No."

"Where did you guys hang out?"

"Clubs, like Greystone or Lure. And restaurants. We came here a few times."

Those were some pricey clubs. And Tower wasn't exactly a cheap date, either. "Who paid?"

"Paige." She twisted the stem of her wineglass.

"Did you ever hear her talk about a guy she called Mr. Perfect?"

"Mr. Perfect? No. But I heard that the others told you about the guy on the motorcycle. I saw him drop her off at work a couple of times. She didn't talk about him much, just said he was an ex but they were kind of still friends."

But if an ex doesn't want to be an ex anymore . . . I'd been focused on Mr. Perfect, but an ex-boyfriend could work just as well. "Do you know his name?" Tonya shook her head. "Can you describe him?"

She gave virtually the same description as the one I'd gotten at the restaurant—right down to the helmet with the flames on the sides. Except she added, "He's really cute."

"Did Paige tell you what he did? Was he an actor?" But Tonya didn't know, and she couldn't tell me anything else about him.

I took another tack. "You said you hung out at her place sometimes?" She nodded. "Did you ever happen to see her jewelry?"

She shrugged. "Probably, but I don't remember anything in particular."

I pulled out the photos of the jewelry that'd been stolen. "By any chance, did you ever see jewelry that looked like this?"

She looked at the photos and her face brightened. "Oh yeah. I had to borrow a T-shirt, and I saw the pieces in her drawer. Seemed weird that she kept them there, buried under everything."

I'd been right. The jewelry was Paige's. "Maybe because it was such expensive stuff."

Tonya's eyes got huge. "You mean they're real?"

"Seems so. Did she say where she got them?"

"Just said they were gifts."

"But not who gave them to her?" Tonya shook her head. We talked a while longer, but I'd gotten all the information she had to give. I motioned for the waiter to bring the check. "Tonya, would you mind showing me your ID?"

"Why?"

"Trust me, okay?"

She took the ID out of her wallet and handed it to me with a wary look.

I studied it with my cell-phone flashlight, then handed it back to her. "This is not a good fake. I don't know how it fooled your manager." Though having met that dim-witted prune, I supposed I did. "But trust me, a cop will spot it in ten seconds. Have they talked to you about Paige yet?"

"The cops?"

I nodded.

She shook her head. "They came to the restaurant on my day off."

"They probably won't come back, but if they do, stay away." They'd send her back to the hell she'd run from in a fast second.

Tonya hugged her body and leaned forward. "What if they do get to me?"

I pulled out my card. "Then you call me. You don't talk to them; you don't tell them anything. The only thing you say is that you want your lawyer. I don't care what time it is or where they take you, I'll be there. Got it?"

Tears sprang into her eyes. She nodded and looked at my card. "Thank you, Ms. Brinkman."

I leaned in and looked at the card. "Doesn't it say Samantha on there?"

She gave a little smile and wiped the tears away. "Yeah."

I slipped her a couple of twenties. "For the ride home." She started to protest. "Don't argue with your elders."

When she'd left, I called Alex. He was my ride.

He answered the phone without preamble. "How'd it go? She give us anything good?"

"A little. Are you close?"

"You might say that."

I looked up to see Alex walking into the bar. We hung up. "You waited in the other lounge?" He nodded. I told him what I'd learned—about Tonya as well as Paige.

He shook his head. "What a fucked-up world we live in. But now we know for sure what's up with that jewelry. And Chloe reported it stolen because Paige didn't want the cops asking her questions about who'd given it to her. You were right."

"Try not to sound so surprised about that." Alex gave me a sheepish look. "Anyway, we definitely have to get a line on that motorcycle friend of hers."

Alex had a confident smile. "Someone's going to give it to us."

His confidence made me smile back. "That book of yours say so?"

"Sometimes I just know things."

"That so?"

He nodded. "I knew you'd take my case. And I knew you'd get me a deal."

I pushed away my glass of wine, flagged down the waiter, and ordered a real drink.

TWENTY-SEVEN

When I got home, I made the mistake of turning on the television. A photo taken of me back in my public-defender days was in a box next to a photo of Dale in uniform. The anchor announced the "*stunning* new development!" in the Pearson case. I changed the channel, but twenty seconds later, our mugs were on the screen again as a reporter made the breathless announcement, "He's her *father!*" When it happened a third time, I gave up and went to bed. I knew it'd blow over when the next freak show arrived, but it couldn't be soon enough for me. I fell asleep praying that Donald Trump would announce he was planning to become a woman.

Surprisingly, I had a dream-free night's sleep, but I knew better than to turn on the television the next morning. I thought about the interview with Tonya. Her information definitely qualified as progress. All in all, I was in a pretty good mood. I drove to the office singing "Gangsta's Paradise."

But my spirits sank when I heard the sound of ringing phone lines before I even opened the door. Just because I'd tuned out the madness at home, that didn't mean it'd stopped. I found Michelle staring at her computer, her expression stricken. "You look like you just saw my tax returns. What's up?"

"The news. They're saying Dale was accused of rape a year ago. Supposedly by a prostitute."

"What?" The next freak show had arrived. And it was Dale. I sank onto the edge of her desk, and she turned the monitor toward me. But I couldn't bear to read. "What happened with it? Did they ever file the case?"

"No. It got washed out as unsubstantiated. No physical evidence."

"Then how the hell . . . ?" Civilian complaints like that might wind up in a cop's personnel file. But those personnel files are supposed to be confidential. "Those assholes. They leaked this on purpose."

I'd wondered what kind of player Zack Chastain was. Now I knew.

But I'd have to deal with this. Fast. "Michelle, get us on calendar tomorrow."

She picked up the phone. "What are we going to do?"

Good question. I started pacing. This story was going to spread like poison. I could spin to the press all I wanted, but it wouldn't matter. "For starters, I'm going to rip Zack a new one for leaking this." But proving Zack was a dirty player ultimately wouldn't matter. I had to come up with proof that Dale hadn't raped her. I paced faster, stomping back and forth in front of Michelle's desk. I was pissed at Zack for being a sleaze, but I was one hell of a lot more pissed at Dale.

Alex had come out of his little office. "I just read the story. I can track her down. Maybe we can try and get her to say she lied . . ."

"Hopeless. She'd get busted for making a false report. No way she'll do it. I need to get downtown and see Dale, find out his side of the story."

And why he hadn't told me about this. I'd been blindsided. Again. This shit was getting old, fast.

"Want me to go with you?" Alex asked.

"Thanks, but no. I have to kick some ass, and it's best not to embarrass a client by doing it in front of someone else." And I *really* didn't need company while I asked my newfound "dad" about raping a hooker. I borrowed a twenty from Michelle for gas—I'd given Tonya all my cash—and headed for my car.

I spent the drive downtown fuming—partly at myself. I'd stupidly let myself start to trust him. What was I thinking? I didn't know Dale Pearson. He was a stranger. A criminal who happened to be my mother's sperm donor. Not the superhero I'd fantasized about when I was a kid.

What a lovely family I'd landed in. Mommy the narcissist and Daddy the sociopathic cop. Our holiday newsletter would be extra spicy this year.

I could tell when they led him into the attorney room that he'd heard the news. His whole body sagged, and his expression was miserable. I didn't care. I picked up the phone and gave it to him right between the eyes. "Why didn't you tell me about that hooker?"

He looked down and spoke quietly. "Because I was afraid you'd believe it." He met my eyes. "It's a lie, Samantha. I'd never do a thing like that."

Dale sold it well. I'd give him that. But I wasn't about to get reeled in by him. My voice came out harsh, flat. "What's the story? She wanted to get even because you busted her?" It was what the cops always said when they got a citizen complaint. But Dale was a homicide dick. He had no reason to be busting hookers.

"No, I didn't arrest her. I brought in a tweaker one night, and she was in the next cell. She was crying. Her pimp wouldn't bail her out, and she had no one left. I felt sorry for her. I checked her rap sheet. It didn't look like she'd been in the life very long. So I told the desk sergeant to cut her loose, and I gave her a referral to county services. Told her they'd help her get a real job. A few weeks later, I ran into her at the Coffee Bean on Sunset. She said she was getting her act together, had a few job applications pending. I was about to knock off for the night, so I bought her a drink to celebrate . . ." Dale gave a sigh so deep his whole body seemed to deflate.

"You had sex."

Dale nodded miserably. "*Consensual* sex. But afterward, she asked me for money—"

"You refused and she reported you."

"No. I didn't refuse. I gave her a hundred dollars. I figured it was more than what she'd ordinarily get. But she said that wouldn't cut it. She wanted ten thousand, and if I didn't pay, she'd say I raped her. I didn't believe her, and I didn't think anyone else would, either. So I said, go ahead."

And she did. "They just dropped it without any follow-up?"

"Internal Affairs set a meeting for her, but she never showed."

That explained why it hadn't gone any further. But I saw a common thread here. "So you'd been drinking when you slept with that prostitute, and you'd been drinking when you had the fight with Chloe—"

Dale shook his head. "It's not a drinking problem; it's a judgment problem." He frowned. "And maybe a bit of an anger-management issue."

Sounded like both to me, but it wasn't my job to psychoanalyze him. "That prostitute, what's her name again?"

"Jenny. Jenny Knox."

"Right. That doesn't sound like a hooker name."

"Like I said, I don't think she'd been in the business long. And she didn't look like your typical hooker." He frowned as he stared down at the counter. "I don't want to come off like I'm defending what I did. I should never have slept with her. But I certainly didn't rape her. I've never raped anyone in my life." His eyes were pleading. "I swear."

Dale looked entirely sincere. I could feel myself falling for it, believing him. But I pulled myself back. He'd looked sincere the last time he told me he wasn't hiding anything. I knew it shouldn't matter whether I believed him. It definitely wouldn't have with any other client. I had to stop thinking of him as anything more than just another client. All that mattered was that the jury believed him. And with that performance, they would. "The next issue is, who might've leaked this story? Does anyone in IA hate you enough to leak this?" It'd have to be quite an enemy to want to see him go down for a double.

Dale rubbed at a spot on the window between us. "I can't think of anyone in the department who'd have that big of a beef with me." He looked at me. "I was thinking this sounded more like your neck of the woods."

Prosecutors weren't supposed to have access to those personnel files without a court order. But if Zack had a buddy in IA, he could get the information under the table. I nodded. "I'll get into that in court tomorrow. Michelle's going to put us on calendar so I can do some backspin." I thought about whether I should have Dale in court with me when I thrashed about this leak. The cameras would do close-ups on Dale's face while I argued that my client—my father—was being unfairly maligned with a bogus rape charge. But all the public would hear was "Dale" plus "rape." And seeing Dale's image would only reinforce the connection. "I want to keep you as far away from this as I can, so I think you should waive your appearance tomorrow. Okay?" Dale nodded. I pulled the waiver-of-appearance form out of my briefcase.

I leaned in. "Look, I need you to get this: You can't keep hiding shit from me. One more bomb explodes in my face and I'm out. I don't care who you are. So what else is there?"

His expression was earnest. "There's nothing else. I swear."

I didn't know whether to believe him. I just knew I didn't want to care so much.

TWENTY-EIGHT

I went back to the office in a somewhat calmer mood than when I'd left. Not because I necessarily bought Dale's story, but because I had bigger, more immediate minefields to navigate.

I told Alex and Michelle to come into my office. The phones were so constant it sounded like one long, continuous ring. Michelle came in looking frazzled. "It's been like that all morning. News shows, cable shows, print reporters, and of course, the usual psychos—but a lot more of them, and they're a lot meaner. At least the story about Dale being your dad got us some sympathy calls. This time it's a whole raft of no-life nutjobs saying Dale's a monster and you're a scumbag for representing him."

I'd been wishing something would happen to take the story about Dale being my father off the radar. Now I realized I should've been more specific. "Any threats?"

"Not so far."

I supposed that'd have to pass for my good news of the day. "We need to get all the information we can on this hooker—"

Alex read from his iPad. "She's thirty-six, five foot seven, one hundred thirty pounds, blonde hair, blue eyes, and has a tattoo of Taz, the

Tasmanian devil, on her left shoulder. Only a couple of busts for hooking, a couple of old busts for shoplifting, and one joyriding that got dismissed for insufficient evidence. The two prostitution arrests were in LA; the rest were all down in Orange County."

"Damn, that all you could get?" I smiled. "Nice job, Alex. Any information on where she is now?"

"Working on it. Her last known address was in Orange County, but that was as of two years ago, and the apartment building is a senior living facility now."

"But she got busted in Hollywood a year ago. Didn't the cops get a new address?"

"No. She gave the same old one, and for some reason, she got released that night with no charges filed, so they never got around to checking it out."

"Yeah, and I know why." I told them what Dale had said.

Alex shook his head. "That's some kind of bad luck."

If Dale was telling the truth. "You might want to check the area where she last got busted, see if she lived nearby. And Dale said he brought in a tweaker that night. Go see Dale and see if he can help you track down that tweaker. You also might want to talk to the desk sergeant on duty that night. See if he backs up Dale's story."

"Zack sure screwed us hard," Michelle said.

I nodded. "I'm kind of surprised. He doesn't have a rep as a dirty player, but . . ."

Michelle looked disgusted. "A big case can be a big motivator."

We all went back to work. I had to get ready for tomorrow, and I still didn't have a solid zinger for the preliminary hearing. I didn't know whether I'd put Chas Gorman on the witness stand at trial, but I sure as hell wasn't going to trot him out now. The less time Zack had to dig up dirt on him, the better.

I put myself to bed by midnight, hoping to rest up for tomorrow. But I had the nightmare again. I woke up at three a.m., my heart pounding, struggling for breath. It took me an hour to get back to sleep. When I crawled out of bed at six, I was tired and achy. I pounded three cups of coffee in rapid succession—though angry as I was, I didn't need the caffeine bump.

And given my state of mind, Xander did the world a favor by driving me to court. I was thinking about what I'd say to the press when my cell phone rang. Maybe Alex had already come up with something. I was so desperate for good news I didn't stop to think that it was too early for him to have gotten anything. And so, when the obnoxiously familiar, ever-entitled voice of my mother came through the phone, it was a double crusher.

"Didn't I tell you so, Samantha? A murderer *and* a rapist!"

"Mother, if you saw the news, then you know I'm on my way to court. I can't—"

She railed on, heedless. "You have to get off this case! Surely now you can see who he is? I told you, there was a reason I broke it off with him. Maybe now you'll believe me!"

I knew I shouldn't engage with her, that I should just hang up. I needed to stay focused. But as usual, I let her get to me. "You told me no such thing. And believe what? You broke up with him because he didn't have money. Not because you knew or cared what kind of person he was—"

"I *did* know. I always knew there was something . . . off about him."

"Then why didn't you tell me about him before?"

There was a long silence. "Because I didn't want to upset you."

I laughed out loud, though a part of me felt like crying. My feelings about anything had always been the least of her concerns. "So you thought it was better for me to find out on the news than to tell me yourself?"

"I didn't necessarily know he would turn out to be *this* bad."

"Celeste, you didn't know diddly-squat. You were just hoping to make me get off the case so no one would find out he was my father. Because you were worried about how it'd make you look—"

"It's not fair that I have to suffer for what that . . . disgusting criminal has done! The least you could do is get off this case and distance yourself!"

We were nearing the freeway exit. "I'm not getting off the case, Celeste." I'd been planning my good-bye speech in my head, thinking of how I'd finally tell her how much she'd hurt me, belittled me, and made it so obvious I wasn't wanted. But in that moment, I knew it'd just be an exercise in frustration. She'd never admit to anything, never change. She'd argue, deny, and turn it back on me, call me ungrateful . . . and a whole lot more. This was probably the worst time to do it, but I didn't want to wait. It'd just give me more time to dream up useless speeches. It was time to bite the bullet. "I don't want you to call me anymore. We have nothing to say to each other." I ended the call and saw that my hands were shaking. I leaned back against the seat and closed my eyes. I couldn't believe I'd actually done it.

I was scared and a little bit in shock. I felt disoriented, like an unseen tether had suddenly been cut and sent me into free fall. But I wasn't sorry. I felt stronger, triumphant. I hadn't realized how much I'd felt like a victim until that moment—when I decided not to be one anymore. By the time Xander pulled up in front of the courthouse, my hands had stopped shaking.

I'd scheduled this appearance at the last minute, so I wasn't surprised to see that there was less of a throng outside this time. It didn't matter. There were enough cameras to guarantee today's proceedings would go far and wide. Brittany and Trevor spotted me as I got out of the car.

Trevor got to me first. "Samantha, what's your response to this rape charge?" I saw Brittany's cameraman move in behind him and train the lens on me.

I forced a calm expression and looked directly into the lens. "There is no truth to the charge whatsoever. The accuser is a prostitute who hoped to extort money from Dale." The other reporters came running and were gathering around me, mikes held out in front of them. "I'm frankly disgusted by the cheap, underhanded tactics employed by the prosecution in leaking this bogus charge. It just shows how desperate they are. And they should be. Dale Pearson is innocent, and we will not let this smear campaign stop us from proving it. Now if you'll excuse me, I have to get to court."

They shouted questions at me as I sidestepped through the crowd, but I'd given them enough of a sound bite for now. I wanted to save the rest for court. As I pushed in through the door, I saw Edie near the elevators. She waved to me and mouthed, "I'm sorry."

Brittany ran up to me. "Samantha, this is terrible. You must be devastated. If you want more airtime, just let me know, okay?"

"Thanks, we'll see what happens."

This time I didn't take the stairs. I wanted to save my energy for the fight. So I squeezed into the ever-packed, slow-moving elevator, and by the time it reached my floor, I was in full boil. I stomped into court, ready to rip flesh from bone. I didn't even look at Zack. I didn't trust myself not to throw something at him. I was glad to see that the courtroom had a fair number of reporters. They were going to get their money's worth today.

Which was too bad for Judge William Tollinberg. People liked to say he was "gentlemanly." But it was just a nice way of saying he was a pussy. When lawyers push the envelope—a near-daily occurrence—it's up to the judge to rein them in. But Judge Tollinberg had no stomach for it. When the fur started to fly, he ducked. So I knew I'd get to swing freely, and I was planning to take full advantage of it.

The minute he called the case, I burst out of the gate like Secretariat.

"Your Honor, I told my client to waive his appearance because he doesn't need to witness this shameful day for our system of justice. I've seen a lot of dirty tricks in my time, but what the prosecution has just pulled is probably the sleaziest. This charge was so bogus the victim herself wouldn't back it up. The deliberate leaking of a totally unfounded rape charge is much more than outrageous. It's a deliberate sabotage of Dale Pearson's right to due process and a fair trial. I'm moving for a dismissal of all charges. Barring that, I want the prosecutor sanctioned for this despicable smear campaign!"

When Zack stood up, his face was red. He bounced the end of his pen on his legal pad, his lips pulled tight. When he finally spoke, his voice was rough. "Your Honor . . ." He cleared his throat. "Your Honor, while I can well understand why counsel's upset, that does not give her the right to go throwing around baseless accusations. I did not leak that rape report, and I don't know who did. I think it's ironic that counsel calls it a smear campaign, because that's exactly what she's just launched by accusing me without any facts to back it up—"

I jumped to my feet. "No facts? Who else has access to confidential personnel files? Who else has the motive to taint the jury pool?"

Lawyers are never supposed to directly address one another in court—we talk to the judge and, on occasion, the jury. But Zack lost it. He turned to face me and fired back. "Obviously someone besides me!"

"Then you should welcome an investigation!"

"I *do* welcome an investigation. And while we're at it, we should find out why Jenny Knox didn't show up for her IA interview."

Finally, about ten clicks too late, the judge held up a hand. "Now counsel, you're both officers of the court, and I know you're aware of your ethical duties—"

But I wasn't done yet. "Your Honor, Zack Chastain obviously doesn't think he has any ethical duties. It's not enough to sanction him. He should be removed from this case!"

Zack's eyes narrowed with fury, and his face flushed an even brighter red. "If anyone should be removed, it's Samantha Brinkman. She's obviously too close to this case. She can't be professional. After all, it's her *father*—"

"That's a disgusting, cheap shot—"

The bang of the gavel cut me off. It was probably the first time in the judge's career he'd ever used it. I thought I saw his hand shaking. The bailiff's mouth hung open.

Judge Tollinberg's voice was strained, but I could see real anger in his pale-blue eyes. "No one's getting taken off this case. But I do not approve of these personal attacks. I will expect written apologies to the court from both of you, and I want them in my hands by five o'clock this evening." He looked from me to Zack. "However, this is a serious breach, Mr. Chastain. I'm ordering the sheriff's department to look into the leak. In the meantime, Ms. Brinkman, my clerk tells me you have discovery matters to take up?"

I appreciated him ordering the investigation, but it was the least he could do. And besides, the damage was done. The rape charge was all over the news. There was no way to un-ring that bell—other than to prove it was a lie.

"Thank you, Your Honor. Yes, I do. I want the victims' cell-phone records, the downloads from their laptops, and their navigational systems' records—"

Zack cut in, his voice cold. "We're working on it, Your Honor. It may take a little while."

I glared at Zack. "I remind the prosecution that we're not waiving time. We want the preliminary hearing and trial set within the statutory limit."

The judge nodded. "Mr. Chastain, how long will it take you to get those records to Ms. Brinkman?"

"I probably can't get all those records before the preliminary hearing." Zack stared down at his legal pad for a moment. "But Ms. Brinkman won't have to worry about discovery for the moment. I'm going to scrap the preliminary hearing altogether and take this case to the grand jury instead." He glared at me. "Since Ms. Brinkman's in such a hurry, that should move things along a little faster."

I returned his glare. "It figures Mr. Chastain would prefer to put on his evidence in secret, where he doesn't have to worry about a judge throwing out this feeble excuse for a case—"

Zack shot me a dagger. "Feeble excuse? This is a slam dunk, no-brainer—"

The judge banged his gavel again. He had the expression of someone who's slipping out of the saddle on a horse that's galloping at full speed. "Ms. Brinkman, is there anything else?"

"Other than putting a stop to the smear campaign? No."

"Then we'll be in recess."

TWENTY-NINE

Reporters had gathered downstairs, but I'd had my say in court—and then some. When I got outside, I gave a shortened version of my earlier statement, adding only that I was "confident the jury would know better than to be swayed by these underhanded tactics."

Edie and Brittany waved to me, but I wanted to get out of there. I waved back and pointed to Xander, who was idling at the curb. As I made my way toward the car, Trevor came up and spoke to me in a low voice. "Why didn't you come to me first with the story about your father?"

"Sorry, Trevor. I just thought it was more of a face-time story. I promise you'll get the next one."

He gave me a measuring look. "What'll you give me if I find out who leaked?"

If I could prove Zack was the leak, it'd really hurt his credibility. That wouldn't necessarily be a game changer. But with a case this tough, every little bit helped. The only problem was, I didn't really have anything to trade yet. "Get me the information and we'll talk."

"I'll be in touch."

I got into the car. Xander slowly pulled away. "I watched you on my phone. You're having quite the day." He pulled into the left-turn lane.

"Yeah." I sighed, thinking he didn't know the half of it. "Thanks for driving me, Xander. At least I get to suffer in style. Is this helping your business any?"

"Not yet, but I'm sure it will."

Alex and Michelle were watching the news on the television in my office when I got back. Alex gave me a thumbs-up. "You really reamed that prosecutor—"

"And that was nice work with the press," Michelle said.

I set down my briefcase. "How'd Zack do with the reporters?"

Michelle sighed. "Unfortunately, pretty well. Said he had no idea who would've leaked that report, and he hopes the guilty party is caught immediately, blah, blah, blah. But he sold it."

I glanced at the screen and saw a reporter standing on the courthouse steps. They'd be chewing on this story all night. "You sure you're not just a sucker for a pretty face?"

"Oh, I most definitely am. But so is your jury pool."

Unfortunately, true. I turned to Alex. "What'd you think?"

Alex gave me an apologetic look. "I agree. Sorry. What can you do about him going to the grand jury? Can you object?"

"No, but I don't want to."

Michelle's eyebrows lifted. "You don't? But the grand jury always indicts. A judge might—"

"Dismiss?" I asked. Michelle nodded. "No friggin' way. It's a solid case, and most of the testimony is going to come from experts talking about DNA and fingerprints. Janet's the only civilian they'll call, and a nuclear bomb couldn't shake her testimony. So all a prelim does is get the bad stuff out there where the jury pool can chew on it for the next couple of months. A grand jury keeps it quiet."

Michelle deadpanned, "Unless there's a leak." She saw my expression. "Too soon?"

Alex stood up and put on his jacket. "I'm on my way to go talk to Dale."

"Just in case you can't get a decent address for that tweaker, have Dale tell you where he busted him. He might still be hanging around there—"

"You want me to talk to the tweaker if I find him?" I nodded. "How am I supposed to get him to talk to me?"

"Michelle, give him a twenty." Dale's retainer check had cleared, so I'd replenished our slush fund. She fished out the bill and gave it to him. "And give him my card. You've got some, right?" Alex shook his head. Michelle gave him a stack. "Always keep these on you. It's a nice carrot for guys like that." I wouldn't necessarily represent him if he called, but he didn't have to know that.

Alex tucked the cards into his jacket pocket. "Any chance I can get some of my own cards? It'd give me a little more credibility."

Michelle nodded. "Already ordered. Should be ready for pickup in a couple of days."

The cards couldn't say he was licensed, but that wouldn't be much of a problem. Most people don't really look.

Alex smiled. "Thanks, Michy." He started for the door, then turned back. "If I find Jenny, do you want me to talk to her?"

"No. Hold off on that one. We need to do it together." That would be a tricky interview. If Dale was telling the truth about her, she was a dangerous person to tangle with. I didn't need the state bar investigating me for some bullshit charge that I'd threatened or pressured her. "But find out where she lives, see if you can find people who know her, and get them talking."

"Got it."

I looked at his khaki pants and navy-blue blazer. "And for God's sake, change into something grungier. Put some street on your back."

Alex made a face. "Fine."

"We don't have a lot of time to waste on this rape charge. So get done what you can today and report back."

After he'd left, I told Michelle about my phone call with Celeste—and that it'd been my last. I hadn't been sure if I'd be able to talk about it. I'd thought I'd be too upset. But I wasn't. I'm not saying I was in the mood to light fireworks or lead a conga line. I was just . . . at peace.

When I finished, Michelle gave me a long hug, then stood back and gave me a searching look. "I've been hoping to hear you say this for years. She's poison. I can't remember you ever coming off a phone call or a visit with her that didn't leave you feeling like shit."

No question about that. "But shouldn't I be at least a little torn up about this? I feel kinda okay with it."

"Like you stopped beating your head against the wall?"

I smiled. "A little bit, yeah. But still . . ."

"Look, you might feel lousy at some point, but if you do, it'll only be because you finally admitted that you never had anything close to a real mother." Michelle put her hands on her hips. "Or it'll be a guilt trip, which I will not allow."

I owed Michelle so much. She was a friend like no other, and I loved her like a sister. But that thought brought me to the likely repercussions of cutting off Celeste. "Her friends are going to think I'm the monster. So will Jack." I didn't like most of her friends, so that was no loss. But my stepfather had saved me from myself when I was going down the drain in high school. I'd only wished he'd met Celeste sooner. "For some reason, no one else ever seems to see her ugly side."

Michelle frowned. "I'm not sure that's true, but think about what you just said. If her friends don't get the same treatment, what does that tell you? She *chooses* to treat you the way she does. And I disagree about Jack. He's a good guy and a smart guy. He'll get that you must've had a damn good reason for doing it. And you have no idea what he's seen. He might know more than you think. After all, she lives with him. It's harder to keep up a good act with the person who shares your bathtub."

I covered my ears. "Ick. Thanks for that."

We laughed, and after a few minutes, we got back to work.

I still had the rest of my caseload to worry about, so I dug out my files and got to work. I was halfway through a sentencing memo when Michelle buzzed me.

"Remember our buddy Ricardo Orozco?"

The gangbanging asshole murderer. "Wish I could say no."

"His father wants to make an appointment."

I thought about it for a moment. "Did he say what he wanted?"

"No. Want me to tell him you're not taking any new cases?"

I shook my head. "Go ahead and make the appointment."

Michelle said she would, and I went back to my sentencing memo.

It was seven thirty by the time Alex got back. It'd been his first day operating on his own, and I could see he'd loved it. When he sat down in my office, his expression was serious, but his eyes were shining. And he'd taken my fashion advice to heart: his jeans were sagging, his T-shirt looked like it'd been used at a car wash, and his Converse sneakers had no laces. "Nice threads, man. Way to blend."

Alex glanced down at his clothes like they were made of roadkill. "They're not mine. I borrowed them from my sister's boyfriend's kid brother."

"Whatever. It worked, didn't it?" Alex nodded reluctantly. "So what've you got?"

THIRTY

Alex pulled a notepad out of his pants pocket. "The desk sergeant who was on duty that night wasn't around. But Dale told me where he'd busted the tweaker, so I went there and pretended I was looking to score. And you were right; he was in the same place Dale busted him—on Hollywood Boulevard in front of Grauman's Chinese Theatre. He was dressed up like Luke Skywalker, posing for pictures with the tourists."

A lot of speed freaks made their money that way. While they were putting an arm around Susie from Dayton, Ohio, and smiling for the camera, they were slipping a hand into her purse and stealing her wallet. "Did Dale tell you why he busted the guy?" Dale worked homicide, not petty street crimes.

"Dale got him—his name is Flip, by the way—on a failure to appear on a jaywalking ticket. But the real reason was because Flip was an eyewitness to a drive-by, and he'd been dodging the detectives."

"So what'd Flip tell you?"

"Turns out he and Jenny bonded a little when they were in jail. Her pimp wouldn't bail her out because he caught her skimming. So he dumped her and she had no place to stay. Flip said she could crash with him at"—Alex thumbed a page in his notepad—"Hotel Washington on Sunset Boulevard just off Coronado Terrace."

"She was scamming her pimp? That sounds promising." If she had the balls to do that, she might've had the balls to try and shake Dale down, too.

"Yeah, that's what I thought. So I headed over there and pretended to be looking for my connection."

"An inspired choice, Alex."

He dipped his head. "Thank you. The book says sometimes you have to—"

"Just tell me what you got."

"It's a good book, Samantha; you should check it out." I stared at him. He sighed and continued. "I found a guy who used to be friends with Jenny." He looked down at his notepad again. "He calls himself Bozo—no last name—but I think I can find him again. He's been there for a couple of years. He said she liked to talk about the scams she'd pulled down in Orange County. He wasn't sure how much of it was true. But she also told him she'd figured out a way to make big bucks off the county."

I sat up. "As in, by claiming she got raped by a cop?"

"Almost. Said she knew a girl down in Orange County who'd been roughed up by a cop and sued the department. They wound up settling for fifteen thousand. Jenny said she wanted to get in on a sweet deal like that."

I sat up. This was sounding better and better. "Oh yeah, baby. So how come he 'used to' be friends with her? She move away?"

"More likely ran away. Jenny ripped him off. The last night he saw her, they were hanging out in his room. He was getting high; she was drinking—"

"What was he using?"

"Oxy."

"Oxy? Pretty high rent for that bunch."

Alex nodded. "Which is why he was so pissed. He'd scored the pills—well, actually, stole them—from his sister. She had a prescription because of a car accident. Anyway, Bozo nodded off, and when he woke up, his stash was gone and so was Jenny. He hasn't seen her since."

"And that was when?"

"About a year ago."

That would've been right around the time she blackmailed Dale. "Does he know where she went?"

"No. He says he's been looking for her, but . . ."

I smiled. "He's no Alex Medrano. Sounds like Jenny had to find a new place to be. As in, a whole new place."

"Yeah, I was thinking she probably went back to Orange County." Alex shook his head. "She's a real *puta*—and I don't mean the kind who has sex for money. That girl burns everybody she gets close to."

I didn't want to get too happy too soon, but it sure sounded like Dale had been telling the truth. I was relieved, and I knew it went way beyond my concern for the case. "Great job, Alex."

"Do I keep looking for her?"

"No. This woman's never going to admit she lied. If she crawls out from under her rock now, it'll only be to claim the rape charge was righteous." The farther away we stayed from her, the better.

"You want to give this to the press?"

"It's risky. Trashing her might make Zack decide he's got nothing to lose by digging her up."

And if the cops found her and she cleaned up well, he'd put her out in front of the tent to say she was telling the truth about Dale. It'd make our already bad press even worse.

"But he might not find her. Zack's no Alex Medrano, either." He smiled. "And even if he does find her, this intel will cream her credibility."

Now that I thought about it, Alex was right. Bozo couldn't be Jenny's only enemy. She probably had a whole passel of Bozos looking for her, which meant a whole passel of reasons not to want to be found. Which meant Zack had almost no chance of finding her. And the sooner we gave people reason to doubt this rape charge, the better. "Good point. I'll give this one to Trevor."

Print was better than the camera this time. I wanted the public to get all the details. And I wanted the story to circulate for a while. If I put it out now and let the public soak it up, they'd be less likely to buy her claim even if Zack did find her.

THIRTY-ONE

I called Trevor. "I'm giving you payment in advance for getting me the leaker."

"Let's hear it."

I gave him the story on Jenny Knox. "And you can verify all of it. Where are you on the leak?"

"Nothing yet, but I'm working on it."

When I ended the call, I saw that it was after eight. I went out to the anteroom and announced, "Time to knock off." Alex came out of his office. "I'm thinking we should hit Paige's modeling agency tomorrow. Michy, how's my day look?"

Michelle pulled up the calendar on her monitor. "You've got a ten thirty in Department 125. It's the follow-up on Deshawn's case."

That wouldn't take long. The sheriff's crime lab had checked the gun for prints and DNA. Nothing matched up to Deshawn. But the video-surveillance footage for the evidence room at LAPD was a no go. The camera had supposedly—and suspiciously—"malfunctioned" sometime during the week before the gun turned up in Deshawn's car. There was no record of who'd taken the gun out of evidence. So Deshawn would get his dismissal, but Officer Ambrose was off the hook.

"I'll swing by Twin Towers first to give Dale the news on Jenny. Deshawn's hearing will take about five minutes, so we'll have time to hit Paige's modeling agency afterward. Alex, I'll need you for that. You can either ride with me or meet me at the agency."

"I'll ride with you. Dale and I are bros now."

I raised an eyebrow. "You and Dale . . . I guess I've seen stranger things."

"Not lately," Michelle said.

I'd asked Alex to get to my apartment by seven thirty. Between morning rush hour and the waiting time at the jail, I figured it'd be nine thirty by the time we got to see Dale.

I was close. It was nine forty-five when the guards brought Dale up. He looked pretty good. If it weren't for the ankle-to-waist chains, I'd almost have said he had a bounce in his step.

I picked up the phone. "That punk-metal thing is really working for you."

He smiled and studied his handcuffed hand. "I'm thinking of getting some ink while I'm here. Couple of spiderwebs on the neck. Maybe a biceps bracelet."

"Just no hearts with daggers."

"Think the jury might take that the wrong way?"

"No, I'm just sick of them. I'm guessing you heard about the dirt we got on Jenny."

"I did. A couple of guys from the station came by this morning." He looked at Alex. "Was that you?" Alex nodded. "Nice work, buddy."

I'd wondered whether he was getting any visitors. "How is that? Seeing them in here?"

Dale looked down at the counter. "It's good to see them. Not so good to be seen."

I could only imagine what it must be like to have his cop friends see him this way. "Are you getting any flak from the department?"

Dale shook his head. "And I've been finding out that I had more friends on the force than I ever knew."

I was glad to hear it. "What about in here? The guards treating you okay?"

"Better than okay. I can't complain. Other than . . . you know, being hooked up for something I didn't do." He gave a brief twist of a smile, then looked closely at me. "How about you? I've been worrying about what kind of heat you're getting."

"From whom? The public or Celeste?"

He gave me a deadpan look. "I feel pretty confident your mother won't be sending you death threats."

"That makes one of us. And she knows where I live." Dale had a puzzled look on his face, but I didn't want to tell him I'd cut her off—not with Alex there. I moved on to the news that Zack had decided to take the case to the grand jury. Dale agreed that was for the best. Then I told him about our plans for the day.

"Okay, just be careful. People on the street are going to start recognizing you more and more, so watch out." He flashed a look at Alex.

Alex nodded. "I've got her back."

I looked at my watch. It was after ten. "I've gotta get to court. I should be back tomorrow or the day after to give you an update." I glanced at Alex. "Or my bodyguard will."

We headed to the courthouse. I told Alex to park Beulah around the corner and wait for me there. "This won't take long."

And it didn't. I skidded into Judge Raymond's court with less than a minute to spare. Rita Stump read the crime-lab report into the record, I made my motion to dismiss, and the judge granted it. Officer Ambrose wasn't there, but the judge told Rita to let Ambrose know he'd been "suspiciously lucky" with that surveillance camera.

When I got downstairs, a reporter I didn't recognize, a young Asian guy with a nice smile, ran over to me and asked if I had any updates on the case. I hadn't intended to do a TV spot on the Jenny story, but since it fell into my lap, I figured it couldn't hurt. I gave him the CliffsNotes version.

When we finished, the reporter—whose name was Kendall—practically kissed my hand.

"I was covering a meeting at City Hall." He rolled his eyes. "Bo-ring. Edie's husband, Aubrey, was the only thing that kept me even half-awake. I just decided to jump over here in case anything interesting happened." Kendall grinned at me. "And I got lucky."

I'd heard Edie was married to a state assemblyman. "Don't tell me; let me guess: they were arguing about how to give themselves raises."

"No, Aubrey's stumping for the young vote, making a lot of noise about funding for state colleges."

It might get me some credibility points with the jury pool to be seen shaking hands with someone like that. Edie owed me. I should ask her to set it up. After all, I'd given her the scoop on Dale being my father. But that story was so "ten minutes ago." I'd need to dangle something new under her nose. "Well, I'm glad I could spice up your day." I headed for the sidewalk.

"Thank you, Ms. Brinkman!"

I waved over my shoulder. "Call me Sam." I trotted down the block and found Alex around the corner.

"Want to drive?" he asked.

"You know where Models Inc. is?" He nodded. "Go for it."

Alex headed for the freeway. "For what it's worth, Dale's story about Jenny seems for real to me."

"Sociopaths—especially the smart ones—can be pretty slick." I was trying hard to hold on to my objectivity. I couldn't let my need to believe in him get in the way of the truth. He hadn't told me about his breakup with Chloe or about the rape charge. There might well be more. Just because Dale's story about Jenny looked like it was panning out, that didn't mean he was innocent—of anything. "And Dale has every reason to perform for us. We're all that's standing between him and life in prison."

Though in all honesty, very few clients seemed to get the logic of that. They usually start out mistrustful, and it goes downhill from there. People always think defendants are out to get the prosecutor or the judge. The truth is, your client is the one most likely to really want to wear your skin.

"You're right." Alex blew out a breath. "But if you're worried that he might be gaming you, I just wanted you to know that he's got me believing, too."

"Thanks, Alex." I smiled. "That means he's good enough to play us both."

He glanced at me and smiled back. "I guess so."

Paige's modeling agency was in Hollywood. The name, Models Inc., had me expecting something sleek and modern. Then I noticed the address.

It was in Tweaker-Junkie-Hooker Central. I'd never expected it to be the Wilhelmina Agency, but when Alex pulled up to the curb, I couldn't believe it. The place was a dump that looked like it'd been condemned years ago. What few windows I could see were either caked with dirt or covered with cardboard. There was some faint evidence that the door might've been red at one time, but now it was just a slab of splinters, and the little window set near the top was so grimy I didn't want to get close enough to even try and see through it.

Alex turned the knob, then shoved it open with his foot—and rubbed his hand on his jeans. The door opened onto a dark, narrow stairway that stank of mildew and desolation. When I put a hand on the railing along the stairway, it swayed. Our shoes scratched on the bowed, dusty stairs as we hiked up to the second floor.

The agency was one square room, dominated by a desk and an ancient-looking computer. A squat woman wearing heavy makeup and tortoise-framed glasses was typing on it. A few young, unspectacular-looking girls sat in chairs along the wall, under movie promo–size posters of famous models like Cindy Crawford and Gisele Bündchen. The young girls stroked their hair and scrolled on their cell phones. A couple of them glanced at us, then went back to scrolling.

I went over to the woman at the desk and pointed to the posters. "Former clients?" Not for one second did I think so, but I wanted to score some brownie points to get her cooperation.

The woman gave me a flat don't-bullshit-me look. She scanned us, then shook her head at me. "You, I can't use. Too old and I've got enough brunettes." Her eyes landed on Alex. "You, I might be able to do something with. You do underwear?"

"We're not models." I introduced us and told her why we were there.

Her eyes slipped back to Alex. "Too bad." She moved some papers on her desk. "I don't get involved in my models' personal lives, so I don't know who Paige's friends were."

"Can you tell us anything about her last shoots? Who she worked for the most?" Alex had found a couple of photos on Paige's Facebook page that looked like they'd been taken at shoots. One of them showed Paige with two other models, but she hadn't given their names.

The woman tapped some keys on her computer, then pushed up her glasses and peered at the monitor. "She did a lot of work for HipHot. com. And it looks like we sent her out with Amaya Horrigan more than anyone else." She looked up at us. "Anything else?"

Alex gave her a smile so warm it would've bent steel. "Do you know how we might get in touch with Amaya?"

The woman looked from him to me. I thought she was going to tell us she wasn't a dating service, but she tapped a few more keys on her computer, then pulled out a business card and wrote something on it. She held it out to Alex. "That's the number I use to get ahold of her. And our number's on the bottom—in case you change your mind."

We were on the sidewalk thirty seconds later. I'd hoped for more, but I couldn't say I was sorry to be out of that stink hole. "At least it was easy."

Alex made a face and handed me the card. "And sad and disgusting."

We got into the car and I pulled up Amaya's bio. A pretty, dark-skinned girl with long, straight hair, her head tilted to one side, smiled back at me. "She looks like one of the girls in that model photo on Paige's Facebook page." When Alex stopped at a red light, I showed him the photo.

"Yep, that's one of them."

I called Amaya. No answer. I left her a message saying we needed to talk to her about Paige. I didn't tell her we were working for the defense. No reason to overwhelm her with information. I felt my stomach rumble. "I'm hungry. Want to hit Pinks?" Pinks is a little family-run stand that makes the best hot dogs in the world. And their chili dogs and hamburgers are a religious experience. I've never seen the place without lines down the block.

"Just hearing the name made my mouth water."

We were almost there when my phone rang.

THIRTY-TWO

It was Amaya. "Are you that lawyer? The one with the dad who—"

"Yeah." Silence. "Don't hang up. I'm not out to dig up dirt on Paige. I just have a few background questions." More silence.

Finally, she spoke. "I hadn't seen her in at least a month. I don't know how I can help you."

"That's okay. Where are you?"

"At work. Spikes. It's on Melrose."

I knew the place. It was a skull-and-dagger-style clothing boutique. And it was close. "Want to meet us at Pinks? I'm buying."

"Be there in ten."

The magic of Pinks.

Alex and I got in line. I was next up when Amaya got there. She was even prettier in person. I'd have thought she could do a lot better than the Models Inc. agency. But what did I know?

We all got chili dogs and bottled waters and found a table at the back of the little shack. The dogs were too good to let conversation get in the way, so we ate first. When we'd finished, I asked Amaya how well she knew Paige. As it turned out, they weren't super tight.

"I always liked to go out on calls with her because she was human, you know? It's pretty competitive, and most of the girls will chew you up and spit you out for a job that basically pays pennies. But Paige was cool."

"Did you know any of her boyfriends?"

"Just Marc, and I'm not really sure he was her boyfriend. He worked for Super Talents. She met him at a shoot."

"So Marc was a model?" Amaya nodded. "What did Paige say about him?"

Amaya wiped her mouth. "Not much. I just got the feeling they were pretty close because I did a shoot with them a few months ago. They seemed pretty . . . relaxed around each other." She sighed and stared off to the left. "So sad what happened to him."

I leaned forward. "What?"

"He drowned. They just found his body a few days ago. It washed up onshore down by the Colony."

"The Colony in Malibu?" Amaya nodded. "Do you know Marc's last name?"

"Palmer. I just read it on the Internet. I only had the one shoot with him, but . . ." Amaya paused. "I feel like a jerk for saying this, but it didn't surprise me that much when I found out he was dead. Paige said he was a hard partier, and when I met him, I could tell, just by the way he talked."

"Why? What'd he say?"

Amaya shrugged. "Just talked about how high he'd been the night before, about how the party went on for, like, two days." She shook her head. "Party for two days? And the night before a shoot? That's crazy. I never even drink a glass of wine the night before a shoot. You can get so bloated and puffy, you know?"

"Yeah, I hate that. Did he say who he was partying with? I take it, it wasn't Paige."

"No, Paige never did stuff like that. She took the job seriously. He didn't say who he was with. But the way Paige reacted, it was obvious that was Marc's MO. Paige just kind of laughed it off, said Marc was lucky he had good genes."

Alex had been scrolling on his phone. Now, he showed the screen to Amaya. "Is that him?" Amaya nodded.

It was a professional head shot of a very handsome—actually, pretty—young guy who had a sexy smile and black hair that fell over one blue eye. His right shoulder was to the camera, and he was looking into the lens through long, dark lashes.

A name *and* a face. Great. Except we couldn't talk to him. It figured. "Did you ever hear Paige talk about a guy she called Mr. Perfect?"

Amaya frowned and shook her head. "But really, we didn't talk about our personal lives. I think the only reason she said anything to me about Marc was because I was there at the shoot with them."

I kept at it for a little while longer but got nothing else useful. I thanked Amaya and let her go. She headed out the back door that led to a parking lot, and I watched her weave her way through the cars. Marc and Paige, both friends, both dead, and pretty close in time. I might be able to do something with this. "Look into Marc Palmer. See if any of his friends knew Paige. But don't make it your life's project. If it doesn't pan out in a day or two, let it go."

Marc hadn't turned up in any of the discovery I'd gotten from Zack, so he was probably a fringe player. We didn't have time to waste on distant maybes.

As we headed for Alex's car, my cell phone rang.

It was Michelle. "Have you seen the news?"

"No, we've been out partying with supermodels, remember?"

"They found Jenny Knox. She's dead."

THIRTY-THREE

I stopped abruptly, and a young kid on a skateboard almost rammed into me. It took me a second to process what she'd said. "Hang on, let me get in the car so I can put you on speaker." When we were settled in the car, I asked, "Where'd they find her?"

"In the morgue."

"What? How long has she been there?"

"About a year. She'd been strangled to death. Her body had been found in a dumpster."

I held my breath as my brain tried to push away the implications. "How come . . . why are they only finding out about it now?"

"Because she didn't have any ID on her when they found her body. She was in the morgue as a Jane Doe—"

"Does the paperwork say why they only just found her?"

"I didn't get any of this from discovery. I got it on the news. It's everywhere. On TV, the *Daily Beast, Deadline*, Twitter."

I wanted to bang my head on the dashboard. "You've got to be fucking kidding me."

"Yeah, that's me, always kidding about dead hookers. Anyway, I'm guessing Zack will fill you in. He just called a few minutes ago."

"Did they say how long after the rape charge she got killed?"

Michelle sighed. "Yeah. They said it was about a week after she made the report."

I ended the call and sat staring through the windshield. I felt sick as the obvious connection sank in. Dale had one hell of a motive to kill this woman. And the timing was hideously perfect.

"Goddamn it!" I leaned forward and put my head in my hands. I felt like a mountain had just rolled on top of me.

Alex sighed. "I know the timing looks bad, but Dale wasn't the only one who had a reason to hate her. This lady had a lot of enemies, Samantha."

"But none of them had been accused of raping her, and none of them stood a chance of losing his career because of her."

"The DA can't put this in at the trial, can he?"

"It doesn't matter. If our jury pool thinks Dale killed one woman . . ."

Alex swore softly. "So now it's not just the rape. We've got another murder to get him out of."

I nodded, too miserable to speak. And we didn't have much time. The indictment would come down any day now, which meant we'd be in trial within sixty days. "We'd better head to Twin Towers and find out what Dale has to say about all this."

I didn't want to see him. I didn't want to have to confront the fact that he'd probably held out on me *again*. And lied straight to my face about it *again*. The thought of having to see his earnest expression, to hear his "heartfelt" apology, made my stomach turn. And just like all the other times, it'd be nothing more than the command performance of a sociopath.

While Alex drove, I took out my cell and found Zack's number. I wasn't anxious to talk to him. But I needed to get some information before I saw Dale.

"DA's office, Zack Chastain."

"It's Samantha—"

"I didn't let this story out. I don't know who—"

"Okay, whatever." Jenny Knox's murder was a matter of public record. Anyone could've dropped a dime on this one. "When and where was the body found, and what's the time of death?" I was back in lawyer mode, searching for the gaps. If Dale had any kind of alibi, I could muddy the waters.

"Hang on." I heard papers shuffling. "They found her at a little after five a.m. on January eighth. She was in a dumpster on Selma Street in Hollywood. Coroner makes her time of death anywhere after ten p.m. on the seventh, to two or three a.m. on the eighth."

"What've you got on the suspect? Any prints? DNA? Fibers?"

"Not that I know of so far. They're going back over everything."

"How come they just found her now?"

"I told my IO to rerun all the Jane Doe prints from the coroner's office in the past year. But I'm giving you fair warning—if I can tie this to Dale, I'm going to try and get it in at trial."

And if he succeeded, we'd be toast. I heard someone in the background telling Zack the meeting was starting. "I've gotta jet," he said. "Just so you know, the sheriffs are moving on the leak investigation. I gave them my statement yesterday." He paused for a brief moment, then cleared his throat. "I keep forgetting how messed up this whole thing must be for you. I can't imagine what it's like."

"Yeah, me neither. When are we going to get the reports?"

"You'll get everything we've got in the next hour—"

"Okay, thanks—"

"Wait." He cleared his throat. "I just wanted to say I'm sorry about that low blow in court. About this being too personal for you and . . . all that. It was over the line."

Was he trying to soften me up for the kill? Trying to get me to let my guard down? Or . . . unbelievable and improbable as it was, did he really mean it? "Thanks."

I spent the rest of the ride downtown fantasizing about the ideal alibi. That Dale would say he'd been working at a soup kitchen for the homeless that night, or working at a shelter for runaways, or providing free security at a fund-raising party for the oncology ward of Children's Hospital.

Since he'd never done any of the above—or anything remotely like it—I knew these fantasies were unlikely to materialize. As a backup, I'd settle for him being tied up at another crime scene where fifty cop-hating (makes the alibi more credible) civilians had seen him. But hell, let's face it, five civilians . . . or three . . . or even one old drunk would do.

Alex paused as we neared the entrance to Twin Towers. "Samantha, I don't mind waiting out here if you want—"

"No. You're investigating this case. You need to hear what he has to say about this." And I didn't want to be alone with Dale.

I could feel the acid churning in my stomach as we made our way up to the attorney room. It was the rape charge all over again—but worse, so much worse. I didn't want to believe Dale had killed Jenny Knox, but I knew the odds were that he had. No matter what he said. I couldn't let myself fall for his act again. Having my belief in him get shattered over and over had left me feeling bruised and battered inside. I couldn't do it anymore.

When the guards brought Dale up, he was smiling. He didn't know. Good. It'd give me a chance to gauge his reaction.

I picked up the phone. "They found Jenny Knox." I paused and watched his face. "She's dead."

His eyes widened. "What? How the fu . . ." He rubbed his forehead. It took him a few seconds before he looked up again. "Who killed her?"

I stared at him.

He leaned forward and put a hand on the glass between us. "Samantha, I didn't do this. I swear. You've got to believe me."

It was a good performance. But then again, it always was. I waved the "Lawyer 101" flag. "It doesn't matter what I believe. Your jury pool is going to think you did it because you had the motive. I heard she was strangled, but I haven't seen the autopsy report yet. I need you to think back about what your schedule was like a year ago. Specifically on the night of January seventh into the early morning hours of January eighth."

"What day of the week—"

"Tuesday." I paused to give him time to dredge up any memories. "Do you have any idea whether you might've been on call?"

He stared over my shoulder for a few seconds. "I could've been. But I'm not sure."

"And I guess you can't remember right now whether you were at a crime scene." He thought for a moment, then shook his head. I didn't really expect him to. It'd been more than a year ago. "I'll get your work records from the department. Assuming for now that you weren't at a crime scene, who were you most likely to have been hanging out with?"

He rubbed his temple. "Rick Saunders . . . Nate Flemming . . . Ignacio Silva . . . Larry Scofield." He paused and stared at the counter in front of him for a few seconds, then shook his head. "That's all I can think of."

Alex wrote down the names.

"Are they all detectives?" He nodded. "In Hollywood?"

"Rick and Nate are. Ignacio's in Rampart, and Larry is . . . I'm not sure where he is now. He was hoping to transfer out to Wilshire Division." He ran a hand through his hair, which made it stand up on top.

"We need some decent counter-spin right now. Who can we put on camera to say good things about you? Cops won't help; everyone expects them to stick up for you. We need some civilians. Like family, childhood friends, college friends—maybe neighbors? And it'd be a twofer if any of them were women."

Dale shook his head slowly, looking depressed. "Mom passed away a while ago. Dad's got dementia. He's in a nursing home in Phoenix. My sister lives out there, too, but we haven't spoken in years."

"Why?" Even as the words left my mouth, I knew it was a question I would never have asked any other client.

He looked away. "Just kind of lost touch. Different lives . . . she's not a big fan of the police." His voice trailed off, and he was silent for a moment. When he finally looked at me, he sighed. "Karen got busted for an illegal grow when she was living up near Sacramento."

"Did you help her out?"

"I put in a good word for her, but I couldn't do a whole lot. Sacramento PD doesn't care much about what an LAPD cop says."

But it sounded like she'd held it against him anyway. "These are what you might call extenuating circumstances. You don't think she'd step up?" He shook his head. Too bad—a sister would've been a nice touch. And having a bust for growing marijuana would've helped us with the young jurors. I finally told him that I'd met Lisa, that she was a great kid and would probably make a good impression. "From what she said, I doubt her mom would be much help, but Lisa's way in your corner—"

Dale's eyes flashed and he slapped the counter. "No! I told you already. I won't have her dragged into this!"

The guard put a hand on his Taser. I shook my head at him and held up a hand. I mouthed, "It's okay." I looked at Dale. His face was closed, hard. "Lisa could really help you. But if you're willing to pay the price—"

He stared directly into my eyes and spoke quietly but with a hint of menace. "I am. Let it go."

I didn't have to let him make this call, but I decided I would. Unlike a lot of my other clients, I knew Dale wouldn't use it against me if he got convicted. And I have to admit, I admired his willingness to make the sacrifice. "What about friends?"

"I didn't keep in touch. I had a college buddy—Louie D'Angelo—but we lost contact when I got into the police academy."

"Any old girlfriends?"

Dale had a sad half smile as he shook his head. "Just ex-wives. I hadn't been on a date in almost fifteen years when I met Chloe."

Damn. No women, no civilians, so we were screwed on the PR front. And it looked like the only shot we had at an alibi was a fellow cop. I was losing ground fast. I had to wrap up so I could think of a way out of this.

I gave Dale the update on what Alex and I had dug up so far. As I spoke, I could see he was having a hard time focusing. The news about Jenny Knox had really shaken him up. That made two of us. When I finished, I asked Dale if he remembered hearing Paige or Chloe mention a guy named Marc.

"I . . . no. I don't."

Of course not. I stared at him. "You need to think hard about your alibi. Your indictment's going to come down any day now. When it does, I need—*you* need me—to be able to say you have an alibi."

Dale looked at me, his expression forlorn. "I'm sorry, I know this is hell for you, Sam."

I scanned his face. It radiated nothing but apology and sadness. It was such a great act that even now, I could feel myself getting drawn in by it. And that was the scariest part of all. I hung up the phone and walked out.

THIRTY-FOUR

There was a leaden feeling in my chest as I headed out to the car with Alex. Neither of us spoke. I didn't want to let my thoughts coalesce. If I did, I'd sink even further.

But I wanted to know what Alex thought. I waited until we got into the car. "Did you believe him?"

He shrugged. "If I didn't know about the rape charge, I probably would. He really sounds sincere. But now? I don't know. I'm not sure."

So even Alex was feeling differently about Dale. I had to find a way to stanch the bleeding or Dale would be DOA by the time we got to trial. I'd gotten onto the 101 Freeway and was heading back to the office when I saw the Warner Bros. water tank towering above the freeway. I remembered we still hadn't cornered that writer, Geoffrey Brocklin, the guy Chloe had been seeing at some point. I had less hope than ever that he'd do us any good, but I was feeling desperate. He was our last thread to pull with Chloe. And besides, I needed the distraction. I asked Alex if he was up for a fight.

"Hell, yeah. I don't know if he's back yet, but it's worth a try."

The last time we visited the set, Alex had made a fan of Ramie, the showrunner's assistant. Now, he called her and found out that Geoff was in the writer's room. She agreed to get us onto the lot.

When he ended the call, I told him to give Michelle the information we'd gotten from Amaya and let her follow up on Marc Palmer.

"You don't want me to do that?"

"No. Marc's a side issue. I need you to move on Dale's alibi witnesses."

Alex nodded and pulled out his phone. He looked almost as grim as I felt. As Alex spoke to Michelle, I faced the fact that there were just too many "coincidences" happening around Dale and the women in his life. The truth was, Dale had probably killed them all—Chloe, Paige, and Jenny. And if I could do the math, so could the cops. They were probably already pulling up all the unsolved homicides in every division Dale had worked—which was all over the county. That's what I would've done.

Dale was probably a serial killer. My throat tightened as tears threatened to well up. I forced a deep breath. I couldn't afford to let this get to me. I was fighting a war on two fronts now that Jenny Knox's murder was out in the open.

I pulled onto the lot and found a parking space close to the building that housed the writing staff. When Ramie saw us approaching, she smiled and waved. It had nothing to do with me. She was twitterpated with Alex. She walked over to us, then glanced around and whispered to him, "I'll tell Geoff someone's waiting for him in the director's office. You'll have to take it from there."

She led us to the office, then went to get Geoffrey Brocklin. I braced myself. Any friend of Chloe's was bound to be an enemy of ours.

Geoffrey stopped in the doorway and frowned. "Who are you?" His hair was shaggy, his wire-rimmed glasses sat too far down on his nose, and his clothes looked like they'd been slept in.

"I'm Samantha Brinkman and this is my associate, Alex Medrano." I figured *associate* sounded better than *investigator*.

Geoffrey's eyes widened. "You're that killer's lawyer? No fucking way am I talking to you—"

He turned to go. Ordinarily, I would've let him. There's no point in trying to beat down a witness who doesn't want to talk to you. But I was in an angry mood and more than willing to share it.

"That's fine. Then here's how it's going to go: Ladies and gentlemen of the jury, ask yourselves why Geoffrey Brocklin wouldn't even give us five minutes to tell him why we thought Dale Pearson might not be the killer? Wouldn't an innocent man, one who has nothing to hide, want to do all he could to make sure the real murderer is brought to justice? Because we all know the police can get it wrong. We've all seen the stories about men and women who spent twenty, thirty years in prison for crimes they didn't commit. But Geoffrey Brocklin didn't want to hear it. Because Geoffrey Brocklin knew who did it—and he knew it wasn't Dale Pear—"

"Are you kidding me? No one's going to buy that!"

I tilted my head. "You sure? You and Chloe were close. Everyone knows it. So when she dumped you for Dale, you got jealous." I actually had no idea whether that was true. "And you don't have an alibi for that night." I was bluffing about that, too. If I was wrong, he'd call security and we'd be bounced out on our asses. At this point, I didn't care.

Geoffrey set his jaw. "We were never a couple. I was just a friend."

Yes. Like they say, I'd rather be lucky than good. "What did she tell you about Dale?"

"Just that he was a pain in the ass. She kind of liked the idea of dating a cop; it was a change of pace for her. But she said he gave her a lot of shit."

"About what?"

A defiant look crossed his face. "I don't know. She didn't really say."

"Bullshit. It was about using. She was back on the needle."

Geoffrey stared at me for a long moment, then slowly nodded. "I was actually on his side about that." He looked out the window, his expression bleak. "I couldn't believe it when I found out. She went through hell to get clean and put her life back together. Watching her slide back down, inch by inch . . . it killed me."

"You tried to get her to stop?"

He sighed. "It was maddening. She'd promise, I'd believe her. And then I'd catch her on the nod." Geoffrey shook his head. "The day she died, I heard she'd had to leave the set. I found her in her trailer. Getting sick." He looked at me. "I knew that meant she'd just shot up. But this time she didn't try to deny it. She said she knew she was out of control." He swallowed hard. "She asked me for help. She'd never done that before."

"Then her source had to be on the lot." She wouldn't have waited to shoot up in her trailer if she'd scored before she got to work.

Geoffrey's eyes moved from me to Alex, then back again. "I'm pretty sure I know who it is. But if I tell you, you'll have to cover me."

Studio lots were little Peyton Places, and Geoffrey didn't want to get branded as a snitch. "If we can't find anything to link him up to Chloe's murder, this goes nowhere."

Geoffrey looked behind him, then spoke in a low voice. "It's not a 'him,' it's a 'her.' Jaylene Thomas. She's a PA—uh, production assistant."

Low on the totem pole, it was a job that involved running around the lot all day. A great gig for a dealer. We got a description: five foot six, medium build, short black hair, and a nose ring. "Do you know whether Chloe saw her after you two talked in her trailer?"

"No, but she could have. Chloe was scheduled to do the last shot of the day, so she was here pretty late."

Geoffrey told us we could probably find Jaylene somewhere between Building 26 and the trailers. I thanked him. He gave me a curt nod and headed back to the writers' room. We went out to see if we could head Jaylene off at the pass.

"You crossing him off the list?" Alex asked.

"For now. He doesn't feel right to me. You?"

"Agreed. I think he probably did want to be more than a friend, but I don't buy him as a killer. You really think a five-foot-six girl could've killed two women?" Alex asked.

"I can't afford to be picky—or sexist—right now. I need suspects."

But as it turned out, Jaylene was a better prospect than I'd anticipated. We found her coming out of Building 26 with a cigarette behind her ear and a lighter in her hand. Perfect.

I stepped up to her, just out of swinging range. "Jaylene?"

She turned and peered at me. "Angus is up now; I'm on break." She pulled out the cigarette and lit it.

"I'm not on the show. I just wanted to talk to you for a minute. We're looking into Chloe's death and—"

Jaylene blew out a stream of smoke. "You a cop?"

"No. I'm Samantha Brinkman—"

Jaylene stared for a moment, then moved closer and poked a finger at my chest. "You're that fucker's lawyer, aren't you? Well, you can go screw yourself."

I pushed her hand away. "Yeah, 'cause you were such a *good* friend to her."

Jaylene dropped her cigarette and came at me, her right fist cocked. Alex jumped between us and pushed her back, saving me from a trip to the hospital. He held on to her, his back to me.

Safe now, with Alex holding her in check, I got in her face. "You're the one who was ruining her life, selling her that—"

"You're full of crap!" Jaylene spit her words at me over Alex's shoulder. "She was about to have a nervous breakdown, but no one cared. They just wanted to use her. I was the only one who gave a shit about her. I don't care what anyone says. She couldn't have made it through one fucking day without me!"

She threw Alex's arm off her shoulder and stomped away. I watched her go.

"I get the feeling Chloe was more than just a customer to our buddy Jaylene," Alex said.

I nodded. "Let's find out if Jaylene has an alibi."

"I'm on it."

THIRTY-FIVE

When we got back to the office, Michelle greeted us with an announcement. "The grand jury just handed down a true bill. Dale's been indicted."

I just nodded. It was a measure of how shitty things were that this almost qualified as good news. At this point, any news that didn't include yet another dead woman in Dale's life was cause for celebration.

"And I actually got somewhere on Marc Palmer—the guy who did some modeling gigs with Paige. He was pretty active on Facebook, and his friends are still posting on his page. I got some background." Michelle read from her monitor. "He moved out to LA from Blencoe, Iowa, three years ago, but he just started modeling last year. Seems like he met Paige at his first modeling gig."

"Did you find any articles about his death? Any indication how he wound up in Malibu?"

Michelle shook her head. "It was just a local news story. The coroner couldn't be sure how long he'd been in the water. Said it was more than a day, maybe as long as ten days. There were signs of blunt-force trauma, but that might've happened after he fell into the water."

"Any information on whether he was drinking or drugging?"

"Both. He had a .13 blood alcohol level and a pretty high level of cocaine. Plus, he was nude. It sounds to me like he was partying on the beach and went for a swim, or maybe fell off a boat."

"But no one reported it."

"Maybe because everyone else was high, too, and didn't notice he was gone until it was too late," Alex said. "And then they were afraid to get involved."

That sounded sadly plausible. "When did they find his body?"

Michelle looked back at her monitor. "March fifteenth."

"Six days after Paige died," Alex said.

What had been just a vague notion now seemed to be solidifying into a real possibility. I might actually be able to sell a connection between Marc's and Paige's deaths. "I want to talk to Marc's buddies. Michy, do you have enough there to track them down?"

"Sure, if they're in the mood to cooperate. If not . . . all I have are Facebook handles."

Alex smiled. "I can probably work with that."

I put my hands on my hips. "You're on probation, remember? I can't afford to lose you."

"They'll never catch me."

I didn't like the idea of him taking any risks, but I knew he was that good. And besides, we needed to see where this led. "Okay. But if anyone bitches about how you got their number, have a good cover story ready."

Alex put his hands on his hips. "Please. I started social engineering when I was eleven."

Of course he had. "Okay, but keep it tight. It's not about Marc per se. It's about Marc's connection to Paige. So we only want people who knew Paige."

Michelle stood up and rolled her shoulders. "How'd you guys do today?"

I didn't feel like talking about Dale, so I just told her about Geoffrey and Jaylene. When I threw out the possibility that Jaylene might be the killer, Michelle raised an eyebrow. "You're saying a *woman* stabbed both of them?"

"I know," Alex said. "Believe me, I didn't buy it either at first. But let me tell you, that woman is pretty strong—and kind of crazy. And it wouldn't have been that hard. Whoever did this probably got the jump on both of them."

I nodded. "And a knife doesn't make noise. Plus, Paige was probably in the shower when Chloe got stabbed."

Michelle shrugged. "I guess . . . I just never thought . . . it always felt like a man to me."

I couldn't disagree. "To me, too. And Jaylene might be a tough sell, but no one's going to buy Geoffrey."

Alex nodded. "That guy really liked her." He stood up. "I'm going to get to work on Dale's alibi for the Jenny Knox murder."

"And let me know the minute you have something solid. Amanda Trace is going to go batshit with that story."

Amanda Trace, cable news's most nasty pit bull of a host, existed to shred anyone accused of a crime. No evidence? No problem. She'd stitch together rumors, innuendo, and irrelevant garbage; slap some graphics on the screen; and spit and snarl her way through the story. She'd been teeing off on Dale all along, but now, with Jenny's death, Amanda's fangs would be dripping blood.

Alex moved toward the door. "I think I can get most of them to see me tonight. You want to come?"

I shook my head. "You can handle them alone." These cops were friendly witnesses. Alex didn't need backup. "If Dale's actually got an alibi, I want to be able to tell the press tomorrow. Report back to me tonight; I don't care how late it is."

"You got it." Alex headed out and I went to my office.

I worked on a few other cases, then went through all the autopsy and crime reports on Dale's case—or rather, cases—with an eye toward what I could say to the press tomorrow. I had to do more than give the usual "Dale's innocent" line. I had to make people think we really had something cooking. No names. I never mention any names till the very last second. The less time I give the prosecution to dig into my witnesses, the better.

Michelle wanted to wait with me, but when we still hadn't heard from Alex at eight thirty, I sent her home. There was no sense in all of us getting thrashed. It was almost ten o'clock by the time Alex got back. I gestured for him to have a seat. "Just tell me, are we hosed?"

He blew out a long breath and plopped down sideways, his legs hanging over the arm of the chair. "I don't think we're golden, but we're definitely not hosed. Dale owes Ignacio Silva a great big kiss and a hug." He opened his iPad and scanned his notes. "Ignacio says he and Dale were at Hoops the night Jenny was killed." Alex swiped a finger across the screen of his iPad. "That's a sports bar in Culver City. They got there at ten p.m. and closed the place down. Ignacio was driving. He dropped Dale at home at about three a.m."

And Dale lived in Porter Ranch. There was no way he could've gotten from there to Hollywood in time to do the murder. "So far, so good. How come Ignacio remembers all this more than a year later?"

"Because there was a big basketball game, and this coach"—he looked down at his iPad—"Shawn Haley, got into a fight with the referee. Chest-bumped him. Got fined more than a quarter of a million dollars." Alex looked up at me. "Chest-bumped? Seriously? Why not just slug the guy?"

"Because that would've cost him two million."

Alex shook his head. "Whatever. Anyway, Ignacio said Patrick, the bartender, would back him up, so I went to see him. That's what took me so long." Alex paused.

"Did he?"

"Sort of. He didn't specifically remember that night, but he said it might be true. Dale and Ignacio—and a bunch of other cops—were regulars."

Hardly a slam dunk. "So it's a cop bar." Alex nodded. I supposed it was better than nothing . . . but just barely. "What did you think of Ignacio?"

"He's good, a little tightly wound—"

"As in, if he gets pushed he's going to push back?"

"Yeah. When I nudged him on the details, he got a little . . . edgy with me."

If Ignacio was "edgy" with Alex, who was on his side, I didn't like his chances of keeping it together with Zack on cross—or with the press. I'd need to keep both him and the bartender under wraps. But that required them to cooperate and keep a low profile. I wasn't worried about Ignacio; he'd do what was best for Dale. But Patrick was an unknown.

Some witnesses will trample their crippled grandmothers to get on camera; others would rather shove hot pokers in their eyes. "Does Patrick seem like the type to want his fifteen minutes?"

"Definitely not. But just to be on the safe side, I told them both it'd be best to keep this quiet—"

"What reason did you give them?" I didn't want Patrick telling anyone that we were trying to hide him—though we were.

"I told them it'd hurt their credibility if they talked to the press."

I smiled at Alex. He was so good it was scary. "Perfect."

"Actually, it was just the truth. The book said that in high-profile cases, it's best to—"

I held up a hand. "Just take the credit, Alex."

Alex gave me a triumphant smile. "But you've got to admit it was right, wasn't it?"

"Even a clock that's broken is right twice a day."

"You've got to believe me, Sam. It's a great book." I stared at him. Alex sighed. "Fine. You know, what would really help is if I could dig up some other suspects for Jenny's murder."

"What about Bozo? That guy she ripped off for his oxy?"

Alex shook his head. "He's too puny. And whiny. No one would buy him as a strangler. But I bet if I go back to her 'hood, I can find others. From what I've seen, that girl must've had a buttload of enemies. She ripped everyone off—"

"No. Let it go. I'll take it from here."

THIRTY-SIX

The case was already hot, but the news of Jenny Knox's murder had turned it into a blazing inferno. And that meant lots more loony-tune court gawkers. The tinfoil-hat brigade was drawn to these big cases like nerds to a *Star Trek* convention. Usually all they did was mill around outside the courthouse and shout and wave signs, but now that Amanda Trace had spent her entire show last night snarling about this "rapist, serial-killer cop" who was a "rabid dog that needs to be put down," things were going to get scary.

So I was glad Xander was driving me. I didn't want to have to make the long trek from the parking lot to the courthouse through those hordes.

But when we pulled up in front of the courthouse, I saw that I'd underestimated the mob scene. It was even crazier than I'd predicted. From the courthouse doors to the sidewalk, it was wall-to-wall bodies. People were waving signs that read: **HANG THE KILLER COP** and **LAPD: MURDERERS' ROW**. Thanks, Amanda. There were a couple that more benignly read: **JUSTICE FOR CHLOE AND PAIGE**. But I only spotted one that I could even pretend to chalk up for our side—it had **RUSH TO JUDGMENT** in a circle with a line through it. Not exactly a ringing endorsement.

Xander circled around the car and opened the door for me. The moment I got out, someone in the crowd yelled, "That's her! That's the lawyer!" Heads began to turn toward me, then others joined in. "Yeah, look! That's his lawyer!"

This could get very bad, very fast. I leaned toward Xander. "Do me a favor. Don't take off till I get inside."

He gave the crowd a wary look. "I'd walk you, but they'll ticket me in five seconds if I leave the car."

I started to move forward, but the crowd surged toward me. I backed up and started to reach for the handle of the car door when three sheriff's deputies broke through and surrounded me.

They kept me inside the circle as we moved, but even so, I was worried that someone in that mob might throw something at me. But as I headed toward the courthouse doors, I saw that the only things in their hands were cameras. And they were pointing them at me. They wanted my picture? Then I noticed that some were waving pens and photos that'd been taken of me in court.

"Can I get your autograph?"

"Hey, Samantha, sign my picture?"

I couldn't believe it. No knives, no rocks. I smiled and waved to them as the deputies herded me inside. It almost made me laugh. No one cared that I was the bad guy's lawyer. I was famous.

Nearly broke, probably out of business after this case, but famous.

The courtroom was packed with reporters. Zack, looking slick in a black suit, his hair a little mussed and his tie loosened, smiled at me. I gave him a chin bob. *Très* cool. But it was good that we were getting along now. It's one thing to have a blowout; it's another to have an ongoing bitch fight. It gets old fast and makes both lawyers look like cranky two-year-olds.

The bailiff brought Dale out. I'd insisted on having him dressed in a suit and tie for this arraignment, and it really helped. He looked like a respectable businessman. This was the man I wanted the public to see. I went over to say hello, knowing the press would eat up the image of father and daughter together. Sure enough, the clicking of cameras followed me like a swarm of locusts. But Dale was watching the gallery as though he were searching for snipers. I had to make him stop.

"Dale, look at me." He dragged his eyes away from the spectators. "Deep breath, calm mind. Pretend you're at a seminar."

"So you want me to fall asleep?"

"Good. Keep that thought. This will be over in a few minutes." I was going to tell him about Ignacio, but I didn't want him to smile. I'd wait till after the arraignment.

Judge Tollinberg took the bench with solid, heavy steps and gave the gallery a sour look. "I'll call the case of *People v. Pearson*."

I moved back to counsel table, and Zack and I stated our names for the record.

The judge read the charges, and Dale entered his plea of "Not guilty" in the strong, clear voice we'd rehearsed. We set the trial for forty-five days from now. The judge looked from me to Zack. "I'm assigning you to Judge Traynor for trial. Any objections?"

I'd never had a case with him, but I'd heard he was tough. If that was true, I wouldn't get a lot of leeway. But I could do a lot worse than just "tough."

We both accepted Judge Traynor. The whole thing took less than two minutes. But when it played on television sets across the country tonight, it'd be drumrolled as though Dale had just confessed in open court.

I went into the holding tank to talk to Dale. Since he was maximum security, he was alone in the cell. "You did great."

He gave a weak smile. "You're a great coach." The smile faded. "I heard the DA say he was going to try and get Jenny's murder admitted at the trial."

"Yeah, but I have some law on my side. We've got a fighting chance to keep it out on legal grounds. And we may have enough evidence to clear you. Ignacio came through with an alibi."

Dale's face broke into a broad smile. "He did? That's great. What'd he say?"

"You guys used to hang out at Hoops?"

"All the time." He frowned. "But I don't remember what was going on that night. Was there a big game?"

"Not exactly." I told him what Ignacio said. "Ring a bell?"

His eyes shifted to the left for a moment, then he nodded. "Yeah, I think so. Will Patrick back him up?"

"He said you guys are regulars, so it might be true. But he can't specifically remember."

Dale's eyebrows lifted. "That's the best he can do?"

"For now. He might be more solid by the time we get to trial." Witnesses could go either way. Some got better. Others faded like cheap prints. I gave Dale the rest of the updates. When I got to Jaylene Thomas, he shook his head.

"So Chloe's source *was* on the show. I knew it." He looked away, his expression sad and worn.

"What's wrong?"

"I wanted Chloe to make it so badly. She had her problems, but deep down, she was a really good person—and so talented. But her mother just . . . ruined her." Dale sighed. "From what Paige said, she was a real monster. Chloe never wanted to talk about her, though. Whenever I tried, she pushed me off."

A sudden bolt of anger shot through me. "What's there to say? It's a short, ugly story. Once upon a time there was an evil friggin' bitch of a mother who hated her daughter and treated her like shit. The end."

Dale stared at me intently. "You really don't like your mother, do you?"

The bailiff came over. "Time to wrap it up, Counselor. The bus is here."

I nodded to him. "I'll come by in the next day or so with an update."

Dale nodded. "Okay. Take care."

I headed for the elevator and thought about my sound bites. I was going to keep it short and punchy. When I got downstairs, I saw that the court-gawker crowd had dissipated, but the press was still there in full force. A sheriff's deputy came over to me as I crossed the lobby.

He stepped to my side and said, "Just stick with me, okay?" I nodded. "Can I ask you not to talk to the press?"

"You can ask, but I have to do it. I promise I'll make it quick."

Edie was at the front of the crowd. She gave me a sympathetic look and spoke under her breath. "Do you even want to talk? I know this must be horrible for you."

"Sure, I've got good news, actually."

She blinked rapidly. "Oh. Okay." She nodded to her cameraman, then turned to me and spoke into the microphone. "This is very dire news for the defense. Jenny Knox's murder, and now the prosecution saying he'll offer it into evidence. What are you planning to do about it?"

"Dale has an alibi for the night of Jenny Knox's death. So that case should now be a nonissue. Dale joins me in hoping that Ms. Knox's killer will be brought to justice very soon."

A chorus immediately rose up.

"Who's your alibi witness?"

"What's the alibi?"

"Give us a name!"

I shook my head and gave my charming "I'm-so-sorry!" smile. "I can't get into the details right now, but I promise you'll hear about it very soon!"

I knew Zack would start calling the minute he heard my sound bite, but I'd tell him I wasn't sure who I was going to put on the stand yet. I spotted Alex on the curb, next to his car. I waved to him and pushed my way through the crowd. Trevor moved toward me. "I hear you were talking to Geoffrey Brocklin. What's your new angle?"

I wanted to ask him who his source was, but there was no way he'd tell me. I noticed that Edie had left her cameraman behind and was pushing her way through the crowd to get to me. Brittany was right behind her. "What makes you think I'm working a new angle?"

"Because the word on the set is that he was pretty tight with Chloe."

Edie poked her head forward. "Are you going for a jealousy motive?"

Trevor threw an irritated glance behind him, then turned back to me. "What's your angle?"

I had no intention of using Geoffrey as one of my fall guys, and for his sake, I wanted to nip this one in the bud. But I couldn't afford to dump any possibilities at this point. "Sorry, guys, I'm not able to discuss it just yet."

Brittany leaned in. "But it has to do with Chloe, right?"

I needed to push them off the Geoffrey connection. If they kept digging into it, they might sniff out my real angle: Jaylene Thomas. I didn't think she'd talk to anyone about our "meeting"—the last thing a dealer wants is publicity—but you never know. So I threw out the best mislead I could come up with. "Off the record?" They all nodded. "I can't give you details yet, but my investigation has uncovered that Paige was the real target. Not Chloe."

I turned and hurried through the crowd before they could ask any more questions.

Of course, that was bullshit. About the only thing my investigation had uncovered was a few lame straw men and some pretty shaky fringe witnesses. But hopefully, it'd make them let go of Geoffrey. More important, I hoped it'd make them focus on Paige.

The idea of making Paige the focus didn't just pop into my head. I'd been giving it some thought. If Paige was the target, then Dale was an unlikely suspect. He had no motive whatsoever to kill her. So the more I could beef up the Paige angle, the better. If I could come up with even one more witness to make that theory stick, I'd keep beating the Paige drum to the press every chance I got. And after hearing it on the news over and over again, the jury would be more inclined to buy it.

As they say, a lie repeated often enough becomes the truth.

THIRTY-SEVEN

I got into Alex's car. "Get me out of here."

He pulled away. "How'd it go?"

"It was nothing." I told him what I'd said to the reporters about Paige being the target. "I just wish it were true."

"We might be able to make it true *enough* if we get something out of Marc's buddies."

"Who've you lined up?"

"Marc had a lot of friends, but only three had connections to Paige. Golden Crossman, Julie Berger, and Ashton Laflame. Golden's a model, too, but Julie's a graphic artist and Ashton's a personal trainer."

"Who did you tell them we are?"

"I told them the truth. As far as I could tell, none of them was real tight with Paige. So they may not love the idea of talking to us, but they don't hate it as much as Paige's buddies."

Good. It's always easier that way. Especially if we eventually needed to drag them into court. "Where are we going?"

"Silver Lake. I told them to meet us at the Starbucks on Sunset. It has an outdoor patio. We'll probably get enough privacy out there."

No question about that. It was a typical March day: some blue sky peeked between the clouds, but the sun was too weak to take the chill out of the air. Only dedicated smokers would be sitting on the patio.

"You didn't schedule them all at once, did you? Even your damn book must have said—"

Alex sighed. "Of course not. We should have Golden first, then Ashton—"

"Ashton Laflame? Is that for real?"

"Every bit as real as 'Golden.'"

As predicted, we practically had the patio to ourselves. Our only company was two young girls in tank tops and low-rise jeans who shivered over their cigarettes. Alex and I had just settled down at a table in the far corner of the patio with our grande-size coffees when Golden showed up. His blond hair was slicked back off a face so perfect it could only have belonged to a model. Beautiful skin; straight nose; a wide-ish, sensual mouth; and deep sapphire eyes. On him, the baggy, beat-up jeans; T-shirt; and flannel jacket looked like haute couture.

Alex introduced us. Golden leaned back in his chair and gave us a measuring look. "I wasn't going to meet with you. I was a friend of Paige's, you know."

Alex stepped in smoothly. "We do know. And I understand completely. So if at any point you feel uncomfortable talking to us, just say so, okay?"

That seemed to relax Golden. He dipped his head. "Fair enough."

I nodded at Alex, a signal for him to keep going. "Did you already know Paige before you met Marc?"

"Yeah, we did an ad for JC Penney together." He swiped a crumb off the table. "Paige was good people. We didn't hang all that much, but whenever she came across possible gigs for me, she'd pass along the info."

Alex took out his notepad. "How'd you meet Marc?"

"He lived in the guest house next door to my building. Part of his rent was walking the dog for the owners. I was heading out to the liquor store down the street one day, and he was like, 'I could use a beer.' But he was flat broke, so I spotted him the beer and we got to talking. He'd been bouncing around, doing whatever he could. At that point he was a busboy at Oasis, but the money was lousy and he was looking for a better deal. You've seen his photos?"

I nodded. "He definitely had the looks for modeling. How come he didn't think of modeling?"

Golden shrugged. "It just wasn't in his lexicon. He was twenty-two, born and raised in Blencoe, Iowa—population three—and he'd only been out here a year. Maybe less. I hooked him up with his first gig." Golden paused. "Well, actually, it came from Paige. She'd offered it to me, but I was already booked, so I asked if she'd push for him. She did, he got the gig, and he started making real money."

"And she and Marc got to be friends?" I asked.

Golden had a sad smile. "Of course. That was her thing, always looking out for the strays."

Like Chloe and Tonya. "Was it ever more than that?"

"I seriously doubt it. Marc always claimed to be bi, but I think he played more for our team than yours. They might've occasionally been friends with benefits, but nothing more."

"Were you and Marc ever . . . ?"

Golden shook his head. "Marc was too much of a player for me."

"How often did you see Paige?"

"Not often. We'd hang out after a shoot, help each other find gigs. But we could go for weeks without talking. I guess you'd call it a work-ship. Work with a skosh of friendship."

I probably wouldn't call it that—a little too cute. "Did she ever talk to you about guys she was dating?"

"No." He paused and stared at the table. "But I think I saw one of them. He rode a bike. I saw him pick her up at a couple of shoots."

"A bike, as in motorcycle?" Golden nodded. "You ever talk to him?"

Golden shook his head and gave a little smirk. "He seemed like the macho type. Probably wasn't all that excited about meeting some fag model."

If so, then Paige's motorcycle buddy was an asshat. Good to know. "His loss," I said. "What else can you tell me about Marc? I mean, besides the fact that he was a player."

Golden sighed and shifted in his seat. He took a moment before answering. "He was basically a good guy. He'd never screw you over or anything. And he was a lot of fun. Pretty artistic, too, had a good eye for color. He talked about getting into graphic design. But he was . . . reckless. He'd hook up whenever, wherever—at parties, in bars. Hell, he even wound up in bed with someone he met grocery shopping." Golden shook his head. "I can't say I expected something bad to happen to him, but it's not that big of a surprise."

"Did you ever get the impression he did it for money?"

Golden's eyes flickered at Alex, then came back to me. "Sometimes, yeah."

I didn't know where this was heading or if it had anything to do with Paige, but I decided to let it spool out. "Did he ever tell you about the people who paid him?"

"No. Marc never named names. He just dropped hints every once in a while about having an extra income source. And he never expressly said it was money for sex, but I could read between the lines."

"Did he and Paige do a lot of modeling work together?"

"I can't say it was a lot, but it was more than Paige and me. I started getting more magazine work, so I didn't need the online gigs as much."

"When was the last time you saw Paige?"

Golden rolled his eyes. "God, it's been a while. Three months? Maybe four."

"What about Marc?"

"The last time I saw him was on March sixth. I remember because it was the day before my birthday. He came by with a couple of beers and we watched that reality show about the pawnshop in Vegas—he loved that show." Golden smiled to himself for a brief moment, then his smile dropped. "Anyhow, that was a Monday. A few days later . . . Thursday, I think, the agency called and said Russell was looking for him."

"Russell?"

"Russell Kitson, the photographer. He was calling around looking for Marc because he didn't show up for his shoot. That's when I knew something was wrong. Marc was a party boy, but he never bailed on work. About a week later, Ashton told me they'd found his body." Golden pressed his lips together and blinked a few times.

I gave him a few moments to recover. "Did you know of any friends Marc had in Malibu?" Golden shook his head. "When you saw him on Monday, did he mention any plans he had to go out there? Maybe to go to a party?"

"No. That's what was so weird to me." He shook his head. "When I heard they found him in Malibu, I was like, seriously? It seemed so random." Golden sighed. "But then again, Marc definitely did get around, so . . ."

I asked some more questions, but Golden had run out of answers. When we'd finished, I thanked him for meeting with us.

Golden looked from Alex to me. "Do me a favor? If you ever find out what happened to him, will you let me know?"

"Sure." Golden left and a few minutes later, Julie Berger and Ashton Laflame showed up—together. Julie, a thin, pale-skinned, black-haired Goth type, apologized. "Alex said you wanted to talk to us separately. But we've already been talking about it for months, so we figured, what's the point?"

I gave them a little smile. "You're probably right." I asked how they knew Paige. They'd met her through Marc, when they all went out for dinner after a shoot. But they didn't know her well at all. "How did you meet Marc?"

Ashton was buffed, but very lean and tan. "At the gym where I work."

"And I used to work at the juice bar next door," Julie said. "That's where I met Ash. He brought Marc over, and we all got to be friends." Her mouth turned down. "I really miss him. He was such a blast, so funny . . ."

Ashton nodded. "Kind of a wild child, but a really good guy."

"So he was into weight lifting?"

Ashton shook his head. "Not at all. He came to the gym because the agency wanted him to put on some muscle. He was pretty skinny."

Ashton and Julie filled out the picture a little more but not much more. They both had the impression Marc's family didn't approve of his "lifestyle," but that was a guess. He didn't talk about his family much.

The last time they'd seen him was the beginning of March, and he'd never said anything about having friends in Malibu or going to any parties there.

Ashton tapped a finger to his head. "I do remember him saying he went to a beach house once." He frowned. "But that was a couple months before he . . . died."

"And he just mentioned it that one time?" Ashton nodded. "Did he give you any details, like who he was visiting or where?"

"No, sorry. But that was typical Marc. He'd just toss out stuff like, 'I went down to the desert for the weekend,' or 'We went up to the mountains.' In the beginning, I'd ask who he'd been with or where they stayed, but he always kind of dodged the question, so I got the message and stopped asking."

"Did you ever get the impression he was getting paid for taking those trips?"

Julie shrugged. "It's possible. He was pretty, uh, relaxed about hookups. And he always needed money. Don't we all?" Julie paused and shook her head. "But Marc loved to party, and he could be a little . . . careless."

It all fit with what Michelle had read in the local news. A young guy who partied too hard one night and fell overboard. Or went for an ill-advised swim.

"When did you first notice he was missing?" Alex asked.

"Not till after they found his body," Julie said. Ashton nodded. Julie's eyes filled with tears. "I felt so bad for him. I just hope he wasn't conscious. That he passed out and just . . ."

Ashton took her hand and squeezed it. "We kind of hoped you'd be able to find out how it happened."

"We'll try. And if we do, I'll let you know."

We thanked them and headed back to Alex's car. Alex took the freeway—which right now was an endless sea of red taillights. "It sounds like Marc died within a few days before or after Paige was killed. But other than that, I can't see any connection."

"Me neither. But I'd like to take a run at that photographer. It sounds like he knew Paige."

"Russell Kitson." Alex held up his phone. "Already got his contact info. Where to now?"

I glanced at Alex. Man, he was good. "Home sweet home." Michelle had scheduled an interview for me at five o'clock with an actual paying client. Things might finally be looking up.

But before Alex could make it to the freeway, I got a call. When I ended the call, I told Alex to turn around. "Dale's in the infirmary. He's been stabbed."

THIRTY-EIGHT

We rode to the jail in silence. I couldn't talk. My brain kept circling around *How?* and *Why?* Dale had said no one was giving him any trouble, and the guards were good to him. Not good enough. According to the nurse, Dale was stabbed multiple times.

When we got to the infirmary, I saw that Dale was hooked up to an IV, and he was asleep. I studied his face. His skin looked gray, and there was a furrow between his brows. A nurse came over to check his monitors, and I asked her how he was doing.

"He's stable. But he's in a lot of pain. He got stabbed three times. Luckily, no vital organs were injured."

I asked her if she had any idea how it'd happened, or who'd done it. The nurse shook her head. "I don't know. We don't have the report."

A few minutes later, Dale woke up. He gave me a weak smile. "Hey. I guess this is the benefit of having my daughter as my lawyer."

Ordinarily, civilians don't get to visit inmates in the infirmary. I nodded. "What happened?"

"On the way to dinner." He paused to catch his breath. His voice was low and rough. I was about to tell him I'd come back later, but he waved me off. "Hallway was crowded. Someone came up from behind . . . shivved me."

"You didn't see who it was?" Dale shook his head. "He didn't say anything?" Dale shook his head again. "Where the hell were the guards?"

"Not their fault." He paused to breathe again. "Got there fast as they could. Saved me."

I was furious. I was going to sue everyone in this fucked-up jail. But I knew better than to rant about it here and now. "You sure you don't have a beef with someone in here?"

"No. No one. Keep to myself."

But he was a cop, and anyone could know that because his face was on television. They didn't need any better reason than that. "How are you feeling?"

"Hurts, but they say I'll live."

"Do you know how long they plan to keep you here?" I wasn't impressed with the security in this infirmary.

"A week?" Dale closed his eyes. He opened them with an effort. "Think that's what they said."

I told him I'd be back tomorrow. "Go easy on those jumping jacks."

He tried to smile, but it came out like a wince. I checked with the nurse on the way out, and she confirmed they expected to keep him for a week. "But he's strong. It might be less."

"Can you get more security for him?"

She gave me a tired look. "Ms. Brinkman, I don't blame you for asking, but we're way understaffed. I'll do what I can, but no guarantees. There's a lot more of them than there are of us."

I didn't like it, but there was nothing I could do about it. "Can I call you for updates?"

The nurse sighed. "I guess. But no more than once a day."

I needed her on my side, so I gave her the nicest, most ass-kissy thanks I could muster, and then got out of there before she could change her mind.

Alex and I didn't speak until we got into the car. "You think the press will find out Dale got shivved?" he asked.

"I sure hope not." It might get Dale some sympathy, but more likely, it'd just look like even the inmates hated him. I was worried that we might be late for my new *paying* client, but we hit a light pocket in the traffic and made it back to the office with a half hour to spare.

When I told Michelle what'd happened to Dale, she was almost as upset as I'd been. "What the hell are those guards smoking? Don't they realize—"

"Right. I know." It pissed me off all over again. "I talked to the nurse about extra security. But there isn't much we can do, other than threaten a lawsuit." The problem was, that'd only piss off the jail staff, which was the last thing Dale needed.

Michelle shook her head. "Well, hopefully it'll dawn on someone in that place how much you can cost them." She looked at her monitor. "You've only got fifteen minutes till your five o'clock gets here, so give me a quick update: What happened with Marc's friends? Get anything good?"

I told her about the interviews and that we got a lead on a photographer named Russell Kitson who seemed to know Paige. "I want to talk to him. The sooner the better. Alex has his contact information."

"Got it. And do you want me to try and get the police and autopsy reports on Marc?" she asked.

"No. If you start asking for that stuff, someone's bound to tip off the DA." I didn't want to leave tracks for anyone to follow. My best bet was to see if my cop buddy Hank could get the reports on the down low. "I'll take care of it."

And I had another reason to talk to Hank. I wanted to find out more about Ignacio Silva, see if he had a downside that might come back to bite me in court. That was another thing I didn't want Zack to know about. If he heard I was asking around about Ignacio, he'd figure out why pretty quickly. Hank could snoop around under the radar.

My five o'clock was right on time. Lane Ockman announced himself on the intercom, and Michelle buzzed him in.

Michelle always has new clients fill out an information sheet before bringing them in to see me. But when I heard him tell Michelle he wasn't going to fill anything out until he had a "face-to-face" with me, I knew it was trouble.

There was one sharp rap on my door. Before I could say anything, the door opened and Ockman filled the doorway. He was tall, about six foot one, and he was built like a heavy bag—square and solid. He had small, dark eyes; short, dark hair; and a soul patch. I opened the left-hand drawer of my desk, where I kept my .38, and stood up.

He paused for a second to give me the once-over, then closed the door behind him and moved to the center of the room. With a smile that was more like a grimace, he introduced himself, and I motioned to the chair next to him. "Have a seat, Mr. Ockman."

"I'm okay. Thanks."

I leaned closer to my desk drawer, my hand open and ready to grab for the gun. "What do you want?"

He folded his arms. "For now . . . just to talk." His eyes slid over to the open drawer. "So you won't be needing that."

I didn't budge. "I guess that'll be my call to make. Get to it."

"You harassed a very dear friend of mine, and I want to make sure you understand what it'll cost you if it happens again."

"I don't know what you're talking about."

"Does the name Jaylene Thomas ring a bell?"

The drug dealer on the studio lot. Now I had a pretty good idea what this was about. "I don't know what she told you, but she was the one who lost her shit. She took a swing at me."

"She tells it a little differently. But she's a big girl; she can fight those battles herself. My concern is that you might be planning to unjustly accuse her of being involved in the drug trade. My boss can't have that."

"I have no intention of getting her busted for dealing."

He gave me a hard look. "But you *are* about to set her up to take the fall for killing those girls."

"Who told you that?"

He gave me an impatient look. "I don't need to be a lawyer to figure out why you wanted to talk to her."

I supposed that was possible. "I'm just following up on all leads."

"Good, then I'm here to help you with that. As of this moment, you realized that lead was going nowhere. Jaylene is off your radar. You're not going to subpoena her, you're not going to talk bad about her to the press, and you're not going to point any fingers at her."

I glared at him. "Or else?"

"Or else your father won't be so lucky next time."

I froze. Dale's stabbing hadn't hit the news. I'd been checking ever since we left the jail. Ockman had set it up.

Ockman nodded at my expression with a cold smile. "If you don't back off Jaylene, your daddy won't have to worry about going to court anymore."

I stared at him. My hand itched to reach for my gun. He held my stare for a moment, then turned and left. I came out of my office just in time to see the front door close behind him. Michelle and Alex were staring after him, their expressions a mix of puzzlement and alarm. I told them what he'd said.

Alex set his jaw. "So he's Jaylene's boss. And he didn't want his operation to wind up in the spotlight."

I nodded. "That's my take." I looked at Michelle. "When did he call you to get this appointment with me?"

"Yesterday."

"Right after we had the run-in with Jaylene. That was plenty of time to set Dale up to get stabbed. And there's no other way he could've found out about Dale this fast."

Alex shook his head. "Ockman's probably got more than one inmate working for him. What are we going to do?"

"*We're* not going to do anything. At least not right now."

Michelle was irritated. "So we're just going to do nothing?"

"I didn't say that. I might have someone on the inside who can help."

Tuck Rosenberg, a former client and one tough giant of a man, was a high-ranking member of the Aryan Brotherhood—a notorious prison gang. He'd been facing twenty-five to life in prison for a murder, but I put together enough evidence to persuade the DA that he'd acted at least partly in self-defense. He wound up with manslaughter and a short enough sentence to do his time in the Twin Towers jail.

Michelle frowned. "How? I kind of doubt Lane Ockman was his real name."

"I'm sure it wasn't. But I'll find out soon enough." I held up my cell phone. "When I heard him say he wouldn't fill out the information sheet, I thought he might be trouble. So I propped up my phone behind the money tree." The little jade tree Michelle had given me for inspiration.

I hit play. The picture wasn't great—the little bells on the tree got in the way—and the voice was somewhat muffled. But it might be enough to figure out who he was.

Michelle's brow furrowed. "Who knows how long it'll take to get his real name with that? And in the meantime, Dale's just lying there in the infirmary."

I was just as worried. He couldn't be more vulnerable. "Yeah, I know. The only thing I can do is back off Jaylene and hope my inside guy can get Dale some protection."

Michelle shook her head. "It seems like every time I turn around, something else is blowing up. First Jenny Knox's BS rape charge gets leaked, then her murder, now this."

Alex frowned. "It is a lot of bad luck. But this Ockman asshole just strikes me as business. He doesn't want his salesman in the spotlight. The leak . . . that's a different story. Still no luck with Trevor?"

I shook my head. "My guess is it's probably a low-level civilian employee, and the LAPD has more than three thousand of them. The only thing Trevor might be able to do is figure out who's paying for it—"

"Like a tabloid?" Michelle said.

I sighed. "Or someone else who's got it in for Dale."

"Doesn't seem like he's got any enemies in the cop shop," Alex said. "I got to all the guys he gave as possible alibi witnesses, and they gave me more cops to talk to. No one had a bad thing to say about him."

I thought about that. If it wasn't professional, maybe it was personal. "Michelle, can you get me the contact information for Dale's exes?" A cop's ex-wife might know whom to bribe and how to get to them.

If I could prove an ex-wife with a vendetta was going after Dale, I might be able to garner a little sympathy for him. Unless it turned out he'd been beating her every day. In which case I'd forget I ever met her.

I thought about Lane Ockman again, how Michy had been so excited that we were getting another paying customer, and shook my head. "Ockman was supposed to be the new client who'd help keep us in the black. And he turns out to be Scarface—"

Michelle looked furious. "Worse. At least Scarface paid his lawyers."

Alex gave an ironic, half twist of a smile. "Well, I'm sure Ockman has money."

I nodded. "Guess I should've given him my card."

THIRTY-NINE

"So what are we going to do with the Jaylene angle?" Alex asked.

I wasn't about to let Ockman shut down a viable straw man. "Do what you can to check out her alibi without getting caught." No reason to risk life and limb if she was reading to blind orphans the night of the murders. I looked at my watch. "Oh jeez, I've got to move." I picked up my purse and blazer. "I need to see how Dale's doing."

Michelle sighed and went back to her desk.

It took less time to drive downtown than it did to get through security. I was relieved to see that Dale was already looking better. And he said they'd had a guard posted by his bed all night.

"Did he stay awake?"

Dale smiled. "Mostly."

After our visit, I went to the attorney room. I had to find out what I could do to beef up Dale's security a little more.

When Tuck Rosenberg walked into the attorney room, his wide mouth spread into a smile. He was a Viking-size man, and he filled the little cubicle. The phone looked like a Barbie-doll toy in his hand. "How you doin', Counselor?"

"I'm good. How're they treating you?"

"I got no complaints. It's good to be among friends."

Meaning: he'd hooked up with some Aryan Brotherhood clique. Which I expected and hoped would come in handy right now. "I need to ask a favor."

"You kidding? Anything you want, just name it."

"I have a client who had some . . . trouble with someone here." I gave him Dale's name and told him about the stabbing.

"That the cop who's in for murder?" I nodded. "Where is he?"

"In maximum. And this is what I know about the guy who set it up." I told him about Ockman—according to Alex, real name Glen Ricker—and his visit to my office, then held up my cell phone and showed him a still shot I'd made from the video. "He talked like he had a big dope operation. It might be true; it might be bullshit. But he's threatening to sic his dog on Dale again, and I need to make sure that doesn't happen."

Tuck stared at the photo for a few seconds, then nodded. "I don't know the guy, but I can ask around. See if I can find out who he's got in here."

"In the meantime, do you have anyone in maximum?" Tuck had a short-term sentence. He was in the general population.

Tuck thought for a moment. "I think I do. Want someone to keep an eye on your man?"

"If you could."

"Consider it done."

"Thanks, Tuck. I owe you. And if you happen to run into the jerk who did the stabbing . . ." The chances of that were slimmer than my bank account, but you never can tell. Stranger things have happened.

Tuck smiled. "I'll be sure to tell him you said hello."

"That'll work."

FORTY

I'd planned to check in on Dale every day, but with the trial getting closer by the minute, I had less and less time to spare. Alex had taken over the visitation duty for me.

And as usual, now that I was pressed for time, no one had time for me. During the next three weeks, Michelle tried to track down Dale's second ex-wife, Bobbi, and Russell Kitson, that photographer friend of Paige's.

According to his assistant, Russell was booked solid and wouldn't have a day off for at least a month. Bobbi was no easier.

I didn't make Dale's first ex-wife, Tracy, as someone who'd go to the trouble of leaking the Jenny story to hurt him. From all I'd heard and seen, they were getting along just fine. Besides, they had a child together, Lisa. The last thing Tracy would want to do was ruin Lisa's father.

His second wife, Bobbi, however, checked all the boxes. They'd been married nine and a half years—plenty of time to rack up all kinds of grudges. But more important, Bobbi had been a 9-1-1 dispatcher. She was an insider. She could've found a way to get her hands on Dale's personnel records.

At first, Bobbi seemed willing to meet. I'd thought maybe my suspicion about her was wrong. But after she made and broke four appointments, I was starting to believe I'd found the leaker.

And then, with just one week to go before the trial started, Bobbi finally agreed to see me. She suggested a Denny's near her house. I'd been so wrapped up in the case, I hadn't thought about whether I was personally curious to see what kind of woman Dale had married. But now, waiting for her in that diner, I realized I was.

I recognized her the moment she walked in the door. Bobbi was a little shorter than I was—and curvier, with a golden tan, shoulder-length blonde hair, and blue eyes that smiled when she did.

Dale definitely had a type. If you took away the warmth of that smile, she could've been my mother.

But there was something shadowed about Bobbi's expression, and there was a nervousness in the way she looked around the diner. I decided to edge in slowly with her, so I started with general questions about how long she and Dale had been married, how they'd met (at a retirement party for her boss), and where they'd lived (Granada Hills—another bedroom community in the North Valley).

Finally, I asked whether they were still on speaking terms.

She looked surprised. "Of course. Why wouldn't we be?"

Too stunned to come up with a lie, I stammered out the truth. "I—I . . . Dale told me that . . . you wouldn't have anything good to say." Now that I'd gone this far, I might as well tell her the rest. "He doesn't know I'm meeting with you."

Bobbi looked perplexed at first, then she nodded and gave me a sad little smile. "Can I trust you to keep what I'm about to tell you to yourself?"

"If you're sure that won't screw Dale."

She looked into my eyes for a long moment. "It won't screw Dale. First, let me assure you, there's no bad blood between us. None whatsoever. Our marriage broke up because he was married to the job, and

I desperately wanted out of mine." Bobbi stared out the window for a long moment. "9-1-1 is a twenty-four-hour line of death and ruination and misery. Some people can take it, even thrive on it. I wasn't one of them. Over time, it wore me down. I was depressed all day and up all night with gruesome nightmares. And finally, the constant fatigue and stress caught up with me. I blew a domestic-violence call. The woman landed in the hospital with four gunshot wounds." Bobbi swallowed. "She didn't make it. Dale kept telling me it wasn't my fault, that there was no way anyone could've gotten to her in time. Her ex-husband was holding the gun on her when she called. But I still think that if I'd acted faster . . ." Bobbie swallowed again.

"So you had to get away from law enforcement? And that included Dale?"

"Not law enforcement. Crime. All those victims. I just couldn't take it anymore." She looked at me. "I still loved him, but I had to get away. I quit my job and moved out. Six months later, I had a nervous breakdown."

"Bobbi, I'm so sorry."

She gave me a brief nod. "Thanks. Things got pretty bad. I had to check into an inpatient facility for a while." Tears glistened in her eyes, but then she smiled. "But Dale showed up every single day. And when they released me, he was the one who moved me back to my apartment." Bobbi looked away as she swiped at the tears on her cheeks. "He wanted to get back together. And I did, too, but . . ." She stared down at the table and shook her head. "But just looking at him was a constant reminder. There was no way."

"And you're afraid that if you testify, the press will dig into your life and find out about it."

"They will. I mean, I've seen stories about everyone who has anything to do with the case. It's all over the news every day."

I hated to admit it, but she was right. "They probably would, but I don't see that it's anything—"

"To be ashamed of? Maybe not, but I am. And Dale knows that. That's why he told you not to talk to me. Because he knew it'd put all my history out there and how much I'd hate that." Bobbi looked out the window for a long moment. Then she took a deep breath and set her jaw. "But I'll do it. If you need me, if it'll help at all, I'll do whatever I can."

It was a noble sacrifice, and if I got desperate enough, I might ask her to make it. The client's welfare comes first. But not yet. It wasn't worth what it'd cost Bobbi. It would've been good to have a civilian—a woman—say nice things about Dale, but I could already hear Amanda Trace claiming that Bobbi had either been threatened or bought off to get her to whitewash her ex-husband.

"As of now, I don't see the need to put you through that. But just to give you fair warning, I might later on."

She gave me a wan smile. "I'll try not to skip town."

So much for Bobbi being my leaker. But she might have some ideas about who it was. "You've seen the stories about Jenny Knox? The prostitute?"

"Yeah. Any clue who leaked that rape charge yet? That was really shitty."

"It is, and I don't. Do you have any ideas?"

Bobbi blew out a breath. "I've got thousands of 'em. The LAPD is a big ocean with lots of little fish who wouldn't mind making some extra money. But I don't know of anyone in particular." Bobbi sighed. "You know, Dale's a good guy. I don't believe he raped that prostitute. And I really doubt that he killed her." She looked at me steadily. "Just in case you were wondering."

I could tell she believed that. And I wanted to believe it, too. But it was just an opinion. I smiled. "Good to hear."

"Sure. But just between you and me, Chloe had to be about the worst choice in the world for him."

I looked at her, confused.

"Because of the drugs." Bobbi gave me a meaningful look. "Dale's mother."

"But she's dead. Isn't she?"

"Yeah. Of an overdose. She took a header down the stairs and messed up her spine when Dale and his sister were young—maybe ten, eleven years old? They put her on painkillers and she got addicted. She OD'd right after Dale graduated from high school. The insurance payout put Dale through college for a couple of years."

And when the insurance money ran out and he had to get a job— my mother left him. "Then his issue with drugs isn't just a cop thing."

"No, it's personal. He really has zero tolerance. And apart from that, he has one heck of a temper."

"How bad?" I searched Bobbi's face. "Did he ever—"

"No, he never hit *me*. But he'd hit the walls, kick the furniture. It could get scary. Especially because it'd come out of nowhere. He'd be okay one second, and in the next he'd just explode. So when I heard Chloe had a drug problem and they'd been fighting about it that night, I thought . . ." Bobbi shrugged.

"He might've done it."

She nodded. "I'm sorry."

For a few moments there, I'd started to think I was wrong about Dale. I sighed. "Me, too."

FORTY-ONE

I didn't know whether I was glad I'd met Bobbi—though I supposed it was best to know all I could about Dale, for a lot of reasons. But I did know I felt sorry for her, and I liked her. And I was relieved to find out she didn't hate Dale. Unfortunately, that only made her suspicions about his guilt that much more credible. If she'd hated Dale, I could've dismissed it as ex-spouse bitterness.

But Bobbi obviously still loved him—more than that, she still liked him. And I could see why. Flash-point temper or no, he'd been there for her in every possible way. And he still was. Even now, when he was facing life in prison—when anyone could be expected to get a little selfish—he'd put her needs first. So to hear even someone like Bobbi say she thought Dale might be guilty was a real gut shot.

It didn't stop me from working night and day on his case. Nothing short of his televised confession could do that. But it was one more thing weighing on me. On all of us. And time was running out. I couldn't afford to chase any more dead ends.

So when Michelle said she had a call from an inmate at Men's Central Jail on Bauchet Street who claimed he had something that'd be "super important" to me, I told her to have him write me a letter. I had just three days to go before we started jury selection, and I had a stack of two hundred juror questionnaires to read. I wasn't about to waste a minute on some goofball who was looking for a free ride.

But Michelle told me to take it, that I needed the break. "Besides, he's only got five minutes left on his call."

I sighed and picked up. "Samantha Brinkman. Remember this call is being monitored—"

His voice was high and pressured. "Yeah, I know. You're the lawyer for that cop dude who killed those girls, right?"

"For that cop who's *charged* with killing those girls—"

"Yeah, whatever. I'm Scott Henderson, prisoner number 1011432. I'm in for possession for sale of coke. I need you to take my case—"

"Why don't you get the public defender—"

"'Cause you're better, and I've got something you need."

"Write me a letter. If it works out, I'll substitute in—"

His voice got even higher. "I don't have time. I've got a lot of enemies in here. You've gotta get me out. And trust me, you'll want to jump on what I have."

The recording came on saying this call was being monitored. I looked at my phone. We had only one minute left. I was sure this wasn't worth my time. But I did have to go see Dale. I'd been sending Alex to keep him company for the past two weeks. It was more than my turn, so I'd be in the neighborhood. But visiting prisoners was a huge time suck. I didn't want to commit. "Maybe I'll come by later today."

"Don't tell anyone you're coming to see me."

I sighed. "Scott, you already did."

There was a beat of silence. "Oh."

It was eleven o'clock. I decided to spend the next hour getting started on the juror questionnaires and leave for Twin Towers at noon. But after I'd gotten through the first ten, I thought I saw an alarming trend.

I quickly checked the first page of the next fifty questionnaires. I was right. Almost all of the jurors were in their twenties. That *never* happens. The twentysomethings are working, or they have little kids, or they're in school—or all of the above. They don't have time to sit in court all day.

That's why older, retired people always dominate jury pools. Plus, older folks are more inclined to feel like they should do their civic duty. And usually, they're the bane of my existence. If this were any other case, I would've been in heaven with this jury pool. But in this case, with a cop as my client, I needed those senior citizens. They had a more benign view of cops. And they'd been my best hope.

By noon, that hope was dead. I fumed to Michelle about it as I packed up to leave for Twin Towers. "That friggin' jury commissioner must've sent the summons to every college campus in LA County."

Alex offered to go downtown with me, but I needed him to keep working on the questionnaires. I had him and Michelle looking through them so I could get their feedback. The more eyes the better. "Dale's seen enough of you. This is just a hand-holding session anyway."

And thanks to Alex, who'd been doing all the driving, Beulah had a full tank of gas. So I had a shot at making it downtown and back before I had to refuel. More luck, the traffic gods were with me. I flew down the freeway and got there in record time.

But the multitiered parking lot was packed. I couldn't find a space till I got to the top level. Even that was pretty crowded. So it really chapped my butt to see a silver Bentley parked diagonally across three spaces. "Asshole," I muttered under my breath as I got out of the car. Then I saw the personalized license plate, A1 LAWYER, and realized I knew this particular asshole. Sherman E. Cross was a high-priced loudmouth with an elephant-size ego and a pellet-size brain. He was the reason lawyers should never be allowed to advertise. Thanks to his ubiquitous TV ads, billboards, and bus benches, he'd managed to bilk millions out of unsuspecting clients who largely got sold down the river. Jerks like this are proof that there is no justice.

But seeing his license plate gave me an idea. A way to make Sherman E. give back. I went to my car, fished my shaver out of the glove box, and took out the razor blade. I looked around to make sure there were no surveillance cameras or anyone else nearby, then strolled casually over to the Bentley. After one last look around, I knelt down and scraped off the registration stickers. I'd probably need to use Scotch tape to make them stick to my plate. But that was one less bill I had to worry about. I smiled as I slipped the stickers into my wallet.

In a much better mood than I'd expected to be, I decided I might as well go visit the coke dealer first and get it out of the way.

Scott Henderson was the only inmate I'd ever seen who managed to walk on his toes in those ankle-to-waist chains. I watched him roll down the hallway in a side-to-side lope, his long blond hair swinging. He was tall and slender, with a mustache and short beard. He reminded me of Ted Neeley in *Jesus Christ Superstar*.

The deputies plopped him down in the chair across from me and locked his handcuffs and ankle cuffs to the ring on the floor. As they left, the heavier-set deputy told me we had twenty minutes.

I figured that should be more than enough time, but I didn't want Scott to think he had time to dawdle. "I've got somewhere else to be, so talk fast."

He snorted back what sounded like a wad of phlegm and licked his lips, which looked cracked and dry. "Okay, uh, here's the thing. If I tell you I did something that's, like, a crime, you can't tell anyone, right?"

I looked at him steadily. I knew I couldn't possibly get lucky enough to have him confess to the murders. But just in case, I had to let him know that I couldn't keep that confidential. I had a preexisting relationship with Dale, and I had a duty to present any evidence that would help him. "Depends on what the crime is."

Scott swallowed hard and took a deep breath. "It involves those girls."

My heart thudded in my chest. Had the incredible happened? Had I really gotten that lucky? I wanted so badly to hear him tell me he'd done it—for so many reasons. My emotions warred with my ethics for a long moment. But I couldn't do it to him. It wasn't right. "If you're about to confess to the murders, I'm afraid I can't keep that confidential, so I'd advise you—"

His eyes flew open. "What now? No!" He shook his head so hard his hair got stuck on his beard. "I never killed nobody."

I'd had a moment of such intense hope it took me a few seconds to recover from the crash landing. "You had nothing to do with the murders?"

He tilted his head back and sniffed hard. "No way. I wasn't even in LA County when that went down." He looked at me impatiently. "So now can I tell you?" I nodded. "I was the one who did the burglary. I ripped off that jewelry."

I stared at him.

"They had a nice flat-screen, but I couldn't get that thing out of there—"

"So you grabbed the jewelry. I get it. Did you pawn it?"

"Fenced it. Got about five thousand for it."

"Which means it was probably worth about fifteen."

Scott shrugged. "Whatever. It was safer than a pawnshop. Really boosted my business—for a while, anyway." Scott had a dreamy look on his face as he relived better times.

Those times were probably what landed him in Men's Central Jail. "Can we cut to the chase? What do you think you have for me?"

"I also took a cell phone."

"From where?"

"From the top drawer of that girl's dresser. The one where I found the jewelry. I kept it—thought I might be able to use it. Then I forgot about it. But after I got busted, I saw you on television in the day room, and I remembered about that phone. I got to thinking maybe you could use it."

And then he could use me. "What was on it?"

Scott sniffed and wiped his nose on his forearm. "Don't know. I never looked. Maybe phone numbers or something."

I thought about that. He'd found it in Paige's dresser. It had to be an extra phone, one Paige didn't use anymore. Zack had given me the cell-phone records for the phone the police had found—the one she *did* use—and they went back for more than a year. The likelihood that an old phone would have anything of critical importance was slim. But I didn't think I could afford to pass up the chance to look.

He leaned forward and dipped his head to my eye level. "What do you say, Ms. Brinkman? Will you do it?"

"What're you in here for?"

It turned out to be a routine car bust. Traffic stop, cop sees white powder on the console, cop calls K-9 unit, dog alerts, they find five grams of cocaine under the passenger seat. I probably couldn't bitch about the search, but five grams wasn't that much. I should be able to get the DA to break it down to straight possession.

I asked about his priors. Clients never get this right. It's always "I got almost nothing. I think they busted me for joyriding once when I was fifteen, then I got busted a year ago for pot. That's about it." Then I check the rap sheet and find robberies, a burglary, and an attempted murder.

So while I hoped he could give me some idea of what I was up against, I wasn't about to take his word for it. Much as I wanted to see what was on that phone, it wasn't worth getting into bed with Pablo Escobar.

Scott frowned and drummed his fingers on the arm of his chair for a moment. "I'm pretty sure all I've got is a DUI and one pot bust."

See?

"If that's right, I'll substitute in as soon as you get the phone to me."

He gave another loud honk, wiped his nose on his sleeve, and nodded. "I'll get it to you today."

I gave him my office address. "See you later. Maybe."

FORTY-TWO

I headed to Twin Towers, which was just a couple of blocks away from Men's Central Jail.

I had a fifteen-minute wait before they brought Dale up, so I texted Michelle and told her to keep an eye out for someone who said he was delivering a package from Scott Henderson. Then I went through my e-mail. I'd just finished deleting my cyber junk mail when they brought Dale out. He still moved a little slower than usual, but he looked much better now. He'd regained most of the weight he'd lost when he was in the infirmary, and his face had filled in somewhat. Just in time for jury selection.

I picked up the phone. "You look good." I studied his neck and arms. "Still haven't gotten those tats, though."

Dale smiled. "My favorite artist got transferred out to Delano. I refuse to settle for anything less than the best."

"And why should you?" I told him about the Marc witnesses—Golden, Julie, and Ashton—and that we were still trying to track down the photographer, Russell Kitson. "But if he's not willing to meet in the next day or so, we might have to let that go."

"Don't sweat it. I never heard Paige mention him."

"And I just got a call from someone out of the blue." I told him about the burglar, Scott Henderson. "Even if he really has Paige's old phone, I'm not sure we'll find anything of value on it. But I have to check it out. Hopefully it'll get dropped off today."

Dale chuckled and shook his head. "I guess that's the upside of a high-profile case. All the weirdos come crawling out of the woodwork."

"How obnoxiously true. Everything okay?"

"So far." Dale looked into my eyes. "I heard you met Bobbi."

"She's really cool."

"She liked you, too."

A rush of sadness made my throat tighten.

Dale had a look of concern. "What? Are you okay?"

I stared down at the counter. Meeting Bobbi had reminded me of the way I'd felt when I was a child. The sadness of meeting my friends' mothers, wondering why I couldn't have a mother like that—and inevitably feeling that somehow, it was my fault. I never told anyone about that. But now for some reason, I blurted out, "I guess I couldn't help thinking . . . all the Bobbis out there, and I get Celeste." I was shocked to hear the words come out of my mouth. "Please, just ignore my self-pity party. I don't know what made me say that."

When Dale spoke, he looked into my eyes, his voice low. "Why do you hate her so much? I'm pretty well aware of Celeste's shortcomings. Believe me, I'm no fan. But it's not like she abandoned you—"

In that moment, something snapped. A flame of anger seared through me. "How the hell would you know?"

Dale looked stricken. "What happened? Tell me. Please."

I'd never intended to tell anyone about it. But for some reason, the dam that'd held back the memories broke. "I was twelve. I'd just finished seventh grade. That's when Celeste met her ultimate dream guy. Sebastian Cromer. He owned a string of real estate agencies—Cromer and Associates. They're all over Southern California—"

"I've heard of them. He sold her a house?"

"No. She was a real estate agent. She worked at the branch in Studio City. She was doing pretty well but not nearly well enough. You know Celeste; she wanted the huge bucks, not the 'good enough' bucks. And she'd never planned to work for it."

Dale sighed. "I'm very familiar with her life plan."

"So even though the guy was, like, a thousand years old and she was thirty-two, when he asked her out she thought she'd died and gone to heaven. I hated the guy from jump. I told Celeste there was something creepy about him. But she wouldn't listen. She dragged me to his mansion in Bel Air practically every friggin' weekend. And after just one month, we moved in."

Dale lifted his eyebrows. "One month?"

I nodded. "In late August. I remember because school started two weeks later. I'd always been a straight-A student. But by November, I was flunking just about every class except art. I got busted three times for having ecstasy, pot, and Jack Daniel's in my locker. But you checked my background. You didn't see any juvie history on me, did you?"

Dale shook his head, his expression dark. "Sebastian bought you out of it?"

"Sure did. And I got sent home almost every other day for wearing 'inappropriate attire.' That went on through all of eighth and most of ninth grade."

They were all the classic signs. Being a cop, Dale knew them well. He was squeezing the phone so hard I heard the plastic crack. "And she said nothing?"

"Nope."

The knuckles on his hand holding the phone were white. He didn't look at me. "Did you say anything to her?"

"No. I was afraid she'd dump me. Put me in foster care or something. His life, his money—that's what she wanted. Not me. And I knew for sure that she'd blame me."

Dale rubbed his temple. "So no one else knew?"

"Lettie, the housekeeper, did. I think she suspected for a while. But she found out for sure when she caught Sebastian 'tucking me into bed'—with his tongue down my throat and his hand up my blouse. She called the police, God bless her."

His voice was raw. "So he got arrested."

I could hear the bitterness in my voice as I answered, "No, of course he didn't get arrested. The Sebastian Cromers of the world never get arrested. Mommie Dearest told the police it was a misunderstanding, that Lettie had been mistaken. And she made Lettie back down and lie to the cop. I felt like a piece of shit for not telling that cop that Lettie had been right. But I could tell he was a big fan of Sebastian's. He was all, 'Of course, Mr. Cromer. So sorry to disturb you, Mr. Cromer.' Lettie left that night and never came back."

"So Celeste didn't do anything about it?"

The look of horror and disgust on Dale's face was like salve on an open wound. Finally, someone believed me. And cared.

"She refused to believe Lettie—or me. But one month later, she saw it with her own eyes. He came after me while I was in the shower—"

"How? Didn't you—"

"Lock the door?" Dale nodded. "I couldn't. He disabled all the locks on my doors."

Dale's face and neck had turned bright red. "*Then* did she believe you?"

"No. She accused me of trying to seduce him, of setting him up. I told her I couldn't take it anymore, and that if she didn't get me out of there, I'd report him to the school police. And I'd tell them that she'd known about it all along and wouldn't stop him."

Dale's eyes bored into mine, his gaze burning hot. "What did she do?"

"She knew the school police probably wouldn't bow down to King Sebastian. And I think some part of her lizard brain knew he'd do it again—and that eventually, he'd get caught by someone who wouldn't let it go. Then she'd be on the hook, too. So she finally moved us out."

Dale stared at the counter as he slowly shook his head, his chest heaving. Suddenly, he pushed back, his face flushed a dangerous red. He screamed as tears gathered in his eyes. "That sick fucking bitch! Goddamn her to hell!" He banged the phone down on the counter—and kept banging it again and again. Plastic shards flew as the phone disintegrated. Spittle flew from his mouth, and his eyes were wild as he shouted over and over, "That goddamned whore! That filthy piece of shit! I'll kill them both!" By the time the guards came running, the receiver was nothing but a mouthpiece and wires.

They yanked him up by his waist chain and threw him down on the floor. I jumped up and pounded on the glass. "Stop! Let him go! It's not his fault!"

But they never even looked at me. They trussed him up and dragged him out. I stood there staring after him, my hands still on the glass. Dale's fury was a wild, terrifying thing. I didn't want to think about what it meant.

But I couldn't deny that when I saw his rage unleashed—for me, for what they'd done to me—a part of me had rejoiced.

FORTY-THREE

When I got back to my car, I sat there for a few minutes. I needed time to recover. I couldn't stop seeing the image of him pounding that phone receiver on the counter with wild-eyed fury. As much as I feared what it meant, I loved that fury. It was *my* fury, and I'd carried it by myself for so many years. And now, finally, there was someone else who felt it, too, someone who knew I told the truth, who believed me. I felt vindicated. I felt strong.

But I knew that was the face of a man who *could* stab two innocent women to death. As much as I wanted to believe he was innocent, the evidence kept stacking up against him.

After a few minutes, my head cleared enough to drive. Ordinarily, I hate the drive from downtown. It's long and monotonous. But now, the boring normality of it brought me back down to earth. Freeway therapy. By the time I passed the Hollywood exits a half hour later, I was feeling pretty steady. But I knew I couldn't talk about what'd just happened. I'd regained my balance, but only just. If I had to relive any part of it now, it'd totally derail me. So I did what I'd always done since childhood: I shut it all out. I spent the rest of the ride back thinking about what else I had to get done before the trial started.

When I got back to the office, Michelle smiled and held up a hand for a high five.

"You know I hate high fives, Michy." Because when I miss, it feels so lame.

"Oh, cope." We slapped hands and I managed to hit hers pretty squarely.

"What are we celebrating?" Other than the fact that I'd nailed the high five.

"Russell Kitson will talk to you if you get out there right now. He's in the Valley." Michelle handed me a Post-it with the address.

"Hey, Alex," I called.

He came out of his little room. "You don't have to shout. I'm only nine feet away."

"Let's go hit up the photographer." He went back to his office to pack up. "Did anyone come by with that phone?"

"Not yet. But it's only three thirty."

I decided I'd asked enough of Beulah for one day and let Alex do the driving. As he headed up the onramp to the freeway, the sky was a dull gray. But as we moved north and east, the sun broke through, and by the time we made it to the San Fernando Valley, the sky was almost completely blue. Just a few wispy clouds floated above us.

Alex got off the freeway at Winnetka and headed north for another five miles. He made a series of turns into a bland, suburban neighborhood and finally pulled up in front of a two-story Tudor-style house set at the top of a steep driveway. As we hiked up to the front door, I noticed that the large picture window was covered with a heavy blackout drape.

When a young woman in heavy makeup, a kimono short enough to wear to the gynecologist, and stiletto heels answered Alex's knock, I knew what kind of photographer—or, rather, videographer—Russell was. The girl ushered us in and pointed to a man sprawled on the couch near the front door. He stood up when we walked in. Russell was at least six foot four and thin as a Flexi straw, with long, greasy black hair. A nose ring with a real-looking diamond rested on his left nostril, and several chains with a variety of medallions hung around his neck, which was covered in multicolored tats. When we shook hands, I noticed he wore leather bracelets and heavy silver rings on every finger. The word *overkill* probably never came out of his mouth.

We followed him past the set—a dungeon that featured a rack suspended from the ceiling, a chair equipped with leather straps, the requisite four-poster bed—with handcuffs, of course—and I even spotted a red rubber ball on the pillow. A man in an executioner's costume—leather head covering and all—sat in a rocking chair next to the bed, scrolling on his cell phone. Two women in G-strings and nothing else watched a cooking show on the television a few feet away. Just another day in a sleepy bedroom town.

As we took seats in the dining room, I saw Russell check me out. There was nothing lascivious about it. He was just scoping out the inventory. He offered us a drink, but I declined. I didn't even want to risk bottled water here. Russell looked more than a little stoned, with eyes at half-mast and a voice that sounded like a tired lawn mower.

I thanked him for meeting with us and jumped right in. "How'd you meet Paige? I assume you knew her before you met Marc."

"Yeah. I've known Paige for about five years. Back then I only did print ads, online ads, that sort of thing."

"She never did porn?"

"No. I tried to bring her over. It's good money. But she wasn't into it." He pulled a pack of Marlboros out of his vest pocket and held it out to us. We shook our heads. He lit up and took a deep drag. I could practically hear his lungs screaming.

I was hoping he could give us a line on who Mr. Perfect was, so I asked if he knew of any boyfriends who were married—and generous.

He shook his head. "Uh-uh, Paige didn't do the married-man thing. At least not that I ever knew. Only guy I ever saw her with was a guy in the industry. Used to pick her up at the shoots sometimes. Drove a motorcycle."

"You happen to know his name?" I asked the question with zero hope.

Russell tipped his head back and stared through the smoke that circled up toward the ceiling from his cigarette. "It was weird . . . like, Cloud . . . Rain . . . no. Storm. Yeah, that's it. Storm . . . Cooper."

At last. I couldn't believe I'd finally gotten a name. But . . . "Seriously? Storm Cooper?" He nodded. I looked at Alex and we did a mental fist bump. "Did you know him at all?"

He pulled on his cigarette like it was a joint, holding in the smoke till the very last second. "Not really. We didn't talk. Maybe like 'Hey' and 'See ya.' I just remember because I dug the name."

I asked a few more questions about Paige, and a couple about Marc, but we'd gotten all there was to get from Russell. I thanked him for his time. He took another drag and stood up. "Not a problem. Well, gotta get back to the salt mines." Russell gave us a salute. "The porn must go on."

I tried not to make a face. As he walked us to the door, one of the girls was getting hoisted onto the rack. Another girl in thigh-high black-vinyl boots picked up a whip.

Russell opened the door. "Such a bummer what happened to her. Never would've thought someone that sweet could end up that way." He shook his head. "Fuckin' world we live in."

A whip cracked behind him. "Yeah, what a world."

FORTY-FOUR

Our trip back to the office was slow going. We'd hit the freeway at the heart of rush hour. I dragged my eyes from the mesmerizing river of lights and searched on my cell phone for Storm Cooper.

Alex glanced at me. "You looking up—"

"Storm Cooper. Yeah." But the Internet connection was slow. I made myself look away from the little spinning blue wheel of death. I read a study that said watching those things increases your risk of heart attack. Of all the ways to go, that had to be a top-five contender for the stupidest. Right behind a roller coaster accident and autoerotic . . . anything. When I looked down at the screen, I found a bunch of results. Storm Cooper was on Facebook, LinkedIn, Snapchat . . . everywhere. "He's a stuntman—"

"The name sure fits."

"And he's definitely single. He's not bad looking. I get what Paige saw in him." I read his description on IMDb, an entertainment-industry website. "Five foot nine, brown hair, and he looks buffed out. Kind of reminds me of one of those gladiators in a Spartacus flick." I pushed the link for his phone number and listened to the line ring. It went to voice mail. I left a message saying I needed to talk to him about Paige and gave him my number.

"Kind of weird that we haven't heard anything about him," Alex said. "It seems like he's known Paige for a while, but he's not on the DA's witness list, and he didn't give a statement to the police. At least not that I saw."

I shook my head. "He definitely didn't." I called Michelle and told her to put Storm Cooper's call through to my cell the minute it came in.

She'd sounded fine when I'd talked to her on the phone, but when we walked into the office, Michelle gave us an ominous look.

Oh hell no. *Another* dead woman in Dale's past? I didn't want to ask. I stared at her.

"You're not going to like this. I know I sure don't. I just got a call from your burglar boyfriend, Scott Henderson. He's not going to give you the phone until you substitute in on his case."

Relief that it wasn't another dead body mixed with irritation. "Wait a minute, let me get this straight: That little douche nozzle doesn't trust *me?*"

Michelle had a sour look. "I'd tell him to go piss up a rope, but I assume you still want to find out what's on that phone?"

"I do." I didn't like getting played like this. But it was just a low-level dope case. I should be able to get rid of it in one appearance. "Tell him I want proof—"

"He said he'd send by a 'compatriot' to show it to us. But we'd better not 'try anything' because his buddy wouldn't be alone."

Now I was good and pissed. "You have got to be kidding me. That putz . . . tell him if his 'compatriot' tries to pull anything, I'll tell the cops he did the burglary."

Alex had a worried look. "What about the privilege?"

"There's no privilege if he threatens me."

Alex frowned. "It didn't exactly sound like he—"

"It will when I talk to the police. Michelle, I assume he's going to call back?"

"Any minute. I spoke to him right after you called from the road, so he knows you're due back around now."

"I'm not talking to him until I see that phone. But get his case number and all the info. If someone shows up with the phone, try and get me on calendar tomorrow so I can substitute in and get rid of the case."

"Got it. Oh, and your cop buddy Hank said she'd be coming by."

"Great." I'd added Scott Henderson's rap sheet to the other information I'd asked her to get. Now was the perfect time to find out whether all this hassle over the phone was even remotely worth it.

Michelle gestured to the stack of juror questionnaires on her desk. "And I'm about done with those." She blew out a breath. "I don't know how it happened, but more than half your panel is under the age of thirty-five. A solid third are in their twenties."

"How bad are they?"

Michelle shook her head. "They don't trust cops, they think the system is 'rigged,' and they're not big fans of lawyers. The only good news is that they don't seem to like prosecutors, either."

"So we'd probably get along great at a party, but they'll tank me in trial."

Michelle nodded. "Exactly."

Perfect. "Alex, let me know what you think when you get done."

"I've only got about twenty more to go. I'll be done by tonight." Alex turned to go back to his office, then paused. "Hey, do you want me to call my uncle and get us backup for when Scott's guys show up?"

"Your uncle?"

"He's a bail bondsman. He's got muscle that helps him out when he needs it."

"I have a feeling Scott's pretty lightweight, and he needs us right now. So I think we're good. But thanks. I'll remember that."

And I meant it. Ever since Lane Ockman had managed to penetrate our airtight security system—AKA, the intercom—I'd been thinking that moving into better digs might be more necessity than luxury. And I'd hoped this damn case would generate the income to let us do that. But so far, all it'd generated were death threats, hate mail, and pissed-off drug dealers.

Alex hovered in my doorway. "Uh, Sam?" I looked up. "That cell phone. Aren't we supposed to turn that over to the judge . . . or the cops? It's physical evidence. The book says—"

"That we're not allowed to hang on to physical evidence. Yeah. So what? How're they going to find out? You think Scott's going to fink on us?"

"No, but if we get caught—"

I waved him off. "We won't. Chill out."

Alex gave me a worried look, but he went back to his office.

I might have to burn that damn book of his. Turn over that cell phone. As if. I went back to work and plowed through the rest of the questionnaires. Michelle was right. Our jury pool was young, skeptical, and unsympathetic. The only question was who they'd hate more: Zack's cops—or mine.

I'd just finished the last depressing questionnaire when Hank showed up.

We sat down in my office. "How's Naille doing? Has he started school?"

"Started it and already kicking ass. One of his teachers asked him to do a special project."

"I'm not surprised. He's an amazing talent."

"How about you?" She eyed the stack of questionnaires on my desk. "How's it look?"

"Like they'll be ready to vote before Zack calls his first witness."

"Well, that sucks." Hank pulled a file out of her purse. "I checked out Ignacio Silva." Her expression said I wasn't going to like this. "When he was on patrol, he had a rep for being baton happy. He's got some use-of-force complaints in his file—"

"You didn't pull his file, did you?" That might get back to Zack and tip him off to check out Ignacio.

"Give me some credit."

"Sorry. Are any of the complaints recent?"

"The latest one was two years ago, and there were a couple more before that. I talked to Jay Gerber about him. Jay was my firearms trainer in the academy, and I know he's a straight-up guy. He worked in West LA with Ignacio for about a year. Said he didn't care for Ignacio's style, but he didn't give me any specifics."

"Damn. Ignacio's my alibi witness—"

"For the double?"

"No, for the murder of the hooker. You're sure this is solid information?"

"As solid as rumors and opinions can be. Though Jay's usually pretty reliable."

It didn't mean Ignacio was lying. But it might mean there were more problems in his past than Hank could find just by snooping around. I'd have to think long and hard about whether I wanted to use him. "Were you able to get any reports on Marc Palmer?"

Hank tapped the file folder. "They're all in there. I didn't read it line for line, but I saw that the coroner called it an 'inconclusive.' He was a friend of Paige's?" I nodded. "I don't know what you'll do with it, but it is interesting."

I didn't know what I'd do with it, either. So far, it looked like nothing. "What about Scott Henderson?"

Hank raised an eyebrow. "How'd you wind up with this guy? He looks like public-defender material to me."

"He might be doing me a favor. I need to make sure the favor is worth my time."

Hank paused for a beat, but when I didn't elaborate, she continued. "He's got two DUIs, one receiving stolen property that wound up getting dismissed for insufficient evidence, and one possession for sale of weed that got busted down to straight possession."

"Was he on probation when he got that last bust?" If he was, he'd probably do time on the probation violation no matter what kind of deal I made.

Hank pulled out the rap sheet and studied it. "No. Matter of fact, he completed probation a year ago." She looked up. "Not bad."

Scott's rendition of his criminal history had been semi-accurate. Shocking.

Hank's phone rang. She looked at the screen. "Sorry, got to take this."

I gestured for her to go ahead and went out to the anteroom to give her privacy. She came out a minute later. "I've got to go."

"Thank you, Hank. I really appreciate it."

"My pleasure." Hank headed for the door, then paused. "Hey, I've been meaning to ask. That check I wrote for Naille's defense . . . it hasn't cleared yet. You lose it or something?"

I shrugged. "Might've accidentally shredded it."

Hank shook her head, then gave me a smile. "Thanks."

I waved her off. She left and I got back to work. At six thirty, the intercom buzzed, and a voice that sounded like a high school girl's said, "Scott sent me."

I got my gun and hurried out to Michelle. I whispered, "I'll be right inside my office. Pick up your phone and dial *9-1*. If anything looks funny, hit the other *1* and leave the line open. I'll come out and hold them off."

Michelle nodded. I stood against the wall in my office and held my gun next to my chest with both hands. I heard her hit the buzzer. The door opened. A skinny, long-haired boy who looked about seventeen and a girl who looked to be maybe twenty walked in. They both bore a stunning resemblance to Scott. I checked their hands for weapons.

I didn't see any, but the girl had her right hand in the pocket of her hoodie.

I came out with my gun behind my back just as Alex came out of his office. The two backed up and gave us wary looks. The boy spoke first. "Scott said to just show you the phone. He said you couldn't have it yet."

I looked at the girl's right hand and lowered the gun to my side. "Let's see that hand. Slowly."

Her eyes got as wide as silver dollars when she saw my gun. She slowly pulled out her hand. Which was holding the cell phone. Alex and I moved forward. She took a step back. "D-don't try anything."

I rolled my eyes. "We're not trying anything. How can we tell if that's the phone if you don't let us see it?"

It was a flip phone. She opened it, punched a couple of keys, and held it up so we could see the screen. It showed Chloe and Paige, their arms around each other, in glittery party hats that said HAPPY NEW YEAR! The girl lowered the phone, tapped another key, and held it up again. It showed Chloe lying on the couch, a script in her lap, her palm held out at the camera in a "Stop" sign. I recognized the couch as the one that'd been in their apartment.

Screw these bullshit games. I should just take the damn thing. I had a gun and they didn't. I took a step toward them, but the girl dropped the phone into her pocket, backed up to the door, and opened it. She was about to bolt. I couldn't shoot her, and I didn't want to get caught chasing her down the hall trying to tackle her. "Fine. But tell your brother if that phone isn't on my desk the minute I substitute in, I'll dump his case and tell the DA he did the burglary."

They nodded and ran out the door. I noticed they didn't deny being Scott's siblings. I went back to my office and put my gun away.

Alex followed me into my office. "That was a flip phone."

"Yeah. I would've thought she'd have something newer."

"Not if it's a burner."

I stared at Alex. A burner is what you get when you want privacy, when you don't want cell-phone records that show who owns the phone. You know, in case someone's wife decides to check his cell-phone bill.

FORTY-FIVE

It took Michelle two days to get Scott's case on calendar. I made sure to be in court early so I could work out a deal with the DA. I was anxious to get this over with. Dale's trial was starting tomorrow, and I wanted to spend the day getting ready.

But the courtroom was packed and Walt Carbahal, the senior prosecutor, had a line of lawyers waiting to talk to him. I sat down in the jury box and pulled out the police reports on Scott's case. There wasn't much to barter with. The traffic stop looked clean, the K-9 search was okay, and the cop read Scott his rights. The only thing I had in my favor was that a jury might think it was a waste of their time.

A young guy with military-short hair, wearing a navy-blue suit that looked like it'd been his big brother's, called out, "*People v. Scott Henderson.*"

I held up my hand. "Over here."

He came over in quick, officious strides, a case file under his arm. "I'm Paul Wesson. I'll be handling this case for the prosecution. I understand you're substituting in?"

Oh God, help me. A newbie. I should've said no and gotten the hell out of there. But I didn't. I stupidly ignored my better instincts and introduced myself. "Shall we talk dispo? It's only five grams and he doesn't have a bad rec—"

"I'm not interested in making any deals. Mr. Henderson has already had the benefit of too many deals. Unless he wants to plead to the sheet, we'll have to set this case for trial."

I stared at him. "Seriously? Are you an intern or something?"

Paul reddened. "No. I'm a deputy district attorney, Grade One."

Even worse. A baby DA who wanted to prove how tough he was. "Look, Paul. I know you want to make a good impression. Good for you. But no one's going to thank you for taking up court time on a piddly case like this."

He straightened his tie. "I don't consider a felony quantity of cocaine to be a piddly case. That's how the drug trade proliferates, by us not taking these cases seriously enough—"

"Then you're going to have a long wait on your hands, because I'm starting trial on the Pearson case tomorrow."

Paul started to say something, but the judge called for the bailiff to bring out the custodies. After a case is sent out to a trial court, the only place to put inmates is in the jury box. So I got up and moved out to join the throng on the defense side of the courtroom.

Scott smiled when he saw me, and I went over to give him the bad news. "We got stuck with a newbie DA who's hot to go to trial."

He swallowed hard. "He won't give me a deal? He has to! I can't do time! I'll die in there!"

I was skeptical. "What, are you claustrophobic or something? 'Cause you're certainly not big-time enough to have that kind of enemy."

Scott looked frantic. "I can't be in there—"

The judge called out, "*People v. Scott Henderson.* I understand Mr. Henderson has retained private counsel?"

I moved back to counsel table thinking I could still bail on this case. But then I'd never know what was on that damn phone. "Yes, Your Honor. Samantha Brinkman appearing for Scott Henderson."

Paul Wesson stood up. "Your Honor, I oppose this substitution. Ms. Brinkman just told me she won't be able to take this case to trial for months. She's on the Pearson case and—"

The judge gave him a weary look. "Yes, Mr. Wesson. We all know what case she's on. Don't worry, I strongly suspect we'll find something else to do in the meantime." The judge gave me an imploring look. "Can't we dispo this case? It's five grams of cocaine."

"I tried, Your Honor. But Mr. Wesson seems adamant about taking this case to trial." Out of the corner of my eye, I noticed Walt watching us. When I glanced at him, I saw he had a mischievous grin. The evil douche had deliberately sicced his gonzo geek on me.

The judge threw a glance at Walt and shook his head. "Ms. Brinkman, give us a time estimate on the Pearson case. A month? Two months? A year?"

"I think three months should do it. So, June twentieth?" The clerk gave the thumbs up, and the judge okayed it. "And I'm asking that my client be released on his own recognizance. He's got ties to the community, no history of violent crime—"

Wesson jumped to his feet. "I object! He's a drug dealer; that's a major danger to the community, and—"

The judge looked over his glasses at the prosecutor. "Mr. Wesson, we don't even have enough beds to house people charged with murder. I think society will manage to survive if I release a low-rent drug dealer." The judge looked at me. "I'm assuming he can't make bail." I shook my head. The judge banged his gavel. "Defendant will be released on his own recognizance. Next case."

Paul Wesson fumed and marched out of court. I went over to Walt, who was doing a bad job of suppressing a grin. "I'm so going to make you pay for this."

"Come on, it's kind of funny."

"Yeah, and I'm laughing. Way deep down inside. Call off your boy wonder, Walt. I want straight possession for time served."

"Sorry, Brinkman. No can do. The boss says it's a 'must go.'" He chuckled.

I glared at him and headed for the lockup. But one of us was happy. Scott was beaming. "Thanks for getting me out, Ms. Brinkman. You're saving my life."

"That phone's in my office within the hour. Got it?"

"Absolutely. I'll make the call as soon as I get back to Bauchet Street. You're the best, man. I mean it."

I remembered a question I'd had. I glanced around to make sure no one was listening and spoke in a low voice. "What made you choose Paige's apartment?"

Scott stared at me for a moment, then licked his lips. "I . . . uh, I knew Chloe lived there and I figured she'd have good shit, 'cause she was, like, famous." He snorted back some nasty-sounding phlegm. I leaned away.

The bailiff called out, "Wrap it up; we're moving 'em out."

I talked fast. "Listen, I'll be setting pretrial dates so I can keep pressuring the DA to give you a deal. You'd better show up. I mean it; don't be messing around. Be there and be on time. That guy wants your head on a spike. If you play it smart, I may be able to talk him down." Truthfully, I didn't like my chances. I just wanted to make sure Scott had plenty of incentive to behave.

"You got it." Scott gave another of his honking snorts.

It made me wince. "That's gotta hurt. You ever talk to a doctor about that?"

"About what?"

"Never mind."

* * * *

I headed back to the office and told Michelle about my ordeal. "If Walt doesn't make that little doofus back off, I might have to cut him."

"I'll hold him down for you." She shook her head. "That phone better be worth it."

I pictured Paul Wesson's fierce glare. "I don't know how it could be."

I went back to work, going over my questions for the jury and my opening statement. I kept looking at the clock, wondering where Scott's minions were. When they still hadn't shown up at six o'clock, I stomped out and fumed to Michelle. "He's got to be home by now. Maybe I should go out there and remind him that I can get off his case as fast as I got on it."

"I wouldn't get all twisted up about it yet. Scott's a flake, and now that he's out of jail, he's in no hurry."

"Guess getting him out on OR wasn't my smartest move."

"Probably not. But he still needs you. He'll come through. Go home, have a drink, get some rest."

I started to head back into my office to take her advice, then paused. I hadn't told her or Alex about my last visit with Dale and how he'd gone ballistic. But if I did, I'd have to explain what'd caused it, and that would mean telling them about Sebastian Cromer. I'd never told anyone about him before Dale. Not even Michelle.

Back when we were kids and I was in the middle of the nightmare, I'd told her things were bad and that I hated Sebastian, but I was ashamed, so I'd never come right out and said what was happening. I'd blamed myself, figured it had to be my fault—that there was something wrong with me. And Celeste only reinforced that belief. I eventually got over that, but I never wanted to even think about it, let alone talk about it. So I'd never told Michelle the whole story.

For some reason, I wanted to now. "You have plans tonight?"

"Big ones. Wash my hair, rewatch some *Mad Men* episodes, do laundry. My life is very full."

"Mind if I tell you something? I mean ancient history, childhood stuff."

She gave me a curious look and sat down in front of my desk. "What's up?"

"Remember when we were in eighth grade and I was always in trouble?"

"How could I forget? You made me hide your stash of Jack Daniel's in my locker for a week. I was so paranoid I couldn't sleep the entire time."

"You drank some of it."

She laughed. "Hey, I needed to calm down."

"I guess you were entitled." I smiled briefly. "Anyway, I thought I should tell you why I was such a . . . mess." I told her about Sebastian, about my mother, about all of it. When I finished, Michelle had tears in her eyes.

"I knew something was going on at home, but jeez, Sam." She shook her head. "I had no idea it was that bad." Michelle sighed. "Though, now that I think back on it, it all fits. Why didn't you tell me? My folks would've taken you in."

"Celeste would never have let me do that. It'd make her look bad."

Michelle had a disgusted look. "You're right. It's always all about her. You know, I used to get the feeling she was jealous of you."

"What? Why?"

"It was just a feeling I got whenever she was around. And now I know I was right—and I know why. *She* didn't snag Sebastian. *You* did. He didn't want her. He wanted you. With her ego, I bet that really chapped her ass."

"That's so gross I don't even know what to say."

"Anyway, I don't think she's jealous anymore. She's gotten a little more human—or at least better at imitating one—since she married Jack."

"Yeah, he's a good guy." Which was just a fluke. Celeste had gone looking for money and accidentally fell on a guy who happened to be decent. "Anyway, I told Dale about it."

Michelle's eyes got wide.

"He lost it completely." I told her about his meltdown.

She sank down in her chair and shook her head, her expression sad. "It's so strange. He's the perfect dad in so many ways. And if he'd been around, he would've shut Sebastian down in a heartbeat. But then there's this other side."

I nodded. "Jekyll and Hyde was a true story, after all."

FORTY-SIX

We packed up and I went home. I made myself go to bed at eleven, but I was so keyed up I didn't manage to fall asleep until one a.m. Good news: I didn't have the dream. Bad news: I only got about five hours of sleep.

But I still woke up wired. I always do when I'm in trial. It doesn't matter how late I stay up or how much I drink. I pop out of bed like someone zapped me with a Taser.

I tanked up on coffee anyway. The adrenaline wouldn't last all day, and I needed to be sharp. I was about to start the hardest part of the case: picking the jury. It's an old saying that you win or lose your case during jury selection. But for a change, that old saying is absolutely true. And I think of it as a game of trying to catch the liars. Not necessarily deliberate liars. Most people who say they won't hold it against your client for being a gangbanger or a drug addict—or a cop—really mean it. They're wrong, but they're not lying.

Others really are just flat-out lying. Either because they want to get off the jury or because they want to get on.

In a case like this one, there'd be a lot more of the latter. Some because they hope to sell their story later; others because they want a front-row seat to the biggest show in town.

Don't get me wrong, the fact that some people want to be on a jury doesn't necessarily mean they're bad news. But I have to dig a little harder to figure out how they really feel about my client, because they're more likely to lie about it.

I put on my only good suit, which was starting to show signs of serious wear and tear around the seat and elbows. But it was my good-luck charm, my confidence armor. I was just finishing my usual bowl of oatmeal when Xander called to tell me he was downstairs. A jolt of adrenaline made my stomach lurch. I dumped out the bowl, grabbed my briefcase, and headed out, heart pounding, brain running two hundred miles an hour. This was it.

I slid into the backseat.

Xander smiled into the rearview mirror as he pulled away. "Big day! You nervous? I sure would be."

"Yeah, I am."

I always had first-day-of-trial jitters. But they'd be gone once we got down to business.

My cell phone buzzed in my purse. I pulled it out and saw that the caller ID said BLOCKED. I knew who that was. I let it go to voice mail. When I checked the message, I found out I was right. It was Celeste. I clicked off and deleted the message the moment I heard her say, "Samantha." I didn't need this right now—or ever. I could tell by her tone that this message would be like all the rest. This was the fourth time she'd called me since I told her not to call me anymore, and her messages were always the same: she ordered me to call her back "immediately," said I was a "thoughtless ingrate" who didn't appreciate all she'd "sacrificed" for me, and accused me of being a "disappointment and a spiteful, terrible daughter."

Why she thought messages like that would persuade me to call her left me completely befuddled. "Why on earth does she think that will work?" I asked Michelle.

"Because it always has. You've been putting up with that kind of behavior all your life. Do you honestly expect her to change? If you're waiting to hear her say she's sorry—for anything—you're living in some alternate universe. And you need to stop listening to those messages. The only thing you'll get from them is more proof that you should've done this long ago. Do you really need it?"

No. I didn't. And I really needed to stop hoping she'd say something that even remotely showed she gave a damn about me. So I stopped listening and just deleted her messages.

The courthouse steps were more packed than ever. The same posters were there, demanding justice for the victims and saying unkind things about Dale—like **PEARSON'S A RAPIST, KILLER!** and **LOCK UP THE SERIAL-KILLER COP!** But this time I noticed two **JUSTICE FOR DALE!** posters that sported a pretty decent-looking photo of him. That was probably as good an omen as I could hope for, all things considered.

This time, I wasn't taking any chances. I didn't get out of the car until the deputies were at my door. And when I did, I made myself stand up straight. A few in the crowd closest to the sidewalk noticed me and shouted out, "It's the lawyer for the murderer!" They started to boo and yell. "You're defending a serial killer!" and "You're a scumbag!"

I guess being famous wasn't going to cut it anymore. It had never been this ugly. A chant went up: "Guilty! Guilty! Guilty!"

So much for presumed innocent. I wondered how much of this my jurors had seen.

It took ten minutes to get an elevator, and when I finally made it to Department 106, I saw that every seat was filled. The benches on the prosecution side of the gallery were filled with Chloe's and Paige's family, friends, and other supporters (*that is*, actors hoping for exposure) and some press. But the defense side was all reporters. That's because there was a lot more room. Dale's family wouldn't be coming, and most of his friends were working. But I spotted Detective Rick Saunders and waved to him.

Zack was already set up at his side of counsel table. I headed to my side and dropped my briefcase on my chair, intending to go into lockup to see Dale. But the bailiff stopped me, saying the judge would be out any second.

In fact, the very next second, as it turned out. Tall, with slicked-back gray hair and an aquiline nose, he moved to the bench with a long, firm stride. The moment he sat down, he ordered the courtroom cleared. "Let's make room for the jurors." No "Good morning, counsel," or "Anything you'd like to take up?"

But it was exactly what I'd heard about him. Judge Traynor—also known as the Freight Train—didn't believe in wasting time. Los Angeles had been forced to close courts down for at least one day a week because of budget shortfalls. Traynor hated it—openly. He'd written a few op-ed pieces calling for an end to this "absurdly poor set of priorities."

While everyone filed out, a bailiff brought Dale out of lockup. He was dressed in a good navy-blue suit, but his eyes were red, and his face looked puffy. When he sat down, I leaned toward him and whispered, "Are you okay? Did those guards bounce you around?"

His eyes were full of apology. "No. No more than they had to. I'm so sorry, Samantha. I—"

"Not now. I just wanted to make sure—"

Dale shook his head. "I just got no sleep is all. They get us up at three a.m. to make the court bus, and I'm surrounded by snorers. It's like a motorboat convention." He smiled. "Got any makeup?"

"Sure. A little blush and some mascara and you'll be good to go."

The courtroom had emptied quickly; the prospective jurors were coming in.

Dale looked over his shoulder at them. "What did you think of their questionnaires?"

There was no point trying to hide it from him now. "We've got a really young bunch."

"That can't be good for me."

"But it might be just as bad for the other side." And that was about as optimistic a statement as I could make.

Michelle and Alex came in and joined me at counsel table. I always like to have as many eyes as possible during voir dire. While I'm talking to one juror, they can be watching the rest of the group to see how they're reacting to me. I passed out legal pads for everyone—including Dale—to write on.

Judge Traynor did most of the questioning and gave Zack and me just fifteen minutes each. Some lawyers bitch about getting so little time. I don't mind. Especially when you have questionnaires, it only takes a few minutes to figure out whether a juror is good or bad for you. After that point, you're just wasting time second-guessing your gut instinct.

Zack seemed to have the same theory. He took only ten minutes to question the jury, and I did the same. I'd hoped to get a quick recess to talk to Michelle and Alex before we started kicking jurors, but no such luck. That was okay for now. I had a few I was absolutely sure of. The young woman in the ponytail who'd graduated from California State University at Northridge had seemed okay. Until she said her ex-boyfriend was a cop and she'd almost taken out a restraining order on him. A young black man had sounded good. Until he admitted that he thought Dale looked guilty. I appreciated the honesty, but still . . .

I'd gone through all my must-gos and was heading into my list of not-sures before Traynor finally gave us a break. As the jurors started to leave, Alex whispered to me. "That truck driver guy in the number-one seat should be okay for you."

I glanced at the man. He had shoulder-length hair and a pierced nose. "You sure?"

"Truck drivers are usually good for law enforcement, according to the book—"

"Wait a minute. That PI wrote about jury selection? You've got to be kidding me—"

"No. It's a different book. It's by a lawyer: *How to Influence Juries and Win Your Case—*"

"Written by one of the dumbest losers in the business. The truck driver's history."

Michelle nodded toward a young woman who'd just stepped out of the jury box. "What about the Barbie doll with all the hair extensions?" They were blonde and down to her waist.

I thought she was pretty good. "She seems like the open-minded type. I like her."

Dale looked worried. "She's awfully young."

I nodded. "They all are. Are you okay with her otherwise?"

"Yeah, I guess."

By my count, six had to go. Three could stay. The rest . . . I'd see who we got after the six I planned to toss. But so far, not one—and I mean not a single *one* of those jurors—remembered having a positive experience with a cop.

We worked well into the lunch hour—which Judge Traynor decided should be a lunch *half* hour—and by three o'clock, we had our jury. Six women, six men, not one above the age of forty-five. Just shoot me now.

Judge Traynor had the clerk swear them in. We picked four alternates, the judge gave introductory jury instructions, and then he announced that we'd do opening statements after a fifteen-minute break.

Zack and I exchanged "Huh?" looks across the courtroom. Any other judge would've sent the jury home and let us do openings tomorrow.

Not the speeding bullet that was Judge Traynor.

The prosecution goes first, which would give me a chance to see how the jury responded to Zack. The minute he stood up, three of the women gave him hundred-watt smiles—probably picturing him in boxers. I mentally kicked myself for leaving them on.

The courtroom was set up with a screen on the wall at the end of the jury box for PowerPoint or videos. Zack started by telling the jury about how Chloe met Dale when he responded to the burglary call, about the strains in their relationship that started to surface almost immediately, and then moved on to the night of the murders. He started with the witnesses who heard Chloe and Dale fighting. "One of them heard Chloe say she was breaking up with him. And earlier that night, Chloe told her sister that's what she was going to do. That's motive, folks. One of the most common motives there is."

Zack moved on to the crime-scene video. The big screen made it even more dramatic. He paused on the ugly frame showing Chloe's lifeless body.

"Dale Pearson punched her in the face, knocked her to the floor, and then he stabbed her to death—buried that knife up to the hilt, straight into her chest, *four* times. I know the defense is going to say a burglar did this. But, ladies and gentlemen, this is *not* what a surprised burglar does. This is what an angry lover does."

Zack let the image linger on the screen as long as he could, then moved on to the frame showing Paige's body. Though she was facedown, the blood trail that showed how she'd tried to crawl away from her killer was even more gruesome.

"Paige wasn't supposed to be home. But after Pearson stabbed Chloe to death, she became a witness who couldn't be allowed to live. Paige was a classic example of collateral damage. The evidence will show that Dale Pearson came up behind her, stabbed her in the back, then jabbed the knife into her throat. Now, he knew the women had just had a burglary, since he'd been the cop who handled the call. So he decided to make this look like the work of the burglar, and he began to ransack the room. But then he saw Paige move. She wasn't dead and she was trying to crawl away. He couldn't have that. He went back and cut her throat . . . and finished the job. It was a cruel, brutal way to kill, and a torturous way for Paige to die."

Then Zack went through the physical evidence—the DNA, the hairs and fibers, and the fingerprints. He wrapped up with the usual prosecutorial flourish. "In sum, ladies and gentlemen, the evidence will prove overwhelmingly, well beyond a reasonable doubt, that Dale Pearson is guilty of these heinous murders. And the next time I talk to you, I'll be asking you to do what the evidence demands. Convict Dale Pearson as charged of the murders of Chloe Monahan and Paige Avner."

It wasn't a good opening. It was a great one. If I'd been on the jury, I knew what my vote would be. And I could see that I wasn't alone. The jury stared at him, their expressions rapt. A few had even nodded. They were with him all the way.

As a general rule, I don't give an opening statement. I like to keep my options open. But I had to do it now. I couldn't let the jury go home tonight without giving them a reason to question Zack's story. I didn't have much. But I had to make the most of it.

I walked over to the podium and looked at each of the jurors as I spoke. "I don't usually give an opening statement. That's because the defense doesn't have to prove anything." I paused and made eye contact with each one of the jurors to hammer that point home. "The prosecutor did a great job of making his case look airtight. But it's not. In fact, it's riddled with holes. The truth is, the case against Dale Pearson is based on assumptions. But as you all know, verdicts have to be based on *evidence*, not assumptions."

I pointed out the fact that since Dale had been dating Chloe, his prints were bound to be all over that apartment. And of course his DNA was under her nails, on her skin. They were a couple and they were fighting. Dale wasn't proud of that, but he'd never denied it.

"And the prosecutor somehow forgot to mention the fact that they found fingerprints and hairs in the apartment that couldn't have come from Dale. But that's key evidence. It shows someone else was there. And when all the evidence is in, you'll see that this person—not Dale—was the one who committed these murders."

I moved on to hammer the point about motive that'd been so popular on the Internet. "Now here's one of the assumptions the prosecutor made. He wants you to *assume* that a veteran detective suddenly flipped out and killed two women just because a woman he'd been seeing for only two months wanted to break up with him.

"But if a breakup was so devastating to Dale Pearson, then how come he has two ex-wives who're alive and well? The prosecution assumed that had to be his motive, but the assumption doesn't make sense. Not only is it illogical, I'm going to prove it's not true. The truth is, Dale knew their relationship was over, and he was more than good with it. He was ready to move on."

I'd have to put Dale on the stand to prove that—something I never like to do. But I'd known from the start I'd have to do it in this case. No juror would forgive a cop who was afraid to take the stand.

"Here's the next assumption the prosecutor wants you to make. He said a burglar couldn't have done this. But how does he know that? He doesn't know all the burglars in Los Angeles. Just because a criminal breaks in to steal, that doesn't mean he won't kill, too. It's not like he's some kind of specialist."

I got a few small smiles out of that one.

"We've all heard of cases where burglars kill homeowners who walk in on them. And there's nothing about this crime scene that shows the killer wasn't a burglar. Again, the prosecutor wants you to just *assume* that a burglar didn't do it. Next assumption: that Paige was 'collateral damage.' In fact, she wasn't. I'm going to prove to you that she was the target. And Dale had no motive whatsoever to kill Paige. No one, not even the prosecutor, thinks Dale had a reason to kill her."

I stepped closer to the jury box for my final salvo. "So the evidence will *not* show that Dale Pearson is guilty. What the evidence will show is that the People's case has assumptions where there should be evidence, gaps where there should be proof, and illogic where there should be reason. So the next time *I* talk to you, I'll be telling you that the prosecution has failed to carry its burden. I'll be telling you that the evidence has shown Dale Pearson is *not* guilty. And I'll be asking you to do the right thing and acquit him."

I looked at each of the jurors. There were a few skeptical faces, but a few seemed intrigued.

I could see I wouldn't be able to convince all of them. But I never thought I'd be able to pull off an acquittal. Not with this evidence. No, the only real question was, did I have my holdout? I only needed one. As I scanned their faces, I thought I spotted two or three possibles.

I went back to my seat. Only time would tell.

FORTY-SEVEN

We recessed for the day, and I stood as the jurors left the courtroom. It's meant to look like a sign of respect, but it's mainly an excuse to watch them. When they were gone, I huddled with my team at counsel table.

Dale had a proud smile on his face. "After that prosecutor's opening, I didn't know what you were going to say. But you really brought it back." He glanced around the courtroom, then whispered, "But how are you going to prove Paige was the target?"

An excellent question. Alex and Michelle looked at me expectantly. "I don't have all the answers yet." Or any, actually. "But I will. Right now, I need to get going."

I had to get out and talk to the press, give them a quietly-confident-but-not-arrogant statement. I patted him on the arm. "I'll get in earlier tomorrow so we can talk. Try to get some rest."

He nodded. "You, too."

I stood up. "Guys, want a ride to your cars?"

Michelle made a face. "And climb through that mob out there with you? No, thanks."

"That's no mob—those are my peeps, my adoring public—"

"Many of whom, according to Twitter, think you're a sleaz—"

"I'll win them over."

Michelle rolled her eyes.

The bailiff took Dale back into lockup, and I herded Alex and Michelle away from the spectators still lingering in the gallery. "Any word on our burglar boy and the phone?"

Michelle shook her head. "I left him a message telling him to call and tell me when he planned to come by. Nothing."

I looked at Alex, but he shook his head, too. "How about if I go to his house? If he doesn't pony up with the phone, I'll just take it."

And he could. Alex was slim, but he was almost six feet of lean muscle. Still, I didn't like the idea of him getting into it with Scott. "The jerk might not be alone, and what if he has a gun? Just tell him I'll walk away from his case."

Alex nodded.

I packed up and we walked out to the hallway. A small knot of reporters was near the elevators. I spotted Trevor, Edie, Brittany, and Kendall in the crowd. Zack had probably just finished giving his quietly-confident-but-not-arrogant statement.

I smiled at the crowd as I walked Michelle and Alex to the elevators. I turned to Alex. "I'll be going straight back to the office, so if anything breaks, you can reach me there."

Their elevator arrived. As they stepped inside, a voice behind me said, "Keeping long hours now, huh?"

I turned and saw it was Trevor. I sighed. "I'll probably be pulling all-nighters for the duration now."

When I got outside, there was a batch of reporters with cameras, so I made sure to keep a pleasant smile on my face that I hoped exuded confidence. Edie was setting up on the front steps. My town car was at the curb right behind her. If I was going to squeeze her for a photo op with her husband, now was the time. And with a jury pool barely old enough to vote, I needed the help more than ever. I walked over and she looked up and smiled. "Hey, Sam. Got a statement for me? Or better yet, a new lead?"

"I might in the next day or so." If not, I'd make something up. "Does your husband want to sit in on the trial?"

She paused, then shrugged. "Maybe. Can you get him in?"

Seats were prized commodities. Members of the public had lined up for passes at six this morning. "I think so. And I'd be glad to chat with him."

Edie gave me a knowing smile. "And maybe take a photo together? Yeah, I saw a lot of young faces in that jury pool."

A photo with the man trying to get cheaper tuition for those young faces couldn't hurt. "The free publicity wouldn't be bad for him, either. Kind of a win-win, don't you think?"

Edie gave a little laugh. "I'll see what he says."

I gave her a quick statement and headed for the town car. I wanted to relax, maybe even take a quick nap, but I couldn't stop the wheels from turning. I mentally reviewed my opening statement. I'd done my best to stitch together what little fragments of evidence I had into a quilt that looked like reasonable doubt—but I knew it wouldn't hold up. If something didn't break my way soon, I'd be standing next to Dale listening to the judge put him away for life.

Michelle was at the office when I got back. Alex had dropped her off and headed out to Scott's place—a small duplex on the east side of Hollywood. Zack told me he was going to start with the neighbors tomorrow. Janet and Nikki were two-hundred-pound boulders; they couldn't be pushed around. All I could do was use them to point out possibilities, like: Isn't it possible Dale was just looking for the burglar when he was driving around the neighborhood? And isn't it possible someone else came to the apartment that night?

And that got me thinking about my last conversation with Scott. I knew he'd been lying when he told me why he'd chosen to burglarize Chloe's apartment. I thought I'd figured out the truth. I stood up and stretched, then saw that it was almost ten o'clock—and heard Michelle still typing at her desk.

I walked out and put my hands on my hips. "Michy, what are you doing here?"

She stopped and stared at me. "Getting a facial. What does it look like I'm doing?"

"No word from Alex?" She shook her head. "Remember I was wondering why Scott chose Chloe's apartment to break into?"

"Yeah, what'd he tell you?"

"That he chose her apartment because he knew she was famous and figured she'd have good stuff. I knew he was lying at the time, but I let it go. Then it occurred to me. He doesn't live that far from their apartment. He's a dealer, and so is Chas Gorman—the guy who lives a few doors down from Chloe and Paige. It's just a hunch, and it might be a coincidence. Maybe Chas and Scott don't know each other. But if they did, it'd explain how Scott happened to target the girls' apartment."

"Makes more sense than Scott's story, that's for sure." Michelle's brow furrowed. "You think Chas told him to rip them off?"

"No, he liked the girls. And he really liked Paige. I think it was all Scott's idea. He either saw Chloe at the building, or maybe Chas told him she lived there."

Alex finally came back. "I knocked, I waited, I knocked again and waited some more. No answer."

Damn it. "Does it look like he split?"

"I couldn't tell. It felt empty, though."

I was good and pissed. "That friggin' asshole."

Alex held up a hand. "Before we make any moves, let me have another day or so."

"I'll give you two days. If we don't have that phone by then, I'm getting off the case. But I do have an idea of where you might want to look for him." I told him about my Chas Gorman theory.

Alex smiled. "My stoner buddy. I miss him. And I bet you're right." He shook his head. "Small world. Want me to go out and see him now?"

"It's after ten. Take the rest of the night off. Tomorrow's soon enough."

The truth was, tomorrow was soon enough because it was probably already too late.

FORTY-EIGHT

I'd thought—*hoped* was a better word, I guess—that I wouldn't have the nightmare. I was bone tired and the past two nights had been peaceful. But it came back with a vengeance. This time when his hands clamped around my arms, I felt a hot laser beam drilling into my stomach. When I woke up—at five a.m.—I was clutching my belly. I didn't even want to try for any more sleep and give that dream a chance to come back.

But on the upside, it gave me time to pound a lot of coffee, so I was fully operational with all systems go by the time Xander picked me up at seven thirty. Nikki—the Pussycat Doll of the neighboring building (I could just picture her singing, 'Don't cha wish your girlfriend was hot like me? Don't cha wish your girlfriend was a freak like me?')—and Janet Rader were scheduled for the morning session. I ran into them just outside the snack bar across the hall from the courtroom.

Nikki was ready for her close-up—false eyelashes, plunging neckline, and all. This was her chance for major-league camera time, and she wasn't about to waste a second of it. When she saw me walking up the aisle, she approached me with a nervous look. "Where do they have the camera?"

It was tempting to lie and watch her pose for the wrong angle, but I decided to give her a break. "It's in the wall above the jury box."

You'd think she'd be grateful, but she just nodded and turned away. I should've gone with my first impulse and lied. I headed into the courtroom and knocked on the door of the holding tank. The bailiff let me in and warned me, "You've got five minutes."

Dale looked a little better today. His eyes weren't so red. "I see you managed to get some sleep. Nice tie."

He nodded and looked down as he straightened it. "Thanks. My next-door cellie picked it out."

"The juicehead? Really?"

"Yeah, he's got surprisingly good taste." Dale smiled. "Kidding. What's on today?"

"Nikki, Janet, and then some crime-scene cops and techs."

"Have you heard back from the stuntman yet . . . what's his name—"

"Storm Cooper." Dale nodded. "No, we haven't. He's got a website, but it doesn't look like he ever updates it."

"And he's not with an agency?"

"Not anymore. According to our research, he fired his last agent a couple of years ago. I guess he's doing okay on his own."

"It's weird that the IO didn't track him down."

"Kind of. But Wayne Little isn't exactly a fireball. And from what I've heard, Storm was kind of a fringe player in Paige's life."

The bailiff tapped me on the shoulder. "Let's move. The judge's about to come out."

I nodded and whispered to Dale, "Remember, no laughing, no smiling, no frowning."

Juries always watch defendants for their reactions. Laughing is never okay. No innocent man on trial for murder laughs. At anything. And unless someone tells a riotous knee-slapper, smiling's off the table, too. Frowns make them look—you know, like a murderer.

I noticed that Zack had his main man, Detective Wayne Little, with him today. I'd wondered more than once if he was the one who'd leaked the rape charge. He struck me as the lazy but ambitious type who'd pull a stunt like that. But he had a lot to lose if he got caught. Hard to imagine he'd think it was worth that risk.

The gallery was so packed I didn't see two inches between the bodies. I noticed Edie and Brittany weren't there. They were probably still at Chloe's apartment building doing standups. I'd seen Edie on the morning news before I left for court. She'd been gesturing to the apartment building behind her and speaking in tragic tones about the first day of testimony.

The air in the courtroom crackled with energy, and the voices of reporters and spectators created a dull but rising roar. It should've come to a grinding halt when the bailiff announced the judge. But instead, the roar only lowered to a loud hum.

Judge Traynor stomped up the stairs to the bench and stood glaring at the crowd, looking like Moses on the Mount. He thundered, "You will be silent or you will be banned from this courtroom."

All voices stopped abruptly. Then one titter leaked out. The judge zeroed in on the source and pointed to a young guy in a brown bomber jacket. "You. Leave my courtroom now. And don't come back."

I could see the furious red spread across the young guy's face as he stood up and sidestepped out of his row. The courtroom was silent as a tomb. The only sound was the chafing of his jeans and then the squeak of his sneakers as he moved down the aisle. When the door closed behind him, the judge sat down and scanned the gallery. "I want you all to make note of this silence. This is the way it will be from now on—whether I'm on the bench or at sidebar." He looked at Zack. "Call your first witness."

That episode had a chastening effect on everyone. Like a bunch of third-graders after the class cutup gets sent to the principal's office, everyone sat up and looked straight ahead. You could practically see the haloes over their heads.

Zack did the typical prosecutorial trick of calling a family member to pull on the jurors' heartstrings. And Chloe's little sister, Kaitlyn, was the perfect one to do it. She was a sweet, somewhat paler version of Chloe. She testified to her phone conversation with Chloe the night of the murders.

I could've objected when Zack asked her if Chloe said she was going to break up with Dale during that phone call, but I let it go. I knew it'd come in when Janet Rader testified. And Zack returned the favor by not objecting when I got Kaitlyn to say that the jewelry stolen in the burglary—a gift from an unknown admirer—belonged to Paige.

Next up was Nikki, who acted like a *slightly* less slutty version of herself, though when the judge told her not to answer until he ruled on the lawyers' objections, she looked up at him and batted her eyelashes, Marilyn Monroe–style. Still, I got her to admit Dale might've been looking for the burglar when he was driving around, and she cut back a little on her "creepy" description of him.

When we broke for lunch, I called Michelle at the office. "Have we heard from Alex?"

"Yes. He went to the apartment building and talked to Chas Gorman this morning. You were right. Scott was a friend of his, but he swore he didn't know where Scott was hiding out."

"Where's Alex now?"

"Staking out Scott's place. We tried to find an address for his brother and sister, but the ones listed in Scott's last probation report are no good."

This sucked. I had a plan, but it was drastic—and risky. It might lose me any chance of ever getting my hands on that phone. I decided to hold off for now and told Michelle I'd call when I got out of court.

Zack put Janet Rader on the stand. I tried like crazy to get her to admit someone could've come to the apartment after Dale left, but she refused to budge. My only hope was that someone on the jury would be skeptical of her absolute certainty.

The rest of the day held no surprises. Crime-scene testimony is always a combination of boring and horrifying. But since none of today's witnesses were there to talk about test results, there were no fireworks.

When we broke for the day, I told Dale I had to get moving.

"Sure, okay. How do you think we're doing?"

"Pretty much as expected. It's way too soon to get a grip on what the jury's thinking. For now, just try to get some rest, okay?"

Dale nodded and I stood up to go. "Samantha? I just wanted to tell you again that I'm sorry I lost it like that when you told me about Sebastian—"

I sat back down and looked around. "Careful." We couldn't talk about it at Twin Towers in case they decided to file charges against him. But it wasn't that much safer here.

Dale scanned the area behind me then whispered, "And I don't want you to think that's how I got with Chloe. I was mad at her, but not like that. I don't know what made me hit her. I'd never done that before. Maybe it was because I was a little drunk. But . . . anyway, that's what I've been wanting to say. I didn't mean to upset you. I don't think I've ever been that angry in my life. I hope you'll forgive me."

I looked into his eyes. I didn't know whether to believe him about Chloe—or whether he'd ever been that angry before. But I knew his fury had been genuine. "It's okay. I . . . I kind of appreciated it in a way."

The bailiff put his hand on Dale's shoulder. "Time to go."

I stood up. "I'll see you tomorrow."

I wanted to skip the circus act with the press. I had a lot of work to do to get ready for the witnesses tomorrow, and I was anxious to see if Alex had found Scott. But I didn't dare piss off the reporters—or miss a chance to counter whatever Zack had been saying.

I slapped on a smile and got through it as fast as I could, then called Michelle from the car. "And?"

"Nothing. Alex doesn't think he's been home since he got released OR. There're some fliers and throwaways on the doorstep."

"Where's Alex now?"

"Still staking out the place. What do you want him to do?"

I stared out the window at the passing cars on the freeway. "Good question."

FORTY-NINE

I called Alex and told him to stop. "Let me handle it."

But he wanted to stay. "You gave me two days, remember? If I can't get him after tonight, I'll give up. I promise."

I had to give in. "Fine, but if he's not there by midnight, I want you to pull the plug."

"How about two thirty? After the bars let out?"

"No. Midnight. And I want you to call me." Not that I would be able to tell from his voice whether he was still at Scott's place. But it might be harder for him to lie about it if he had to talk to me. What the hell, it was worth a shot.

Alex sighed. "Okay, I'll call you."

Michelle was smiling when I got back to the office. I glared at her. "What's with the happy face? Knock it off."

"We might have a paying customer. A real one."

As opposed to the one who had threatened to kill Dale. "No way. Who? What?"

"It's white collar. Computer and bank fraud."

"Ugh."

Michelle gave me an indignant look. "White collar is where the money is. And you have Alex now. He'll handle the workup."

He'd probably love it. "How do we know he has money?"

"*She*, you sexist. I asked for all her numbers—checking account, credit cards, debit cards, the works. Nina Lederman is in good shape."

"Assuming those accounts aren't all fake."

"Go work on your trial. You're bumming me out."

At six o'clock, we got a delivery. A big FedEx box that'd been designated for overnight delivery. I put my ear to the box to listen for ticking, then frowned at Michelle. "What on earth could this be?"

Michelle handed me a pair of scissors. "Gee, if only there was a way to find out."

But she looked puzzled, too. The only deliveries we ever got were from Staples. I sliced through the tape, feeling apprehensive. As I pried open the box, my mouth was dry. I had a lot of haters lately. But this was an awful lot of trouble and expense to go to. I hesitated before pulling out the filler paper. Maybe it was a dead animal? I didn't smell anything. Or maybe it was some of those ugly posters people had been waving outside the courthouse? Or maybe there was a spring-loaded bottle of acid inside? Was there even such a thing? Enough. I made myself pull out the paper.

And there lay a pile of gorgeous suits. The packing slip said they'd come from Barneys. As I pulled each of them out, I could feel the richness of the fabric. These suits cost more than a year's rent. They were the right size, too.

I was furious.

Michelle examined the packing slip. "Who . . . ?"

"Fucking Celeste. That's who." I'd been taking some heat in the press for my somewhat battered, hugely out-of-date wardrobe. "She's embarrassed because people are saying her daughter looks like a rag doll."

Michelle sighed and nodded. "But you know what? Free clothes are free clothes. And your wardrobe could use a little . . . refreshing."

"I don't care. Screw her. I'm not wearing this shit." I repacked the box and closed it up. "How do I return this?"

Michelle folded her arms. "I am not going to help you cut off your nose to spite your face. Figure it out on your own."

I didn't have time to fool around with this. "Fine." I stomped into my office and threw the box on the floor.

I went back to work. But an hour later, my cell phone rang. It was Jack, my stepfather. "Are you still at work?" I said I was. "Guess you'll be burning the midnight oil until it's over. I hope you're taking care of yourself and finding a way to get some rest."

"Thanks, Jack. I'm trying." Jack was always doing this—showing me how a normal parent behaves. It would've been easy for Celeste to put on a better act. All she had to do was copy him. But that would never occur to her. "I hope all's well with you?"

"Fine, just fine. Look, I know you don't have time for jibber-jabber; I just wanted to make sure you got the package."

"The FedEx package?"

He cleared his throat. "That's the one. I hope the suits are the right size. I asked your mother. Do you like them?"

Jack bought them? I glanced at the box. "Uh, yeah. I mean, who wouldn't? They're gorgeous. Thank you, Jack." But I was suspicious. Jack was no fashion maven. He didn't even shop for his own clothes. "How'd you pick them out?"

"I . . . uh . . . got some advice from the salesperson. Good. I'm glad they worked out."

When we ended the call, I told Michelle that Jack said he'd bought the suits. "I think he's just covering for Celeste. He knows I won't wear them if they came from her."

Michelle raised an eyebrow. "But you can't be sure of that. And if he really did buy them and you send them back, you'll hurt his feelings."

I picked up the box. This was one hell of a bind.

Michelle smirked. "I'd say Jack played that nicely. Now hang up those suits before they wrinkle."

I shot her a dagger, but I took them out and laid them across a chair. Then I buried myself in fingerprint and DNA evidence for the next four hours. At ten thirty, I told Michelle to go home. "Someone around here should get some sleep."

"If you're staying, I'm staying."

She had that don't-mess-with-me look I'd known since seventh grade, so I didn't bother to argue. "Want me to go pick up some dinner?"

A police siren that'd been a distant wail was getting louder and louder. I glanced at my watch. Right on time. This was when our Barrios Van Nuys gang neighbors tended to get busy. Michelle looked out the window and shook her head. "Probably not a good time for us to be out walking around. I'll order pizza."

The cops had found whatever they were looking for just a block away, and more were coming. It was getting too noisy to think. I closed my window and went back to work. When the pizza came, we took a break. I decided to keep going until Alex called. But midnight came and went, and I got no call. I went out to Michelle's desk. "Did Alex text you?"

"No."

I took out my cell and called Alex. The call when straight to his voice mail. It was twelve fifteen. "I don't like this."

"Me neither. Let's go."

I knew that Scott's place was in an even lousier neighborhood than this one. I put my gun in my briefcase and we headed out.

But I hadn't even reached the freeway when my cell phone rang. I gave it to Michelle.

She looked puzzled, but she took the call for me. "Yes, this is her phone. I answered because she's driving." After a pause she said, "I'm Michelle . . . yes, Michelle Fusco." Another pause. "Oh my God. Yes, we'll be right there. Thank you."

My stomach tightened as I took in Michelle's stricken look. "What?"

"Alex is in the hospital. Someone attacked him."

Panic filled my brain. "Where is he?"

"He's at Saint Vincent Medical Center."

I floored it. "What did they tell you? Is he going to be okay?"

But Michelle didn't have any other information. At that time of night, we could fly, and I took full advantage of it. We got there in twenty minutes flat. I parked in a doctor's space, and we ran to the emergency room.

Alex was in a bed at the far end. His left arm was in a sling, and his head was so heavily bandaged I could barely see his face. His eyes were closed. I looked up at his monitors. His heartbeat was slow but regular. I turned to go find a doctor, but Michelle grabbed my arm.

She leaned down. "Alex? I didn't quite hear you."

Alex's eyes were open, but they were just slits, and he whispered through swollen, bloody lips. "Don't tell. Okay?"

I nodded.

"I went inside to look for the phone. Someone . . ." He stopped and tried to lick his lips. I grabbed a Kleenex, poured some water on it from a bottle on the table next to his bed, and gently patted his lips. After a few seconds, he said, "He was looking for Scott."

I poured some more water on the Kleenex and swabbed his lips again. "The guy who beat you up thought you were Scott?"

"Yeah. When he saw it was me, he ran." He closed his eyes, then slowly opened them. "No phone. Sorry."

"No. You don't get to say that word. I do. I'm sorry. I should never have let you go out there alone. I'm so sorry, Alex—"

A doctor walked up and pulled the curtain around the bed. "Are you Michelle and Samantha?" We nodded. "He's got a few cracked ribs, a concussion, and his arm is sprained, but it's not broken. He'll be out of commission for a little while, but there shouldn't be any lasting damage."

"Did you call his family?" Michelle asked.

"Yes. His uncle is on the way."

I stared at his battered face. "When are you going to release him?"

"If everything stays stable, probably tomorrow morning. I'd guess by about ten a.m. So if you two plan to take him home, come back then."

The doctor left. I sat down next to Alex's bed. "I'll take him back to my place—"

Michelle shook her head. "And then what? You're in trial. You can't take care of him. He can stay with me—"

"How is that any better? You've got to be in the office."

"I can forward the calls—"

Our bickering got cut off by the arrival of Alex's uncle—who made it clear that he'd be taking Alex home with him.

Tomas Medrano looked like the kind of guy you'd be glad to have on your side. Height clearly ran in the family. He was more than six feet tall. But unlike Alex, he was barrel-chested and had thick, heavy features. Jutting cheekbones; a wide, broken nose; and heavy brows combined to make him look like someone you didn't want to piss off. His biceps and thick hands said how much it'd hurt if you did.

And when he said Alex would be staying with him, we didn't argue.

FIFTY

It didn't take long for rage to crowd out the sadness. Maybe Alex shouldn't have broken into Scott's place, but he'd only done it because that dickweed was jerking me around.

Which made Scott the dumbest tool on the planet. Lesson *numero uno* if you're a criminal: when you're facing state prison, the one person you cannot afford to piss off is your lawyer. It was a lesson Scott was about to learn the hard way.

The next morning, I made an early stop at Department 125. I told the clerk I needed to put Scott's case on tomorrow morning's calendar to handle some "serious discovery issues."

That left me with two minutes to get down to Department 106. The elevators were backed up, so I took the stairs and ran all the way. I knew Judge Traynor, AKA the Freight Train, wouldn't hesitate to chew me out in front of the jury if I was late. I wound up huffing and puffing my way into court with just seconds to spare.

I was still breathing hard when the bailiff brought out Dale. He looked at me curiously. "You jogging to court now?"

I answered between breaths. "Just had another appearance up in Department 125. Had to take the stairs."

Dale raised an eyebrow. "Maybe you *should* be jogging to court, then. You're too young to be this strung out by a few flights—*downstairs*. You don't smoke, do you?"

I shot him a dagger. "No. I don't smoke." Dale looked relieved. I stared at him. "But I do shoot up. That's okay, right?"

Dale sighed and rolled his eyes. The bailiff stood up and announced the judge, and I quickly unpacked my briefcase.

Zack was putting on his DNA witnesses today to prove that the scrapings under Chloe's nails and the small blood swipe on her neck had come from Dale. The case was moving fast. Too fast. I needed to slow things down and buy myself some time.

Zack had warned me that he was going to make a motion to get Jenny Knox's murder into evidence when he finished his DNA witnesses. If the judge let that in, it was game over for us. And I wasn't sure Ignacio would be able to sell Dale's alibi. What Alex had said about him, as well as what Hank had dug up on him, worried me. I had to find more backup for his testimony—or at least make sure there wasn't something really ugly in his background that'd shred his credibility. And now that Alex was laid up, I had to do my own digging. So I'd prepared some lengthy cross-examination for the DNA witnesses to try and stall the motion for a couple of days.

But for a change, I got a break. Zack had decided to do a whole dog and pony show, starting with, "What is DNA?"

By the end of the day, it looked like someone had blown sleeping gas through the air vents. The whole courtroom was fighting to stay awake.

I could tell the judge wanted to throttle Zack. But I wanted to send him a bottle of Patrón Silver. And that went on until Thursday—when I had my appearance on Scott's case. I told Judge Traynor I had another appearance Thursday morning, so we'd have to start late. He didn't like it, but he couldn't say no.

When I walked into Department 125, I saw that my nemesis, Paul Wesson, was fired up with righteous indignation—which was just what I'd expected. And counted on. The judge called the case of *People v. Scott Henderson.* "Ms. Brinkman, you put this case on calendar for a motion to suppress. Do we have the defendant?"

I shook my head and cast a worried look behind me. "No, Your Honor. I called him several times and left messages, but he hasn't responded. I even had my investigator go to his residence. It appears he hasn't been there since his OR release."

The pit bull was practically gnashing his teeth. "This is exactly why I opposed his release, Your Honor! I ask that his OR be revoked and that a bench warrant be issued forthwith!"

The judge raised an eyebrow. "Counsel? Any reason why I shouldn't make that order?"

I gave a fake deep sigh. "None that I can think of, Your Honor."

He banged his gavel. "OR is revoked; bench warrant to issue forthwith—"

Paul interrupted. "I'd ask that you make this a no-bail order, Your Honor!"

The judge looked at me again. "Seems a bit extreme. Counsel?" I shrugged. "I'll set bail at one million for now. That should be sufficient. The bailiff will notify you when the defendant is picked up."

I smiled at Paul. "Have a great day."

He frowned at me, confused. I was still smiling as I headed downstairs. The payback wheels were in motion. What a nice way to start the day.

And another stroke of luck was waiting for me. Zack came over as I was unpacking my briefcase. "I hate to do this to you, but I left out a whole area on contamination. I'm going to ask to reopen direct."

I pretended to be annoyed. "How long will it take?"

"A while. I probably won't finish until around two or two thirty."

Perfect. I shrugged. "It's not like I have a choice. But thanks for telling me."

And as it turned out, his estimate had been light. Zack didn't finish until the end of the day. Tomorrow was Friday; the court was dark. That gave me three days. It wasn't nearly enough time, but every extra minute meant another chance for something good to happen.

At the very least, I figured I'd get my hands on Scott. I'd given the bailiff every single bit of information I had on him. And sure enough, Friday morning at eleven thirty, I got the call. Scott was in custody. They were bringing him to court to reset bail and pick our next court date.

I gave Michelle the good news. She set her jaw. "What're you going to do to him? It'd better be horrible."

I stared at her. "Seriously? You're worried I might be too *nice* to the little peckerwood?"

Michelle shook her head. "Really, what *is* wrong with me? I don't know what I was thinking." She sighed. "Anyway, make sure you get back by two thirty. Orozco's coming in."

My gangbanger Ricardo's father. I wasn't looking forward to it.

I nodded. "Got it."

I headed to court with a little over a quarter of a tank of gas. I'd make it there, but I probably wouldn't make it back. Michelle had forbidden me from using credit cards. But I had no choice. It was either use my gas card or leave Beulah on the street and take the bus home. That potential new computer-fraud client was looking like a better idea by the minute.

When I got to court, I told the bailiff I needed to see my client.

"Scott Henderson's yours?" I nodded. "He's pretty freaked out."

"He giving you guys problems?"

The bailiff rolled his eyes. "He won't shut up. He's bitching and whining like a little tweeny whose mommy won't let him go to the One Direction concert."

I smiled. "I'll see what I can do." When Scott saw me, he ran to the front of the cell and gripped the bars. "You've got to get me out of here!"

"Is that right?"

"Look, I know I fucked up! I meant to get you that phone. But I had to lay low for a while. I've got some people—"

"Who're after you. You owe them money."

"How'd you know?"

"Because thanks to you, my investigator is in the hospital."

His eyes got big. "Oh shit. He was staking my place?" I nodded. Scott hung his head. "That's fucked up."

"You're about to be just that. And I assume whomever you owe has connects in Men's Central."

He swallowed and nodded. "Are you going to dump me?"

"No." A surprised smile trembled on his lips. "I'll be your lawyer until death do us part." I gave him a cold stare. "Which also happens to be when I'll announce 'ready' for trial. And I think your bail's going to have to stay at one million. As an officer of the court, I had to tell the truth about how you dodged my calls and never showed up at the address you gave me. So I'd advise you to make some friends. You're going to be there awhile."

The tremulous smile faded as comprehension sank in. "No! Please! You can't do this to me! I'll give you the phone, I promise! I can get it to you in one hour—no, less!"

I raised an eyebrow. "Oh, you promise? Well, that's a different story. I mean, why wouldn't I trust you? It worked out so well before." I glared at him but kept my voice low. "Tough shit. You jerked me around and put my investigator in the hospital. See you in court."

I called for the bailiff to let me out and left him clutching the bars. Scott could make a motion to have me relieved as counsel. But I was betting he wouldn't. If he got rid of me, he'd have to roll the dice with a public defender or a court-appointed lawyer—and that's exactly what he didn't want. Sure enough, when the judge called the case, Scott never said a word. Other than, "I apologize to the court."

I said I thought the June twentieth date we'd set for trial was turning out to be way too optimistic. We reset it for August nineteenth. Scott looked pale and shaky as the bailiff escorted him back into lockup.

It was one forty-five by the time I got out of court. I headed for my car at a fast trot. I didn't want to keep Orozco Senior waiting. Especially since Michelle was alone in the office.

FIFTY-ONE

On my way back, I thought about what he might want from me. Or want to do to me. I told myself not to be paranoid, that I'd gotten that gangbanging asshole Ricardo a hell of a deal, and that he'd be stupid to shoot me in the office in broad daylight. But his son was a psychopath. There was a distinct possibility the apple hadn't fallen all that far from the tree. And after the fun time I'd had with Lane Ockman, I decided there was no reason to take any chances.

When I got to the office, I put my .38 Smith & Wesson in the pocket of my blazer. Michelle raised an eyebrow. "I think if you don't want to take his case, a simple 'no' will do."

At that moment, the outer door buzzer sounded. Michelle cast a critical look at my waist. "It totally shows. Just put it in your desk drawer like you always do."

Michelle went to get the door. I supposed she was right. I dropped the gun into my drawer. But I left it open.

A few seconds later, Michelle escorted in an older man whom I assumed was Ernesto, and a younger man who looked a lot like Ricardo—tats and all—but he was thicker in the chest and arms. They were taller than Ricardo; I figured they were both about five foot nine or ten. The older man, who had the head of a buffalo and slightly stooped shoulders, extended a leathery brown hand. "I am Ernesto Orozco, and this is my son, Arturo."

I reached out and shook his hand. It felt like a chunk of asphalt—rough, solid, and heavy. "Pleased to meet you, Ernesto."

Arturo, who had the same slicked-back hairdo as Ricardo, stretched out a hand that was inked from pinkie to thumb. "Thank you for seeing us."

As we shook, I noticed the muscles move under his black T-shirt. He'd taken a bath in cologne for the occasion, and the sweet scent mixed with the smell of hair grease made me queasy. It brought back memories of Ricardo. I gestured for them to take the seats in front of my desk. I was glad to have the advantage of my big lawyer's chair so I could look down on them. The old man's eyes were black and flat, like a shark's—just like Ricardo's. But Arturo's eyes were hot, and they glittered with malice. The air felt heavy, like the moments before a thunderstorm, and I could feel the weight of it in my chest. Out of the corner of my eye, I clocked the position of the gun in my open drawer. If I had to grab it, I didn't want to wind up with a handful of paper clips. I made my face relax and did my best to sound confident. "What can I do for you?"

Ernesto's eyes grew watery. He spoke slowly in a deep, rumbling voice. "We have had a terrible tragedy. My son Ricardo. Someone killed him in prison."

My heart gave a dull thud. I pulled on a look of concern and surprise. "Oh my God. I'm so sorry. How did it happen? Was it a guard?" I kept my gaze steady.

Arturo shook his head with a venomous look and bit off his words as though he were tearing through flesh. "A *pinchi* Southside motherfucker shivved him."

Ernesto dabbed at a tear that leaked out of the corner of his eye. "They put Ricardo in with the Southside Creepers."

His rival gang. My palms were sweating. I wiped my left hand on my thigh and let it dangle off the arm of my chair, within closer reach of the gun. Barely breathing now, I looked from Ernesto to Arturo. "How did that happen?"

Ernesto shook his head, his hooded eyes narrowed. "They tell me it was an accident. Someone made a mistake, put his name on the wrong list."

Arturo leaned forward with his elbows on his knees and cracked his knuckles. "We don't believe it. That was no mistake. I think some Southside *pendejo* got friends in high places."

I wanted to swallow, but I couldn't let them see they were getting to me. I moved my left hand a little closer to the open drawer and kept my expression neutral. "So you think a guard who was on Southside's payroll did it?" They both nodded. "I assume you want to file a lawsuit. But I'm sorry, I don't do civil cases."

Ernesto stared at me for a moment, then nodded. "We can find another lawyer to sue. But we want to find out how this happened. Who did this. Who killed my son."

Arturo's hands curled into fists. "*And* who put him with those Southside *putas*."

I must have looked alarmed, because Ernesto patted Arturo's arm heavily. "Don't worry about him. He gets a little hotheaded sometimes. We just need to know for our own peace of mind. We don't mean no harm."

The hell they didn't. They wanted revenge, and they wouldn't be picky about how they got it. They weren't going to buy that it was just a computer glitch or a typo. They wanted names. And if they didn't like my answers, they'd take me out, too. Having anything to do with these two animals was a bad—possibly fatally bad—idea. But I had no choice. I had to take the case. "I understand. But you know I'm not an investigator."

Ernesto slowly nodded. "*Sí.* But you did a good job for Ricardo. And you are famous now. We think maybe the cops will be afraid to lie to you." He looked at me with his hooded shark eyes. He spoke to Arturo in Spanish.

Arturo translated. "He says he has faith in you."

Arturo leaned back in his chair and stared down his nose at me—just like Ricardo had. Everything about him, from the curl of his lip to the hands that lay on his thighs, radiated menace. I started to take a deep breath, but it got stuck in my throat. I couldn't let them see me sweat, so I quickly stood up, my left hand still dangling near the open drawer. "All right. Send me everything they've given you. I can't promise results, but I'll do what I can."

Ernesto slowly stood. "That's all I ask."

I nodded. "Michelle will work out the payment schedule with you."

Arturo held out his hand. When I took it, his eyes bored into mine. "And I'll be doing some digging of my own. One way or another, I'm going to find out who's responsible for my brother's death. No matter what it takes." He held on to my hand for an uncomfortable moment longer as he continued to hold my gaze.

Scared as I was, I refused to let him intimidate me. I stared back at him. "I understand." I pulled my hand away and walked them out to Michelle's desk.

When I went back to my office, I closed the door, sank into my chair, and took big gulps of air. I was in business with a pair of maniacs who were out for revenge. There was no way this was going to end well. I just had to figure out how to make it end worse for them than for me.

A few minutes later, Michelle came in. "Since it's not a trial or a case per se, I took a five-thousand-dollar retainer. Sound about right?" I nodded. "So what's the story?"

"Ricardo has shuffled off this mortal coil. Got stuck in the wrong tank with a rival gang. They want me to find out how that happened and who killed him."

"Alex is going to love this one."

I shook my head. "I won't need him." I had to handle this one myself.

Michelle raised an eyebrow. "Well, when you find out who did it, let me know. I'd like to buy the man a drink." She gave a little chuckle. "When they had to give Orozco that deal, I was so pissed. I mean, where's the justice?" She smiled and shook her head. "But I guess you never know."

I returned her smile. "Justice moves in mysterious ways."

Michelle blinked, then returned my smile. "Funny, that's what you said when the guy who mugged me got killed in a hit-and-run."

I was still distracted, so it took me a moment to answer. "Is it? I can't remember that far back. But anyway, it's true, isn't it?"

"In ways both good and bad." She looked at me closely. "What's going on? You don't seem like yourself."

I frowned and pushed some papers around on my desk. "What do you mean?"

"You seem kind of . . . shook up. I admit, that Orozco clan's pretty gnarly. But you've had scarier clients. What's the deal?"

I gave a casual shrug. "No deal. I'm okay, just got way too much going on." I smiled. "I'm fine."

Michelle had a skeptical look. She gazed into my eyes. "Whatever it is, you know you can tell me, Sam."

I made myself hold her gaze. "Seriously, there's nothing to tell."

The phone rang and Michelle went to get it. Two minutes later, she rushed back into my office. "Finally, some good news: Scott came through. Chas Gorman has the phone."

FIFTY-TWO

I was glad we were about to get the phone, but I wasn't jumping for joy. It'd cost way too much. "Yeah, great."

She folded her arms. "Samantha. I'm still pissed off, too. But this is what Alex put himself on the line for."

I gave her a sullen look. "Exactly." Getting the phone didn't make up for what he'd been through. "I've got a two-thirty meeting with Detective Rick Saunders. Tell Chas I'll get there around five."

I was hoping Rick Saunders might be able to give me more information on Ignacio, the alibi witness for the Jenny Knox murder.

But at noon, I got the call I'd least expected.

Michelle buzzed me. "We must be on some kind of a roll. I've got Storm Cooper on the line."

The stuntman who'd been Paige's boyfriend once upon a time. We'd been leaving him messages for the past three weeks. I clicked over. "Samantha Brinkman here. Thanks for returning my call."

His voice was cold, hostile. "I wasn't going to call you back, except I heard you said Paige was the real target."

"You've been watching the trial?"

"No. A friend told me. I just got back from a shoot in Helen's Bay yesterday."

Where the heck was Helen's Bay? "Then you never spoke to the police?"

"Of course I did. I called 'em the minute I heard about Paige's murder on the news."

But I hadn't seen his statement in any police report. "Can you spare me a few minutes to talk? You can come to my office. Or I'll meet wherever you want."

"Meet me at Mel's Drive-In on Sunset."

That was about thirty minutes away. "How about twelve thirty?"

"That'll work."

Mel's is a retro-style drive-in diner on the Sunset Strip. The wall-to-wall windows that face the street give customers a view of the boulevard—and give the whole world a perfect view of everything and everyone inside the place. I would've preferred something more private, but I didn't want to risk bartering over the location. Storm was curious, but I could tell he'd blow me off in a hot second if the meeting was too much of a hassle.

I told Michelle to wish me luck and took off, hoping I could score a booth away from the window. But when I got there, I saw that all the back tables were filled. I was stuck with the row of booths against the window. I took a seat at the end and ordered coffee. Twelve thirty came and went. At a quarter to one I took to checking my phone every five minutes. When he hadn't shown up at five to one, I figured I'd been stood up. But since I didn't have to meet Rick Saunders until two thirty, I decided to give it another few minutes.

At one o'clock, Storm Cooper finally appeared. He clomped in on worn-out motorcycle boots, a black helmet with flames on the sides tucked under his arm.

He was handsome in a rugged, manly man kind of way—dark eyes that crinkled into crow's-feet; a weathered tan; and long, wavy brown hair. I held up a hand, and he stomped over and slid into the booth across from me.

I'd considered how to approach this. I doubted Paige had told him about "Mr. Perfect." Storm was an ex, but that didn't mean he wanted to hear about her other lovers. So I decided to take an open-ended approach. "Thanks for meeting me." He grunted and pushed back his hair. "Where's Helen's Bay?"

"Northern Ireland. Been there for the past couple of months."

The waiter came over, and he ordered a cup of coffee.

"Were you in town when Paige was killed?"

His eyes hardened. "Yeah, I left a few days after. What makes you think Paige was the target?"

The honest answer was wishful thinking. I knew that wouldn't cut it. But being the defense attorney means you get to play your cards close to the vest. "I can't really talk about the defense. It's privileged. But I promise I'll tell you when it's all worked out. Deal?"

He gave me a narrow stare. "I'm outta here at one thirty regardless. So fire away; it's your dime."

The waiter brought Storm's coffee, and he dumped five packets of sugar into it.

"I'm going to need you to start at square one, because I never saw any police report with your statement in it." Storm frowned and gave me a skeptical look. "I have no reason to lie about that. Especially with the time limit you just gave me."

He took a sip of his coffee as he mulled that over. "Fair enough. I've known Paige for four years. Met her when she visited Chloe on the set of *Hard Times*. Chloe had a bit part."

"So you and Paige dated?"

"Yeah. For two years, off and on. Off and on is about the only way I ever get to date. I'm on the road a lot, on location."

"Who ended it?"

He slouched down in the booth. "She did. Said she couldn't take all the coming and going. Can't say I blamed her, but I've got to make a living." He pushed around some stray sugar granules that'd fallen onto the table.

"But you remained friends?"

Storm nodded. "I kept hanging around. I guess in the back of my mind I was hoping she'd want to get back together. But we wound up seeing less and less of each other. She never seemed to have time for me. This past year I barely saw her at all."

"Did you know if Paige was dating someone else?"

He set his jaw, a dark look on his face. "Toward the end, yeah. It was maybe a month before she . . . died." Storm paused and stared down at the table for a moment. He took a deep breath, then continued. "I stopped by her place to see if she wanted to have dinner. She was on her way to some big party, and she was dressed up in heels and diamonds, the whole nine yards." I pulled out my phone and showed him the photo of the stolen jewelry. "Yeah. Can't say that's exactly the same necklace, but it looked like that. I asked where she got it, and she said some rich guy gave it to her."

"Did she tell you who he was? Or say anything about him?"

He shook his head. "I asked, but she dodged me, said it was none of my business. Which I guess it wasn't."

"Did you tell the police all this?" He shook his head. "Why did you call them?"

"Because when I heard the story on the news, I realized I saw her that day." He folded an empty sugar packet into an accordion. "I thought they'd send someone out to talk to me, but they just took my statement on the phone."

"You saw Paige the day she died?" Storm nodded. "Where?"

The waiter came by and offered to refill our coffees. I shook my head. I hadn't touched mine. Storm signaled for more.

"I was driving north on Malibu Canyon and I stopped for a red light at the intersection of Malibu Canyon and Mulholland Highway. I was about to turn right onto Mulholland when I saw her. She was stopped at the light, across the intersection from me. And she was heading toward Malibu."

Malibu. Where Marc had been found.

I leaned forward. "What time?"

"About six thirty."

"Then it was almost dark. You're sure it was her?"

He took a sip of coffee. "Definitely. There're streetlights at that intersection. Plus, I recognized the car. I waved to her, but I guess she didn't see me. That's when I noticed there was a guy in the passenger seat."

"Did you recognize him?"

"No. Never saw him before." Storm's phone rang. "I gotta take this. Excuse me." He got up and walked outside.

I quickly pulled up Marc's Facebook page.

Storm came back. "Look, I gotta jump."

I held up my phone. "Is this the guy you saw in the car with Paige?"

He took the phone from me and studied it. "Yeah, I think so. Who is he?"

"Marc Palmer. He was a model who worked with Paige. His body washed up on the shore in Malibu about a week after Paige died."

He frowned as he gave the phone back. "Hell of a coincidence. So that's why you said Paige was the real target. You think they're connected."

I nodded. "Especially after what you just told me."

"Then it's important?"

"Very. But do me a favor, don't tell anyone about this, okay? I'd rather not have your statement get tossed around by the press." Or the cops—who'd probably wind up proving that it was nothing more than the usual defense red herring.

He nodded slowly. "Yeah, the press is all over this case, isn't it?"

I gave him a weary nod. "It's nonstop."

He stood and picked up his helmet. "Later."

Actually, *I* wasn't so sure the two deaths were connected. But with Storm's testimony, I thought the jury might. It was exactly the kind of intriguing sideshow juries loved.

Or, as I'd call it in my closing argument: reasonable doubt.

FIFTY-THREE

I asked Rick Saunders to meet me at Mel's since I was already there and it was close to his station. I was glad I'd saved myself a trip. He didn't know Ignacio. He offered to ask around about him, but generating talk about my alibi witness was the last thing I needed.

By three o'clock, I was ready to go see Chas Gorman. I wasn't supposed to get to his place until five o'clock, but I had a feeling he'd be around. Chas seemed like the kind of guy who was always around. And I was right.

As an added plus, he was almost sober. Either he was getting a late start or his stash was running low.

Chas smiled when he opened the door. "Hey, thanks for coming over."

"Hey, thanks for having me." He'd offered to bring the phone to me, but I wasn't about to take any more chances with the damn thing.

He led me to the living room and gestured for me to take a seat on the lumpy brown couch. "I'll be right back."

He was as good as his word. In less than a minute he was back, an old flip-style cell phone in his hand. It looked like the one Scott's siblings had shown us.

"Just so you know, I had no idea Scott did that burglary. I was really pissed when I found out."

I opened the phone and checked out the photos, just to make sure it was the right one. It was. "How long have you guys known each other?"

"A few years. And I've never known him to do shit like that. But I think he got himself in debt to some heavy dudes, and it's making him act crazy."

I could well believe it, but I didn't care. His "crazy" had landed Alex in the hospital. Screw him. "Thanks, Chas." I headed for the door.

He followed me. "The press was all over this place a few days ago."

That would've been the first day of trial. I paused at the door. "Anyone try to talk to you?"

"Not that day, no."

"But another day?"

"Yeah. Not sure if it was a reporter, but it was right after Alex came by."

I'd sent Alex to the building to find out if Chas and Scott were friends. "Who was it?"

"Dunno. But whoever it was banged on my door for, like, a half hour. It was really weird."

"Male or female?"

Chas shrugged. "Female? No, male." He sighed. "I'm not sure."

"He didn't give you a name?"

"No. I didn't answer the door, just played dead."

As always, talking to Chas was an exercise in frustration. His fried brain coughed up tantalizing fragments, but they never coalesced into a solid piece of information.

I thanked him again and left. When I got to my car, I opened Paige's phone and checked her voice mails. *Nada*. There were a few texts between Paige and Chloe sent a couple of days before they died. But they were just mundane messages about picking up the dry cleaning and Taco Bell for dinner. I went through the photos.

Again, nothing intriguing. Just Paige and Chloe horsing around and joke-posing. I felt a pang of sadness looking at their young faces. I scrolled more quickly. I didn't need any more reminders of what a tragedy this was. And then I found a photograph that got my attention. It'd been taken two months before the murders.

I looked at my watch. It was three thirty. The perfect time to go see Alex. I'd been planning to check in on him, and I knew he'd want to see this photo.

Alex's uncle, Tomas, lived in Arcadia—about fifteen minutes northeast of downtown. In rush hour, that fifteen minutes could easily turn into an hour. But I thought if I got on the road right now, I'd beat the worst of it.

I didn't. It took me more than an hour to get there.

Alex's uncle lived in a modest fifties-style ranch on Bella Vista Drive, a quiet suburban street that hadn't changed much since the homes were built. An older woman who said she was Maria, the housekeeper, ushered me into the living room where Alex was set up on the couch. She told me Tomas was at work but he'd left instructions that Alex was not allowed to move. I took that as the warning it definitely was and promised her I wouldn't even let him leave the couch. She nodded. "*Bueno.* Can I get you something to drink? Or eat? Are you hungry?"

"No, thank you. I'm good."

Alex looked 200 percent better than when I'd last seen him. Which wasn't saying all that much, since the last time I'd seen him, he'd looked like roadkill. His dark skin hid some of the bruises, but his lips and right eye were still badly swollen.

I sat down in a chair next to the couch. "I hope you feel better than you look."

He deadpanned, "Let me say on behalf of the world that it's probably a good thing you chose the law instead of medicine. Your bedside manner sucks."

"Seriously, how are you feeling?"

Alex blew out an exasperated breath. "Bored. Nobody lets me do anything, and really, I'm fine. I'm just sore. I can move around. I can drive—"

Maria called out, "No you can't!"

Alex gave me a pleading look. "If I don't go back to work, I'll lose my mind." He put his hands together prayer-style. "Please tell her you need me."

"I do. But I'm with Maria and your uncle on this one. You shouldn't push it. Besides, I've got something you can do lying on your back." I pulled Paige's cell phone out of my purse.

"Hey! How did you—" Alex sat up too fast. He winced and held his side.

I raised an eyebrow. "Yeah, you're obviously good to go." I gave him the whole story and ended by saying, "Our boy Scotty's going to be in Men's Central for a good long time."

"I'd like to be the bigger man and say he shouldn't have to pay for this, but—"

"But if you did, I'd knock you out myself."

Alex smiled. He flipped the phone open and examined it. "Just your basic burner. You check for texts and voice mails?"

"Yeah, nothing of interest. But I found a photo." I held out my hand. He gave the phone back to me, and I pulled it up again and showed him. "It's a little distorted, but this looks like Marc to me." It was a selfie taken at a bad angle that made his forehead look huge.

Alex took the phone and studied the photo. "Yeah, it does. That's the ocean right behind him. Malibu?"

I nodded. "What I was thinking." I told him about my meeting with Storm that afternoon. "But if he took that photo in Malibu, he wasn't in the Colony." Malibu Colony is the most built-up area in Malibu, where all the stores and most of the restaurants are. The area behind Marc in the photo looked less inhabited. And the house behind him looked too modest—and isolated—to be in the Colony.

Alex pointed to his laptop that was on the coffee table. "Could you hand me that, please?" I gave it to him, and he Google-mapped street views of Malibu Colony. I watched as he moved from one block to the next. "You can see he's standing on a street, but none of these streets look right. Must be farther up the coast." He studied the photo again. "But this was taken in late January. Almost two months before the murders."

"True, but Storm said they were heading toward Malibu. So maybe they were going back to that same place the day she died."

Alex set the phone down on the coffee table. "Maybe. But Paige wound up in Laurel Canyon."

"So? We're the defense, Alex. We don't have to prove anything. All we need to do is connect enough dots to scare the jury out of convicting."

Alex nodded. "Well, it's definitely worth checking out. Let me get into this phone and see if I can find anything else. And I'll do a closer check of Malibu neighborhoods. How much time do we have?"

I sighed. "Zack's going to wrap up by Wednesday at the latest. So we've got to be ready to start calling witnesses on Thursday."

Alex blew out a breath. "Can you stall?"

"With this judge? Are you kidding? If I ask for more time, I'll be sharing a cell with Scott."

"Hold on." Alex pointed to the television. It'd been playing on mute. "Isn't that your boy Storm?"

I turned and saw Storm holding forth to a circle of reporters. "Oh shit . . ."

Alex raised the remote and turned up the volume. A woman I didn't recognize asked, "Why didn't you come forward sooner?" She held the microphone up to Storm.

"I did. I called the police right away. I guess they didn't think it was that important. But the defense attorney sure did."

The reporter asked Storm what he'd told me, but he shook his head and smiled. "I can't tell you that. The attorney asked me to save it for the courtroom, and I promised I would. But I can say that my testimony is going to prove for sure that Paige was the real target."

The reporter turned to the camera and threw it back to the anchor. "This might be a real bombshell, Terry. If you recall, Samantha Brinkman did say in her opening statement that she intended to prove Paige Avner—not Chloe Monahan—was the one the killer was after. If Storm Cooper's testimony establishes that critical fact, it's a lot less likely that Dale Pearson committed these murders. And that's the latest, most up-to-the-minute development in the Dale Pearson case. Back to you, Terry."

Alex muted the television and threw the remote down on the couch. "Son of a bitch."

When we'd talked, Storm hadn't been all that excited about being my witness. I guessed it didn't dawn on him until after our meeting that being a witness in this case meant free advertising.

"At least he didn't give up what he told you about seeing Paige and Marc together."

"Not on camera. But we don't know what he might've told them off the record."

Reporters could make big promises when a hot story was at stake. Storm wouldn't be the first to get sucked into telling secrets.

I stood up. "I'd better get back to the office—"

Alex turned off the television. "Can you give me a few more minutes? I need to talk to you about something."

Alex had an anxious look on his face. Whatever it was, I had a feeling I wasn't going to like it. I sat back down.

FIFTY-FOUR

The phones were ringing nonstop when I got back to the office, and Michelle was looking frazzled. She punched a button, said, "Brinkman and Associates, please hold." Then another line rang and she did it again. After the third time, with all lines blinking, she finally looked up. "The minute Storm gave that stupid interview, the phones started going crazy."

"Press looking for comment?" Michelle nodded. "I'll take them."

She readjusted her scrunchie and blew out a breath. "I can split them with you if you tell me what to say."

"Just say that as of this afternoon, Storm Cooper is on our witness list. Period."

I stomped into my office, pissed off and frustrated. Now I'd have to turn over Storm's statement to the prosecution. I wasn't worried that Zack would be able to shake Storm's ID. Alex had Googled that intersection. Storm could easily have seen inside a car stopped at that light.

The problem was, once Zack found out about Marc Palmer, Zack would try to prove there was no connection between Marc's death and Paige's. And if he succeeded—and with this much lead time, I strongly suspected he might—that'd end my best shot at winning this case. Or at least getting the jury to hang.

I'd have to move fast to keep that from happening. I had to get out to Malibu, find the place where Marc had taken the photo, and see if I could lock down some witnesses who could help me. But I couldn't go out there alone, and if I took Michelle, we'd have to shut down the office. Not a great idea with all that was going on. But screw it. This was more important. We'd get through the bulk of the press calls and then head out there.

But by the time the phones slowed down, it was dark. No way I could hope to find the location in that photo at night. Michelle came in and flopped down on one of the chairs in front of my desk. "Well, that was insane. And Zack called. I had a feeling you wouldn't want to talk to him yet, so I took it. Says he wants the discovery on Storm. Want to clue me in?"

"Damn skippy I didn't want that call. Thanks, Michy." I gave her updates—on Storm and on Alex and my fear that Zack would take a wrecking ball to the whole story.

Michelle shrugged. "I don't mean to be a buzzkill, but he probably will anyway. Don't you think it's possible that Paige just gave Marc a ride out to Malibu that night? That she dropped him off at someone's house and then went out to do her own thing?"

The fact that Paige ended up in Laurel Canyon did tend to make it look that way. "That's a possibility. But if I can come up with just one weird detail—like a witness who thinks he saw them together in Malibu later that night—I'll have a shot at making at least one juror get stuck on the coincidence of their deaths. And if I can find out where Marc took that photo, I have a shot at finding that goofball—uh, I mean witness. The problem now is, I've got to do it before Zack has a chance to send in the cops."

If something *had* happened to both Paige and Marc out there, the kind of witnesses who could help me probably weren't the type who liked to talk to police—or we'd have heard about them already. And if they saw cops around, they'd scatter. Or lie.

"Then you should get out there tomorrow."

"I plan to, first thing in the morning—"

"And you'll need backup in case you get lucky and find your dream witness. I'll go with you."

"Right. Thanks, Michy. And maybe Alex has managed to narrow down our search area. I'll check in with him now and find out."

She gave me a warning look as she stood up and stretched. "He'll want to come."

"No doubt." I smiled, remembering how he'd begged me to get him out of the house. "But he'll have to climb over his uncle to do it."

Michelle smiled. "I don't see that happening anytime soon." She went back to her desk.

I called Alex. "Any luck finding where Marc took that photo?"

"Not exactly. I can rule out the Colony. And it definitely wasn't farther south, so we should hit the northern parts of Malibu."

"No, Alex. Not 'we.' Me. Now that Storm opened his big yapper, the DA's demanding discovery. I've got to get out there ASAP, and you're in no shape to be out running around."

"I'm in fine shape to do it. Really. I look a lot worse than I feel. Besides, we're not scaling mountains; we're walking around neighborhoods. And I'm moving back to my place tonight, so we can meet at your apartment in the morning—as early as you want."

Alex lived in West Hollywood, just a few miles away from me. I didn't love the idea of him getting out of bed—especially if his uncle found out he'd done it because of me. But I didn't think it was going to be a major undertaking, either, and I could use his help. "If you're sure you're up to it, I was planning to get on the road by eight o'clock."

"I'll be at your place at seven forty-five."

After we ended the call, I went out and told Michelle she was off the hook. But she shook her head. "He can't be well enough. What if he fades on you? We're out of time, Samantha. We won't get a second crack at this. I'm coming."

I smiled, relieved. I'd need her if I had to toss an exhausted Alex in the trunk. "Maybe we'll hit Neptune's Net for lunch."

"Sounds perfect." The phone rang and Michelle answered it.

I went back to my office and put in a call to Storm. I wanted to find out what he'd told the reporters when he was off camera. But the call went to voice mail. I had a feeling he was dodging me. It probably didn't matter. I doubted he'd tell me the truth anyway.

I got busy preparing for the next witnesses. The rest of Zack's case was all physical evidence. I'd be doing back-to-back cross-examinations of experts. There wouldn't be any time to regroup between them, so I had to be on top of all of their reports. But it was tedious work, and I was already tired. My eyes kept closing. I shoved my window all the way open. The night air was cold, but it kept me awake.

I didn't look up again until Michelle came in. The digital clock on my desk said it was almost eleven. "Damn. I didn't realize how late it was. How come you're still here?"

"Same reason you are. But . . ." Michelle looked behind her. "Can you smell that?"

"Smell what?"

Michelle's brows were furrowed. "Smoke, I think."

I followed her out to the anteroom and sniffed the air. "Maybe." Even as I said it, the smell got stronger. I went to the front door and put my hands on it. The smell of smoke was stronger there. And the door was hot . . . and getting hotter. I turned to Michelle. "I think it's a fire."

Michelle stared at me, her face white. "Shit!"

The front door was our only exit. And our only way out of the building was the stairway down the hall. I had to see if we could get to it. I opened the door a crack. A wave of heat and smoke rolled in. I shielded my face as best I could and looked into the hallway. Flames were shooting out through the open door of the stairway and reaching across the hall. We were cut off. I slammed the door shut. "The fire's in the stairway!"

But Michelle was already screaming into the phone. "There's a fire! We can't get out! You've got to get someone here right now!" She gave our address, then listened. "No! There's no way out!"

I thought for a second. Actually, there was. I grabbed Michelle's hand and yanked her toward my office. Our only way out was the window. We'd probably break a few bones, but we'd survive. "We have to jump—"

But just as we stumbled into my office, something flew in through the window and smashed into my desk. A ball of flame exploded in front of us. I staggered back. We ran out and I slammed the door shut. We were trapped in the anteroom.

Smoke was flowing in through the cracks around the front door. I took off my jacket, rolled it up, and stuffed it into the opening at the bottom. But that wouldn't work for long. I could hear the fire roaring just outside. In minutes, we'd be engulfed. Panicked, I looked around the room. There had to be some way to get out of here. I pictured the hallway outside the office. Did it have any windows? No. There had to be a fire escape somewhere on this floor, didn't there? But I couldn't remember ever having seen one. And there was no way to get through that wall of fire in the hallway to find out.

The smoke was clouding my eyes and searing my lungs. It was getting harder and harder to breathe. I'd heard people actually died of smoke inhalation before the fire got to them. Now I knew why. It was like drowning on dry land.

We got down on the floor and huddled at Michelle's desk, coughing and hacking. I listened for the sound of sirens. I thought I heard one, but it was faint, probably too far away to get here in time—assuming it was even coming for us.

I felt weak, light-headed. I tried to think of something to do. But there was nowhere to go, nothing I could do. All our exits were blocked.

And now smoke filled the room. Michelle, just three feet away, was only an outline. She pointed to the copy room—Alex's office. "In there!"

The fire might not reach it as fast. And maybe it still had some clean air. We crawled on all fours, trying to stay below the worst of the smoke. But when we got there, I saw that the tiny space was already filled with smoke. I shook my head and backed away. "Better out there!"

But not much. As we crawled back out, I could hear the fire in my office snapping through the cheap furniture. In minutes, it would eat through the thin wall. I was dizzy and sick to my stomach. Gasping for air, I sagged against the wall. Michelle sank down next to me and crumpled to the floor. I tried to shake her awake, but I had no strength. I tried to call out to her. "Michelle!" But the roar of fire drowned out my hoarse croak.

My lungs burned as they strained for oxygen. Every breath felt like I was inhaling fire. I could feel my body sliding down to the floor. I covered my head and curled up in a ball. Then everything went black.

FIFTY-FIVE

I woke up with something over my face. I tried to grab it, but someone grabbed my hands and said, "It's oxygen. Just breathe." The sound of a siren pierced my ears, and I realized we were in motion. My chest burned and my eyes were streaming so badly everything was a blur. Then I passed out again. The next time I woke up, I was in a hospital bed. And ironically, Alex was standing next to it.

Disoriented and nauseous, I stared up at him, wondering if I was dreaming. "Alex? What're you doing here?"

"The cops. They were in the 'hood when the fire broke out, and they knew that was your office. That's how come the firemen got there so fast."

For a change, being in the middle of gang turf had paid off. "But how'd they reach you?"

Alex gave a little smile. "You're famous, remember? They know who you are, and they know who works with you. I think they called to find out where I was. How're you feeling?"

Something pinged in my head when he'd said "called." But I couldn't focus long enough to figure out what it was. "I'm okay." Dizzy, nauseous, and still breathing fire—but alive—which was a lot better than I'd expected. "Michelle?"

"Yeah, she looks the same as you. Kind of a mess, but still with us. What happened?"

Michelle was okay. Tears of relief leaked out of the corners of my eyes. My throat was raw and it was hard to talk. I croaked out slowly, "Don't know. Fire in the stairway. Then, someone threw . . . something through the window."

I could tell Alex was struggling not to sound alarmed. "Like a Molotov?" I shrugged. "Why? Who would do this to you?"

I had to take a deep breath to force out the words. "Don't know." I thought for a moment. Since the Molotov—or whatever the hell it was—had been thrown through my window, I was pretty sure I'd been targeted, but now it occurred to me there were other possibilities. "Might not be me. That copy service."

"The one right below our office?"

I nodded. "They're sinking. Owe money—"

"You think it's an insurance scam?"

"Or bangers . . ."

"Like maybe someone in the building might've pissed off some gangbangers?" I nodded. Alex looked skeptical. "Then why throw a Molotov through *your* window?"

"Only one open." I paused to take another deep breath—as deep as I could manage anyway.

Alex looked skeptical. "I guess it's possible." Alex fell silent for a moment. "But this case has generated an awful lot of attention. I don't have to tell you there are some crazies out there with real strong feelings about Dale—and *you*."

He was right. He didn't have to tell me. But would the nutballs go this far? It seemed a bit extreme. I shrugged. "Could be."

"Anyway, the cops have someone posted outside your door, and you should be here for a while, so I think you'll be safe."

A while? "No! Got to get out!" I only had one day to look for witnesses, and I wasn't going to let this damn fire ruin it for me.

Alex was exasperated. "Sam, you can't win this case if you're dead."

"I'm okay . . ." I had another coughing fit. "When can I get out?"

"When you stop doing that." I gave him a look. Alex sighed. "The nurse said if nothing goes wrong, they'd let you go after twenty-four hours."

I shook my head. "I don't have time—"

"Come on, even that maniac judge has to cut you some slack now."

"No." I paused to wheeze in another breath. Now that I'd been conscious for a little while, the possibility that I'd been targeted seemed more and more likely. And I didn't think it was by some whacked-out loony-bin reject. It wasn't that the firebombing was exactly a sophisticated effort. That stupid building was easy pickings. But it had taken some planning—not a lot, but some. "If someone's . . . trying to stop me . . . got to figure out why. Maybe we're onto something."

Alex didn't look happy, but he didn't argue. "I see your point. But if that's true, then you can't go home. You and Michelle should stay with me."

I waved him off. "Can't find me. My address . . . not public."

Alex was impatient. "If people are willing to burn down your office to get to you, what makes you think they wouldn't find a way to get your address?"

"It's blocked." Ever since my days as a public defender, I've had a block on my address. Even cops who stop me for speeding have to jump hurdles to get it.

"Want me to show you how fast I can find it? And they don't even have to be as good as me."

I held up a hand. "Please don't." I didn't need to see how wrong I'd been to feel so secure all these years. Especially right now.

He folded his arms. "It's my place or my uncle's."

"Okay. Thanks."

"*De nada*. Just give me the key to your place and a list of what you need."

I tried to draw another deep breath and went into another coughing jag. When it finally stopped, I said, "Keys were in my purse, but . . ." They'd be a melted mess by now. Everything was gone. I couldn't absorb it all. I closed my eyes. Alex's voice yanked me back.

"You don't have a spare anywhere?"

I forced myself to think. "I . . . wait, yeah. Taped on the ledge . . . above door." I still had my apartment. I hadn't lost everything. That thought made me feel a little better. I wrote down a list of what I'd need for the next couple of days.

Of course the press got ahold of the story. I had a television in my room, and it was showing the footage of my office building going up in flames. Michelle and I had been the only ones inside, and we were reported to be in "stable condition." But the building was a total disaster. One of the firemen said multiple code violations allowed the fire to spread as fast and hard as it did. That came as no shock. But the sight of it was devastating. Tears rolled down my cheeks as I watched all my hard work for the past seven years dissolve into ashes.

Alex had a mournful look as he watched with me. But after a few moments, he snatched the remote and turned it off. "Stop watching that. It's just a building. You're still a lawyer; you still have cases. And there'll be more." I nodded and wiped my cheeks. Alex handed me a Kleenex. "Have the police called you yet?"

Police. I hadn't thought about that. But his mention of the police calling made me remember what'd pinged me before. "Phone!" My heart was hammering in my chest. Paige's cell phone had been in my purse—the purse that was now a puddle of ashes and soot. We'd never find the place now. "Paige's phone . . . the photo . . ."

Alex put a hand on my shoulder. "Samantha, it's okay. You left the phone with me. Remember?" It took a moment to register. That's right. I'd left it with him when I went to see him at his uncle's house. The relief was so sharp I couldn't speak. I closed my eyes and focused on breathing. Alex patted my arm. "Get some rest. I'll be back tomorrow to pick you both up."

I slept as well as anyone can in a hospital, with nurses constantly checking this and probing that. But I didn't have any other visitors that night. Reporters had been calling the hospital, and the next morning, some even tried to see me. I told the nurses to throw them out and refused all calls. But there was one person I couldn't keep out.

Jack tapped on the door, which was standing open. As always, his round, smiling face and rosy cheeks lifted my spirits. The full head of auburn hair he'd had when he'd married Celeste was just a monk's fringe now, and it was all white—like his neatly trimmed beard and mustache. But he moved like a man half his age, and he exuded good energy. His marriage to my mother was proof that darkness seeks out light.

The smile froze on my face when I realized his appearance might mean Celeste was there. But when I looked over his shoulder, I saw he was alone. My smile relaxed into the real thing, and I told him to come in.

He came over and kissed my forehead. "How are you feeling? You look remarkably good, all things considered."

"Getting better by the minute." And I was. It had been a long, fairly sleepless night, but now my voice was almost back to normal, and the coughing fits were nearly gone.

He pulled up a chair and sat next to my bed. "I assume the police will be investigating. Do you have any idea who might've done this? Or why?"

"No. It might just be a scam by one of the other businesses in the building."

"Can't pay the rent?" I nodded. "Wouldn't surprise me. Well, I'm just glad you're okay. Can I get you anything to eat? I'm sure the food here really sucks."

I laughed. "They brought me scrambled eggs that tasted like cardboard. How do you mess up scrambled eggs?"

Jack smiled. "It's a medical miracle. But you're not hungry?" I shook my head. "What about clothes, shampoo? I'd be glad to bring you anything you need."

"Thanks, Jack. I should be getting out pretty soon, so I'll be okay."

"What time? I'll pick you up—"

"I really appreciate it, but no worries. I've got it covered."

Jack patted my hand. I saw a shadow pass over his face. I had a feeling I knew what was coming. I was right. "Your mother wanted to come see you, but we thought it might be best not to right now, given how . . . strained things have been between you two lately."

This was the time to tell him that things weren't just strained between us—they were over. Forever. But for some reason, I couldn't bring myself to do it.

I gave him a twisted smile. "Bet it wasn't too hard to talk her out of coming." Celeste hated hospitals. And it would never have occurred to her to come just to check in on me. Had she really said she wanted to come? I doubted it. But if she did, it was only so she'd look good—probably knowing full well Jack would take her off the hook. Win-win for Celeste.

Jack's expression saddened. "Come on, Samantha. Your mother loves you. Surely you know that."

I knew Jack believed it, and I didn't want to hurt him. But I didn't want him to think I believed in that fiction. I put it as mildly as I could. "I think you see a different side of her than I do."

He frowned briefly and looked away. It was an understatement, but it was the truth. Would he ever be able to see that? Or was it possible he already suspected it? I couldn't tell. But even if he did, I didn't think he'd ever know what a monster she really was. And maybe it was better this way. He got his dream. She got hers.

FIFTY-SIX

That night, when the nurse told me I could leave, I was so happy I raised an arm to do a fist pump—and almost ripped out the IV needle. The nurse shook her head as she removed it. "I'm probably talking to myself right now, but you need to take it easy. Your body's been through a lot." I nodded and tried to look compliant.

Her expression told me she wasn't fooled. She probably got lied to as much as I did.

When Alex arrived to pick us up that night, I told him I didn't think I'd ever been happier to see anyone in my whole life. He'd parked at the back door, which was empty at that time of night, to make sure no one saw us leave. We made it to Alex's place in no time, and when he opened the door, Michelle and I stood in the doorway and stared. His apartment, decorated in a modern, minimalist style, was sparkling clean. "You didn't have to spiff up for us, Alex."

He looked puzzled. "I didn't."

I looked around at the spotless kitchen, the dustless living room. "You will not be allowed to see my place unless you're drunk."

Alex smiled. "Don't worry. I don't judge. Much." Then his smile faded. "Sit down. I've got some bad news."

Michelle and I sank down on the beige sofa in the living room. I didn't know if I could take it. "What now?"

"Someone broke into your apartment. It's . . . pretty bad. I couldn't tell if anything was missing. But the place was really turned upside down. It looked like they were searching for something. Did you keep any files there?"

My heart began to pound. "No." The import of it hit me like a sucker punch. The tiny sliver of hope I'd had that the fire wasn't meant for me vanished. But there was an upside to that. "Then I was right. We're onto something." And it had to be something we'd gotten recently—something the public would know about. I forced my tired brain to backtrack. "Storm."

Michelle nodded, her face pale and pinched with fatigue. "Right."

Alex nodded. "Did you ever find out what he told the reporters off the record?"

"No. He never called me back." I paused. "And I'm not sure he did say anything off the record. But maybe he didn't need to."

Michelle rubbed her temples. "That's true. If we're right about this, he obviously said enough to make someone think he was a threat."

Alex narrowed his eyes. "And Storm might know more than you— or he even realizes."

I agreed. "But given what he said to the press, we know one thing for sure: my theory that Paige was the target must be close to the mark."

Alex met my gaze. "Exactly."

But that made it clear I couldn't stay here. "I think I'd better go to a hotel, Alex. If they could find my apartment, they could find—"

"No, they couldn't. Because I know how to hide." He gave me a pointed look. "Remember how we met, Samantha." He'd hidden those two BMWs beautifully. "No one knows where I live except my uncle. You're safe here."

"But we've got to tell the cops," Michelle said.

"And we will," I said. "Just not yet. Whoever's after me won't know where I am until I go back to court. That means we have tomorrow. And it's all we've got, so I want to use it." I'd been too thrashed to feel anything but pain and exhaustion. But now that I was better, I had energy to spare for anger, and it felt like a red-hot spike in my gut. Someone had tried to kill us—and destroy our evidence. And whoever that was wanted me to run and hide. Well, to hell with that. "I'm not just going to let the asshole who did this back me down. I don't know if it'll pan out. I just know I've got to see it through." I looked from Alex to Michelle. "But you guys don't have to go with me. This is *my* insanity. I don't want to drag you down with me."

Michelle still looked pale, but she shook her head. "Save it. I—" She had a coughing fit. When she'd recovered, she took a deep breath. "I'm going."

Alex gave her a skeptical look. "Uh-huh."

She waved him off. "I'll be fine. One good night's sleep away from that damn hospital and I'll be good as new. What time are we getting up?"

I pulled my phone out of my purse. It was ten thirty. "I'd like to aim for seven thirty. Sound okay?"

They both nodded. Alex looked from me to Michelle. "Okay. You two can either share the foldout couch in the guest room, or one of you can sleep on this one." He pointed to the sofa we were sitting on. It was nice to look at, but it was hard.

Michelle and I exchanged a look. "We'll share," I said.

We talked for a little while about our plans for tomorrow, then called it a night.

Michelle and I hadn't shared a bed since we were in ninth grade, and I was always leery of sleeping with someone because I never knew when I'd wake up screaming. But it wasn't a problem. We were so tired, we fell asleep within seconds, and I didn't wake up until Alex knocked on the door the next morning.

FIFTY-SEVEN

Alex had coffee waiting. We gulped it down and got on the road by eight o'clock. There were a few things I'd forgotten to ask Alex to pick up, so we had to stop at my apartment. Alex wanted to go in for me, to spare me the bummer of seeing how badly it'd been thrashed, but that would take longer, and I didn't want to waste the time. Alex had put a padlock on the door because the flimsy door-handle lock had been broken. When I got the padlock off and pushed the door open, I stood there, frozen.

It was a horrible sight. The place had been turned upside down, and a violent energy still hung in the air. It felt as though the burglar was still there. I got out as fast as I could. I'd have to call the police and report it soon. But there was no point wasting time with it right now. Anyway, a report was just a formality. The odds of them catching the burglar were about as good as my winning the lottery. And I've never bought a ticket.

I got back to the car within minutes, and we headed for Malibu. The good thing about doing this on a Sunday was that there was no traffic. We'd make good time, and it'd be easier to see if we were being followed. We watched for any suspicious cars all the way to Pacific Coast Highway. The road behind us was clear.

It was one of those sparkling fall days when all the colors seem too vivid to be real—the cornflower-blue sky, the golden sunshine, the azure ocean that shimmered like glass.

The beauty of the day and the hope for our mission buoyed our spirits. We started our search at the northern edge of the Colony, energized and optimistic. We drove up one street and down another, working our way up the coast, sure we'd be able to find the house in the background of Marc's photo in no time. But as we traveled up and down block after block, our spirits sank like a punctured air mattress.

By noon, we were tired, stumped, and demoralized. And I was starving. I spotted a sandwich shop across the highway from the ocean. "Let's take a break. I'm buying."

We ordered at the counter and took our sandwiches to the little metal table on the front patio. There was an older couple at the table next to ours who wore the unflashy tans and bleached cotton T-shirts and shorts of locals. I told them we were looking for a house that our friend had visited and asked if they might recognize the area from a photo. They said they'd give it a try. I showed them the photo on Paige's phone.

The woman squinted at it and tilted her head. "I don't know where this is, but it's not this neighborhood." She passed the phone to her husband.

He stared at it for a few beats. "I couldn't tell you what street this is, but it kind of reminds me of Broad Beach. You know where that is?"

I'd heard of it. Broad Beach was multimillionaire territory, where humongous mansions sat right on the sand. Mega-celebrities like Barbra Streisand and Danny DeVito lived there. "It's a little north of here, right?"

"Yeah. Just head up the coast."

I thanked them and we got back into Alex's car. "There you go. Progress at last."

Michelle gave me a tired look. "Unless there's more than one street in Broad Beach."

I sighed. "And more than one house on that street. But at least we're getting closer."

We found the road the man had told us about. It was exotically named Broad Beach Road. But we couldn't find a spot that looked like the one where Marc had been. We showed the photograph to everyone we saw, but none of them recognized the area.

It was almost five o'clock, and we were running out of energy—and daylight. I suggested a last-ditch effort across the highway, where there was a Rite Aid, a liquor store called Beachside Bevs, and a gas station.

The clerk at the liquor store, a tall, skinny young guy with acne, studied the photo, then shook his head. "Nah. Doesn't look familiar to me."

We struck out with all the clerks at the Rite Aid, too. The gas station was our last chance. I showed the photo to the cashier. She stared at it, and I could see she was really trying. But she shook her head. "No, sorry."

We were about to leave when I noticed a mechanic working on an old Mercedes. I nodded toward him. "What the hell, it's worth a try."

Alex and Michelle followed as I headed toward the service bay. He had a tat on his neck that said Live Free or Die, and he wore a leather necklace with what looked like an animal tooth.

I asked him if he might recognize a street in a photo I had. I held up the phone, and he wiped his hands on a dirty rag as he studied it. His face brightened. "Yeah. I know that place. It's at the end of Sea Smoke Drive."

A jolt of electricity ran through me. I tried to act casual. "You know the address?"

"The last house at the end of the road. It's one of the smaller cribs in this community. You can't miss it. Sits by itself out there."

"How do you know the place?"

"Been taking care of their cars for the past couple of years. I pick 'em up and deliver 'em."

"Then you know the people who live there?"

"Sure. Cory and Sarah Larsen. But if you're looking for them, you're out of luck. They're in Thailand. Took off at the end of January. Won't be back till next year."

The end of January was right around the time Marc had taken the photo. But that meant these people—the Larsens—had been gone for months by the time he and Paige got killed. Marc and Paige wouldn't have gone there if no one was home. Unless someone else was staying in the house. "Has someone been house-sitting for them?"

"Nope. They told me they were locking it up, asked me to check the place when I had a chance. Matter of fact, I'm storing their cars for them."

How could this be? I felt like an anchor had lodged in my chest. I'd been so sure I was about to hit gold. Not only didn't I hit gold but my one solid hope had been crushed.

Depressed, I thanked the mechanic and we trudged back to Alex's car.

Alex leaned over the steering wheel and stared at the ocean. "Someone else might still have access to the place."

I sighed. "I suppose."

Michelle rallied. "And maybe Crocodile Dundee over there was wrong. Maybe it's another house."

Alex nodded. "She's right. Either way, it couldn't hurt to look."

"Sure," I said. "We're here. May as well."

It took us a while to find Sea Smoke Drive, and when I saw the house at the end of the road, I knew he'd pegged the right place. This was where Marc had taken the photo. The mechanic hadn't been exaggerating when he said the house sat out there by itself. There were an easy fifty yards between it and the next-to-last house on the street.

Alex drove past the house, then parked farther up the road. "Let's get out and look around."

By now the sun was close to the horizon, and the ocean had a red glow. I wandered down the street behind Alex and Michelle, trying to figure out if there was still a way to resurrect the Marc angle. But without some evidence that Paige had been here with Marc that night, I didn't see how it could work. It'd just come off sounding like a flimsy distraction. Which it was.

Alex and Michelle were circling around behind the house to the backyard—fifty feet of sand that led straight to the ocean, a private beach. I walked up to the front of the house and looked for a gap in the drapes. I found a small one a few feet to the right of the door, but it was completely dark inside. I couldn't see a thing. Just for the hell of it, I knocked on the door. No answer.

Then, without thinking about what I was doing, I grabbed the doorknob and tried to turn it. It gave. It wasn't locked? How could that be? The mechanic had said no one was house-sitting for them. Something was wrong. My palms started to sweat. I didn't want to call out to Alex and Michelle. It didn't look like anyone was home, but it'd be bad to get busted for breaking and entering. I looked around. I didn't see anyone nearby.

I put my head to the door and listened for signs of life, but I didn't hear anything. I pushed the door open as slowly and quietly as I could and peered inside. The house was dark. All the drapes were closed. I made out a large sunken living room on my right. Straight ahead was a dining area, with a small kitchen to the right. There was a gap in the drapes on the wall of the dining area that let in a sliver of light, and I could see that they covered sliding glass doors that opened onto the private beach.

Slowly, my eyes adjusted to the darkness. The place had been trashed. Table lamps lay broken on the floor, couch cushions were thrown around, and the drawers in the coffee table had been pulled out. I stepped inside, leaving the door open behind me. As I walked into the foyer, I stepped on something that crunched under my shoe. It sounded like glass. I noticed a broken vase lying on the floor a few feet away.

Someone had busted in, that was for sure. But I had no way of knowing if anything had been stolen. I moved through the living room and headed for the hallway that led to the rest of the house. My heart thudded in my chest as I made my way through the gloom, my ears straining for any sounds of movement—maybe by the person who'd busted in here. I came to a bedroom on my right. It was a mess, but it wasn't thrashed like the living room. Clothes were strewn around, the carpet was coated in sand and dirt, the bed was unmade, and there was a sleeping bag on the floor. That, and the empty fast-food wrappers and bottles, showed someone had been staying here, but I couldn't tell how recently.

I paused again to listen for movement. Nothing. I headed farther down the hall. When I got to the end, I saw what looked like the master bedroom on my left. It was big, and it, too, was a mess. There was another sliding glass door at the far end of the room. Drapes covered the view, but from the sand caked into the carpet, I surmised it also opened onto the beach. The duvet on the king-size bed was pushed to the side, the sheets looked rumpled and dirty, and the pillows were squashed. Someone was sleeping here, too. But nothing was thrown around or broken. I stepped inside and opened my phone to give myself more light. To the right of the bedroom door was a walk-in closet. Ahead, just past the bed, was a half wall that separated the bedroom from a large marble-floored bathroom. I was about to go and have a look at the bathroom when I heard a scrabbling sound coming from the sliding glass door. My throat tightened. Then a latch clicked open. Whoever was camping here had come back.

I ran to the closet. I couldn't risk them seeing me close the closet door, so I had to leave it open. I hunkered down against the wall and tried not to breathe.

FIFTY-EIGHT

I heard the sliding glass door open. The sound and smell of the ocean poured into the room. My lungs ached for air. If they decided to hang out in the bedroom, they'd catch me for sure. My only hope was that they'd head into the kitchen.

I heard footsteps on the carpet. Then a voice. "Why would they leave it open?"

It was Michelle. Light-headed, I leaned back against the wall of the closet and let in a long, deep breath. It took a few seconds before my rubbery legs would let me straighten up out of my crouch. I took another deep breath before I walked out into the bedroom. "Hey, guys. Nice place, huh?"

Alex and Michelle jumped, then stared at me. Michelle pointed to the closet. "What were you doing in there?"

"Hiding. It looks like someone—maybe a few someones—are hanging out here. And it doesn't look like they're invited guests. I thought you were them."

It was really dark now. I moved to the doorway, found the light switch, and flipped it. The lights came on. I was surprised. "Kind of weird that they left the electricity on if they're gone for a year. Seems like a waste."

"Maybe it's on a timer," Michelle said.

"I guess. Did you guys see the rest of the place?"

Alex shook his head. "We didn't think it'd be open. I just tried that sliding glass door for the heck of it. The hasp on the latch is broken."

Michelle moved through the bedroom toward the hallway. "What does the rest of the place look like?"

"Like Whitesnake and Ratt partied hard. Come on." I turned off the bedroom light. I didn't want to attract any attention—from the squatters or any security patrol. I held up my phone and led the way out to the living room. Now that I could see better, I noticed this was more than just a really bad mess. I moved around the room, looking at everything closely. The broken vase in the foyer had sent glass flying into the living room. And the table lamp seemed to have fallen off a side table that was knocked over.

Michelle took in the scene. "Kinda looks like the squatters had a disagreement."

"Does." I moved around the room and took some pictures, but I was getting nervous about hanging around this place. "We should get going. I have a feeling we don't want to meet whoever camps out here."

Michelle followed me down the hall. "Assuming they still are. Don't you think it's weird they haven't been caught? A 'hood like this must have some kind of security."

"Some kind, sure. But we didn't notice anything wrong from the outside, so unless security patrol actually checked doors and windows—which obviously they didn't—they wouldn't know. And the nearest neighbors aren't that close." The more I thought about what we'd seen in that house, the more sure I was that the squatters still called this place home. Which meant they could come back any minute. I wanted to get out of there. I motioned for Michelle to follow me and headed back to the master bedroom.

Alex had turned the light back on. He was standing on the bed and staring at the ceiling.

"You okay?"

He glanced down at us. "See this smoke alarm?" I looked up at the round plastic fixture Alex was studying. I nodded. "It looks just like the one my uncle uses at his workplace."

"So? Look, Alex, we need to get out of here. This is someone's crash pad, and they might be back any second." And with the lights on in this bedroom, the squatters would know they'd been invaded even from a distance.

Alex reached up and pulled on the plastic casing. "Just give me a sec."

I took a closer look around the bedroom. The flat-screen television on the wall facing the bed looked fairly new. The furniture was average, nondescript—somewhere between high-end and yard-sale quality. I wondered if this was a summer home. It had the look of a place that got secondary attention. When I got to the nightstand on the left of the bed, I saw a notepad. There was a phone number written on it. I snapped a photo.

I noticed a couple of framed photographs on the dresser. One showed a slim, not necessarily pretty, woman, with long hair parted on the side that dipped over one eye. She was wearing a short sarong skirt with a bikini top, and she was sitting on a man's lap with her legs crossed. He had a hand wedged between her thighs. It was just a few inches shy of a crotch grab. They looked like they were in their twenties. The photo next to it showed the same couple, but older—by about twenty years. The man was standing behind the woman. An arm wrapped around her waist held her against his body, and she was bent slightly forward, half sitting on his leg. They both wore broad smiles. The poses in both photos were obviously intended to be sexy, but something about them felt kind of . . . creepy. I took pictures of them, then looked through the drawers. When I got to the bottom right drawer,

I found a stack of what looked like color printouts. I pulled them out. One showed a picture of a woman on her hands and knees with a dog mounted on her back. Jeez. I looked through a few more and saw that they were of the same ilk—some with horses. After the first few, I didn't need to see anymore. I held one of them up. "Whoever these owners are, they're real sickos. Check it out."

Michelle came over, looked, and made a gagging sound. "Put those things away." She moved to the closet and turned on the light.

I put the printouts back and closed the drawer. "Anything in there?"

Her voice was muffled. "Just some old clothes." Michelle came out. "Thank God, no dog collars—"

I stood up. "Or bridles."

Michelle made a face. "You're disgusting."

I gave a short laugh. "*I'm* disgusting? *I*—" I stopped. I heard voices. Male voices. They were coming from just outside, near the front of the house, and they were getting closer.

Michelle's eyes got wide. "Holy shit."

Alex was still fiddling with the smoke alarm. I tapped his leg and whispered, "Alex, forget that thing. We've got to get out of here."

"Turn off the light. You guys go. I'll be okay. It'll just be a minute."

I turned off the light, but I wasn't about to leave him there by himself. "Michelle, take off. They won't see you if you go out that way." I pointed to the sliding glass door at the far end of the room that opened onto the beach.

She looked from me to Alex. I could tell she didn't want to go, but her face had drained of color, and she was shaking. I could feel my heart pounding, too. If the condition of that living room was any indication, these guys were not the peaceful type. And I didn't have my gun. The voices got louder. It sounded like they were nearing the front door.

Alex looked down at me. He whispered, "Can you get me a pair of tweezers? There might be some in the bathroom."

Michelle pulled on his pants leg. "No! Alex, forget it. We've got to get out of here."

But Alex shook his head. There was no point wasting time arguing. I ran to the bathroom and searched the drawers, found an old pair, raced back, and handed it up to him. "Hurry. Please."

Alex used the edge to unscrew the plastic plate. But the alarm was attached to the ceiling by wires. "Alex, I don't know what you think that is, but it looks like a real smoke alarm to me. Let it go."

And then I heard the front door open. Heavy footsteps thudded on the wooden floor and headed into the kitchen. I heard a male voice say, "Put this in the fridge for later." Another male voice laughed. The refrigerator opened, then closed.

Michelle moved toward the sliding glass door and whispered, "Come on, Alex!" She opened the door and took a step out. Then suddenly, she jumped back inside. Her voice shook as she said, "There're two more right outside."

"Two more . . . what?" I asked.

"Guys." Michelle was so white I thought she was going to faint. "And they don't look like they belong in this 'hood."

I pulled Michelle away from the door, slid it, and shoved her toward the closet. "Alex, we've got to go!"

"Just one more sec. Almost got it."

I wanted to yank him off the bed and drag him out of there, but I was afraid to make noise. Exasperated, I went over to the bed and held my phone up to give him light. I whispered with as much heat as I could, "Wrap it up, Alex. Or we might not live to see whatever you think you've got there."

I listened for the voices of the men outside the house. They were faint. It was hard to tell how close they were over the sound of breaking waves. Should we wait? If we did, maybe they'd move on. But I could hear the others moving around in the kitchen. If they decided to come and kick it in the bedroom, we were toast. And that could happen any second now. "Alex, come on!"

Finally, Alex pulled the alarm free. "Got it!" But he'd spoken out loud.

A voice just down the hall said, "What the fuck was that?"

There was no choice now. I went to the closet, grabbed Michelle by the hand, and headed to the sliding glass door. I listened again. The voices outside sounded like they were coming from the right. I turned back to Alex and pointed to the left. He nodded.

I slid the door open and stepped out as quietly as I could. Michelle was right behind me. I whispered to Michelle over my shoulder, "Go!"

I ran as fast and hard as I could. But running through sand feels like one of those nightmares where your feet are lead weights and the monster's breath is hot on your back. I heard the men shouting behind me, but I kept going. Over my right shoulder, I could hear Michelle wheezing as she tried to keep up. My throat and chest were burning and I noticed that I was wheezing, too. When I glanced back, I saw that Alex was at least twenty feet behind Michelle. I knew he was faster than both of us. He was deliberately hanging back to give us cover.

I kept running, though now every breath felt like a knife scraping through my lungs. Finally I reached the nearest neighbor's backyard. I ran through it on purpose, hoping someone might see us and call the police but I didn't see any lights on inside. No hope there. It was getting too painful to breathe, and I could feel my footsteps slowing. When I got to the far edge of the property, I turned left and headed for the street. Michelle was right behind me. As I neared the street, the shouts grew louder. I turned to look over my shoulder and saw two rough-looking men coming up fast behind Alex.

The car was only twenty yards away, but they were gaining on him—and he had the car keys. I did the only thing I could think of. I pushed a button on my phone to make the screen light up and held it over my head. I took a deep, searingly painful breath and screamed, "I'm calling the police!"

The men slowed, but they didn't stop. I glanced at the nearest houses. Surely the neighbors must've heard me? If they did, they were ignoring me. No one came out. I tried to yell again, but my throat was raw and I could barely breathe. All that came out was a strangled croak. The only thing I could think to do was to keep holding my phone up as I backed toward the car. Alex was running at full speed, and I saw that he was finally pulling away from the men. As he drew near, he reached out, the remote in his hand, and I heard the beep beep of the car alarm. We were only ten yards away from the car, but the squatters had started to run again. I tried to yell, "Hurry!" but my voice was shot. Frantic, I waved my arms at Alex, then turned and raced to the car. Michelle had already run past me; she was getting into the back seat. I turned back and saw that Alex had made it out to the street, but one of the men was right behind him.

I got to the car and stopped. What could I do? Frantic, I looked around for something to throw. I saw the extra bottle of Diet Coke I'd bought at lunch on the passenger side floor. I yanked open the door, snatched it up, and hurled it at the man. It was the Hail Mary pass of all time. But somehow, I managed to hit him on the head. It startled him—probably more than it hurt him. But it stopped him just long enough to give Alex time to get to the car. We both jumped in. Alex fired up the engine and hit the door lock just as one of the men slammed his body into the rear driver's-side door. Michelle screamed. But Alex punched the gas and the man fell back. We sped out of there.

I lay back in the seat, gasping for air. I didn't have enough wind to talk until we turned on to Pacific Coast Highway. My voice sounded like sandpaper scraping concrete. "Alex, that smoke alarm better be linked to the Pentagon or I'll kill you."

"I don't know what it's linked to. Maybe nothing. But I do know this much: it's definitely not a smoke alarm. It's a camera."

FIFTY-NINE

We were just about to head into Santa Monica when Alex's cell phone gave a loud *ping*. He handed the phone to me. "I've got a Google alert tagged to Dale's name."

The alert was a link to a news banner that read: "Tragic Accident on Mountain Road. Death Linked to Pearson Murder Case." My heart gave an agonizing thump as I read it aloud.

Michelle, her voice sounding as bad as mine, echoed my thoughts. "Oh God, no. *Now* what?" I wished I didn't have to find out. I hit the link and held the phone so Michelle could watch with me. A blonde anchor wearing a plunging neckline announced in dire tones, "A tragic accident has claimed the life of a witness who recently surfaced in the Dale Pearson case. Experts are saying it's bound to be a serious blow to the defense. Jim Martinelli has the latest. Jim?"

The blonde anchor threw to a reporter standing on the shoulder of a road.

Behind him, the sun had faded to a dim glow, and the mountains loomed dark and ominous. "Laura, I'm standing just forty feet away from the spot where stuntman Storm Cooper's motorcycle went off the road here on Mulholland Highway. There were no witnesses, but police believe he lost control and drove off the embankment, then plunged to his death three hundred feet below. Authorities were alerted to look for the body when a hiker familiar with the area noticed new tire marks that seemed to skid off the asphalt, continue across the dirt shoulder, and go straight off the cliff. This road is very popular among bikers. Friends of the stuntman say it was one of his favorite rides. Now, it seems this was his last ride. Back to you, Laura."

I closed the link.

"An accident," Michelle said. "I can't believe it."

I stared at the screen. "I *don't* believe it." Not after the fire. And the burglary of my apartment.

Michelle looked at me, stricken. "But he didn't really tell you all that much."

"No. Either he knew more than he told me, or someone thought he did."

Alex glanced at me, his expression worried. "Samantha, if you're right, we can't put this off anymore. We've got to call the police."

Michelle sat forward, her arms wrapped around her torso. "He's right. Someone just killed a friggin' witness, for God's sake. And almost got *us*."

I nodded. I was plenty scared. And a little in shock. The thought that someone had killed Storm—in part because of me—was horrifying. But the likelihood of it was undeniable given everything that had happened, and the timing of it all. "Okay, we'll call the police." I looked at Alex's phone. It was only six o'clock. I couldn't believe it. It felt like midnight. "Let's just hold off until we see what's on that camera." I gave Alex a pointed look. "Since it almost got us killed."

When we got back to his apartment, he examined it and explained. "It's a motion-activated camera with a built-in DVR that records onto an SD card. Pretty simple device. I should be able to hook it up to a television and play whatever it captured."

Michelle had poured herself a glass of wine to stop her hands from shaking. "How'd you know that thing was a camera? It looks like a garden-variety smoke alarm to me."

"Because my uncle has one just like it in his office. He uses it for security . . . and to spy on his employees."

Michelle took a sip of her wine. "Maybe they put it in as a security thing, too, since they're gone for . . . what did that mechanic say? A year?"

Alex nodded. "That's possible. But then I'd expect to see other surveillance gear outside the house, and maybe in other rooms, too. When we walked around the outside of the house, I didn't see any cameras."

Alex went to a cupboard in the kitchen and pulled out a plastic tub filled with all kinds of power and electrical cords. He chose one, took the alarm over to the television in the living room, and plugged it into the television. "Okay. Let's see what we've got."

Alex changed the input on the television and started the camera. An image flickered on. A paunchy, dark-haired man in his forties was looking up at the camera. He waved his arms, then got up on the bed. Then the screen went dark. I pointed to the television. "That's the guy in the photos. The ones I saw on the dresser." I pulled up the photos I'd taken in the bedroom and showed them to Alex and Michelle.

Alex nodded. "Mr. Larsen, I'm guessing."

"Yeah," Michelle said. "What was he doing? Was he testing the thing?"

Alex nodded. "Looks like it."

The camera continued to play. The next image showed a handsome blond man in a silk robe moving around the bed. There was a bottle of champagne in an ice bucket on the nightstand. A woman lay on the bed behind him. "How come there's no sound?"

Alex frowned. "I don't know. My uncle's has sound. It might not have that feature. Or it might be a malfunction."

I hoped it didn't matter. "Pause when we get to a better shot of the woman."

Alex nodded and restarted the camera. The blond man sat down on the bed, picked up a small mirror and a rolled-up bill, and held it to his nose. He snorted a couple of lines, then passed it to the woman behind him. When she took the mirror, he left the room. Now we had an unobscured view of the bed. Alex paused the video. I stood up and walked over to the television. I stared at the woman's face. "Oh my God. That's Paige."

Michelle leaned forward and looked closely at the screen. "You're right."

We were all silent for a few moments as we studied the image. But it was too soon to tell whether this would do anything for us. There was no date or time stamped on the video. I stepped back. "Okay. Let 'er rip."

Alex hit play. The blond man came back, followed by a younger-looking man. I grabbed Alex's arm. "Can you pause again?"

As I stared at the frame, my heart began to beat hard and fast. I pointed to the younger man. "That's Marc, isn't it?"

Michelle looked closer. "It sure is."

Alex nodded. "Yeah. But who's the blond guy?"

"No clue. Okay, hit it, Alex."

The blond man dropped his robe and got on the bed next to Paige. He looked tall, and he was lean but well muscled. Marc, who was a lot thinner and shorter than the blond man by several inches, lay down on the other side of her. Now I noticed that there were three glasses next to the ice bucket. Paige got up and slid off the bed. Based on my memory of the place, it looked like she was heading for the bathroom.

As soon as she left, the blond man rolled Marc over, facedown on the bed, and started to climb onto his back. Marc shoved him off, looking angry. He pushed Marc back down and tried to get on top of him again. This time, Marc bucked him off and swung out his arm, hitting the blond guy in the throat.

They started to grapple. Paige must've heard them fighting because she came running back into the bedroom and tried to pull him away from Marc. Marc seized the opportunity and took another swing at him, but he failed to connect. The blond man suddenly twisted away, grabbed the champagne bottle, and raised it over his head. But before he could swing it, Marc tumbled to the floor and scrambled out of view.

The blond man followed, holding the bottle like a club, and also moved out of view. Now Paige was alone; she grabbed a towel off the floor, wrapped it around her, and hurried out after them. The camera flickered for a second, then we saw Paige run back through the bedroom and head for the bathroom. She was sobbing. I asked Alex to pause. "What the hell? Why did it flicker like that? Is it broken?"

Alex shook his head. "No. It's motion activated. When it doesn't detect motion, it shuts off. That means when everyone moved out of range, it stopped recording. So there's a time gap here. We know they all left the bedroom, but we don't know for how long."

I nodded. "But from the looks of things, whatever happened outside the bedroom wasn't pretty." I remembered the condition of the living room. "Maybe that mess in the living room wasn't just because of the squatters. That blond guy looked hella pissed—"

Michelle stood up, still staring at the television. "And the other rooms weren't anywhere near as thrashed."

Alex restarted the camera. In the next frame, Paige was fully dressed and moving from the bathroom toward the bedroom door. Her makeup ran in black streaks down her face. She picked up her purse off the dresser and ran out.

The camera flickered again, and now we saw someone entering the bedroom through the sliding glass door that opened onto the beach. It was the blond guy, and he was bare-chested, wearing only jeans. And he was soaking wet. He moved slowly and seemed to be breathing hard. He stripped off the wet jeans, went to the dresser, pulled out a pair of pants and a T-shirt, and put them on. Then he walked out of the bedroom. The camera flickered again.

I had a feeling I knew what had just happened as I waited for the next image.

He came back into the bedroom holding his robe in one hand and a cell phone in the other. He dropped the robe on the bed and punched in a number on the phone. He stood listening for a few seconds, then punched the keys again. He raked a hand through his wet hair and paced as he listened. I saw his lips move; then he lowered the phone and paced some more. It looked like he'd gotten someone's voice mail and left a message. A few seconds later, he punched in another number. He began to pace again as he listened, but this time he didn't speak. Whoever he was calling wasn't answering.

He threw the phone down, sat on the bed, put his head in his hands, and rocked back and forth. A few seconds later, he snatched the phone back up. This time someone answered. I saw his lips move as his hand made sharp, emphatic movements. He picked up his wet jeans and his robe as he spoke. Then he walked out of the room. The camera flickered again.

I held my breath, not knowing what I hoped to see. But the next frame showed a ragged-looking man in a battered trench coat carrying a paper bag. He took a swig from the bag, looked around, then flopped down on the bed. We kept watching, but the rest of the images showed only that man and his friends—probably our not-so-friendly squatters.

Alex finally turned off the camera. "I guess that's all we've got."

I stared at the blank television screen. "Is there any way to retrieve a date and time from that footage?"

"I don't know," Alex said. "I could try." He put down the remote. "But I think I have an idea who that blond man is."

I did, too. "Mr. Perfect." He sure fit the bill, with his well-groomed hair and super-toned body. We knew Paige had started seeing him in January, so this footage was definitely taken after that. I mentally reviewed the images we'd just seen. "Looks to me like he might've killed Marc and dragged his body out into the ocean. That's why he was soaking wet when he came back in through the sliding glass door—"

Alex stood up. "And why we didn't see Marc again—"

Michelle frowned. "But how do we prove that? There's no time or date stamp on that footage. For all we know, Marc just passed out in the living room—or got knocked out—and Mr. Perfect took off."

Good question. I paced as I replayed the footage in my head. "Alex, can you give us the first frame with Paige again?"

He started the camera and paused when Paige came into view. I studied the frame. "Is there any footage before that?" He restarted the camera from the very beginning. When it showed the blond man moving toward the nightstand, I told him to stop. I searched for what I thought I'd seen before. And found it. I pointed to a leopard-print skirt and black blouse on the floor near the nightstand. "That's Paige's skirt and blouse. Remember? They were in the crime-scene photos at her apartment. The cops found them in the hamper."

Alex sat back and nodded. "Yeah, that's right. And those were the only clothes in her hamper. So this must've happened the night she died."

If Paige and Marc died on the same night, it was no coincidence. That meant Chloe really wasn't the target. Paige was. And Mr. Perfect was looking good as the girls' real killer. But as I thought about what we had, I shook my head. "The problem is, Marc's friends weren't specific about when they last saw him, and the coroner was pretty vague about how long he'd been in the water. So we can't say for sure whether that footage was taken the night Marc died. We need more." I started to pace. "But one thing I am sure of: that blond man is Mr. Perfect. Dale said that's who she was going to see that night."

Alex frowned. "You think he killed Paige to keep her quiet?"

I shrugged. "Him, or the person he called." I again replayed the video footage in my mind. "But the pieces fit. We just need to figure out who he is."

Alex added, "And who he called."

Michelle gave me a warning look. "But we agreed whoever's behind all this is out to kill us—and he's already killed Storm. So we're going to let the police take over now, right?" She watched me pace, then repeated with a lot more force, "*Right*, Sam?"

I stopped pacing and faced her. "Here's the thing. As of now, we have some decent theories. But like you said, for all we know, Marc just took off after the fight. In which case, Mr. Perfect had no motive to kill Paige."

Michelle frowned at me. "But he was soaking wet when he came back into the bedroom, and he looked pretty freaked out—"

"So? He'll say he went outside to get some air and fell in the water. He was obviously drinking and coking."

Alex nodded. "And he was freaked out because Marc might talk about their threesome. If we're right that Mr. Perfect's married, that'd be very bad news."

"Exactly," I said. "But that footage doesn't pin him down as Marc's killer. He'll say Marc left with Paige and that's all he knows."

Michelle shook her head. "But when Marc left the bedroom, he was naked."

I shrugged. "He had clothes in the living room. Or he grabbed a kitchen towel when he ran out. No. We need more before we call in the troops. I don't want to give them any room to dust this off as defense bullshit." I paced back and forth in front of the television.

Michelle gave me a sour look. "You have any idea how to do that?"

"For starters, by finding out who Mr. Perfect is."

SIXTY

Michelle sighed and nodded. "He doesn't look the type to just break in, so he must be a friend of the owners. What'd that mechanic say their names were?"

Alex stood up. "Cory and Sarah Larsen. Let me get my laptop and see what we can find on them."

When he came back, I told him to check his phone for the photos I'd taken in the bedroom. "I got pictures of the photos on their dresser and the phone number that was on a pad next to the bed."

Alex picked up his phone and scrolled through his photos. "Let's check out that phone number first."

I sat down on the couch next to Michelle. "You notice how the first image on that camera is the owner setting it up, testing it?" Michelle nodded. "And then the very next image is of Mr. Perfect with Paige and Marc. Looks to me like he set up that camera expecting to get some hot footage—"

Alex looked up. "Yeah. You know, I thought it was weird that he didn't set up any surveillance cameras for the outside of the house. The one in his bedroom is the only one I saw. Now it makes sense."

Michelle made a face. "He invited his buddy over to use his place and then put in the camera to spy on him?"

"Sure seems that way. It didn't look like anyone knew it was there." I thought about those disgusting printouts of women with animals. "But being the lovers of the animal kingdom that they are, it actually makes sense."

Michelle rolled her eyes. "Don't remind me."

Alex sat back and read from the monitor. "Okay, that phone number on the notepad belongs to the Larsens. It's a global plan, and they opened the account in January."

Just before they left for Thailand. "Nice work." I knew having a hacker on the team would come in handy. I started to pace again. I sifted through all the information we had, trying to figure out how we could use this. And got an idea.

"Alex, can you find out whether they're on Snapchat or Instagram, anything like that?"

"For sending photos?" I nodded. "No. No way they'd use Snapchat or Instagram. Not for what they're into."

I stared at him. "Don't Snapchat photos disappear after a few seconds?"

Alex snorted. "Only for the very few who don't know how to get around their so-called security. Snapchat leaks like a rusty sieve. The only thing these guys would use is Wickr. It saves absolutely no data on a server, and everything's encrypted so—"

I held up a hand. "TMI, Alex. I get it. Can you capture a still shot of Mr. Perfect off that video? Nothing too explicit, just something that looks like he took it during that threesome." I wanted it to be believable that he'd send it. No matter how secure this Wickr app might be, no one with half a brain these days believes anything is foolproof.

Alex leaned back and blew out a breath. "Maybe. Assuming they're on Wickr, I could set up a fake account for us and send it to them."

I nodded. "Hopefully they'll give us a name to work with. I assume you have a spare phone? One that's not registered?" Alex smiled. It figured. He probably had a dozen of them. "Send a note with the photo saying he's using someone else's phone for cover."

Alex reached out and turned on the television. Fifteen minutes later, he had a shot of our man with his robe half off. It was cropped to keep out Paige's image. "Perfect," I said. "Let's send that with a message. Something like, 'Thanks for the memories.'"

Alex winced. "Really?"

I put my hands on my hips. "Make up something better, then."

Alex sent out the photo with the message, *Good times. Thanks! LOL.*

I stared at him. "Yeah, like that's so much better."

Michelle shrugged. "Actually, it is."

I shot her a look and went back to pacing. Alex asked if we wanted anything to eat, but my stomach was so tied up in knots I couldn't think of food. Michelle asked if he had any soup.

Alex headed for the kitchen. "I think I've got something in a can that might not put you in a hospital."

A few minutes later, he brought out two bowls of chicken noodle soup. While they ate, I stared out the living room window. It had a reflective covering that let you see out but prevented anyone from seeing in. Alex wasn't kidding about his security. It was almost seven o'clock, and all that was left of daylight were the indigo blues on the horizon. As I watched the rising glow of city lights, I tried to come up with a Plan B if this one didn't work.

Ten minutes later, Alex's spare phone gave a beep. We all turned to look at it. I grabbed the phone and read the message aloud. "'You're most welcome, Aubrey. Keep sharing!'"

Aubrey. That was such a distinctive name. "I know I've heard that name before, I just can't remember where or how. Sound familiar to you guys?"

They both shook their heads. I started pacing again as I tried to squeeze my brain for the memory.

Alex sat down at his computer. He started to read off the screen. "Aubrey, Aubrey . . . wow, lots of girls named Aubrey."

Michelle watched me. "Was it during this case?" I nodded. "Maybe you heard it in court?"

I shook my head. "No, I know I didn't hear it in court." I might not remember my own phone number, but I never forgot what anyone said in court.

"Did it have something to do with this case?" Michelle asked.

I stopped and stared at the floor. "No, I don't think so."

Alex read from the screen again. "Aubrey Plaza, Allison Aubrey, there's a town in France."

I stared at him. "You're not helping, you know."

He glanced up. "Sorry." But he kept scanning the monitor.

"What about outside court?" Michelle asked. "I mean, when you were talking to reporters?"

Something tickled the back of my brain. I had that frustrating feeling that it was hovering just out of reach. I tried to grasp it. And failed. "Damn it!"

"Okay, let it go," Michelle said. "You can't force it. Talk about something else."

But I couldn't. I kept pacing.

Alex picked up their empty bowls. "That guy Marc was a lot smaller than this Aubrey dude. I thought models were supposed to be buff."

I'd noticed that, too. "At least more buff than Marc was. But as I recall, Golden said the agency was trying to get him to buff up."

Alex nodded. "Yeah, I can see why." He shook his head. "And I can also see why Marc had no chance against him."

Aubrey probably outweighed Marc by a good thirty pounds—and all of it looked like solid muscle.

Michelle stood up. "Here, let me help you, Alex. You don't have to wait on us." She took the bowls from him. "I was wondering if Marc shaved his body. I've never seen a guy that hairless. He reminded me of a Ken doll. Except you know, he wasn't all smooth down there."

Something she'd said clicked in my brain. "Say that again!"

Michelle stopped. "Say what? Smooth down there?" I shook my head. "What? Ken doll?"

Ken doll. Ken doll. "Kendall, that reporter! He said Edie's husband's name was Aubrey!" I was about to tell Alex to look it up, but he was already back at his laptop and typing.

Michelle's eyes widened. "Holy shit, Sam. Mr. Perfect's married to Edie Anderson?"

"That's what I—"

"Got it!" Alex read from the screen. "Aubrey Miles, state senator. And yep, he's married to Edie Anderson, correspondent for local news channel KCAL 9."

I mentally replayed the surveillance camera footage. "Can you figure out who he called after Paige left?"

Alex was energized. "I'm on it."

It was a little alarming how fast Alex managed to hack into Aubrey Miles's cell phone account. It couldn't have been more than ten minutes before he looked up and turned the laptop toward me. "Done. These records won't tell us where the calls were made—"

"So you can't get the cell-tower records?" Cell-phone calls ping the nearest towers. The location of those towers gives you the general area where the calls were placed or received.

"I can; it'll just take a little longer."

"Okay, we can wait on that. What do you have for the night Paige got killed?"

"The first call went to a number with a Beverly Hills prefix at eleven thirty-two p.m. The second was made to a number with a West Hollywood prefix right after that. Both numbers are registered to a Brent Farmington—"

Michelle picked up Alex's phone. "Spell that for me." She typed it in as he gave her the spelling.

I remembered the coroner's estimated time of death. "So those were all made before Paige died." Alex nodded. "How long were the calls?"

"Those first two calls were too short to be actual conversations—"

I pictured the footage of Aubrey on his cell phone. "He didn't seem to be talking to anyone. Looked like he just left a message. So there was no answer."

Alex studied the monitor. "Right. And it was late. So maybe the first call was to a landline, and the next one was to a cell phone. Then right after that there was a third call. That one went to Aubrey's own home in West Hollywood. It lasted for almost a minute, so I'd guess someone answered—"

"Edie, probably," I said. "They don't have kids."

Alex continued. "The last call I have on Miles's cell for that night was an incoming. It was right after the call to Edie ended. From one of Brent Farmington's numbers."

"And I got him." Michelle held up Alex's phone. "Brent Farmington is Aubrey's aide."

"Sounds like that's who Aubrey was looking for," I said.

Michelle passed me Alex's phone. "He looks like the serious type."

A LinkedIn photo showed a sharp-featured man in his thirties with slicked-back hair and wire-framed glasses. I thought about the timing of those phone calls—and the order. Aubrey to Brent. Aubrey to Edie. Brent to Aubrey. I gave the phone back to Michelle and looked at the monitor over Alex's shoulder. "Seems like Aubrey actually talked to Edie, and right after that, Brent called him."

Michelle raised an eyebrow. "Isn't it kind of late to be looking for his aide?"

I flopped down on the couch. "Definitely. But you saw him on that video. He was in a panic. If we're right, if he did kill Marc, he needed help with . . . something ASAP, and he couldn't exactly ask Edie. 'Hi, honey, I was having a threesome and got into it with the other guy and killed him. Can you give me a hand?'"

Alex stared at the monitor. "The timing of the calls is awfully tight. Brent called Aubrey almost immediately after Aubrey spoke to Edie."

"You think Brent and Edie were together?" Michelle asked.

I shrugged. "Not necessarily. Brent might've just happened to notice his missed calls right after Aubrey talked to Edie. Or maybe Edie called Brent right after she spoke to Aubrey, and Brent finally picked up."

Michelle looked skeptical. "Heck of a coincidence."

Alex shook his head. "According to the book, there's no such thing as coincidence."

I shot him a dagger. "Really? The book? Now?"

Alex held up his hands. "You say it, too."

That was true. Irritating, but true. "Whatever. But if they were together, that's an interesting wrinkle." It was pretty late for Edie to be hanging with her husband's aide.

Michelle nodded. "They could just be friends. Maybe went to a late movie or something."

"I suppose." Stranger things have happened—like meeting your father for the first time when he's charged with a double homicide. In any case, that was a dead end for now. We had no way to find out tonight if or why Edie had been with Brent. "However it happened, Aubrey connected with Brent."

Michelle looked down at the photo of Brent on Alex's phone. "So Brent's in the middle of this."

I nodded and went back to pacing. I'd been thinking about why Aubrey would need to call him. If my theory was right—that he'd killed Marc during the fight in the living room and dragged his body into the ocean—then there was only one reason I could think of for him to call someone. And it fit with what was on the camera footage. "We saw Paige follow them out of the bedroom, and when she came back, she was freaked. She grabbed her purse and ran. She had to have seen the murder. My guess is, Aubrey was worried she'd call the cops—"

Michelle frowned. "So he told Brent to go kill her? I don't know—"

"Not necessarily kill her." I paused at the window and looked out at the night sky. "I'd guess he just asked Brent to go talk her down and keep her off the phone until he could get there."

Alex shrugged. "Then really, either of them could've killed Paige . . . and Chloe."

Michelle gave me a stern look. "And I'm sure the police will be glad to take it from here, so—"

I shook my head. "Michy, these guys aren't street-corner dealers. They're smart. They've probably already put some kind of story together. Hell, I can think of one right now: Brent never got to Paige's place—or he got there and no one was home. And Aubrey's going to say he only called Brent to go calm Paige down and that Marc and Paige took off together after the fight."

Alex gave Michelle an apologetic look. "She's right." He sighed. "But we're not going to get anything out of Aubrey."

I had to agree. "No, that's probably hopeless. But Brent . . ."

Michelle looked from Alex to me. "If you're thinking you're going to confront either of those guys, you're out of your friggin'—"

I waved her off. "Of course not."

Not yet, anyway.

SIXTY-ONE

Alex had gone to clean up in the kitchen. When he came back to the living room, he had his cell phone to his ear. "Just thought I'd check in with the answering service."

We hadn't picked up our messages since the fire. "Anything exciting?"

"Just the usual bazillion messages from the press. Some nice personal condolences from Brittany and Edie about the fire. And of course, they wanted your reaction to Storm's death."

Edie. That was interesting. "Can you give me Edie's number?" He read it off to me as I tapped it into my phone.

Michelle's brow furrowed. "You're not going to ask her if she was with Brent that night, are you? Because I don't think—"

"Yeah, right. 'Hey, Edie, what's new? By any chance, are you banging your husband's aide?'" I rolled my eyes. "But she might have some inside information on Storm's death."

Alex held up a hand. "Maybe it's not so smart to make contact. What if she knows about the murders?"

I shook my head. "I can't see Aubrey telling her anything." He'd have to trust Edie not to turn him in—or at the very least, not go for a divorce that could get very nasty. I hit the last number and listened to the phone ring. Just when I thought it was going to go to voice mail, Edie answered. She sounded hurried and irritable. "Yes?"

"Hey, it's Samantha . . ."

There was a long pause. When she spoke, her voice sounded brittle and a little high-pitched. "Samantha! Hey! I was just thinking about you. You okay?" I told her I was. "Such bad news about Storm."

Sounds of traffic and loud voices filled the background. "Yeah. Are you covering the story?"

She spoke in a breathless rush. "I am now. They pulled me off a car chase in Pasadena. I had to slog through rush-hour traffic. Took me two hours to get here. Anyway, you want to give me a comment?"

"On what?"

"Anything. On your situation, on Storm. I could send a crew out if you want to get on camera?"

"No crew, but thanks. No comment on the fire. They have no leads. As for Storm, how about, 'This is a terrible tragedy, and my sincere condolences go out to all his friends and family.'"

"What about the case? Doesn't this put a big dent in your defense?"

"No comment on the case. Sorry."

"Okay, off the record, then. What did he tell you? It sounded like he was going to be your ace in the hole."

I couldn't see any reason not to tell her. The video was what mattered, and I wouldn't tell anyone about that until we called the cops. "Actually, he just said that he saw Paige and a young guy heading to Malibu on the night she died."

"But wait . . . didn't he say his testimony would prove Paige was the target? How does that prove anything? She might've just been giving him a ride."

"Yeah. He got a little carried away. Wanted to make his fifteen minutes last." I took a beat. This had to sound casual. "What are you hearing about the accident? Are they sure that's what it was?"

Edie paused, and I heard police in the background shouting for people to get back. "Seems so. One of the first officers said they were looking for signs that he'd been pushed off the road, but so far no one's saying they've found anything."

"Okay, thanks. Well, if you hear any—"

She broke in, her voice rushed. "I'll keep you posted. Studio's calling. I've gotta go."

"No worries. See you in court."

I told Alex and Michelle what Edie had said.

Michelle got up and stretched. "So, now what?"

I thought about what we had and what the cops would do with it all. We'd grabbed the video after breaking and entering, but since we weren't the police, it'd still be admissible in court. The phone records . . . we didn't have to tell the cops we had them. They'd know to check phone calls on their own once they saw the tape.

But I didn't know how fast they'd move, and it was clear that either Brent or Aubrey—or both—were panicking. They'd tried to destroy evidence—and me—and they'd probably killed Storm. The only reason I had the surveillance-camera footage was because they didn't know it existed. And if I'd gotten it just one day sooner, it would've been destroyed in the fire. And then I'd have been left with nothing. The cops would never have taken my word for what I'd seen on that tape.

It was a chilling thought. And that thought raised the next one: Even with this footage, what would the cops do, and how fast would they do it? The video recording had some damning implications, but it didn't necessarily clear Dale. I'd already figured out a way for Aubrey and Brent to talk their way around it. I had to find a way to nail them, and I had to do it now. "Alex, you said your uncle has muscle. What kind of muscle?"

"Four guys, two of them used to be boxers. They all carry. What're you thinking?"

Primarily I was thinking that Aubrey had the motive to kill Paige, but he'd been stuck out in Malibu—about forty-five minutes away from Laurel Canyon. That's why he'd needed Brent. Brent was close. But that didn't necessarily mean Brent had killed Paige and Chloe. "If we tell Brent about the video footage and the phone calls, show him how bad it looks, maybe he'd dump Aubrey out."

Alex leaned back in his chair and laced his fingers behind his head. "If you're going to brace anyone up, Brent's definitely a better choice than Aubrey. And I can promise you we'll have great backup. Tomas and his guys know what they're doing." He looked at Michelle, who was shaking her head. "Really, don't worry, Michelle. This pasty little *huero* Brent won't be a problem for Tomas. It's not like we're dealing with the Mafia here."

Michelle pressed her lips together. "That 'pasty little *huero*' might've killed two women. *And* tried to burn us up. *And* killed Storm."

"And broke into my place," I said. "But—"

Michelle was angry. "But nothing. Let the cops take it from here. They can handle it."

I put my hands on my hips and drilled her with a look. "Really? You trust that slug, Wayne Little, to see past their bullshit? Or move fast enough to put it all together before they do more damage? Or before they run?"

"But if they ran, wouldn't that look bad?" Michelle asked. "Bad enough to get the case thrown out for Dale?"

I shook my head. "Not necessarily."

Michelle sighed. "I don't like it."

I didn't blame her, but I couldn't trust anyone else to put the case together. "It's not ideal. But Alex's right: Brent's no match for Tomas and his guys. We should be okay."

Alex was keyed up and ready for action. "So how do you want to handle this?"

I told him.

SIXTY-TWO

It was almost nine o'clock by the time Alex and I got to Brent's house—a small, older Spanish style that was on the border between Beverly Hills and West Hollywood. Michelle stayed behind at Alex's place to man the computer in case we needed information.

Alex drove slowly as we passed the house. There was a new-looking black Audi in the driveway. I wrote down the license plate. Alex parked a few houses down, then called Michelle, gave her the license-plate number, and walked her through a program that would give us the owner of the car.

"It's his," Alex said when he ended the call. "Did you see any lights on when we drove by?"

"Yeah, at the back of the house." The front of the house had a large picture window. The drapes were closed, but I thought that was probably the living room. By process of elimination, I figured the room that was lit was probably the bedroom. "When do you think Tomas will get here?"

"Might be a couple of hours. It'll take a while to round everyone up. He said he'd call when they were on their way."

In the meantime, Alex and I worked on our good-cop-bad-cop plan for questioning Brent. Periodically, we drove around the block so I could see whether the lights were still on. When we circled at ten thirty, I saw that the house had gone dark. "Ten thirty? Seriously? Damn, those aides lead boring lives." I didn't like the idea of waking him up. That'd guarantee a hostile reception right out of the gate. I'd hoped to at least start out with the friendly approach.

Alex sighed. "I know. But Tomas and his guys should be here soon. When this Brent guy sees his team, losing some beauty sleep will be the last thing he'll want to bitch about."

It was a quiet street with almost no traffic, and most of the residents parked in their own garages. I made a mental note of every car that was parked on the street: a red MINI Cooper, a black Altima, a white Explorer. Only one—the black Altima—hadn't been there already when we showed up, and I'd seen the driver go into the house four doors down from Brent.

We were slouched down in our seats so the neighbors wouldn't see us—a position that didn't do a thing to help my bored, sleepy condition.

So when a silver Prius pulled to the curb a few houses past Brent's, it took me a few seconds to focus. I sat up a little higher and peered over the dashboard to see who got out. But two minutes passed, then five. No one did. "Do you want to check—"

"Already on it." Alex was texting. "I'm having Michelle run the plate right now."

A few minutes later, his phone buzzed. He read the screen and his eyes widened. "It belongs to Aubrey Miles."

We exchanged a look. "Shit. Can you check with Tomas for an ETA?"

"I can try." He texted again.

Two minutes later, the driver got out. I couldn't see a face; the figure was dressed in black sweats with the hoodie pulled up. "Too small to be

Aubrey." As the figure rounded the car and headed down the sidewalk, I caught a glimpse of the face. "Edie?"

"Sure looked like her. And she's trying to keep it on the down low."

"A booty call?" That would explain the late hour and the way she was hiding under a hoodie. I appreciated the symmetry of the playboy politician's wife getting it on with his aide. I sank back down and turned to watch as she walked past the front door and turned left at the side of the house. Probably heading for the back door. I grabbed my cell phone and tapped in all but the last number for Alex's cell. "I've got to see what's going on. I'll just stay back and look. If anything seems dicey, I'll call you."

Alex started to protest, but I didn't give him a chance to argue. I slid out of the car and moved as fast as I could without running. When I got to the side of the house, I checked the street to make sure no one was watching, then followed the path Edie had taken and tiptoed toward the back of the house. I stopped at the edge and peered around the corner just in time to see Edie use a key to open the back door. My heart started to beat faster as I thought about what that meant.

This was more than a booty-call relationship. If she had a key, then she and Brent were pretty damn tight. There was a good chance they *had been* together when Aubrey called on the night Paige died. Still, that didn't mean she knew what was going on, what Aubrey had done—or what he'd asked Brent to do. I crouched down below the windows and moved toward the back door.

The top half of the door was glass, and I saw that it opened onto the kitchen. I could see Edie inside. She was heading toward the area I'd pegged as the bedroom. I took hold of the doorknob and slowly twisted. It was open. My pulse was racing now. This was a bad idea. I didn't know what I was walking into. But I'd come this far. If it turned out to be just a hookup, I'd sneak back out the way I came. And hope none of the neighbors saw me and called the cops. My throat felt tight as I called Alex. When he answered, I whispered, "I'm going in."

"No, wait—"

I ended the call and moved inside in a low crouch, deliberately leaving the door open for a fast exit.

As I passed through the kitchen, I saw Edie. Her back was to me, and she was standing in front of a closed door. I crouched down and hid behind the wall that separated the small dining area from the hallway where she was standing. She paused, her left hand on the doorknob. As I watched her, I noticed that the right side of her sweatshirt was sagging. It pinged a vague alarm in my head.

She turned the knob and opened the door slowly, then took two steps inside. As she reached into her right pocket, I finally realized what that sagging pocket meant. Without thinking, I launched out of my hiding place and sprang toward her. I shouted, "Stop!" just as she pulled out the gun. Startled, she turned toward me, and I rammed into her. The momentum sent us both flying. As we crashed to the floor, the gun went off. The sound of the shot exploded through the house.

I heard Brent scream from the far side of the room. If he jumped into the fray to help her, I'd be dead meat. I had to get that gun. I looked up, hoping she'd dropped it when we fell. No such luck. It was still in her hand. But she'd reached up to break her fall. Her arms were still outstretched. I jumped on top of her and tried to jam my forearm into her neck as I reached for the gun, but she twisted away and threw me off. I saw her start to bring her arm down, putting the gun into firing range. In desperation, I slammed my body into her. She fell back, but she still had the gun. I tried to grab her arm, but my hands were now slick with sweat. They slipped off as she yanked her arm away.

I latched onto her again and pulled myself up, toward the hand that held the gun. She tried to push me back and make room to put the gun between us so she could fire at me, but I held on. As I reached up again to grab the gun, she tried to slam it down on my head. I pulled away at the last second, but I didn't dare let go of her. The blow landed hard on my neck. The force of it choked my windpipe, and I saw stars. Brent shouted something, but I couldn't make out what he was saying. Was he calling to Edie? Frantic now, I clawed at her face. She screamed as my fingers found her eye sockets. Finally, I managed to seize the hand that held the gun. I banged it hard, once, twice, three times. Her hand flew open, and the gun skittered across the floor.

I had one hand jammed against Edie's throat and the other latched onto her flailing arm. I was about to climb over her to get the gun when I heard footsteps pounding toward the bedroom. Alex pulled me away. In one deft move, he flipped her over, yanked her arms together, and zip-tied her hands behind her.

When I stood up, I saw that Brent was staring down at Edie, his face white. His whole body was shaking. He spoke in a voice that was choked, hoarse. "You—you were going to kill me? Why? I've done everything for you—"

Edie, seated on the floor, struggled against Alex's restraining arm as she whipped her head back and forth. She let out a shriek that sounded like a crazed animal and bucked against Alex, her eyes wild, features twisted in a snarling grimace. Alex shoved her to the floor, facedown. I turned to look at Brent, trying to make sense of what he'd said. "You killed Paige and Chloe . . . for *her*?"

Brent's gaze was fixed on Edie, his face slack, numb. "No. But I . . ." His face crumpled. "Edie, why? I never would have—"

Edie screamed, "*He* did it! He did it all! He killed Storm!"

"To protect you, Edie!" Brent shook his head as tears filled his eyes. His voice was choked. "Because I love you!"

I looked from Brent to Edie. And realized I'd had it all wrong. I began to put it together. "Brent?" His eyes briefly flicked up at me, then settled back on Edie. "When Aubrey called you that night, he said Paige was freaking out. He wanted you to go calm her down, keep her from calling the cops. But you never went, did you?" Brent shook his head. "Probably not the first mess you had to clean up for him, was it?" Brent didn't answer. But he didn't have to. I knew I was right. "You told Edie you weren't going to do it again—"

His gaze still fixed on Edie, Brent broke in. "He wasn't worth it, Edie. He wasn't good enough for you. Why couldn't you see that? He doesn't love you. I do! I'm the one who loves you!"

Edie was breathing hard, but she was silent. I pressed on. "So she went instead. Did you know she'd killed those girls?"

Brent's body sagged as he shook his head. "Not at first. She told me no one answered the door. But after Storm came out and said . . ."

Said that we knew Paige was the target, Edie saw it was all about unravel, so she told Brent he had to stop us. "Did Aubrey tell you the real reason why Paige was freaking out?"

Brent finally looked at me, his expression confused. "He got in a hassle with some guy. Paige was coked up, acting crazy."

I shook my head. "No. It was because he'd just killed that guy. And Paige saw it all." Brent's mouth opened, his lips moved, but no words came out. And that told me even more. If Brent didn't know, neither did Edie. "So Edie went there thinking Paige was just another affair. She'd go talk Paige down, maybe promise her a little hush money." I looked at Edie, who'd gone quiet. "Isn't that right, Edie?"

Edie glared at me with a crazed expression; then she gave her body a violent twist, arching her back in an effort to break free from Alex's grip. Alex tightened his arm around her neck and she stopped, her chest heaving. She spoke in a low growl. "That fucking whore! She would've called the cops! After all those years of sucking it up, looking the other way, eating his shit, his lies. All for nothing—because of that stupid little piece of trash? No! No way in hell!"

Edie began to sob. It was a harsh, ragged sound—ugly and raw.

Brent watched her, the agony on his face like a gaping wound.

At that moment, I heard heavy footsteps running along the side of the house. The cavalry was here. Edie, lost in her collapsing world of misery, didn't seem to notice. But Brent did. And as he looked up, I saw something shift in his expression. Before I could figure out what it meant, Brent lunged across the room and grabbed the gun off the floor. Tears streaming down his face, he raised the gun, his eyes fixed on Edie.

I reached out to him and screamed, "Brent! No!"

But Brent never even looked up. He stared down at Edie as in one swift move, he put the gun to his head and pulled the trigger.

The blast rattled the windows. Wet clumps of blood and brains splashed the walls. I stood staring, unable to speak, my hand still reaching toward him. Tomas and his men came running in; their heavy footsteps echoed like thunder in the small house. Then, in the distance, I heard the thin wail of sirens.

SIXTY-THREE

I must've been in shock for a little while, because I wound up on the couch in Brent's living room with no memory of walking to it. The paramedics checked me out and said I was "basically okay," but told me I should go to the hospital "just as a precaution." I politely declined. Well, not all that politely.

It'd been hard to put together any coherent thoughts at first, but Detective Wayne Little wanted a statement now, so we did our best. We knew Brent had killed Storm, so it wasn't a big leap to surmise that he'd set the fire in my office and broken into my apartment, too. Wayne thought they might find prints in my apartment to prove it. And he was hoping they'd find evidence in Brent's house to link him to the fire as well.

But the big question was, how did Edie manage to kill both Paige and Chloe?

That had us stumped at first, but then I remembered what Chas Gorman, the doper in the building, had said. He'd thought he heard someone knock on Chloe's door before she and Dale got home. I hadn't put much stock in his accuracy at the time. But next-door neighbor

Janet was wide awake when Dale left, and she hadn't heard anyone else arrive after that.

So Edie had to have gotten there *before* Dale and Chloe. And the timing of the phone calls with Aubrey and Brent confirmed it. That meant Edie had to have killed Paige before Dale and Chloe came home. But then why kill Chloe? I had to replay the whole scenario to figure that one out. There was only one possible explanation: Chloe and Dale got home before Edie had the chance to escape. Stuck in Paige's bedroom, the only thing Edie could do was close the door and hide—and hope no one came in. That's where she got lucky. Paige had said she probably wouldn't be back until morning, so Chloe had no reason to go check on her. And Chloe was distracted. She and Dale were having one hell of a fight.

Hiding in Paige's bedroom, Edie would've heard that fight and heard Dale storm out. It was the perfect cover. Armed with the knife she'd used on Paige, she caught Chloe by surprise and—based on the crime-scene photos—still on the floor. With Chloe dead, Edie had a little time to figure out how to get out of there without being seen. It wouldn't have taken her long to figure out that the balcony was an easy climb.

Then I remembered there'd been some stray hairs and prints in the apartment—notably, some unidentified prints on the doorknob of Paige's closet, probably where Edie had been hiding when Dale and Chloe came home. Wayne Little said he already had his men pulling up the evidence to see if they matched up to Edie. I wound up thinking it was all pretty simple. But most crimes are, when it comes right down to it. Even the big ones.

By the time the cops let us go, I was so exhausted on every level—emotional and physical—that I could barely keep my eyes open. And now that the adrenaline had worn off, I felt like I'd been stuck in a cement mixer. Alex looked drained, but he seemed in better shape than I was. He drove us back to his place and insisted I spend the night.

I decided not to argue. My place was safe now, but it was still a mess, and the thought of having to confront the ugliness was overwhelming. On our way back to Alex's apartment, he told me he'd called Michelle to give her a quick rundown of what'd happened while I was wrapping up with Wayne Little. She'd been glad we were alive but "pissed enough" to kill us.

Right as she was, I didn't have the energy to deal with it. So when we walked in, I was prepared to tell her to yell at me tomorrow. But we must've looked pretty bad, because she took one look at us and said, "You guys need to get to bed."

Alex went to the kitchen and pulled out a bottle of pinot noir. "We do. But I've been saving this for a special occasion. It's from Adastra, this great winery in Napa. Proximus pinot noir."

It was beautiful. And just what I needed to take the sharp edges off all the trauma we'd been through. I let Alex fill in the rest of the story.

When he'd finished, Michelle stretched out and held the glass on her stomach. "But why would Edie need to kill Brent? She knew he killed Storm. And that he tried to kill us. So what if he knew she'd killed Chloe and Paige? Wasn't it kind of a standoff?"

Alex refilled Michelle's glass. "I'd guess she just didn't know if or when he might have an attack of conscience and decide to come clean. Or maybe blackmail her with it. As long as he was alive, it'd be hanging over her head. She'd never really be safe."

Michelle took a sip. "You think Aubrey knew about Edie and Brent?"

I shrugged. "That one's hard to call."

Michelle sat up and put her glass on the table. "Well, I sure don't blame her for having an affair. But how'd she plan to get away with killing Brent?"

Good question. "I don't know. But she was pretty unhinged. I'm not sure how much real planning went into it."

Alex swirled the wine in his glass. "Even so, she might've pulled it off if we hadn't been there. Unless someone got a good look at her—not so easy considering she was dressed in that hoodie and dark clothing. Plus, who'd suspect her?"

I sighed. "And losing it or not, she sure managed to play me like a kazoo—for months."

Michelle nodded. "But who's in handcuffs now?"

A great point. I smiled. "And more important, look who's out of them." I raised my glass. "To Dale." We toasted to that.

SIXTY-FOUR

I was pretty amped when I rode to court the next morning. Tired, sore, and looking like I'd spent the night in a washing machine on the spin cycle—but amped. Alex and Michelle were with me. They deserved to take this victory lap.

I headed back to the holding tank to see Dale. It was a whole new experience now that he'd been cleared. I could look him in the eye and not wonder whether he'd murdered two innocent girls. I could share a smile with him and not worry that I was in the company of a psychopath. And I could hold my head up without feeling judged for being the daughter of a multiple murderer. It surprised me to realize how much that had weighed on me. It wasn't as though he'd ever been a real father to me. But there was no denying that we were connected by blood. Like it or not, on some elemental, lizard-brain level, his sins were my sins. So knowing he hadn't killed Paige and Chloe was more than just a relief—it was almost as though *I'd* been exonerated.

Dale was beaming. "Does this mean I'll actually get to talk to you with no bars or bulletproof glass between us? I won't know how to act."

I smiled. "Me neither."

His eyes were misty. "I'd say thank you, but it seems so lame. You saved my life." His expression turned anxious. "When I heard about the fire at your office, I thought I was going to lose my mind. If anything had happened to you, Sam . . ." He trailed off, unable to speak.

I waited for him to recover. When he looked up again, I gave him a little smile. "We don't have to go there."

Dale sighed. "No, better not."

But my smile wavered. The image of Brent putting the gun to his head, the roar of the shot, his blood and brains splattering the walls, kept coming back to me, again and again.

Dale watched me knowingly. "I've seen some ugly things—even saw a jumper once—but I've never seen anyone commit suicide that way. How'd you sleep?"

"Not great." That was nothing new. But last night, I got to have a whole new nightmare and dreamed nonstop about blasts of gunfire and torn, bloody faces. I woke up over and over again, breathless and shaking. "I just hope it'll stop sometime soon."

Dale nodded. "I don't know how long it'll take, but I can tell you from experience, it does get better—eventually. And if you want to talk, I'm here."

That's right, he really could be. Now. "Thanks. I'll remember that."

Dale's brow furrowed. "They arrest Aubrey yet?"

I nodded. "Up in Sacramento. He was at a campaign fund-raiser. Guess he'll need those funds for something else now."

As we exchanged grins, the bailiff tapped me on the shoulder. "The judge's about to come out, Samantha. Wrap it up."

I gave the bailiff a salute and turned back to Dale. "Okay. Let's do this."

The benches in the gallery were so packed I didn't know how anyone was breathing. The story had been all over the news, but the audience sat in rapt silence as Detective Little spoke. To his credit, he admitted we'd put it together for him.

When he finished, Zack asked for two weeks to let the crime lab process the evidence at Chloe's apartment and the Larsens' beach house, "Just to make sure it all jibes."

The judge glared at him. "Two weeks? So this man can spend *more* time in custody for crimes he didn't commit? I'll give you three days. You either bring in solid proof that Dale Pearson committed these murders by then, or I'm dismissing this case. And in the meantime, I'm setting bail at ten thousand dollars." He turned to me. "I assume he can make that?"

I'd anticipated the judge might grant bail, so I'd asked Alex to bring his uncle Tomas, the bail bondsman. I looked back at Tomas now, and he nodded. "Yes, he can make that."

"Very well. You're all ordered back Thursday morning. Until then, we'll be in recess."

When the judge left the bench, Dale and I had a long hug. Our first real one. It felt strange but somehow familiar. The clicking of cameras filled the room. For a change, I'd get to go out and talk to the press without worrying about what I needed to spin.

I stood in front of the courthouse in the thin winter sunshine and answered obvious questions like, "Do you feel vindicated?" (Of course) and "Does Dale plan to sue?" (No comment at this time).

This was better than a hung jury—or even an acquittal. Dale was completely cleared. And the story was huge. By tomorrow morning, there'd be no corner of the country that hadn't heard it. Dale would never have to deal with the doubts that always lingered around defendants whose convictions got reversed on a "technicality."

And public opinion had turned on a dime. Now the waving posters touted **DALE PEARSON—INNOCENT!** and **DALE PEARSON, VICTIM OF INJUSTICE!** There was even some comic relief: a woman in high heels and a bikini waved a poster reading: **DALE PEARSON, WILL YOU MARRY ME?**

I took her picture. When I picked Dale up at the jail later that day, I showed it to him. "Just wanted you to know you've got a lot of 'options.' Even if some of them are a little sketchy."

He laughed, then he looked up at the sky. "I can't believe I'm out of that dungeon." We didn't talk much on the ride home. Dale spent most of the time staring out the window. When I pulled into his driveway, he sat unmoving for several long moments as he looked at his house. "I didn't think I'd ever see this place again."

He pulled on the door handle and tried to push the passenger door open, but it stuck. He had to put his shoulder into it, and when it gave, the old hinges let out a metallic shriek. Dale frowned, then leaned over and checked out the mileage. "Don't you think it's time to let this thing go to car heaven?"

I spread my arms across the dashboard. "Do not let Beulah hear you say that. She'll make me push her home."

Dale grinned. "My bad. We'll discuss it later, when she's not listening. Maybe over dinner? We really should celebrate."

"I agree. You get settled and we'll figure it out."

Dale squeezed my hand and got out. I watched him unlock the door. He turned and waved to me, and I waved back. As I drove away, I realized I didn't know whether this was a beginning or an end. And I wasn't sure which one I wanted it to be.

SIXTY-FIVE

The courtroom wasn't nearly as packed on Thursday morning. The hearing was kind of an anticlimax. No one expected Zack to come up with anything, and he didn't. Case closed—for Dale.

Edie's was just beginning. The stray hairs on Paige's robe and in Chloe's bedroom were consistent with Edie's, and the stray prints in Paige's bedroom matched Edie's. And an unexpected bonus: they'd found Edie's prints on the balcony as well. Zack had charged her with two counts of first-degree murder. But even if the jury only went for first degree on Chloe's murder and gave her a second degree on Paige's, she'd still wind up doing life without parole.

After the case against Dale was dismissed, we all walked out together.

Dale gave me a broad smile. "Dinner next week?"

I answered with a lot more certainty than I felt. "Absolutely."

When Dale left, I saw Zack talking to a reporter near the elevators. Aubrey Miles had just been transported to Los Angeles that morning, and it was big news. They'd found his blood and Marc's at the Malibu house. It'd take a little while longer to finish processing the crime scene, but the writing was on the wall: Aubrey Miles was going down. The reporter left and Zack waved to me.

I walked over to him. "You going to let Miles plead to a manslaughter?" Zack nodded. I figured as much. "The cops get a statement from him?"

"Such as it was. He claimed it was an accident; they got into a fight, and Marc fell and hit his head. We probably can't prove otherwise."

"You think Aubrey knew that Edie did the murders?"

"He says he didn't. But unless she talks, which I seriously doubt will happen, we'll never know for sure." Zack shrugged, then smiled at me. "Anyway, that was some nice work you did finding that surveillance camera. You know, you should join the DA's office—"

"Couldn't pass the background check."

Zack laughed. "No, seriously. You should."

"No, seriously. I can't pass the background check." Plus, just the thought of it made me gag. "But to be honest, Alex was the one who found it."

Zack nodded. "I hope you finally believe that I had nothing to do with that leak on Jenny Knox's rape case."

"Yeah, I do." I'd never be able to prove it, but I was pretty sure Edie was behind that.

He tilted his head toward the snack bar. "Want to get some coffee?"

"Next time. I've got to get moving."

I had to set up the new office so I could start seeing clients. I'd thought I'd have to work out of my apartment for the next few years to save up money for a new place. But it turned out the one bill Michelle always paid on time was our insurance premium. We wound up with a pretty nice place in West Hollywood. It wasn't exactly a luxury suite, but it was in a pretty decent neighborhood.

When we found it, Michelle had let out a whoop of victory. "An office that *isn't* in Gangsville. I can't believe it—"

"Aw, come on, Michy, admit it. You'll miss the bangers, the pitter-patter of little feet as they hunt each other down, the nightly gunfire. The exciting dash to your car at night . . ."

She'd ignored me. "And we have a security guard."

I'd given a mock yawn. "Man, it's gonna be boring."

In the days that followed, I was busy nearly 24-7. Setting up a new office was a full-time chore.

We got our phone system up and running, and it looked like I was going to score a few new—*paying*—clients. It helped that the story was still a hot topic with the media. I'd been giving print interviews here and there, but I needed to get into the studio. I wouldn't be a big ticket forever, and I had to squeeze the last drop out of every chance I got to beef up our business. Sheri's producers had been blowing up my cell phone for the past week, offering to give me two solo segments with her. It didn't get much better than that, so I asked Michelle to call the producers and put me on the show today.

But Michelle said I couldn't do it. "You've got a client meeting, and it's at four o'clock."

I looked at my calendar. "How come it's not on the books?"

"I sent you an e-mail. It'd help if you checked it once in a while. Do Sheri's show on Monday. Believe me, she'll make it work."

At four o'clock, I heard Michelle say, "She's in her office." A few seconds later, my office door opened and Dale stood at the threshold. He gave me a little smile as he looked around the room. "I like your new digs."

It took me a second to get over my surprise, but I went over and gave him a hug. "It doesn't have the charm of being on Barrios Van Nuys turf, but I guess you can't have everything." I had a feeling this wasn't just a social call, so I cut to the chase. "What brings you here? I mean, why the office?"

Dale cleared his throat. His eyes briefly met mine, then shifted off to the right. "I think I need to hire a lawyer."

SIXTY-SIX

I gestured for him to sit down in one of the chairs in front of my desk. I had two matching chairs now. I was so uptown. I went around the desk and sat down. I thought I knew what he was here to talk about. And I was afraid it might get ugly—might in fact be the last time I ever saw him. But I was relieved. It was time to put our cards on the table and find out who we were going to be to each other. "What's up?"

Dale cleared his throat again and swallowed. "Jenny Knox."

I nodded. I'd guessed right. This was it.

His face was tight, and I could see it was a strain for him to hold my gaze. He took a deep breath, then exhaled. "I—I killed her." His eyes shifted to the right.

I waited for him to make eye contact again. "Yes. I know."

Dale opened his mouth, then closed it. He clasped his hands in front of his stomach, his body rigid. "How?"

It was Alex's only real rookie mistake. But it was a monster. I gave a deep sigh. "I told Alex to drop the Jenny Knox investigation after Ignacio gave you an alibi. But he didn't. I didn't know it, but he kept going back to Jenny's building to see if he could find a witness who'd point the finger at someone else for her murder." Given who she was,

I couldn't blame Alex for thinking that'd be easy. "But he wound up finding a guy named Cricket who lived in the building next door to hers. Cricket got out of rehab the night Jenny died, and he was on the street looking to score. He ran into a friend who was in pocket, and they were about to do the deal when the friend spotted a cop he knew—a detective he'd worked with before." I paused and looked at Dale. He was staring at me, his lips pinched, his face pale. "It was you. Cricket showed Alex the street where they saw you. It was a half block away from the alley where Jenny's body was found." I took a beat. "And there's one more thing. When I told you that Jenny was dead, you didn't ask me how she died. You said, 'Who killed her?'" I studied Dale's reaction.

He stared at his hands, still clenched together in front of him. After a few seconds, he cleared his throat again in a harsh, rasping grunt. When he finally spoke, his voice was choked. "I'm sorry, Sam. I—I wanted to tell you, but I was . . . afraid of . . . of what you'd think."

A part of me wanted to accept that, to pretend I believed him and let it go. But I couldn't. "Afraid of what I'd think? Or what I'd do? Weren't you really just worried that I wouldn't fight as hard for you?"

He drew back as though I'd slapped him. But then his eyes shifted over my shoulder to look out the window. After a moment, he slowly nodded. "Maybe. I guess it was partly that." He met my gaze now, and I saw pain in his eyes. "But with two murders already hanging over my head, I was afraid you'd pull away, write me off as a . . . criminal. That I'd never get the chance to show you who I really was."

Was that true? I supposed it might be. "But you are a criminal. You killed her. Why? No one was going to buy her bullshit rape claim. They'd already washed it out. That is, unless . . ." I looked him in the eye.

His face suddenly reddened, and he gripped the arms of the chair. "No! I never raped her! I did lie to you, and yes, partly for my own benefit. But that bogus fucking rape charge had *nothing* to do with it!"

I stared at him. "You need to calm down." Dale's eyes widened, but after a few moments, he sat back. I could see he was still breathing hard. "Okay, if it wasn't the rape charge, then why?"

Dale stared out the window. His expression hardened, and his voice was cold, bitter. "A few days after Jenny made the rape charge, she called me and said she was sorry. That she was going to withdraw it. But she needed a ride to the hospital. She'd been jumped by a couple of crackheads, and they'd beaten her up. And she sounded bad, real bad. I was just a couple of blocks away, so I went to pick her up—"

"In that alley?"

Dale nodded as he stared out the window. His hands had balled into fists on his lap. He had a look of disgust on his face. "But of course, she lied. When I saw her and realized she was fine, I told her if she ever called me again, I'd make sure her story about getting jumped came true. She said she was doing me a favor, that she was giving me one more chance to pay up. I told her to go fuck off and started to leave. But then she showed me . . ." Dale reached into the pocket of his jacket and took out a cell phone. He dropped it on my desk. "This."

I looked at it, then back at him. "It's hers?"

He nodded and jerked his head at the phone. "Go ahead, look."

I stared at the phone for a moment, wondering why he'd hung on to it. When I looked up, I found Dale watching me. His eyes were narrowed, measuring. But there was nothing contrite about his expression.

I picked up the phone and refreshed the screen. When I saw the picture, a wave of shock that felt like a thousand needles spread over my body. It was Lisa—Dale's daughter. My half sister. She was looking straight ahead, her hands on the straps of her backpack. It was a candid shot, taken from no more than ten feet away. There was only one reason why Jenny would've taken that photo and shown it to Dale. I put down the phone. "What did she say?"

Dale stared at the phone, his jaw clenched. His voice was quieter now, but an icy fury still lay just under the words. "She said Lisa—"

Holy shit. "Jenny knew her name?"

His eyes were hard as he met my gaze. "Yeah. She said that Lisa looked like a nice kid. That Lisa was lucky to be in a good school like Arthur B. Wright. That . . ." He had to stop. When he continued, his voice was hoarse. "That there was more than one way to get the money I owed her." Dale was rubbing his fisted right hand with his left.

Now I understood why he'd kept the phone. He was looking into her contacts, trying to find out if there was anyone who really might pose a threat to Lisa. I hadn't known whether he'd give me another half truth—a story I could never be sure of. But I'd read about girls—even in good neighborhoods—being snatched off the street and sold. I didn't know if Jenny really had those connections, but it wouldn't surprise me if she did. Dale's story felt true. And I definitely didn't mourn the loss of a foul snake like Jenny Knox. But that didn't answer the final question. "I get it. But why kill her? Why not just turn her in?"

The angry energy drained away as Dale sighed and leaned back in his chair. He stared at the cell phone as he spoke in a slow, heavy voice. "I could tell you I didn't know whether any charges against her would stick. And I could tell you I was worried that even from jail she'd be able to retaliate by getting her connections to go after Lisa. And it'd all be true." He finally looked up at me, and his expression was naked, vulnerable. "But the real truth is, I heard her threat and . . . I just . . . snapped." He frowned and shook his head. But when he looked at me, his expression was frank. "I'm not proud of what I did. But I can't honestly say I'm sorry, either." His eyes softened as he added, "The only thing I'm sorry for is lying to you, Sam. I do hate myself for that."

I was glad he'd come clean. And I believed his story. But I didn't buy the notion that he'd bared his soul to me now just because of a guilty conscience. He'd kept the lie going for too long.

I knew in my gut he'd never have told me if he'd thought he could get away with it. Why risk rejection? What I didn't know wouldn't hurt me—or more to the point, him. No, the only reason he'd told me about Jenny Knox was because he knew, or strongly suspected, that I'd figure it out.

But then it struck me: How did I know that? For all we'd been through, I still barely knew him. So how come I was so sure?

The answer crept forward, like a cowering, guilty child: because it's what I would've done. It'd been my motto since I was a kid: Slide by with a lie; don't admit it till you quit it. It was such second nature I never even thought about it. And that thought forced me to finally confront the bigger, core truth. The one I'd been avoiding ever since I found out he'd killed Jenny.

Dale knew he didn't have to kill her. But he wasn't having any guilt pangs over it. And neither would I. I might not have been as sloppy about it, but if I'd been in Dale's position, I'd probably have killed her, too. I was who I was, and Dale was who he was. And we were a lot more alike than I—or he—could possibly have known. It occurred to me in that moment that it really wasn't such a coincidence that our paths had crossed, after all. To the contrary, it seemed almost inevitable.

I looked at Dale now, saw his tense, worried expression as he looked into my eyes. When he spoke, his voice was tight. "I don't know how you feel about me right now. Maybe you don't, either." He swallowed and took a deep breath. "But I need to know what you're going to do about . . . all this . . ."

The question almost made me smile. Dale knew so little about me. "You know it's privileged. I can't tell—"

Dale waved me off. "Yeah, I know you can't *tell* anyone what I said. But we both know you can get around that if you want to."

He was right. Alex had already put the wheels on the wagon by finding Cricket. It wouldn't take much to set them in motion. All I'd have to do was get Cricket busted and then drop an anonymous call to the cops saying he had information on Jenny Knox's murder. I shook my head. "If I'd wanted to take you down, I'd have done it already."

Dale exhaled and nodded slowly, but his eyes searched my face. He wasn't 100 percent sure of me. But I wasn't 100 percent sure that I could trust him, either. He was a loose cannon with a short fuse, and he had no compunction about lying.

Then again, neither did I.

But his hair-trigger temper worried me. The image of Dale exploding with rage after I told him I'd been molested was still fresh in my mind. I didn't want to wind up sitting next to him in court again. I couldn't afford it—for a lot of reasons. I had to be honest with myself. Being close to him posed a real danger. But being honest, I also had to admit that seeing his fury in those moments, I'd felt a wild, howl-at-the-moon, bloodlust satisfaction. And *that* was what I'd always wanted. Not Superman, not Bruce Lee. I'd wanted that raging, untamed monster who'd shred and tear the limbs off anyone who dared to hurt me.

And I still did. That monster, managed right, could be just what I needed.

Dale glanced down at his hands. They were laced together in front of him. "I'll get it if you don't want to see me again." He looked up and searched my face. "But I'm hoping you will."

I wasn't sure what our relationship would look like or where it would take us. And it might wind up being a disaster—for both of us. But there was only one way to find out. I looked into his eyes. "I'm in."

EPILOGUE

I'd just finished an appearance in Department 130 and was having a cup of coffee in the snack bar when Michelle called. "Put on Channel Four."

I walked over to the television that was bolted to the wall, stepped on the bottom rung of a chair, and changed the channel. Brittany Marston was standing in front of the Twin Towers jail, microphone in hand. To her left, a young kid in jeans and an OBEY t-shirt—his frightened eyes barely visible under a mop of wavy hair—was being led toward the jail by two beefy deputies who gripped his skinny arms as though they thought he might fly away. I turned up the volume. ". . . and prosecutors are saying they intend to try the sixteen-year-old as an adult for the slaying of his older brother. Back to you, Gabe."

I sat back down and spoke to Michelle. "So who was that?"

"Your next client. His mother said she'd come in with the retainer as soon as you sign on."

It was our second new case this week. The fame train was starting to pay off. I got up and threw my coffee cup into the trash. The Twin Towers jail was just across the street. "Tell her I'm on my way."

The guards only gave me an hour with my new client, Jason Stambler. I didn't want to get into the case with him until I saw the police reports, so I introduced myself, gave him the standard warning about not talking to anyone, no matter how "friendly" they seemed, and told him what to expect during the next few days.

By the time I got back to the office, it was almost three o'clock.

Michelle was just getting off the phone when I walked in. I pointed to the leopard-print Scünci she was wearing and made a growling noise. "You're really gonna drive the boys wild today, babe."

She shot me a dagger. "It keeps the hair out of my eyes, smartass." She nodded at the phone. "That was Arturo Orozco, wanting to know what you've come up with."

My heart gave a painful thud. I'd known those guys were going to be trouble, but I hadn't expected it to start this soon. I had to find a way to calm them down, buy myself time to figure out what to do with them.

Michelle broke into my thoughts. She peered at me with a worried expression. "Sam? What's going on?"

I made my face go blank. "Nothing. I just haven't had time to get much done for them yet." I rolled my eyes. "I mean, between the fire, the break-in at my apartment, and such, we've been a little busy."

Michelle shook her head. "Don't dust me off, Sam. I know you too well. It's more than that." Her mouth set in a firm line. "So what gives?" Her expression softened. "Come on. Let me help."

I shook my head as I took in the scar on her forehead and thought about the asshole who'd given it to her. She'd picked him out at the lineup, was 100 percent sure. But the cop had let her see the guy in handcuffs beforehand, and he was the only one in the lineup with a goatee. Michelle said none of that mattered; she knew it was him. But the judge threw out her identification anyway, and that was the end of the case. For them. Not for Michelle.

The day after the case was dismissed, the letters and phone calls started. Ugly death threats, describing how he'd maim her, burn her alive, throw acid in her face. She went to the police, told them she knew who was doing it—and the cops were sympathetic. They were sure she was right, but she had no proof. Their hands were tied.

Michelle wasn't eating, she wasn't sleeping, and within two weeks, she'd dropped ten pounds—weight she didn't need to lose. My best friend was about to go over the edge. I had to do something. I got the dickweed's address from Michelle's copy of the police report and staked out his place, a skuzzy studio apartment in Koreatown.

It took two weeks, but I finally found my chance when he left his place late one night. After having watched him for the past two weeks, I knew his habits, knew he was headed to the local liquor store. And I knew the route he'd take. I still remember the feel of the gas pedal under my foot, the roar of the engine as the car leaped forward, the look on his face as he saw me bearing down on him. When he rolled off the hood, I backed up and ran over him two more times, just to make sure.

But what I remember most of all is the feeling of power. *I* did this. I made things right. It was a liberating, intoxicating feeling, a high like no other. I didn't know it then, but I was hooked.

I took in Michelle's worried expression and wished I could tell her. But I couldn't. I couldn't tell her about any of them. I couldn't put that burden on her. And though I didn't think she would, I couldn't take the risk she'd turn me in.

I'd find a way to handle the Orozcos. It helped that they'd asked me to investigate Ricardo's death. I'd just have to make sure no one remembered that I'd been hovering over the custody list when we took his plea. And I needed to start thinking about a fall guy. Someone else I could pin the blame on. I forced a bright smile. "No worries, Michy. I got this."

Michelle gazed at me. I could see she knew I was holding out. She sighed. "Okay. But if you change your mind . . . I'm here for you."

My smile relaxed. "Yeah, me, too."

In more ways than she'd ever know.

ACKNOWLEDGMENTS

As always, my undying gratitude goes to Catherine LePard. Without her support, I would never have had the courage to reach for the childhood dream of writing novels.

Thank you, Dan Conaway, agent extraordinaire. You're the best in the business.

I totally lucked out to get the most amazing editor on the planet. Charlotte Hersher, my gratitude is boundless. It's been a joy working with you.

Thank you to JoVon Sotak and Alan Turkus for believing in Samantha. It's been a real pleasure working with you.